RUNNING INTO TROUBLE

Elle Spellman is a runner, but finds it more fun to run with friends. She's fond of the seaside and strolling through old cemeteries, and when not working on a novel, Elle occasionally writes flash fiction. She lives in Bristol.

Twitter: @seventhelle

RUNNING INTO TROUBLE

Elle Spellman

TRAPEZE

First published in Great Britain in 2020 by Trapeze
an imprint of The Orion Publishing Group Ltd
Carmelite House, 50 Victoria Embankment
London EC4Y 0DZ

An Hachette UK Company

1 3 5 7 9 10 8 6 4 2

A CIP catalogue record for this book is
available from the British Library.

ISBN (Paperback) 978 1 4091 9154 4
ISBN (eBook) 978 1 4091 9155 1

Typeset by Born Group
Printed and bound in Great Britain by Clays Ltd, Elcograf S.p.A.

MIX
Paper from

*Every time you want to quit, remember
why you started.*

Part One

Three months until race day!

I

Hannah

Like many strange and questionable decisions Hannah had made in her life, it all began with wine.

Red wine, in particular; the perfect ingredient for casual life destruction. As Hannah pulled the bottle of own-brand Merlot from the crumpled Tesco carrier bag, she considered how it would always begin so innocently. You vow to have *one*, with the best of intentions, and before you know it, you're knocking back an entire bottle of supermarket plonk, putting the world to rights while munching through a box of chocolate fingers that was meant to be your contribution to your boss's birthday buffet.

Hannah had a distinct feeling of how the evening would go down even before the ruby-red liquid threatened to spill over the brim of her glass. She watched it intently, totting up the days in her head: eight weeks, three days and approximately two hours since Dan's hasty departure from the house – and quite possibly her life – during which time the occasional glass or gin in a tin had swiftly morphed from post-work treat into a well-heeled evening ritual. It was comforting; that little taste of bliss in an otherwise solitary evening.

Hannah kicked off her shoes in the hallway. A scuffed black pair that made her toes feel as pinched as her smile after a nine-hour day at Travel Town, putting together bespoke holiday packages for lucky jet-setters who'd swoop in, giddy with excitement, visions of infinity pools and Insta-worthy cocktails dancing in their eyes. It was difficult *not* to feel envious.

She headed into the living room, bottle in one hand and glass in the other, and slumped down on the sofa, its scratchy blue material prompting yet another reminder of Dan. He'd insisted on it – she hated it – yet they were still paying off the damn thing. Hannah flicked on the TV, navigating to the crime drama she'd been watching on Netflix, grateful for the background noise that made the house feel that little less empty. She took a long-awaited sip of wine, sighing as the warmth hit her throat.

The sun was still shining, beating down onto the terraced street. The recent summer heat had brought with it a wave of humidity that others welcomed, beckoning them outside. It was too hot to keep the windows closed, so Hannah was forced to listen to the sounds of everyone else's happiness sneaking in, unwanted: children playing, families and friends gathered in nearby gardens, their tinkling laughter floating in past the curtains like an unwelcome ghost. All she could do was endure it, stuck in the living room that was now too big for her alone.

On the screen a mystery was unfolding, a police officer poised and ready to burst into a suspect's run-down apartment, but Hannah wasn't paying attention. She tried, but the story was drifting, drifting until it was out of focus. She'd spent hours longing to come home and retreat to the comfort of her sofa, only to find herself wishing now that she was anywhere else. All it took was a slight reminder – a loved-up couple perhaps, all dreamy-eyed, swanning in to book their honeymoon – and Hannah was jolted back to only months before, when everything was seemingly fine.

Now, she was surrounded by reminders. Dan's belongings were still scattered around the house; his books on the shelf, clothes in the wardrobe, golf clubs in the garage from that month he embarked on another new hobby, one he neglected weeks later. He'd only taken what he could pack in his solitary suitcase. Surely that wasn't enough?

Surely, he'd have to come back?

The memory of the night he told her was still fresh, as if she'd been dealt the blow only yesterday. It wasn't something she could easily forget. Hannah could wake to wailing sirens, orange skies and the beginning of the apocalypse only to see Dan's pitiful expression on that evening. It was etched in there like a recurring bad dream, even worse than that nude-in-the-supermarket one that had haunted her for years.

Dan had come home – a Tuesday, bolognese night – and had wolfed down the meal Hannah had lovingly cooked before blurting out the whole sorry story. *Leaving*. She'd dropped her fork but didn't notice, her gaze fixed instead on her husband, who was saying things that didn't quite compute. His mouth was moving, but the words coming out of it didn't make sense. It was as if he'd been replaced. With what, she didn't know – maybe some kind of reverse Stepford scenario – but he didn't *sound* like the Dan she knew.

So she'd listened, mutely. Waited for him to finish. Blinked, watched, listened some more as the words tumbled from his sauce-stained lips.

'Not happy.'

'Want a break.'

Hannah had sat, numb, as her world descended into silence. Words came but made no sense. They lingered, waiting for her to collect them from the newly cold air and comprehend them.

'Moving out for a while.'

'Best for us.'

And the absolute kicker, the one that made Hannah feel as though her soul were rapidly leaving her body:

'I've been seeing someone else.'

Frozen at the table, she'd tried in vain to formulate a coherent sentence as the life she'd known for twenty-three years – seven years of coupledom before sixteen years of marriage – collapsed around her.

'Why?' she'd muttered finally.

Saying it was a struggle. Hannah knew that she sounded different, mouse-like. She hated it.

Dan's eyes couldn't meet hers. 'It just happened,' he said sheepishly. 'You can't really help who you fall for, can you?'

Hannah had almost laughed and would have if the reality of her situation hadn't rendered her completely numb.

'Seriously, Dan? *You can't help who you fall for?* That's the most clichéd bollocks I've heard in a long time. You *can* help it. By not cheating on your wife, for starters. Why didn't you talk to me?'

Dan shrugged. 'It wasn't intentional.'

'Who is she, then?'

Dan had the grace to look slightly ashamed. 'She's a personal trainer,' he confessed. 'From the gym.'

Hannah's insides turned to stone. A personal trainer. *Is this some kind of midlife crisis?* she wondered. Most victims came home with a cringe-inducing sports car, but here was Dan, her loving, reliable, handsome Dan, running off with a personal trainer from Gym4Less. No wonder he'd been spending so much time there lately. And Hannah thought he had finally started to take exercise seriously, after a wellness day at work had scared him into a health kick. Clearly, she'd been wrong.

Dan *was* looking remarkably fitter, Hannah mused, then regretted it.

He's dumped me for a fit woman, she thought. *Everything I'm not.*

The tears had come then, blurring the scenery, the kitchen they'd decorated together. Their home. Their dreams.

Of course, there were some dreams that hadn't come true. But after everything, Hannah didn't expect *this.*

'I'll pack my stuff, then,' said Dan, dropping his dish into the sink before heading up the stairs.

It's just a blip, Hannah told herself, retreating to the bathroom. She turned on the shower so that Dan couldn't hear her sobbing as he hastily threw as many belongings as he could into their favourite holiday suitcase. *These things happen. It won't last long.*

Sadly, it had lasted for more than two months.

Hannah took another sip. The TV cop had made her arrest, but Hannah felt restless. Tipsy now, her eyes travelled to her phone. *One quick look,* she thought, unable to resist the temptation. She pulled up Facebook.

She typed in his name. Dan had unfriended her – *easier that way,* he'd said – but he didn't realise just how many photos he'd left public.

There he was. Dan Saunders. Sitting in a sunny pub garden in his profile photo, in a T-shirt she didn't recognise. Hannah clicked on the photo, enlarging it.

Dan's smile made Hannah's heart soar with longing before she caught sight of the rogue arm and tendrils of long chestnut hair that fell over a tanned shoulder. She may have been cropped out, but Hannah knew instantly that the glowing, toned arm belonged to Sophia.

Dan hadn't revealed too much about his elusive new fling, but it didn't take Sherlock Holmes to find out what she needed to know. Social media provided all the answers.

7

Sophia Sandford was the polar opposite of Hannah. Effortlessly beautiful; tall and slim with perfect hair and a look so polished that it screamed 'success'. Sophia looked as though she'd stepped out of a glossy magazine. Photos showed her small, super-fit body adorned with fitness gear. A body to show off. Not that Hannah could blame her. *If I looked like that I would walk around Tesco in the buff*, she thought.

Hannah could never look like Sophia. She'd tried over the years before she realised that it was completely impossible. Hannah was naturally curvy, having taken after her mum's side of the family. She was shorter, too, and Hannah had much preferred long jumpers and dresses that concealed her body rather than putting it on display. Unlike Sophia, with her long, cascading hair and tight-fitting dresses that clung to every toned curve. Hannah's own hair, dyed blonde to cover the greys that had been creeping in since her thirties, sat just above her shoulders.

She stared at the profile photo again. Had it really 'just happened', or had Dan been looking for someone else the whole time?

Hannah took another sip of Merlot and clicked the image away. On Facebook, one of her former colleagues reclined on a tropical beach, sipping a vivid orange concoction. *#Blessed.* For a brief moment, Hannah pictured herself escaping. Leaving Bristol for a few days, stuffing her old blue bikini and trusty bum-concealing sarong into a bag and jetting away somewhere sunny. She'd buy the giant, pineapple-shaped lilo she saw in town and float along in the pool, clutching a drink of her own. It was a perfect sun-kissed fantasy – until she realised that her bikini was likely three sizes too small by now and her bank balance could barely get her to Skegness, let alone Portugal.

Facebook was a portal of despair when your life was shit, Hannah knew. Yet, she couldn't help looking. Before she could stop herself, her fingers hovered over the search bar.

Sophia Sandford.

As expected, Hannah felt sick. The wine swirled in her stomach. Hannah had visited the profile almost nightly, somehow unable to stop torturing herself. There was nothing new about Dan on the page, but Hannah's shaking hand ventured to the photos once again, perusing the gym selfies and beach photos and night-out snaps that she'd seen a million times. Not only was Sophia beautiful, but she was also thirty-three. Dan had left Hannah to sample pastures greener. And fitter. And over a decade younger.

In one photo Sophia was mid-run, grinning among a crowd. Hannah swiped. Now, Sophia was holding a medal, glowing with pride.

'If that's who I'm up against, I'm stuffed,' Hannah slurred, defeated.

Glass in hand, she let the tears come. She went to get up, but her head felt light. Hannah looked at the bottle on the coffee table, noticing the mere drip left at the bottom. She'd worked her way through almost the entire thing. She shuffled off the sofa to get to her feet, thinking it might be best to go to bed, but as she stumbled unsteadily to the door with all the grace of a baby learning to walk, she stubbed her toe on the coffee table.

'For God's sake!' she yelled.

Her phone bounced onto the floor.

Hannah bent down to retrieve it, noticing, thankfully, that Sophia's page was gone. Her newsfeed appeared instead. As the room began to spin, something caught Hannah's eye.

The bright advert beamed out enticingly. The words danced in front of Hannah's eyes. A marathon?

Hannah let out a laugh. She stared down at the ad, at the smiling runners who beamed back up at her as if to say *join us*. Then an image of Dan appeared in the forefront of her mind. Dan obviously liked fit women. *Maybe that's where I went wrong*, Hannah thought. *Maybe I should have shown more interest.* She pictured herself as a runner with a medal of her own, smiling as she ran through the crowd, Dan's arms outstretched as he waited for her at the finish line.

It's only a run! It can't be that difficult, surely? If thousands of people can do it, so can I. I'll start tomorrow! I'll run across fields and mountains and be like those women in the sportswear ads . . .

It came to her like a message from the heavens. Suddenly, she knew exactly what she needed to do.

Her hands wavered as she hit 'Register'. She laughed, filling in her card details, wondering why she hadn't thought of this before.

The words were fuzzy on the screen.

'Yes!' Hannah yelled to the air. 'I'm going to run a marathon. I'll be fit and fast and bloody *amazing*.' She posted a quick update on her own Facebook page before flopping back onto the sofa.

Where, promptly, she fell asleep.

The following morning, Hannah awoke to a pounding headache and thirty-eight new Facebook notifications.

Thirty-eight? Hannah thought. *That's unusual.*

Bringing the phone closer to her face, she squinted in a desperate attempt to quell the pain behind her eyes and the sickness in her stomach, not to mention the disgusting furry taste in her mouth. Hannah glimpsed the near-empty bottle of Merlot on the coffee table and felt a momentary hint of shame.

Nervously, Hannah looked at the notifications. Usually she'd have two, six at the most. Maybe as many as thirty on her birthday, but certainly not on a normal day. She waited for the screen to fall into focus and when she finally saw the words, her throat felt tight and the bile in her stomach began to rise.

> So GUESS WAHT??? Gonna be running the GREAT SOUHT WEST MARATHOOOOON! *Go meee! Just singed up, time to get fit & fast!!!*

Oh no.

Please, no.

A vague memory of the previous night began to surface. Hannah looked again, willing the words to disappear and prove she was still asleep, mid nightmare. But she wasn't. She'd definitely typed those words.

Her best friend Bronwen had been first to comment:

> Er, Han? Those typos tell me you're sozzled. Are you?? You need to tell me more when we meet! Anyway . . . GO, HANNAH!!
> XX

Beneath Bronwen, other friends and acquaintances had posted their own good-luck wishes:

> Well done, Han! Wish I was as brave as you!
> A marathon! Wow! that's fantastic, Hannah. Good luck!
> GO HAN! GO HAN! Xxx
> Wow, 26.2 miles! I'd keel over before I got to two.
> Good luck, Han, we'll be cheering you on!

Twenty-six point two miles.

Hannah had signed up to run twenty-six (and a bit!) miles.

Sure enough, sitting in her inbox was the congratulatory email from the Great South-West Marathon team. She hadn't imagined it. There was her name, her registration number, happily reminding her that she'd be running a *marathon*.

And, if that wasn't bad enough, the race was in three months' time.

Hannah felt the colour drain from her face. *Run*. She could barely run to the bottom of the street for the bus without becoming a breathless, sweaty mess. Hannah hadn't done any proper exercise in years. And yet she'd willingly, drunkenly, idiotically volunteered to run an entire marathon, in front of everyone. The room began to swirl and sway in front of her eyes as the jarring light of the morning crept through the curtains, along with the nasty smack of reality.

Twenty. Six. Miles.

Suddenly, the unkind lurch of last night's wine rose to her throat at the sheer thought of it. She made it to the bathroom just in time.

That's it, she resolved. *I'm never drinking again.*

2

Malika

Malika missed the smell of flowers.

It was odd, really; just recently, she'd hated it. Hated the acrid stench of the initial sweetness beginning to ripen and rot. She couldn't stand the way it wafted past her nose every morning, a strange attack on her senses. A harsh reminder. Of course, it had once been pleasant. For a time, the aroma had permeated the office of Rocket Recruitment, provoking fond memories of childhood visits to her grandmother's house. Her beloved gran would buy artful bouquets from the local florist and each week a new arrangement would sit on the hallway table, next to the old telephone. But, as with her grandmother, the charming scent had become cloying, entwined with another feeling – loss.

It was everywhere.

The absence of the sweet smell reminded Malika that it was over. Four weeks on, the bouquets had stopped arriving altogether. Things had started to venture back into the territory known as 'Normal', even though Malika was nowhere near ready. The flowers in the office had grown dry, their crinkled, fallen petals swept into the bin, the vases emptied and relinquished to the back of a cupboard. The unnerving cloud of sympathy that had hovered over the building in recent weeks had started to lift, making way for the summer sun that illuminated the street outside. Malika's colleagues, already a small team of four before it happened, had started to laugh and joke again. It felt almost as though they'd forgotten about Abbie.

Four weeks. That's all it had taken for Abbie to fade into the background. The cool June air had become warmer, bringing forth the promise of summer, evident as people wandered up and down the steep incline of Park Street towards the shops and the cafes and the vast library on College Green; the students, the workers, the casual summer tourists heading up the iconic hill, bathed in a summer glow of hope and excitement. Malika would watch them through the window, almost envious. Just weeks ago she'd looked forward to joining them; these people, these city dwellers out in force among the visitors. She loved summer in Bristol – breezy evenings spent in harbourside bars, watching the lights dancing on the water as the hours stretched ahead; relaxing with her housemates Roz, Dean and Kath, sipping from bottled beer and talking the weekend away.

But now, she dreaded it. The warm air felt sticky and overpowering. The sky wasn't so bright any more.

The day was just beginning as Malika entered the office, hanging up her denim jacket on the coat stand in the corner before heading to her desk. Abbie's desk. Malika had swapped as she couldn't bear to see it empty, awkwardly ignored because nobody wanted to admit that Abbie wasn't coming back. She turned on the PC, carefully pushing aside some clutter that had once been Abbie's: a notebook, a little pot of paper clips, an assortment of Post-it notes covered in Abbie's handwriting. Malika didn't have the heart to throw them away.

'Morning!' Eva, the branch manager, poked her head out from the kitchen. 'Warm out there today, isn't it? Was just about to put the kettle on. Tea?'

'Silly question,' Malika joked, hoping Eva believed the bounce in her voice, the perkiness that she once used to possess, which was now merely an act.

Malika checked her emails, flagging up any new ones she'd have to answer, her eyes flitting towards the window. She enjoyed the quietness as the city opened up for the day, the sun making its morning debut over the tall, old buildings. In less than forty-five minutes, Malika's first candidates of the day would be bustling through the doors, hopeful and eager and in search of a new job, or sometimes a new dream career. The possibility of helping them to find it usually made Malika more determined, more eager to embrace the day, but for now she relished the temporary peace, savouring it.

Until the door opened and in walked Marc. The silence was broken.

'Hey, M!' he announced loudly, winking, hanging up his suit jacket and pulling out his sports bottle. He placed it on the desk, a thick green sludge-like substance swirling inside it. Marc caught her looking. 'New smoothie. Want some?'

'It looks vile,' she said, smiling.

'You're right,' he said. 'Not gonna lie. Looks like I've scooped it out of a swamp. But it does the trick.'

Malika watched as Marc kicked his bag under the desk and stretched, honed muscles straining beneath his pristine white shirt. Marc always turned up to work suited and booted. It made Malika nervously wonder if she should be doing the same. Putting more effort in. Abbie had, after all.

Eva returned from the kitchen with two mugs full of tea. 'All right, Marc?' she asked. Eva looked down at Malika's desk, brow furrowed as she surveyed the clutter, looking for a place to put the mug.

'Oh, Mal, forgot to ask. Did you get round to printing off the new vacancy posters last week?'

Malika's face fell. 'No. I totally forgot. I'll do it right now, Eva. I'm really sorry.'

'Don't worry,' Eva replied, smiling. 'If you could do it later, that'd be fab. But . . .' Her eyes darted around the desk. 'Maybe we should clear some of this stuff away. You can hardly move.'

'It's all right,' said Malika quickly. 'I'll do it soon.'

Eva leant forwards and plucked a business card from a neat stack on the desk: *Abbie Gordon, Assistant Manager.*

'Well, we don't need these any more, do we?' she said.

To Malika's horror, she scooped up the small pile and dumped the cards in the wastepaper bin. Malika reached for them, but Eva stopped her.

'Mal.'

'It's just . . .'

'It's good to de-clutter,' Marc called across the room. 'If you don't, well, that's how hoarding starts. You'll end up on one of those documentaries,' he added with a laugh.

Malika knew that behind his cheeky demeanour he was only trying to help. For once, it was nice; more often than not, Eva and Marc danced so tentatively around the subject of what happened. Or worse still, avoided it altogether.

Eva slipped from the main office, returning seconds later with a small cardboard box. The kind you use when you move house. Or when you get a new job, and have to pack up your mementoes and leaving card full of wishes before your colleagues bid you a happy farewell.

Or the kind your friends put your belongings in when you're dead.

Malika pushed the box away. 'Don't you think it's a bit early?'

Eva shook her head. 'Keeping her things here will only make you feel worse. It'll just get harder the longer you leave it. I know you were fond of Abbie, we all were, but we need to keep things ticking away as normal or it'll be total madness in here. We have to move on at some point.'

Not yet, Malika wanted to say, but she struggled to find the words.

Eva spoke quietly. 'Mal, is everything all right? You just don't seem, well, *yourself*. I know it's only natural to be feeling like this, but if you need to take some time off, don't be afraid to tell me, OK?'

'No, Eva, it's fine—'

Eva held up a hand. 'Mal, seriously. I know you said you're happy to take on Abbie's workload until . . .' She trailed off.

Until you replace her, Malika thought.

'. . . for the time being.' Eva corrected herself. 'I'm just worried it might all be a bit much for you at the moment. Maybe making you assistant manager in her, well, absence, wasn't the best way to go. I've heaped so much on you.'

'No!' Malika almost shouted. Eva's concern, although appreciated, was just too much. 'Honestly. I can do it, Eva. Really. I don't need time off. I'm fine.'

I'm fine. It was her biggest lie of late, one she'd told so many times that she almost believed it herself. To her boss, to her housemates, to her parents, to the strangers who'd entered Rocket asking for Abbie, only to be told she was no longer there. *I'm fine. I'm all right.* What did it matter, anyway? It wasn't about her. Abbie was the one who mattered. Abbie, Malika's colleague and friend.

Their friendship had formed when Malika had joined Rocket, their casual lunchtime conversations turning quickly into post-work evenings out, gigs and shopping trips, wandering the charity shops of Gloucester Road in search of pre-owned treasures. Abbie was always there to talk through Malika's problems, to listen to her housemate-related frustrations, like when Dean got a new girlfriend who'd practically moved in. Abbie was a problem-solver. Abbie was an amazing friend. A wonderful human being.

Abbie was killed when a car ploughed into her bicycle as she cycled home from work.

Eva smiled sadly, proffering the box again. 'All right. If you're sure. But for now, can you please clear some of this stuff away? We can keep it in the cupboard for the time being until we work out what to do with it.'

Malika nodded mutely. *Maybe Eva's right*, she thought. Maybe she needed to let go, after all. Move forwards. It was all about moving forwards.

She placed the box at her feet, took a deep breath and began to place Abbie's possessions in their new home, one by one; carefully, as if they were priceless antiques. She opened the top drawer, which she'd left just the way it was. Stationery, more notebooks, three boxes of herbal tea, a stapler . . . and a small emergency make-up kit that Abbie and Malika kept for impromptu after-work nights out. Malika held it in her hands, smiling at the memory before dropping it softly into the box.

Then, as she lifted out an old folder, something fluttered out from beneath it. A leaflet. Reaching down to retrieve it, Malika noticed it was an advert for a race. Big, bold letters beamed out from the glossy paper, over a photo of a sea of smiling runners. Abbie had been a keen runner, always trying to get Malika to join her. 'Do it!' she'd say. 'Go on! It'll be fun. We can do it together.'

Malika had always turned down the offer. 'One day, maybe,' she'd reply.

'That means never. I know you, Malika!'

'You're probably right. Running just isn't me.'

Abbie had always laughed off her excuses. But Malika wasn't lying; running just wasn't her forte. She'd never been sporty at all, really, besides a bit of netball in high school. She saw exercise as more of a chore than fulfilment, unless dancing in Popworld with Roz and Kath counted.

'Please?' Abbie had asked, appearing at her desk, making a pouty face. 'It'll be fuuun.'

'Fine!'

'Promise?'

'I promise.'

'I'm holding you to that, Mal. Don't go thinking you can get out of it.'

But she *had* got out of it. In the worst way possible.

Malika winced at the memory, wishing she'd done it, wishing she'd done everything possible to spend as much time as she could with her friend. She'd had no idea Abbie's time had been nearly up. If she could go back, she would have done anything. Any sport. Anything.

She looked down at the leaflet. Malika read:

The Great South-West Marathon is happening in October – are YOU ready?
Owing to the huge success of the Bristol and Bath Half Marathons, we're proud to announce a brand-new annual race – 26.2 miles around the stunning city and countryside!

Malika dropped the leaflet into the box and went back to emptying the drawer. A flash of silver caught her eye.

Malika reached in and pulled out something small, round and heavy that was nestled among the old staples and paper clips.

A medal.

Malika felt the sturdy weight of its round surface in her hand. It glinted beneath the light of the window. The medal, attached to a blue ribbon, was engraved with the words 'Great Bristol Half Marathon 2017'. Malika remembered the day Abbie brought it in, holding it up to show everyone. She'd raised over three hundred pounds for the British Heart Foundation. Malika briefly pondered why Abbie had left such an item in her work drawer. If *she* had won a medal, she'd display it proudly at home, telling anyone who'd listen about her amazing feat. But Abbie took part in races all the time. She probably had an entire collection of medals at home and had just forgotten she'd left it there.

Malika clasped her hand around the medal, her fingers brushing the ribbon. She held it over the box, ready to drop it in, but stopped herself. *No.* It was far too special to be left in a cupboard, forgotten, only to be disposed of in time. Instead, Malika put it in her pocket.

She pulled out the leaflet.

A marathon.

The idea swirled briefly in her head before she swatted it away. *No*, she thought. *That would be crazy. What a stupid, stupid idea.*

But her hands were already on the keyboard, typing into the search bar.

The colourful website sprung into life.

Take the challenge!

Runners appeared, a photo slideshow of faces, determination in their eyes, happy and glowing as they raced along a sunny road.

She could hardly believe she was even considering it. A marathon, of all things. One that was taking place in three months. She certainly wouldn't have enough time to train.

Go on! Abbie's voice sounded in her head again.

Malika remembered her words. *I promise.* Stealing another glance at the medal, she realised that here was the perfect opportunity to keep that promise.

Closure. That's what she needed. Eva had told her so. Her mother had told her so, during her regular phone calls. Hearing about Abbie's death had only made Mrs Sade worry more about her daughter. 'I'm fine, Mum,' Malika would say, trying to keep the irritation from her voice.

But now, there was a possibility. Something to focus on. Something, anything, to keep her mind on the road ahead, to stop it from straying down that narrow, winding path of grief, and the constant fear of the inevitable that had already begun to take over Malika's life like a dark, suffocating monster.

Perhaps, she reasoned, she, too, could raise some money. Help to make a difference.

With a deep breath, she clicked 'Sign Up'.

3

Hannah

Never had the front door looked so terrifying.

'I can't do this, Bron. It's scary. I wish I was joking.'

Hannah gripped the phone, edging closer to the door as though an axe-wielding clown was awaiting her on the other side. Through the pane of frosted glass, the clear blue sky and slightly overgrown greenery that lined her short garden path would normally be an inviting image. Hardly terrifying. Until now.

Frankly, she thought, *I'd rather take my chances with the killer clown.*

'What *are* you on about, Han?' Bronwen boomed down the line, over the noise of a school football match.

A roar went up from the crowd.

'Well done, Ethan. Wooo!' Bronwen shrieked, almost deafening Hannah. 'Sorry, Han. He scored a goal. Anyway, of course you can bloody do it. Just go to the door – you know, that big white rectangular thing with the handle? Open it and go outside. Then you put one foot in front of the other, *et voila.'*

Hannah knew her friend was only trying to be encouraging, but *go outside* seemed easier said than done. She took a deep breath and another step forwards, her ancient trainers sinking into the hallway carpet, wishing she could kick them off and rush back to the sofa, where she'd cocoon herself for as long as possible.

'I'm going to make a tit of myself,' she argued.

'No, you won't! Trust me, no one will even care. And besides, even if you *did* make a tit of yourself, would it actually matter?'

It bloody well would, Hannah seethed but kept quiet. Maybe Bronwen wasn't the best person to call for moral support. Then again, who *could* she call now? Dan?

Hannah's muscles tensed at the thought of it. *Running*. Her drunken mind had obviously seen possibilities that her sober mind did not. She imagined herself puffing away slowly, her legs giving up before she'd even run for two minutes. The pitying looks. She pictured herself heaving and panting, in the *least* sexy way, as the runners from the local club whizzed by in a flash of swishing ponytails and pricey trainers. She'd seen them, weekly, hurtling past her window while she watched from the sofa.

It was OK for Bronwen, who was incapable of ever looking terrible, even when lounging around the house. At forty-eight, she could still fit into the jeans she'd worn at twenty-three. If it weren't for the slight lines on her face that hinted at her years, Bronwen had barely changed since their carefree days of the eighties (minus the huge perm, of course). Even the arrival of her two baby boys, now towering, handsome teenagers, had blessed her with an enviable glow. She'd kept her figure the whole time, losing the baby weight quickly afterwards. Just many more ways in which life, to Hannah, hadn't been remotely fair.

No, Bronwen never had to experience what Hannah had; the cruel taunts in the playground, the dismissal throughout her teenage years, when looks were so important. When she was cast aside, unwanted. Bronwen never had to endure shrieks of 'fatty' or 'thunder thighs' from the queen bees at their comprehensive school. Their giggling was knife-like, sinister, as it carried across the playing field and echoed through the corridors. Karen Smith, the ringleader, was by far the worst culprit, her voice like a gleeful foghorn as Hannah struggled to reach the first base in rounders without passing out. Hannah would simply accept it, forcing back the tears until she got home, closing her bedroom door behind her and pouring her thoughts into the glittery, lockable diary that she wouldn't dare show anyone else. Not even Bronwen.

Back then, once Karen Smith tired of the fat jokes for a whole five minutes and strutted off to graffiti the girls' toilets instead, the lovely Bronwen Lewis would be on hand to offer support. 'Just ignore 'em,' she'd say, offering Hannah a sweet from her pick 'n' mix, or a shred of gossip about a teacher. 'They're not worth it.' Yet, however much Hannah appreciated her best friend, the girl she'd grown up with, there were still things that separated them so vastly it was as though they resided in different worlds. Bronwen was a different being: smart, pretty, an unassuming beauty who simply didn't know that cruelty was often impossible to shrug off with platitudes and inspirational slogans, or the fleeting nonchalance that Bronwen was also blessed with.

There were some things she just wouldn't, couldn't understand.

'I'm still impressed you're running a marathon. This isn't . . . never mind.'

Another loud cheer rang out from the football field.

'What, Bron?'

'This isn't about Dan, is it?'

Hannah's cheeks felt flushed all of a sudden. 'No! Definitely not.' She thought about the infallible plan she'd scrawled on a Post-it at work. The Dan Plan: 1. Get fit. 2.

Run race. 3. Show Dan what he's missing! 'I just thought it'd be fun.'

'Fun? A marathon?'

'Why not? OK, *now* I know why not. It's bloody terrifying. That's why I'm stuck in the hallway.'

'I just don't want you to do anything stupid, that's all. But if you insist on doing this, you should actually leave the house.'

'Fine,' Hannah said finally. 'Right, then.' She didn't want to argue; Hannah had witnessed Bronwen's wrath when it came to Ethan and Joshua. There was no way anyone could win an argument with Bronwen. 'But if I pass out then I'm blaming you. It's your responsibility to come and scrape me off the pavement.'

'Duly noted,' laughed Bronwen. 'Good luck, Han. Love you!'

Hanging up, Hannah attempted a stretch. She lifted her arms and bent one knee, hearing a click from her left leg. It wasn't looking promising.

It had to be done, however. It had been two days since her drunken misdemeanour and signing up to the race had made her feel like a nervous wreck. Hannah had experienced drunken regret many times over the years, but *this* exploit was by far the worst. What was she thinking?!

Dan. It was all about Dan.

Her heart leapt when she thought about him, when she envisioned the pride on his face at seeing her at the finish line. The thought had kept her going for the whole day at Travel Town, after she'd crept into work following the Facebook debacle, hoping it would go unmentioned. It did not.

'A marathon!' her boss, David, had declared loudly across the office. 'I didn't know *you* were a runner.'

'What do you mean?' Hannah had asked, almost defensively, wondering what he was getting at.

'Well, you never mentioned anything,' he replied. 'And you're normally the first to tell us what you're up to.'

Apart from the fact my husband walked out on me, she thought. Nobody needed to know about *that*.

And soon, they wouldn't have to.

Of course, it wasn't the way she looked that had shocked David – it was the simple fact that only a complete and utter idiot would volunteer to run 26.2 miles on a whim.

'Yeah, I thought I'd keep it quiet,' she lied.

Lying was the only thing she could think to do. It was either that, or admit she'd made a huge mistake. All those messages of support, the sudden Facebook popularity she'd never encountered before. Everyone was rooting for her to do this. And as barmy and frightening as a marathon seemed, giving up would mean one thing: *I'm not good enough.*

The words stung Hannah, like they did sometimes at night, shouting from the shadows as she tried to sleep. *You weren't good enough for Dan. That's why he left you.*

So she had to carry on.

Which meant going out for an *actual* run.

Hannah owned nothing whatsoever in terms of fitness attire, besides a scuffed pair of trainers that hadn't seen the light of day since the late nineties. She'd pulled on a pair of old leggings that were thinning at the knees and rummaged through some of Dan's T-shirts in search of something that didn't cling tightly to every curve. She'd found one that had Darth Vader on the front. Still snug, but it did the trick.

Hannah stuffed her key and phone into her bra, took a deep breath and reached for the door handle, finding herself face to face with her new-found enemy: the outdoors.

Hannah headed out through the gate and down the street, starting with a light walk. *This isn't so bad*, she thought. She passed the terraced houses, their neat gardens splashed with colour. She focused her attention on the path ahead, trying to ignore the road, picturing passing drivers gawping and laughing at her almost see-through leggings and jiggling boobs that struggled to break free from a bra that had seen better decades, let alone days. She upped her pace, already feeling a dull ache in her legs. At forty-eight years old, she still had that feeling that people were watching. Judging. As though Karen Smith and her cronies were lurking round the corner, ready to leap out and make her feel awful all over again.

It only took a minute for the sweat to start pooling around her body. The leggings felt warm and rough against her skin. Hannah knew her face, soaked with sweat, was the colour of beetroot and she hadn't even really started to run yet. Up ahead, a lamp post filtered into view in the sunny haze, so Hannah made it her goal. *If I can run to that lamp post, I'll be OK.*

But she didn't make it. Her legs gave way.

They surrendered before anything else. There was an ache in her calves, her feet, *everywhere*. Even though her mind wanted her to carry on, to work through the pain and reach the end of the street, her body had other ideas.

Hannah's knees buckled. She gripped a nearby wall for support, feeling her body morph into an unmovable, red-faced, jelly-like being who'd become stuck. Just as she leant over to try to heave herself back up, Mrs Gibson from number sixty-three appeared from behind her own neatly trimmed hedge, face full of concern.

'Hannah! You all right there, love? You look a bit sick.'

'I'm – *puff* – fine, thanks,' Hannah wheezed, trying to force her legs back into submission.

'If you're sure,' said Mrs Gibson, glancing quizzically at Hannah, in her Darth Vader T-shirt, practically on the pavement. She turned towards her front door, then stopped. 'Actually, while you're there, is your Dan about?'

Hannah could feel her face getting warmer. 'He isn't, sadly. He's—'

'Oh? Where is he, then? I haven't seen him in a while. Usually parks his van close by, but it's not been there for weeks.'

'He's . . . away. Lots of work stuff on at the moment.'

Mrs Gibson raised an eyebrow, no doubt wanting to probe further but clearly thinking it impolite. 'Oh! Right, then. It's just that he said he'd do the guttering for me. Could you ask him about it when he gets back?'

'Sure,' said Hannah through gritted teeth.

Lovely Dan, the ever-helpful neighbour, always ready to lend a helping hand. What would Mrs Gibson think if she knew the truth? Hannah wondered. Then again, she had a feeling Mrs Gibson wouldn't keep it under wraps. She loved a bit of neighbourhood gossip.

Hannah made her way slowly back down the street, feeling oddly grateful that her face was dripping with sweat.

At least nobody could see the tears.

Back at home, Hannah collapsed on the sofa and ran a hand through her sweat-soaked hair. Three minutes was all it had taken for her body to quit. She'd failed.

Maybe I'm too old for this, she told herself, thinking of the fresh-faced women with their swishy ponytails, of Sophia, and was suddenly overcome with a painful wave of regret. She'd left it too late. Too big, too unfit to start now. Hannah wiped away more tears as she fished in her bra for her phone and opened Facebook. She typed:

Sorry, everyone, but I am no longer running the
Great South-West Marathon.

Her fingers hovered over the 'post' button as she pictured all of her friends and their well-wishes, and Dan, who'd no doubt hear about Hannah's blunder from their mutual friends. 'You wouldn't expect Hannah of all people to run a marathon, would you? Christ,' he'd laugh, sneaking a loved-up glance at Sophia, thanking his lucky stars that he'd found someone so perfect.

Suddenly, Hannah had a vision of her future. A Miss Havisham type, living in moth-eaten pyjamas in a dusty, silent house. The longer Dan had been away, the colder her – *their* – home had become. Soulless. Hannah's world was changing and there was nothing she could do about it.

Hannah didn't want to start her life again. The one she'd known was happy enough. She just needed Dan to see that he could be happy with their life, too.

Staring down at the Facebook update, Hannah changed her mind. She deleted the maudlin words and instead grabbed her trainers, placing them neatly on the floor before snapping a photo. Being sure to choose a decent filter, making the photo look bright and inspiring, Hannah uploaded it.

Enjoying a run in the sun, training for the big race!
#fitness #marathon #olympicsherewecome #lol

It was wrong to lie. She knew that. But if she wanted her old life back, then she had to make some changes. Starting with herself.

She had to finish that marathon.

4

Malika

'Mal!'

Roz's voice travelled boldly from the hallway, loud enough for Malika to hear through her headphones. She pulled them off as her heavy-footed housemate thundered up the two flights of stairs to her attic bedroom.

'You decent in there, Mal?' Roz called before opening the door.

Roz surveyed the room, taking in the sight of Malika, who was already in bed, one leg peeking out from beneath the duvet. She was watching something on her laptop, propped up on her pile of pillows.

'Bloody hell,' said Roz. 'What's going on?'

'What do you mean?'

'Budge up,' said Roz, flopping down on the end of Malika's bed. 'What I mean,' she continued, gesturing around the cosy bedroom with its slanted walls, 'is *this*. You, in your pyjamas, when it's only eight o'clock.'

Malika hit Pause on the laptop. She'd taken to watching comedy movies lately, in an attempt to lighten her mood. They were a pleasant distraction, at least.

Roz continued. 'We're thinking of heading out in a bit. Kath's not working tonight, so we might go to The Lanes for a bit of bowling and food. D'you fancy it?'

Malika shook her head. 'I think I'll stay in. Going to have an early night.'

'Another one? Come *on*.' She nudged Malika's foot playfully, screwing up her small face in mock sadness, her big kohl-rimmed eyes peering over at her friend. She swung her floral Doc Martens over the edge of the bed and stood, rushing to the clothes rail at the back of the room and pulling a denim skirt and silky top free of their hangers. 'Here you go,' Roz said, throwing the garments on the bed. 'Just change quickly; we can wait. You haven't been out with us in ages and we're missing you.'

Malika looked at the clothes and at Roz's hopeful expression. She was right, of course, but that didn't change anything.

'Thanks, Roz. Not tonight. The week's been so busy and I just want to chill.'

'Are you all right, Mal?'

Roz's words were sudden but not expected. Malika had been asked the question a thousand times already and still the answer was the same. As if on autopilot, that ever-familiar answer tumbled straight out.

'I'm fine.' It was starting to become her personal catch-phrase. 'Totally fine. It's been a busy week, that's all.'

'OK. If you're sure.' Roz nodded, a look of concern flashing so briefly that Malika almost didn't see it.

When Malika did, it made her stomach drop. Just a month ago, going out with her friends had been a regular fixture in her calendar, but now she couldn't face it. Truthfully, she didn't feel much like going out at all once the workday was over; the mere thought of leaving the house again, interacting with people and pretending she was having a fantastic time was an exhausting prospect, one she didn't want to face. Instead, she preferred to stay in her room, her

31

cosy sanctuary at the top of the house, with her headphones drowning out the raucous laughter from downstairs.

Roz smiled, heading for the door. 'No worries,' she said, then stopped. Something had caught her eye. 'What's this?' she asked curiously, reaching for the blue ribbon that hung on the back of the door next to Malika's jacket. 'Ooh, it's a medal. Is this yours, Mal?'

'Mine? Honestly, Roz, do you even know me at all?' Malika laughed. 'No, it was Abbie's. I found it at work yesterday. I thought I'd keep it.'

'It's nice,' said Roz. She twirled the medal round in her hand, running her fingers over its perfect shiny surface. 'God, that takes me back. I used to win medals as a kid. I had loads of them.'

'What for?'

'Gymnastics, mainly. And trophies! So many trophies. My parents still keep them on a shelf at home, which is pointless really, because I'm shit at it now. Can't even manage the splits any more.'

Malika wondered what it would have been like to win trophies, to have them displayed on her parents' mantelpiece back in her small hometown in Gloucestershire, along with her brother's awards that stood in a noble, shimmering line. Malika's lone certificate from a school poetry competition was framed above, but Malika had never been the athletic type, had never scooped trophy after trophy like Khari. Khari, two years older than Malika, had been the star of the high school football team, spending his days being followed by groups of lovestruck girls and his evenings at football practice. Photos of Khari standing tall in his football kit adorned the walls in their parents' hallway and although they were proud of their children in equal measure, there was only one sports star. Where Khari had been athletic since the day he took his first steps, Malika seemed to have missed out entirely. She hadn't even learnt to swim until she was fourteen.

Not that it bothered her; she was grateful for her big brother. Her tall, strong protector who helped her to navigate her first days of school, who supported her creative endeavours, who ran after her when she fled the stage of her Year Eight drama production, when stage fright stole her voice, making her drop her microphone and run.

The Sade siblings were close. They were just nothing alike.

'Well,' Malika said, glancing at the medal in Roz's hands, 'maybe I'll get one of my own soon. I've signed up for the Great South-West Marathon.'

For a moment she wished she could take back the words. As Roz's eyebrows shot up in surprise, Malika's face flushed with momentary embarrassment. A marathon. Even thinking about it made the nerves bubble inside her again. She clutched the duvet tighter, as though the soft material were capable of keeping her shielded from the outside world.

'You what?'

Malika took a deep breath. 'I know, I know. It was an impulse decision. One I kind of regret now. But Abbie used to run, and I promised I'd do a race with her one day and . . . well . . .'

'You never did.'

'Exactly. And I saw the race and thought, *why not?* But now I realise just how stupid I've been. I can't run a marathon, Roz. And even if I do, Abbie's already gone. I can't share it with her. It won't be the same.'

I thought it would be OK, thought Malika. Just like she thought taking part in the school play would be OK. It was the same unpleasant flutter of anxiety all over again.

Roz let out an excited squeal, bounding over to throw her arms around Malika. 'Mal, this is amazing. You're brave.

I mean, *really* fucking brave. I know Abbie can't be there, but just think of how proud she'd be.'

Holding Roz close, Malika tried to stop a tear from escaping onto her friend's oversized canary-yellow cardigan. She remembered how, when they'd first met, she'd been slightly intimidated by Roz, with her loud laugh, the way she carried herself. A way that oozed confidence. Oh! And the ability to rock a pink pixie cut in a cool, sophisticated way.

'If you don't mind me saying this,' said Roz, 'and tell me to bugger off if you want, but I think this will be good for you. You can't lock yourself in this room all the time. The race might help to take your mind off it all.'

'That's what I thought,' Malika replied. 'But now that I'm home it feels stupid, you know?'

'It's not stupid.' Roz leapt off the bed, dropping the medal into Malika's open hand before heading for the door. 'It'll get easier, I promise. In the meantime, if you change your mind about joining us, just let me know. We'll bring back pizza.'

With Roz gone, Malika was left alone with her laptop. She listened to the chatter in the hallways as her housemates readied themselves for their night out, their footsteps loud against the aged floorboards, their laughter travelling like soft smoke to where Malika sat wrapped in silence, in guilt. That's what she felt the most: guilt that she was ignoring her friends, guilt that she was locking herself away, refusing to enjoy herself because Abbie wasn't able to enjoy anything at all any more. The unnerving mixture of thoughts and words collided in her head. They wound together, united, unwanted. *You're selfish. You should go out.*

It'll pass. That's what people had told her. You won't feel this way for ever. You won't feel empty for long.

If only she knew when it would stop.

As the front door banged shut behind her friends, the house became fraught with eerie silence besides the soft thump of the old pipes and the sounds of a summer evening sneaking in from the open window. Light flooded in from Malika's lemon curtains. She found it impossible to close her eyes, to concentrate on anything but the silence, the worries ahead, enlarged by the sounds of life and fun outside that she was no longer a part of.

It was no use. She was fully awake.

Closing her laptop, Malika sat up and kicked off her duvet, annoyed at her sudden restlessness. For a second, she contemplated heading downstairs, maybe watching another movie now she had the living room to herself.

Until she saw it.

Abbie's medal.

Malika picked it up. A crazy idea was forming.

If Malika was going to run the Great South-West Marathon, she actually needed to *run*. She'd planned to start at the weekend, but with her housemates out, and nobody to see her hurrying down the stairs in her trainers and make an unnecessary fuss, tonight was as good a time as ever.

Sadly, convincing herself to get out of the house was a difficult feat. Getting to work each morning was fine; she made the half-hour journey almost without thinking, listening to music as she sat on the top deck of the bus among other bleary-eyed morning passengers until it stopped at Broad Quay.

But this? This was different.

Getting out there, actually *running* – it felt impossible. Anxiety made its presence known, a threatening lurch that made her long to clamber back into bed and stay there. Away from the people, the noise, the traffic. She hesitated, contemplating the possible merits of this strange spontaneous idea, but then she caught sight of the medal again.

I have to do this.

Malika rushed to her rail of clothes, packed tightly with her work outfits and party dresses she hadn't worn in ages. Somewhere, she knew, there were a couple of gym outfits she'd almost forgotten about, bought when Roz had talked her into going with her to a dance fitness class. They'd given up after the second session. Pulling the clothes from their hanger, she rummaged intently in the pile of shoes below for her trainers. Malika stepped from the comfort of her light pyjamas, pulling on the leggings and top, tight and unfamiliar against her skin.

Stepping into her trainers, she rushed down the stairs and was out of the house before she could talk herself out of it.

Outside, the evening sun was still present. Malika squinted ahead, warmth pricking at her bare shoulders. She set off at a slow pace, more walking than running, making her way along the row of terraced Victorian town houses that stood tall on either side of the street. She continued along the pavement, listening out for the sounds of traffic, as if it were tuned into her brain now. Cars that careered down the stretch of road would make her breath quicken, her heart flutter.

It was sudden . . .

Didn't have time to stop . . .

Dead . . .

The words echoed in her mind. Encased there, permanent. They made her jump, made her tense at the sound of any vehicle that was going too fast for her liking. She wished she possessed some kind of power, some superhuman ability to stop them, to make their tyres grind to a shuddering halt before the worst could happen.

All it took was one moment. That nanosecond of distraction to wipe out an entire life. Malika knew this all too well. 'I'm sorry to have to tell you this, but something terrible happened last night. Abbie passed away.' She'd always remember those words, choked out by Eva in their morning huddle as she tried to hold herself together.

Only Abbie didn't 'pass away' in that nice, pleasant way that the well-worn phrase seemed to conjure. She didn't slip away in her sleep surrounded by all of her loved ones. Abbie was killed almost instantly. The local newspaper hadn't spared the imagery; there had been blood at the scene, her injuries fatal. For several days after it happened Malika couldn't sleep, hearing a screech of brakes each time she closed her eyes, picturing her friend being thrown into the air, the sickening *crack* of bones on tarmac as she landed.

Malika quickened her pace and turned down a side road that led round the back of the houses. She moved into the shade, into the alleyway where the backs of the terraces rose above, slightly less imposing than their pointed facades. Malika's path was shrouded by the shadows of trees that reached over tall, neat fences, their branches like waving hands, ready to grab and pull. Malika dashed to the side to dodge an overhanging willow, her feet pounding in a soft, unfamiliar rhythm against the hard ground.

She stayed within the safety of her street, where it was quiet but for the thump of music from a nearby window, or the sounds of a chatter as a group of teenagers walked by. The inviting smell of barbecue smoke hung in the air as Malika wound her way round the block and back again, trying to keep her breathing steady. She had no particular route. She just let her feet, and her mind, carry her away.

Malika ran until the ache that had risen in her calves forced her to stop. *Too much, too soon*, she thought, heading slowly towards home, her skin warm and sweaty. For a moment, Malika marvelled at how good it had felt, even for such a short time. She'd managed to let herself escape the safe, familiar surroundings of her room.

But it didn't take long for another realisation to hit her with force. She'd managed to run for less than ten minutes. How on earth was she going to manage for twenty-six miles?

It was impossible.

The rock-like feeling in her stomach returned. She pondered how she'd been so stupid, so naive as to sign up for a marathon. A quick jog round the block was one thing, where the safety of home was just moments away, but a big race? Among thousands of other people? The thought made her heart pound with absolute dread.

Malika sighed as she pulled her key from the pocket of her leggings and stepped back inside the empty house.

5

Hannah

'We're about to start the five-minute warm-up walk. Get ready!'

The chirpy voice in Hannah's ears made her walk a little faster along the pavement. Almost in a power-walk, she moved quickly, checking her reflection in the window of a parked car as she passed. Her face was half concealed by a pair of giant sunglasses.

After the humiliation of her first attempt, Hannah had decided to take it slow. Very slow. And she wanted to be anonymous. Away from the threat of passing motorists and overly curious neighbours. Which is why she'd decided to come to the park.

'And we're off!'

The voice was replaced by music, all upbeat and inspiring. At least, it was meant to be. Hannah mentally questioned the reality of what she was doing and let out a laugh. Just yesterday, Bronwen had introduced her to the 'Couch to 5k' programme.

'It's great!' Bronwen had said as they'd met in their favourite cafe for their usual weekly post-work catch-up. 'It's designed to help new runners to get off their sofas and get running. It guides you on how to run 5k in nine weeks. Sounds like the very thing you need. Download it, give it a go!'

Hannah did, hastily, only to realise that in just *twelve* weeks she was supposed to be running a marathon. Hannah wanted to cry.

It wasn't a podcast she needed – it was a miracle.

Victoria Park wasn't far from Hannah's house – a huge, sprawling haven among the bustling city. Gathering a bit of speed as the gates came into view, Hannah slipped inside, away from the road and into the safety of the trees and the shade. The park itself was far from empty, which was no wonder given the balmy evening. Dog walkers ambled down the path as their four-legged companions bounded on the grass in their element, tethered to extendable leashes. Teenagers gathered beneath a tree in the distance. Mothers pushed buggies in unison as they chatted, their other, older children hurrying off towards the swings as trains rumbled by on the nearby track, into Bedminster station.

And, of course, there were the runners.

Hannah knew they'd be there. She knew she'd be unable to avoid the runners who followed the park's dedicated route. Today there were only two, but the sight of them made Hannah feel increasingly self-conscious, her legs more jellylike than when she left the house. The first was sprinting along in the distance, poised and serious, as though she were leading an Olympic sprint. The purple hue of her running top matched the stripe on her clearly expensive leggings.

A proper runner.

Hannah briefly imagined herself, running free, slim and poised just like that woman in purple, with a body she was proud of. She slunk back into the shade, watched as the woman headed back, glancing at a fitness gadget on her wrist. At the other side of the park, just in Hannah's field of vision, the second runner made her way along the route, too. The girl looked young, her head down, earphones in, as if lost in her own world. She was slower, Hannah noticed, stopping to drink water before carrying on.

Hannah gripped her own water bottle tightly, contemplating starting her jog in the midst of these two pros. Nobody was looking her way, but that didn't make her feel any less of an imposter. A scruffy novice in her T-shirt and battered trainers about to make a complete fool of herself. This was not her world.

I should have just stayed home.

No, Hannah thought. It had to be done. She started to jog, letting her feet do the work. She tried to ignore the burgeoning pain in her muscles that had started during her walk from the house. It hadn't been that big a distance, but her body, still used to shying away from the mere thought of this much exercise, had started to rebel.

Hannah stole another look at the other runners hurrying along in the sun and suddenly saw herself heaving her large, sweaty body alongside them. The thought was terrifying, as if the ghost of Karen Smith had appeared before her, yelling her insults for all the park to hear.

Nervously, she continued her gradual run. Slowly but surely, she wound her way up the path, keeping to a steady pace, watching the scenery around her as though to stop herself from seeing the daunting route which seemed to go on forever. She watched as a man walked his two golden Labradors on the grass verge nearby. They bounded happily, chasing a ball as the music thumped in her ears. *This is the warm-up*, she thought. *And I'm already sweating.*

Suddenly, the music stopped, replaced by the soft hum of her ringtone. Fishing her phone out of her bra as discreetly as she could manage, Hannah looked at the screen and her heart soared.

Dan.

Shakily, she swiped the screen to answer.

'Hello?' said a bold voice. 'Han?'

It was Dan all right. Hannah knew that voice anywhere. It was the voice that had greeted her every night after work, that had talked to her about anything and everything over the years. That had made her laugh, made her cry with happiness, that comforted her when life was most harsh. It was a voice she hadn't heard for many weeks.

'Dan?' Hannah replied, trying to keep the shock – and the excitement – from her voice.

It made her smile: Han and Dan. They were always Han and Dan. It felt for a second as if he hadn't left, as if he were calling her to ask what she wanted from the chip shop.

'Are you all right, Han?' Dan asked. 'You sound all wheezy.'

Hannah stopped in her tracks. 'I'm fine. Just training, that's all. I've just run 5k. It really takes it out of you.'

She cringed at her lie. But clearly, it had worked. Why else would Dan be calling? He must have seen her posts about the marathon, the 'post-run bubble bath' selfie she'd uploaded the day before. 'Relaxing bath chases all the stresses away!' she'd typed. Clearly, it was working. His interest had been piqued.

'Ah, right. So you're actually doing that race, then? I thought you were winding us all up.'

Hannah's breath caught in her lungs.

'No . . .' she managed, not wanting to let her disappointment show. She couldn't break down in tears. Not now, not in the middle of the park. 'I wasn't joking,' she said defensively. 'I'm actually doing it.'

'That's good, then,' said Dan.

She sensed a smile at the other end of the line.

'Really good.'

That was something, at least.

He paused. 'Can you talk right now?'

'Yes, I can,' said Hannah, ambling along the path.

The other runners were still going, still racing against the heat of the evening sky. A flicker of hope ignited.

'Perfect. Well, I think I've left my good toolbox at the house. Do you know if you've seen it? The blue one. You know the one I'm on about. Could have sworn I'd brought it with me, but obviously I didn't.'

The disappointment welling up inside her was swiftly replaced by anger. All the possible reasons and she hadn't thought of *that* one.

'No, Dan. No, I bloody haven't.' With that, she ended the call, stuffed the phone back in her bra and began to run.

I'll show him, she thought.

I'll show him exactly *what he's missing*.

Hannah's feet pounded against the track. She gave it all she could. Her legs cried in pain, but she no longer cared. Through the shade of her oversized glasses, the park was a blur through the tears, but she continued, pounding and pounding and . . .

'Ouch!'

Startled, she looked down to see what had just hit her in the shin. A tennis ball rolled slowly along the grass.

'Sorry!' shouted a male voice. The dog walker, Hannah noticed.

She squinted at his figure in the distance as he gave an apologetic wave, just as the dogs bounded excitedly towards her in search of their toy.

'Toby!' the man shouted. 'Henry! Come on, boys, get back here, now!'

Hannah stepped back, but it was too late. All she saw was a blur of golden fur before she felt herself hurtling forwards in an awful, sickening slow motion.

Thud.

Hannah's body hit the grass. She scrambled to her feet, but it was no use. She was stuck. She looked round to discover that the dogs' thick red leashes had entangled her legs.

'Toooby!' she heard the man yell in the distance. 'Henry! Oh, God, Tobe, no . . .'

The dogs, who'd ceased scrabbling for the ball, eagerly decided to return it to their panic-stricken master. They sped off along the grassy hill, dragging Hannah along behind them like a sled. She rolled over in an attempt to free herself from the leashes, but only made it worse.

'Er, help?!' she yelled, her knees burning with pain, face ablaze with shame as she felt the whole park turning round to watch.

Toby and Henry, oblivious to Hannah's terror, came to an abrupt halt at their master's feet. The man – elderly, Hannah noticed now, in his thin jumper and flat cap – ambled over as quickly as he could. Hannah lay there, face down on the grass. It had only been seconds but it felt like a lifetime. She looked at her leggings, now sporting some vivid grass stains and a gaping hole on each knee.

Maybe the park wasn't the best idea, after all.

6

Hannah

'Hey!'

Attempting to heave herself up from the grass, her sunglasses broken and skew-whiff on her face, Hannah heard a voice call across the park, over the rumble of a passing train. Looking up, she glimpsed a flash of limbs as someone ran to a stop beside her. It was one of the runners. The tall one in purple. The woman headed straight for Hannah, untangling the leashes from her now throbbing ankles before rounding on the dogs' owner.

'What on earth do you think you're playing at?' she snapped, thrusting the leashes, now resembling a tangled ball, into the man's hands. 'Letting your hulking great dogs jump at people like that. Do you really think that's appropriate?'

Hannah almost felt sorry for the man. Hearing that stern voice would have made her run away herself if she hadn't been lying on the ground.

'I'm so sorry,' he muttered. 'They're not usually like this. Are you OK?'

Both of them turned to Hannah, who let out a pained groan.

'Fine,' she said, looking at the sore, red grazes on her knees. 'Just a bit dizzy.'

'Sorry, love,' said the man again. 'If there's anything I can do . . .'

'Just be more careful in future,' the runner said, brow furrowed.

Naturally, Toby and Henry were now on their best behaviour, sitting quietly next to their master. A perfect picture of obedience. The man turned and shuffled off, the dogs trailing happily behind him.

'Some people are so irresponsible,' said the runner in purple, helping Hannah to her feet. 'Are you sure you're all right?'

'Kind of. My feet hurt. And it's safe to say these leggings are destined for the bin. But otherwise, I'm good.' Hannah took a step and winced. 'Ouch.'

'Can you move your foot? Try to wiggle your toes.'

Hannah did as she was told. 'It's fine. I'd know if it was broken. Broke a toe once and that was bad enough. There'll probably be a nasty bruise or two tomorrow, but I think my pride hurts the most. Everyone in the park just saw me go arse over tit.'

The woman laughed. Her features softened, her small, serious face suddenly glowing. She helped Hannah to a nearby bench, picking up the water bottle and phone that had fallen into the grass. She looked at the slogan on the bottle – 'I swear this is not gin' – and laughed some more.

'Love it,' she said as Hannah slumped back on the bench, defeated once again. 'And don't worry about it. I'm sure nobody filmed it.'

'Oh, God.'

'I'm just kidding. It's fine. And after a rest you'll be back to running in no time.'

Hannah thought about that possibility. Did she actually *want* to run again?

She sneaked a glance at her purple-clad saviour, with her toned legs and expensive kit. She looked to be in her early thirties, a picture of health and wellness, just like the magazines kept pushing. Hannah felt like a joke next to her. A fat, unfit joke who'd just been dragged pathetically through the park by a couple of playful dogs in front of all and sundry. If only Karen Smith could see her now.

Or Dan. Hannah shuddered at the thought.

'I'm Cassie, by the way,' the woman said, prodding her fitness gadget.

'I'm Hannah. Thanks for coming to my rescue. They were pretty harmless pooches, but very strong. It was just an accident.'

'I think they liked you,' Cassie said.

'Maybe. I do have one of those faces, you know? Everyone wants to chat to me at the bus stop. And in the supermarket. I must look approachable. Is that a good thing, or a curse?'

'A bit of both, I think,' laughed Cassie.

At that moment, Hannah saw another figure come hurrying across the grass. The other runner. She watched as the girl, with her matching outfit and bouncing ponytail, sprinted towards them and felt a pang of envy.

The pang subsided when the girl stopped at the bench and almost fell to the floor, trying to catch her breath.

'H . . . hi,' she wheezed, gulping down some water. 'Oh, God, I shouldn't have done that. I can't run that quickly yet. I just wanted to check you were all right.'

'Wonderful,' laughed Hannah. 'An audience. I'm fine. Just a sprain, I think. And I thought coming to the park would help me to blend in.'

She smiled at the runner, who was now seated on the ground, resting. She was young; Hannah guessed at late teens to early twenties.

'I wouldn't worry,' said Cassie. 'I fell over during a race once, in front of a load of spectators. Wouldn't have been so bad if I wasn't caught on camera. That was one race photo I didn't keep.'

The others laughed.

'Thanks for coming to check on me. I'm Hannah.'

'Cassie,' Cassie said, giving a little wave to the newcomer.

'I'm Malika. Don't mind me; I'm just having a little rest. Wow, running can be hard. I don't think I'll ever properly "get it", you know?'

Hannah perked up at this information. If this fresh-faced youngster wasn't getting it either, then at least she knew she wasn't alone.

I know exactly what you mean,' she said. 'I've only just started training. I'm meant to be running a race soon and I've no bloody clue how I'll even make it through one kilometre, let alone the rest.'

Malika's eyes widened. 'Same! I signed up for it and . . . well, maybe I was being a bit too ambitious. It's my first race.'

Cassie rose from the bench to do some leg stretches.

'Well, having a race to train for is really good motivation,' she said. 'What are you training for? A 5k?'

'Er,' Malika began. 'God, I feel so stupid for saying it, but The Great South-West Marathon.'

'Me too!' Hannah nearly squealed.

Hannah watched as Cassie's face yielded a spectacular transformation. A flicker of amusement, followed by complete and utter open-mouthed shock. Cassie stared, her gaze flitting from Hannah to Malika. Despite the heat of the park, Hannah suddenly felt cold, noticing Cassie's eyes drinking in her outfit, her grubby old trainers, her mere *presence*.

'Wait, you're *not* joking?'

Hannah shook her head.

Cassie's mouth opened again as though she was about to say something but decided against it at the last minute.

Probably for the best, thought Hannah, unsure if she could take any more humiliation in one day.

'Your first race is a *marathon*?'

'Hey, you're not helping,' said Malika jokingly. 'I'm already terrified.'

Cassie frowned, making the slight line between her eyes more prominent. A line that was invisible when she smiled and laughed. When she wasn't doing it, she was striking, her big, blue-grey eyes commanding attention, contrasting with her dark brown hair. Hannah wondered if Cassie frowned a lot.

'A marathon is . . . well, it's *hard*. And you do know the race is in three months, right? I'm running it, too.'

'Really? That's amazing,' said Malika. 'All three of us doing the same race. How spooky.'

Both women looked at Hannah, who was sitting on the bench in silence. She'd been stupid. Embarrassingly so. If this random woman, this actual runner, thought she was mad, then she had no hope in finishing that race whatsoever.

'I know how it sounds,' said Hannah, staring at the grass, the noises of the park ebbing away, replaced by the images inside her head. Dan. The scenes she'd imagined, where Dan would see her racing, fist-pumping the air as she pounded the pavement along with thousands of others. A silly fantasy. Suddenly, she felt rather foolish. 'You don't have to remind me.'

'Sorry,' said Cassie. She finished her stretches and perched on the bench beside Hannah. 'I didn't mean to be rude about it. It's just . . . a marathon? That's ballsy.'

All three of them laughed.

'Trust me, you can do it. If you put your mind to it and stick to a training plan, you can do it.'

'Are you sure? I thought I could, but now I really don't know. Do I *look* like a runner to you?' Hannah jiggled her arms as if to prove a point, expecting a peal of laughter from Cassie, but instead she was met with a look of confusion. 'It was . . .' *An accident? A drunken mistake?* Hannah didn't want to admit that part of the story. 'Well, a spur-of-the-moment thing. If other people can do it, why can't I?'

Because I'm not a runner, she remembered, then chided herself for not thinking positively. She wanted to believe what she'd just told Cassie, yet at the same time, something was holding her back. Just one glance would tell anyone that this was new to her, that maybe she wasn't cut out for it, after all. That it wasn't her place. The sudden, shifting feeling from hope to despair reminded her of school PE lessons, where she was always one of the last to be chosen for a team. Last Resort Hannah.

Malika put down her water and smiled. 'Don't worry. You're not the only one. I've never run a race in my life, yet here I am, training for a marathon.'

'Can I ask why you've decided to start with twenty-six miles, then?' Cassie enquired.

Malika looked at the ground, reaching for one of the daisies that dotted the acres of green. She plucked it out, twirling it in her fingers, inspecting it.

'It was last minute,' she replied. 'A friend encouraged me.'

'That's nice,' said Hannah. 'Having a friend to run with. I bet having someone to spur you on makes all the difference.'

Malika discarded the flower in the grass. 'She's not around any more,' she said quietly. 'She died.'

Silence descended upon the group. Hannah went to speak, but no words came. Around them, the sounds of the park could be heard, joyful and serene; the birds tweeting their loud songs in the trees overhead, the determined cheers of people playing football in the fields behind. Hannah felt as though she'd spoilt a happy moment.

50

'I'm really sorry,' said Hannah. 'I have a habit of putting my foot in it sometimes.'

Malika shrugged. 'It's all right. You weren't to know. But yes, I'm doing this alone. My friend liked to run. I promised her I'd run one with her one day and then . . . well, she died, so here I am. I'm doing it now.'

'I'm so sorry,' said Cassie sympathetically.

Hannah turned to Cassie. 'And what about you, then? I'm guessing you do this all the time.'

Cassie's face brightened. 'Yep! I run every day. It's so therapeutic. I've done lots of 10ks and about five half-marathons, but this is my first marathon. It's been a goal of mine for ages and now it's time. I like to challenge myself.'

'Can you bottle that outlook so I can buy some?' Hannah said, laughing.

'Give it a month and you won't need to,' Cassie replied.

Hannah wasn't convinced, but she didn't want to argue. She knew, without a doubt, that she would never be like Cassie. If she hadn't been bitten by the fitness bug now, at forty-eight, then there was little chance of that happening. Hannah had always just put it down to not being *one of those people*. She certainly hadn't been blessed with a runner's body; there was no way she'd ever be able to keep up with Cassie, all fast and strong and lithe.

Even though the comments of her schooldays had followed her into the vast alleyway of adulthood, Hannah had managed to put them behind her – most of the time, anyway. Especially when she'd met Dan. He'd made her feel beautiful, put her at ease. When she'd sometimes plucked up the courage to admit how she felt in the early days, how she'd worried he'd be tempted by someone prettier, someone slimmer, he'd laughed her worries away and enveloped her in his strong, comforting arms.

Even later, when her body had failed to make her dream of a family come true, Dan still stood by her. And when the menopause had made an untimely appearance, making its startling debut not long after her forty-third birthday, Hannah felt a big part of her long-imagined life disappearing in a taunting puff of smoke. As the doctor confirmed it, she'd sat in the uncomfortable leather chair in his beige office, watching her dreams falling straight through her shaking fingers. Yet, she and Dan had stuck together, worked through it as one. Han and Dan.

Hannah had always assumed that she'd other redeeming qualities, attributes that had commanded Dan's attention from the first time they'd met. Her kindness, for example. Her sense of humour, her bubbly, approachable nature and penchant for a bit of fun. But since Dan had dumped her for someone else, someone who fit that 'other' mould so perfectly well, she'd started to second-guess whether or not she'd ever been likable – and attractive, for that matter – in the first place.

Cassie got to her feet, pulling Hannah out of her maudlin reverie.

'Right, I should go. My sister-in-law is coming round later and I'd better prepare myself.'

'Good luck,' said Hannah.

She knew in-law woes all too well. If anything, being away from Dan had at least *one* benefit – she wouldn't have to endure awkward dinners with Dan's overly smug brother, Martin.

'It was nice to meet you,' said Malika. 'You, too, Hannah. I should probably head home as well.'

'Good luck with the race,' said Cassie.

Hannah got up from the hard bench, wobbling slightly, trying to ease the pain of her foot. There was no way she could run now, not until it had fully healed. A hot bath was certainly on the cards.

Hannah and Malika watched as Cassie hurried off down the path. Then, just before she reached the gates, she stopped. Cassie took out her phone from the back pocket of her leggings and stared at it before turning round and rushing straight back towards them.

'Look,' she said, reappearing by the bench, stuffing the phone back into her pocket. 'I know this whole training thing is daunting, especially as it's your first race. I live close by, so I'd be happy to run some training sessions with you, if you like.'

'Are you kidding?' Malika squealed, her big eyes glinting with excitement. 'That would be amazing.'

'Are you sure?' Hannah asked. 'Wouldn't want to trouble you.'

Cassie grinned. 'I'd love to. How are you two fixed for Wednesday evenings?'

'Sounds great,' Malika agreed.

Hannah nodded. She wasn't about to turn down some training. She needed all the help she could get.

Once they'd exchanged numbers, Hannah limped towards the gate, but the pain didn't bother her any more. Now that Cassie was going to help them train, Hannah felt high on positivity. She'd even laughed off the dog debacle, seeing it as a blessing in disguise. As she left the sounds of the park behind her just as the sun was beginning to set, Hannah's phone pinged with a message from Cassie:

Forgot to mention . . . it's exactly three months until race day! Xx

Hannah's evening had become that tiny bit brighter.

7

Malika

Hey, lovely! I know I should really stop posting on
here now. Even if you could see these messages,
you'd probably be getting fed up of them. But
sometimes, it still doesn't feel real. I still expect you
to walk through the door, like you'd just gone on
holiday. Sometimes I'll be scrolling through my
timeline, expecting to see you pop up in a photo,
smiling on a mountain somewhere. I really miss our
office chats – could really do with one now, to be
honest. I just hope you know that I miss you loads.
Hope you're having fun and that you don't forget
about us down here.
Xx

Malika contemplated deleting the message. Just like every
other time she'd posted on Abbie's page – she'd forgotten
how many at this point – she questioned her reasoning. The
weight she felt each day when she thought about it, invisible
but lead-like, returned at its worst when she ventured there,
when her head spun with a thousand unanswered questions.
Why?

That was the worst question of all. The biggest and cruel-
lest. *Why her? Why now? Why not someone else? Why didn't*

she get the chance to say goodbye? But wasn't it better that it was quick? Why am I thinking that?

Each time Malika typed a message into that looming, waiting box, she told herself it would be the last time. One final tribute, then she'd stop. Close the page and refuse to look back. But she always went back, each time more heartbreaking than the last when she saw the page empty of Abbie's words. Noticing how many days had ticked by since Abbie's final status update was harrowing, yet at the same time, provided Malika with a strange sort of comfort.

Venturing onto it, this record full of Abbie's life, from the fun to the mundane, made her happy in a way she couldn't quite comprehend. And as she clicked through the photos she'd seen thousands of times before – Abbie and Malika smiling at a Halloween party three years previously, Abbie sitting on a beach with her boyfriend, James, beneath a backdrop of endless sunshine – Malika felt it was confirmation that her kind, beautiful, lively friend had been there. She'd lived. Despite the silence, she'd lived.

The status updates had ended one Monday – a sunny, calm afternoon that had become memorable for all the wrong reasons. There was still a slight chill in the air, the stifling heat of summer a near distant promise. Malika had said goodbye, leaving Abbie to finish up some emails.

'I won't stay too long,' said Abbie, knowing Malika was playfully about to remind her that she had a boyfriend to hurry home to. 'See you in the morning.'

She didn't even make it home. Abbie was just minutes away from her house when the car collided with her bicycle.

Why didn't she leave just five minutes earlier?

'Remembering Abbie Gordon'. That was all that was left. Abbie was hardly going to come back from the dead and pop up with a message. The 'where are you?' text that

Malika had sent when Abbie didn't turn up for work the following morning (she was *always* the first one in the office) was still left unread, and always would be. So why did she keep looking, keep checking? She knew that by posting tributes, she was merely talking into the void; friends, family, Marc and Eva, they'd all left one sentimental message and left it at that. Except for Abbie's mother. Aside from Malika, only Abbie's mum had remained active, pouring her grief into messages as though her daughter could hear her. Messages that made Malika's heart ache with longing and guilt, because nobody, *nobody* had it worse than Janice Gordon.

Malika took a sip of coffee. It was still too hot and it burned her tongue, but she didn't care. Her eyes were on Abbie, at her friend's smiling face that beamed out of the profile photo. It was the one the local newspaper had used. In it, her blonde hair flowed to her shoulders in beachy waves as she posed with a cocktail, sunglasses pushed up onto her head. Malika stared at the photo as if drinking in every detail, committing it all to memory. She had to stop looking now. Stop leaving messages. Put it behind her.

Life was fragile, Malika knew this now. One second, one wrong turn, and you could be pulled from this world in less than a minute, before you even got the chance to say a proper goodbye.

'Hey, Mal!'

Malika jumped at the sight of Eva, who'd appeared quietly beside her. Malika noticed her boss's glance flit towards the screen. Hastily, she closed the page.

'Sorry, love. Didn't mean to startle you. Just wanted to give you a heads-up about today. We're expecting quite a lot of new registrations; the First Circle jobs went live on Friday and we've already had a lot of CVs sent through. So, if you could start going through them, that'd be amazing. If it gets too busy, I'll jump in and help.'

Malika nodded. 'No problem,' she said, forcing a smile.

On the plus side, she thought, watching Eva head into the kitchen, *a busy day will make the hours fly by*. Maybe afterwards, she could go running.

Running. It was a new sensation, the thought of actually being excited about running. Her legs, sore since the last run and the morning's ascent up Park Street, shifted beneath the desk. Since meeting Cassie and Hannah, the dark cloud of dread had eased slightly and even though the race terrified her, it didn't seem as daunting now she wouldn't be facing it alone.

The door swung open and Marc entered the office, the strong scent of aftershave trailing in his wake.

'All right?' he asked cheerily, stretching, turning on his computer as the sound of the kettle and Eva's lively singing travelled in from the kitchen.

'Yeah. Ooh, before I forget, Eva's just warned us that we're likely to be busy today, so be prepared.'

'Yes, boss,' said Marc, giving a mock salute.

Malika rolled her eyes, amused. 'Very funny.'

Leaving Marc to go and get some coffee, she turned to the computer, clicking back to Abbie's page. The cursor hovered over the tiny cross, ready to close it for the very last time. Just as she was about to close it for good, something caught her eye. A link to a recent news article. Abbie's mum had posted it, beneath a row of broken heart emojis.

BRISTOL LIVE: Concern in city as number of traffic accidents soars – mayor calls for changes . . .

Malika clicked.

Residents have expressed concern over Bristol's busy roads after a number of traffic-related incidents in the last five years . . .

According to government statistics, more than a hundred cyclists are killed on UK roads . . .

Malika's heart thudded. Abbie's death might have been an accident, but it was an accident that was happening again and again. Unless something was done about it, it would only continue to happen.

Determination surged through Malika. She opened up a new search and typed, her fingers hurrying along the keyboard. Within seconds, she found what she was looking for.

Brake – the road safety charity.

Malika saw the 'Fundraise' link.

Could she?

The thought of running the marathon was scary. She knew that. She constantly tried to swat away the mental image of the huge crowd, the people, everyone watching. Malika knew she was likely to finish last, but it didn't matter; all she wanted to do was finish. And with Cassie training her, that goal now seemed achievable.

She wanted to raise money, so what was stopping her? Besides self-doubt, of course. She thought of Abbie's medal, now tucked safely into the pocket of her backpack like a good luck charm.

Quickly, she clicked on the link. *I'll do it*, she thought. *I'll do it for Abbie.*

Malika slid the paper across her desk. 'So, if you could just fill out this form . . .'

The girl sitting opposite, with her wide round glasses and a hopeful smile, took a pen from the holder and began to jot down her details. Eva wasn't wrong: the office was abuzz with activity – so busy that Malika and Marc barely had time to eat lunch, instead munching on the stash of biscuits that Eva kept in the kitchen, whenever they had a spare two minutes. Every seat in the small office was taken and already two of Malika's candidates had turned up late, pushing everyone else behind schedule.

The girl sitting in front of her stopped writing, a confused expression in place of the smile she wore two minutes ago. Malika wished she'd hurry up and jot down her details before anyone else decided to come in for an impromptu chat.

'Is everything OK?' she asked.

'Maybe. It's just . . . I'm pretty sure I've filled this one out before. I registered about three months ago. I was put forward for a job in HR. I had an interview and I still haven't heard any news, and to be honest, I really had my hopes set on that one. Have you heard anything?'

'Oh!' Malika replied. 'I'm sorry. I didn't realise you were already with us. I'll have a look on our system. What's your name?'

'Rebecca Stone.'

Malika typed in the name, watching as the girl's profile loaded in front of her. Rebecca flicked her red hair over her shoulder, a hopeful look on her face. Malika could see the application for the HR job. And the feedback.

She'd been unsuccessful.

'I'm really sorry,' said Malika. 'But it looks like you didn't get the job.'

The hope suddenly disappeared.

'Really?' said Rebecca. 'So why wasn't I told?'

'Well, I—'

'I mean, that's not on! I've waited *ages* to hear about it. I called, but nobody answered. What kind of agency *is* this?'

Rebecca's voice grew louder by the second. Around the room, people glanced in their direction, wondering what was going on. Face burning, Malika took another look at her screen. There it was – the reason. The sinking feeling returned to Malika's stomach. She closed her eyes for three seconds, willing it to go away. Rebecca wasn't prepared to let it go.

'Seriously, I've been waiting a month to hear back. A *month*! That's not acceptable, is it?'

'No, it's not. It's—'

'Where's the woman I spoke to before, then?' Rebecca demanded loudly. 'You know the one. Blonde hair? Shoulder-length? Black blazer? Chatty? I'm sure if I speak to her, she'll have an answer. She'd *better*.'

Rebecca's eyes darted around the room for the mysterious blonde-haired woman, who'd never be coming to her rescue.

Malika began to speak, but the words were stuck in her throat, causing her to emit a tiny croak as she struggled to set them free. 'She's . . . not here any more,' she managed.

'Typical,' said Rebecca under her breath, just loud enough for Malika to hear.

Malika felt as though she'd been punched in the stomach. The anger hit her with such force that it rendered her speechless. She opened her mouth, but the words weren't there. She could see herself grabbing Rebecca by the neck of her fashionably oversized blouse, telling her just *why* Abbie wasn't here to deal with her shitty, unimportant problem.

Because that's all it was, wasn't it? Some minor inconvenience. A First World problem for this woman, who'd be able to stand, walk out into the summer sun and tell her friends what a *terrible* day she'd had, not getting what she wanted. Meanwhile, Abbie was dead, in a coffin beneath the ground. Malika had watched as it was lowered, her friend disappearing for good. Abbie would never be able to walk back in, no matter how desperately Rebecca's beady eyes searched the room as though Abbie would stroll through the door and make everything right for her.

Malika got to her feet, fuelled by anger. Rebecca's impatience had finally broken through Malika's cool, calm exterior. Before she could stop herself, Malika snatched Rebecca's form from her grasp and balled it up in her fist.

'Do you want to listen to me for a minute?' Malika shrieked.

Malika felt the silence that fell across the office. Every head turned to look, including Marc's.

'You OK?' he mouthed, but Malika ignored both him and Eva, and everyone else who was gawping, desperate to see what happened next.

'Abbie didn't call you. Do you want to know why?' She turned the monitor round for Rebecca to see, prodding at the dates. 'The company told us that you didn't get the job the day after you interviewed. Which was the day Abbie died. Abbie's *no longer here*, OK? She's *dead*.'

Marc leapt from his desk. 'Come on now, Mal. I'll deal with this.'

'No!' Malika shook her head. 'If she wants a scene, she'll get one.' She turned to Rebecca. 'Abbie was dealing with it, OK? She didn't mean to get hit by a car. And we didn't answer your call because we closed the office for a few days. Is that all right with you? To take a few days to deal with something like that.'

All eyes were on Rebecca now, who looked panic-stricken. Humiliated. The overly confident anger had seeped away now and she slunk back in her chair, her eyes on the ruined form that Malika was still holding.

'So,' yelled Malika. 'Maybe it's best if you kept your snarky attitude to yourself. Otherwise, *nobody* will want to hire you. Ever.'

The shock on Rebecca's face was a picture. Her pale cheeks turned a deep shade of crimson before she grabbed her bag and hurried out of the door without saying another word.

The regret hit Malika instantly. She'd never been so angry, even with the most difficult of people. And now her boss was hurrying over, her mouth a thin line of concern.

'I think you need a break,' Eva said. 'Go and get yourself a coffee.'

'But—'

'Mal, I'll take over from here,' offered Marc, his hand on her shoulder. 'You sure you're all right?'

Malika nodded, even though she felt anything but all right. She picked up her purse and headed out into the sun-soaked street, realising for the first time ever that the very thing she wanted to do was run.

8

Hannah

Hannah was first to arrive at Victoria Park the following Wednesday, taking a seat on a bench halfway up the grassy hill. She'd taken another entrance this time, traipsing further and further up the bank, trying not to put too much strain on her foot. It had healed nicely, but she didn't want to exert herself.

She sat in silence, observing, enjoying the sight of the city as it sprawled into the distance. The brightly-painted houses of Totterdown stood tall and pretty as though overseeing the park, this haven of calm that existed among the high-rises and the hubbub of busy city life. She admired the houses, with their slanted roofs and uplifting colours that could be seen through the surrounding trees. She liked it here. The peace, the calm, the chance to think. It made her feel safe, somehow.

Hannah watched two mothers strolling along the path. One pushed a buggy as two toddlers hurried on ahead, enjoying the summer sun. One of the toddlers, a little girl in a yellow dress, bent down to pick a dandelion before hurrying back to her mum, beaming with pride, holding it out as a token of love. Hannah was met with a reminiscent sting, one that was strangely raw. Perhaps it was because she was alone, or that Dan was gone, but it was something she hadn't felt in a while. Something she kept locked away in a box, stored at the back of her mind, where she didn't want to venture. *Longing*. That's what it was. A longing for something she couldn't have.

Hannah couldn't take her eyes off the women. It made her feel uneasy, the way her gaze trailed them as they ambled along, chatting away yet keeping their eyes on the toddlers, who were running towards the playground. The children yelled happily, stopping to pick more flowers and weeds. They were at that particular age, curious about everything the world had to offer. What Hannah would have given to have a child at her feet, asking her questions and calling her Mummy. It would have been tiring, she knew that; even Bronwen, with her picture-perfect family life, didn't have it easy. 'I'm knackered,' she'd say. 'All the time, I'm bloody knackered.' Yet, Hannah would have taken it all in a heartbeat – the midnight feeds, the sleepless nights, the inability even to go to the loo without a wide-eyed audience. But life didn't have that in store for her. Her body had seen to that. During the worst times, when the feelings ate at her the most, she'd look at her reflection with disgust, prod at her stomach and wonder why she'd been made to be different. *Faulty*.

She thought she'd put that world behind her. Accepted it, acknowledged that they'd just be Han and Dan from then on. Gone were the days when she'd have to dive into supermarket toilets to cry after glimpsing a newborn baby, or feel as though the world had been pulled out from under her feet whenever a friend or colleague made a special 'announcement'.

And she couldn't deny it – over the past few days her sleepless thoughts had been invaded once again by Sophia. Lying awake in the darkness, she pondered whether such an announcement would come to rip her heart out all over again.

Almost instinctively, Hannah reached for her phone, heading straight for Sophia's Instagram. Each time she looked she felt sick, seeing little hints of Dan.

My man xxx

He was only in one of her photos, but the feed was rife with clues.

Spending another day with my special guy xx

Her friends had responded with a flurry of kissy face emojis and hearts. One had said:

We need to meet this mystery man of yours!!
So sweet, Soph!

Hannah resisted the urge to hurl the phone into a nearby bin, instead focusing on the most recent picture. A table, set with a romantic, candlelit centrepiece and two flutes filled with champagne. The knot in Hannah's weary stomach loosened. If Sophia was happily lapping up the bubbly, Hannah had nothing to worry about.

Yet, she thought.

Glancing round to check nobody was looking, Hannah put on her sunglasses and posed for a selfie, making sure to whack on the best, yet most inconspicuous, filter she could find.

Official training sesh! Feeling more energetic already. #runningselfie #glowing #fitandfast

'Hi!'

Hannah nearly leapt off the bench, the phone tumbling from her grasp.

'Christ!' she said as Cassie appeared in front of her like an overly-enthusiastic ghost. 'You frightened the life out of me. I'm not one for jump scares.'

'Sorry,' said Cassie.

Behind her was Malika, who'd come to join them on the bench, already starting some leg stretches. Hannah hurriedly went to collect her phone, but Cassie got there first.

'You dropped this,' she said.

Hannah felt her face burn with humiliation as Cassie's gaze lingered a little too long on the screen, where the photo was still in full view. Was it just her imagination, or was there a hint of amusement on Cassie's face?

Cassie didn't say anything, simply handed it back. Hannah promptly stuffed it back into her bra.

Now, Cassie laughed.

'What?' asked Hannah. 'It comes in handy when you've got no pockets.'

'It's genius,' said Malika.

'Maybe you should invest in something better for the marathon,' said Cassie. 'A proper belt. Or a backpack. Unless you want to carry round a couple of bottles of water, Vaseline and snacks in those cups, as well.'

'Oh, those'll be in my knickers,' said Hannah seriously, prompting a guffaw from Malika.

Cassie raised her eyebrows in shock.

'Just joking, obviously! I'll buy something better suited.'

'Well,' began Cassie excitedly. 'Are you ready for some training?'

*

Hannah didn't know where the surge of energy had come from, but it was there, coursing through her, spurring her on. Her legs felt heavy, and the ache was present, taunting and throbbing as she followed Cassie and Malika through the park.

'OK, let's get to that tree!' Cassie yelled like a drill sergeant, pointing into the distance.

Sweat dripped from every pore. Hannah could feel her armpits; sweat had soaked Dan's T-shirt just as it had her face and she yearned to stop and simply let her legs collapse beneath her, drop to the grass, give up, just breathe. She knew she'd be feeling it in the morning. Her legs would lock up and she'd be dragging herself through the workday. She'd need to recover. But Cassie's booming voice and Malika – who wasn't faring much better, in all honesty – propelled her to carry on.

Just keep going.

'Aaand *stop!*' yelled Cassie.

Hannah hadn't realised it, but they'd reached the tree. Turning round, Hannah noticed just how far they'd run.

'Wow,' she said before guzzling down the contents of her water bottle.

'See? You're both actually really good. You just need to set yourself goals. I'll help you over the coming weeks. Small goals. Try not to think of the race as a whole – see it in small sections. Otherwise the worry will get on top of you.'

'Easy for you to say,' said Malika between breaths.

'Honestly,' Cassie assured them. 'You're going to be fine. You won't be finishing it in record time, but if you're careful and you take it slow, it's doable. Oh! And one other important thing – don't stop. Whatever you do, keep moving. When you can't run, just walk.'

Hannah let out a nervous laugh. Malika looked more frightened than ever.

'You all right, Mal?' Hannah asked.

'Kind of. It's just . . . I felt so proud of myself for running round the park for half an hour, but that's nothing compared to all those miles we'll have to do. And I need to finish. The thing is, I decided to run for charity. I've registered now and reality has just hit me. Hard.'

'Charity? That's fab,' said Hannah. 'Are you raising money for your friend?'

Malika nodded. 'Yeah. She died in a road accident, so I've decided to try to raise some money for Brake in her memory. I mean, I already had this stupid, crazy idea to run a marathon, so why not?'

'Ooh, send me the details,' said Cassie. 'I can share it, maybe even get some sponsors at work.'

Hannah grinned. 'Me too! Actually, why don't we join you, Mal? We can all run for Brake. What do you think, Cass? You up for it?'

'Definitely,' Cassie replied.

Malika's face brightened. 'Oh my God, that's amazing. Thank you.' She turned to Hannah. 'Hey, we should run together. Cassie will probably want to do her own thing seeing as she's not a newbie like us, but shall we?'

'A million times yes!'

They headed towards the gates, grateful for the afternoon breeze that had descended on the park, making the branches sway. Cassie halted at the gate and Hannah noticed she was back to wearing her serious face, as though running turned Cassie into someone else entirely. Someone carefree and blissful.

'Do any of you fancy a drink?' Cassie asked. 'One of my favourite pubs is just up the street. And I made you some training plans we could discuss.'

Hannah felt her spirits instantly lift. A glass of red was all she needed after that difficult run, the first proper run

68

of many, even though she was trying to cut back on the habit. But while a post-work restock of cheap plonk from the local shop was one thing, having a well-earned drink with friends was something entirely different. Something that meant she didn't have to spend the next hour alone.

'That would be a dream,' she said. 'The only thing is, you ladies might just have to carry me.'

9

Hannah

Hannah had been joking about the carrying part, but Cassie's suggestion of a drink at The Shakespeare had made it somewhat of a reality. It may have been minutes away for a fitness fanatic like Cassie, but for anyone else, navigating the steep hills of Totterdown with already aching legs felt like climbing a treacherous mountain.

They ambled slowly past more pretty terraced houses, their facades painted in an assortment of colours that made Hannah think of seaside towns, of bright things to come. Despite the tiredness seeping into her bones, the rainbow of houses brightened her mood and she considered whether or not she might be experiencing the runner's high that she'd heard so much about over the years. Before, Hannah had refused to believe it existed – a myth, like mermaids or unicorns or perfect men, but now she felt overcome with a sudden rush of positive energy.

The pub was already buzzing with its evening regulars as they made their way inside, spotting a table by the window. Cassie unclipped the running bag from around her waist and rummaged inside for some money before making a grab for the drinks list.

'I'm tempted by a glass of red,' said Cassie. 'Even though I shouldn't. Hmm, decisions. What are you having?'

'Let me get these,' Hannah offered.

But Cassie shook her head, making Hannah feel somewhat guilty at Cassie's never-ending kindness, especially as just days ago they were complete strangers. However, Hannah was relieved to stay seated and not have to shuffle her way through a busy bar in a sweat-drenched T-shirt.

'I'll have a vodka and Coke,' said Malika. 'That'd be lovely.'

'A red wine for me as well, please,' said Hannah.

As Cassie headed for the bar, disappearing into the lively throng of people, Hannah turned to Malika.

'So, what was she like, then?'

'Sorry?'

'Your friend.'

Malika seemed taken aback by the question. She looked back at Hannah, her eyes flitting towards the table as if trying to figure out what to say.

'I've done it again, haven't I? I need to think before I speak. Sorry if I upset you.'

'No! No, honestly. It's fine.' Malika sat back in her chair.

Outside, people walked by the window. Chatting, laughing, holding glasses close as they relaxed in the evening sun.

'It was just a bit unexpected. Hardly anyone talks to me about her, that's all. Not really.'

'Why not?'

Malika shrugged. 'It's awkward, isn't it? They just don't know what to say. Every time I *do* get to talk to someone about her, they put on their best "sad face" and tell me how sorry they are, etcetera. Even Cassie did it. Then they carry on as though nothing's been said. It's like they don't want to feel awkward any more so they shut it out, like it's just a bad day you can get over quickly. It's not.'

'I know exactly what you mean,' said Hannah.

71

She cast her mind back to years before, when she'd spent months in a haze of sadness. The first miscarriage was the worst, she remembered. Nothing felt worse than having to explain to people what had happened. That the bubble of joy she'd been walking around in had eventually burst. She recalled the head-tilting, the endless proclamations of 'I'm sorry. *That must be so hard for you.*'

'Some people just don't know what to say,' Hannah continued. 'Especially if they haven't experienced it themselves. If someone could just say, "Hey, I know you're having a shit time right now. Here's a cake and someone to rant at," things would be so much easier.'

To Hannah's relief, Malika laughed.

'Yes! That'd be perfect. Abbie was only thirty-three. She was so lovely. We worked together, but we were quite close friends too, and she was such a genuine, kind person, which makes it so much worse. She was always happy, funny, had everything going for her. She had a lovely boyfriend, was ambitious, confident, sporty, had just bought a flat . . .' Malika pulled a beer mat from the table, turning it round in her hands.

Hannah had a sneaking suspicion that if Malika looked up, Malika would cry. Hannah reached over and placed her hand on Malika's arm.

'It's all right,' she assured her.

'But Abbie was one of those people you couldn't even hate if you wanted to. She was an all-round great person. I know I'm making her out to be a total saint here, and she wasn't, I know that. She could be bossy and sometimes I had to remind her that work wasn't everything. Maybe if she'd listened, she wouldn't have stayed late at work that evening and . . . well. She was stubborn. Really stubborn. But great.'

Malika lowered her voice. 'I keep seeing things on the news. Murders and knife crime, you know? All kinds of terrible things. I keep thinking, why are those awful people still out there when Abbie . . .' She trailed off. 'Sorry. I must sound so morbid. Didn't mean to lower the tone.'

'Don't be sorry,' said Hannah. 'What you're going through is perfectly normal. And you shouldn't have to avoid talking about her, you know. Talking about her keeps the memories alive.'

Malika looked up from the table and wiped her eyes. 'Thank you,' she said.

'Come to think of it, I remember seeing something in the local news about a cyclist. I thought at the time how tragic it was. There are some really busy roads in this city, and I've seen a few close calls when I've been out and about.'

'Me too,' said Malika. 'Maybe more can be done to stop so many accidents from happening. Some new safety initiatives, perhaps. I hope we can raise enough money to help.'

Hannah smiled. 'We will!'

She reached for her phone to share the link just as Cassie reappeared at the table bearing a small tray of drinks. How she'd managed to wade through the crowd without spilling them was anyone's guess. She placed the three glasses down carefully on the table. Hannah snapped a sneaky photo of hers and uploaded it to Facebook and Instagram.

A well-deserved post-run drink with the girls!
#marathon #yum

Perfect, she thought, in the desperate hope that the news of her new fitness regime would soon wing its way to Dan.

'I don't usually do this midweek,' Cassie said, slipping into the seat next to Malika, 'but a first official training session deserves a treat. Which reminds me – I've just emailed you both the training plans I've made. Most of the plans you can find online work on the assumption that you're already a runner, so I've tailored one to make it more . . . realistic.'

'That's really kind of you,' said Malika.

Hannah shifted in her seat, already opening her emails. 'What do you mean, *realistic*? Do you think we won't finish?'

Cassie shook her head quickly, fidgeting with the stem of her glass. Hannah noticed the subtle sparkle of an engagement ring, glimmering beneath the dim, cosy light of the pub. It was small and intricate. Understated, wrapped elegantly around Cassie's long finger.

'No! As in *no*, I don't think that. You can do it, but you won't be doing it quickly. I've been a runner for years. I run all the time and yet I still find marathon training hard. I can't imagine how difficult it is for a newcomer. You just need to make sure that you take it slowly and don't do anything that'll risk injury. Make sure you eat right and take up some body conditioning exercises like yoga.'

'*Yoga?*'

The pub faded to a blur in front of Hannah and she wasn't even tipsy. *Yoga.* Just thinking about it made her feel sick. Hannah had never set foot in a yoga class. The thought alone made her skin prickle with fear. All those slim, flexible bodies. As Hannah stared down at the email, more frightening words fell into view on the four-page, colour-coded plan. *Hills. Cross-training. Ten-mile run.* Tears pricked the corners of her eyes and before she could stop herself, she was crying.

'What's the matter?' Malika asked.

'This plan,' she said. 'It's so good, Cass. And so . . . detailed.'

At this, Cassie pulled a hilariously smug face.

'But I can't do yoga. Or hill runs. Or faff about making smoothies,' she continued. 'I'm just not one of those people.'

'People like me, you mean?' asked Cassie, a flash of hurt crossing her face. 'It's not so bad, once you get into it. It's just a case of establishing a habit.'

Hannah briefly recalled her most recent habits: the telly, copious amounts of chocolate and a clinking recycling box. Wistfully, she pictured what it'd be like to be Cassie. She wondered if Cassie's fiancé was the same. Tall and outdoorsy.

Hannah reached for her glass in an attempt to quell the disappointment before she realised just what she was doing.

'Ugh! I'm doing it again,' she said. 'I should be careful. It was this stuff that got me into trouble in the first place.'

'Trouble?' asked Malika.

Dammit, thought Hannah. She hadn't meant to blurt that out, but it was too late.

'It's nothing, really,' she said, trying to backtrack, hoping one of them would change the subject.

Because for a moment, Hannah had forgotten where she was. That this wasn't her usual catch-up with Bronwen – this was different. A nice evening drink in the presence of two new friends who really didn't have to know her pathetic life story. They didn't know the real her and in front of these two women, she could be whoever she wanted to be. Like the Hannah she portrayed on social media, where everyone seemed to be lapping up this new transformation. 'Look at you, Fitness Queen!' one person had commented beneath her selfie from earlier.

'Come on,' said Cassie, taking a sip of wine. 'You can't drop a bombshell like that and expect us not to ask questions.'

Hannah paused and contemplated lying. Glossing over the whole Dan story, just like she had online. But then, these weren't her social media friends who viewed her rose-tinted life from afar. Cassie and Malika were actually here, in the pub, witnessing her bedraggled appearance, which was nothing like the sophisticated picture of wellness she longed to portray.

'Han?' Malika tapped the table, eagerly awaiting her confession.

Hannah sighed. 'Fine. Well, the whole reason I'm running the Great South-West Marathon is because I got drunk on a bottle of Merlot and thought it'd be a grand idea to sign up, even though I could barely run across the street.'

Malika stared at her, mouth agape. Cassie, on the other hand, burst into peals of laughter.

'Well, thanks for the support,' said Hannah.

'I'm so sorry!' said Cassie. 'But that's brilliant. You got drunk and signed up to a *marathon?*'

'Oh, come on, Cass,' said Malika, trying not to laugh herself. 'Haven't you done anything weird while drunk? I know I have.'

'Well, many things, but not *that*,' said Cassie. 'Fair play, that's brave. Anyway, do carry on. I guess my big question is *why?*'

Hannah looked from Cassie to Malika and considered keeping quiet, retreating from this conversation altogether. *I made a mistake.* Wasn't that enough of a reason? She suddenly felt defensive, almost shameful at admitting her silliness in front of oh-so-perfect Cassie. Who, she was sure, would never have done something so moronic.

But she wasn't Cassie. And she never would be.

'OK,' she said, drawing in a breath. The pub felt almost too warm now, cloying and sticky. Or maybe it was the fear of actually baring all in front of these two women. 'My husband, Dan . . . well, he left me. We're separated.' She flinched as the word rolled off her tongue. *Separated.* So unnatural a word. So formal. 'He left me for a woman he met at the gym. She's fit, gorgeous, the whole bloody package. She's also a runner. So I had this marvellous idea *not* to do what normal people do while plastered and order some out-there outfit they forget about until it arrives, or even phone a friend and slur down the phone. Nope, I went and signed up for a bloody 26-mile run. Hence why I'm in this mess.'

All of a sudden, both Cassie and Malika burst into more laughter.

'I'm so, so sorry, Han, but you're too funny,' said Malika, managing to stop herself before more tears came. 'Your husband sounds awful. No offence. But on the plus side, I'm in this mess with you. It'll be fun.'

Cassie was still in a fit of giggles. *Laugh it up*, thought Hannah, but through the post-run haze and the dimly lit atmosphere full of chatter that enveloped her in a balmy hug, she soon let the fog clear and felt the laughter bubble in her own throat.

'Oh, Han, I'm sorry for laughing,' said Cassie finally. 'But if anything, you've just put yourself on a new adventure. It could have been a lot worse, trust me. You could have drunk-texted your ex twenty-eight times in one evening, like I did. It wasn't pretty. Not at all.'

'Ouch,' said Malika. 'Yep, got to give you points for creativity there, Han.'

'I guess it *is* funny, when you think about it,' Hannah agreed. 'Years of marriage and he leaves me for his personal trainer. The novelty will wear off, though. It always does with Dan.'

'Do you have children?' asked Malika.

There it was, the question that could knock the wind out of Hannah's sails.

'No,' she answered honestly.

'Oh.'

Hannah saw realisation sweep across Malika's innocent face. Cassie fell silent, turning her attention to her wine glass.

'So!' said Hannah, desperate to revive the conversation. 'That ex you texted, Cass. Did you ever get back together?'

'Oh God, no,' she replied, her face beaming a wide smile that Hannah hadn't seen before.

Hannah recognised it, though; she'd seen it in her own face, years ago. Love at its most intense.

'I ended up dating a man called Jack,' said Cassie. 'Who, thankfully, I didn't mess up with, because he's now my fiancé.'

'Aw, that's lovely,' said Malika.

'Congratulations!' said Hannah, raising her glass.

'So, I think we need a toast,' said Malika. 'In honour of our new running club.'

'Club?' said Cassie in alarm. 'Hey, I never said anything about a club. I've never run in a club before.'

'Why not?' asked Malika.

Cassie shrugged. 'I've never wanted to. There's nothing like running alone, having that solitude, being free to take whichever route takes your fancy. You can just let yourself go, let your feet thump to the beat of your music . . .' Cassie stared dreamily out of the window, while Hannah and Malika laughed uproariously.

'Get you,' said Hannah. 'Solitude? And then you go and offer to train us numpties?'

Cassie's faraway gaze returned to the table. Hannah noticed Cassie take a glance at her watch.

'Well,' Cassie said. 'We can't exactly be a club. There's only three of us, for starters.'

Malika grinned. 'So what? We're all doing this for a reason. I'm running to keep my promise to Abbie. Hannah, you're going to show your ex what he's missing, right?'

Hannah nodded, punching the air.

'And Cassie, you're going to fulfil the ultimate bucket-list goal of running a marathon, yes?'

'Indeed. *And* hit a half-marathon personal best!'

'OK, then. So what's stopping us? Here's to the . . . er, Wednesday Club?'

'Hmm, doesn't sound right,' said Hannah. 'It's a bit boring.'

'Then how about the Running into Trouble Club? Since that's what we're doing. Besides Cassie, of course. She'll be zooming off into the distance, leaving us all behind.'

'But is it really a club, though?' Cassie persisted.

'Definitely,' said Malika, laughing as they all clinked their glasses beneath the low, cosy light of the pub. 'We are *definitely* a club.'

10

Malika

Malika stood before the mirror in the small bathroom at the back of Rocket Recruitment. The light was harsh, as it always was, streaming through the blue-white overhead bulb. It drowned her features in unwanted brightness, illuminating the dark circles beneath her eyes and the small scar on her right cheek, the result of a roller-skating fall as an eleven-year-old. In a rare brave mood, she'd borrowed Khari's skates and taken off down the street, only to fall face-first onto the pavement. It was the last time she'd been so daring. Until recently.

The scar was usually invisible, but not here. Not in this room, where she felt as though she was standing beneath some strange lonely spotlight. She and Abbie used to get ready together in the ladies' room for evenings out, claiming the two cramped cubicles as their own personal dressing rooms. They'd laugh as they applied their make-up beneath the overly bright light, oblivious to the imperfections it revealed. Back then, there weren't any.

Malika normally liked her face, its roundness, her full lips that always looked great with a sweep of lip gloss. But now, the woman peering back at her in the mirror didn't resemble her at all. The tight dark curls that she usually wore natural and loose were tied back in a short ponytail because she just didn't feel like making the effort. In fact, the thought of spending time on her hair now felt needless and exhausting. Her full cheeks seemed thinner. Malika wondered if it was simply a trick of the light, or if she genuinely looked that way.

She hadn't been eating as much recently and she knew that, but when there was no appetite to be found, she couldn't exactly help it. The lead weight in her stomach that had refused to budge for weeks prevented her hunger. It had stolen it along with her energy and motivation. She barely felt like doing anything when she made that much-anticipated step into her house, feeling the warm air wrap around her like a well-loved jumper, guiding her straight up the stairs, only stopping for greetings and unavoidable small talk with her housemates on the way. The only thing she'd been happy to do was run.

Malika was still surprised that she'd managed to drag herself out to run in the first place. She'd chosen the park for more privacy, to try to rid her mind of the inevitable tension that came with being near the road, as though she were running on the thinnest sheet of ice. Meeting Cassie and Hannah was both amazing and nerve-racking at the same time. Here were two people willing to help her, willing to see her succeed. They just didn't know how difficult she found things sometimes.

Still, forming the Running into Trouble Club had been a perfect idea. Now, she *had* to run and she found it easier when she was with the others. She felt positive, moved along by their chatter and their shared experience. With Hannah, Malika knew she wasn't the only one running her first race and at least she didn't have to do it alone. But when she went home, lying in bed plagued by anxiety, she was back to telling herself how wrong she was. The heavy feeling that had started to lift when she ran returned, stronger than ever, and as she sighed at her reflection in the Rocket bathroom mirror, the nervous fluttering in her stomach was back.

Malika straightened her blouse and reached for the door just as Eva burst in.

'Mal! Wondered where you'd got to. Just came to let you know Callum has arrived. He got here a bit early. Are you all right?'

Eva cast a quizzical glance over Malika, no doubt taking in the redness around her eyes. She stood in the doorway, her collection of fashionable bangles clinking against her wrists.

Pull yourself together, Malika told herself. *You're Assistant Manager, for crying out loud!*

She smiled as brightly as she could manage. 'I'm good,' she said. 'Just got a bit of a headache, that's all.'

Malika slipped past Eva and back into the buzzing atmosphere of the office, where the sunlight beamed through the windows. Marc was busy registering a new candidate, his loud laugh booming across the office as he flirted with her. He did it with almost every girl, Malika noticed. Not that he could help it; he was, she admitted, conventionally handsome and charming. And he knew it.

Malika's desk was also occupied. A young man sat quietly in the seat opposite, fiddling nervously with a pen. Malika instantly recognised those smart trousers and shirt, that almost too-professional appearance standing out against everyone else's summer attire.

'Callum,' she said, slipping into her seat. 'Congratulations on getting the job.'

Callum had recently interviewed for an accountancy role, one that he'd pinned his hopes on. He'd been successful. Malika had enjoyed his shriek of 'brilliant!' down the phone when she told him the good news and asked him to come in to finalise the paperwork.

'Thanks,' said Callum, a smile breaking through his usual shyness.

Malika returned it; genuine this time, not the well-practised one she'd used in recent weeks, one she could switch on and off like a decorative light. Callum's demeanour reminded her of her own when she first started out at Rocket; an equally nervous graduate in search of her first job in the city. So she harboured a soft spot for people like Callum, doing whatever she could to help them land the role they really wanted.

'OK, so first things first, the company wants to see you on Friday,' said Malika, pulling open one of her desk drawers. 'I know you don't start until Monday, but this will just be a little introduction to your new team and they'll take you through the basics. They move quickly, so I'll get you the contract, and get a copy of your file sent over and . . . oh.'

Malika stared at the drawer, the one in which she kept all of her candidate files. She knew that Callum's was near the front, because she'd sorted them all out that morning, in order of appointment. Just like she did every day.

Callum's wasn't there.

Malika flicked through a second time and then a third. Panic rose in her chest. Callum's file wasn't in the drawer.

'Shit,' she muttered.

'Um, is everything OK?' asked Callum, peering cautiously over the desk.

Malika's eyes darted from file to file as she searched again. Her hands shook as she rifled through the drawer.

'I . . . I can't find your file. Don't worry, it'll be here somewhere,' she muttered, clinging on to every shred of positivity she could.

She tugged open the other drawers, even though she knew they wouldn't contain the brown A4 folder that comprised all of Callum's documents. When her search proved fruitless, she hurried to the filing cabinet at the back where older paper files were kept, just in case, somehow, it had been misplaced. She searched, her body trembling, growing warmer by the second. *Panic.*

She took a deep breath, reminding herself of all the times she'd 'lost' the TV remote at home, only to find it stuffed behind the sofa cushion. She'd been doing that a lot lately, losing things, because panic made you miss things that were right under your nose.

Malika rushed back to the computer. 'Your info should be stored on the system, so not to worry. I'll just check.' Aware of Callum's worried eyes on her, Malika searched, feeling a rush of relief when Callum's folder appeared in front of her. 'Aha!'

Clicking into it, she realised she'd spoken too soon. Callum's contract was there, along with the forms he needed, but his ID was missing.

I'm sure I scanned it, thought Malika, turning to Callum with a sheepish expression. 'Er, do you by any chance have your passport? I need to take another copy. For some reason, it wasn't backed up.'

Malika wondered why on earth it wasn't there. She usually scanned everything in. But her heart thudded when she recalled the busy week following Abbie's death. When the world still didn't feel real. Where so many tasks were put on hold because they were far too busy dealing with the backlog, as well as grief. Clearly, Malika hadn't got round to it.

'I don't have it with me,' said Callum fretfully. 'It's at home. I live miles away. It's not like I can just pop home today and get it. Can I still start the job?'

Malika tried to halt the oncoming tears of frustration, but it was no use. Through them she saw Marc, who was already summoning Eva.

'Mal, go and take a breather,' she said. 'I'll deal with this.'

Feeling terrible, Malika rose from her seat and hurried out to the office kitchen, where she let the tears flow free.

The five minutes it took for Eva to come and find her again felt like years. Malika sat at the small white table, drinking a glass of water. She was grateful that the glass gave her something to clutch, something to focus on when the pity in Eva's eyes became unbearable.

'Malika,' Eva said softly, reaching across to touch Malika's arm.

It was meant to be a comforting gesture, but Malika didn't move, just stared aimlessly into the glass, watching a lone droplet of water as it trickled down the side.

'I'm worried about you. I know I keep bringing this up, but I need you to be honest with me. I'm concerned, that's all.'

Concerned. Malika didn't like that word, not any more. She'd grown accustomed to its tone; the drop of a voice, the sympathy that came with it that filled the room with an almost shameful echo whenever it was uttered.

'Sorry, Eva. I panicked. I lost the file and—'

'You didn't lose it. Marc found it on the shelf next to the photocopier.'

'What? But—'

'Mal,' Eva interrupted, her bangles bashing noisily against the table. 'I know you're missing Abbie, but if it's affecting your work, we need to talk about it. And determine what we're going to do.'

Malika pushed the glass away. She knew that Eva meant well, but the concern only made her feel worse.

'Eva, I'm good at my job. I know what I'm doing, OK? It was just one little mistake, that's all.'

'You could have cost Callum his job. He could have put in a complaint. And what about that argument with Rebecca the other day? You could have handled that much better. I let that one go, because she *was* being unreasonable, but this? This can't continue, Mal.'

Malika sniffed. 'I would have sorted it out.'

'I think we both know that's unlikely,' said Eva.

The words stung.

'You flew into a panic. Documents went missing *and* you hadn't backed them up. Look, I know things were hectic right after Abbie left us. But I'm your boss, Mal. I'm here to support you. If you're finding things difficult, all you have to do is tell me.'

Malika nodded. 'Thank you,' she said. 'I'm fine. It was just a blip, that's all. I can deal with it. Really.'

Eva smiled and left the room, her wedge heels clicking against the tiles. Malika wiped her eyes, took a final sip of water and returned to her desk.

I can do it, she told herself. *I can deal with this.*

If only she fully believed it.

II

Hannah

'So we just *had* to go back to the Maldives, didn't we, Olly?'

Hannah's latest customer, who was no older than twenty-five, with sleek dark hair and perfect make-up, cast another loved-up look at her handsome beau. She gestured wildly with her hands, almost as if to show off the huge diamond that took up most of her ring finger. 'It was just *so* lovely. We didn't even think of going there until some of our friends told us how nice it was. They only went for a week, so we decided to make it two. And that's when Olly proposed.'

'I did indeed,' said a grinning Olly, taking her hand in his. 'It was day three and we were walking along the beach . . .'

Give me strength, mused Hannah, being sure to keep her wide smile plastered on, telling the cute couple how wonderful it all sounded. Olly and Liv giggled together, staring into each other's eyes as though they were in an intimate booth in a posh restaurant rather than sitting on scratched leather chairs at Travel Town beside a cardboard cut-out of a grinning flight attendant. As though they were the only ones in the world who mattered.

Hannah recognised the bitterness that was creeping into her thoughts of late and she wasn't a fan. It wasn't *her* and it made her worry. She didn't want to end up that way. Yet, glancing at the clock as the couple reminisced, only stopping to ask Hannah if she could recommend any hotels with their own private beach, Hannah couldn't wait for the wholesome onslaught to stop.

'I'm sure I can find something absolutely *perfect* for you,' she said, being careful not to let her smiley, professional demeanour cross the invisible border into sarcasm.

Normally, such a display would cause her to dab at her eyes, being careful not to smudge her mascara. The buzz she felt from making people happy, hearing the excitement in their voices when they knew they were heading off on a new adventure, gave Hannah a frisson of warmth on a daily basis. That, and her love for holidays, was what had kept her in her job for almost twenty-two years. The parents were her favourites, barely able to contain their own glee as they booked their children a surprise trip to Disneyland. As a feisty twenty-something full of ambition, Hannah had joined Travel Town with dreams of jetting off around the world on a once-in-a-lifetime trip of her own. She'd peruse the glossy brochures, taking in the images of beautiful resorts, sparkling clear-blue seas and historical temples in such awe that it made her shake with longing. It was all hers for the taking. Until she met Dan.

Hannah wouldn't forget the first time she ever set eyes on Dan Saunders. She'd noticed him as the door to Travel Town swung open and a group of lads walked in. Dan held the door open for his three mates, who made a beeline for Hannah. They'd come in to organise a stag party in Paris for one of the group. Hannah let out a sigh of relief when she realised the groom-to-be wasn't Dan, even though she didn't know why. She didn't even know his name at first, though she noticed he was the quieter one of the group, his witty sense of humour overshadowed by the others' loud presence and raucous laughter. Mr Sensible, she guessed.

The one who'd no doubt act like the dad of the trip, responsibly stuffing his sozzled mates into a taxi at the end of a booze-fuelled night and making sure they didn't get up to anything *too* stupid.

Dan was tall and lean, with a kind face and a wide smile that Hannah couldn't help falling for. *Just my type*, she'd thought, blushing, handing over their booking details.

'Here's my number,' she'd said directly to Dan as she scribbled it down on a piece of paper. 'If there's anything you need to know about the trip, just give me a ring.'

He called the following day and it had nothing to do with Paris.

Once upon a time, Hannah had had her heart set on working her way up the career ladder, but once she met Dan, her plans changed. Her *life* changed. The idea of marriage and a family, things she'd put to the back of her mind, had come at her with full force. When Dan had proposed – he'd taken her to Prague to pop the question – Hannah had a whole new plan for life. To her boss's shock, she turned down a promotion; after all, Dan was doing incredibly well in his career as a building surveyor, they'd just put a deposit down on a house and Hannah wasn't planning on staying a full-time employee much longer. Not when she'd need to take maternity leave . . .

It was surprising how quickly the years caught up with you, Hannah often thought. They crept up on you before grabbing at you with their sharpened claws, forcing you to acknowledge how fast time flies. How not everything stays the same. What she'd give to go back, to spend more time with Dan, to be happy again.

'Hannah?'

Hannah snapped out of her reverie to see Olly and Liv looking at her expectantly.

'We're really sorry,' said Liv, 'but do you mind if we come back? There are so many options and we want to make sure we're making the right choice.'

Thank god for that, Hannah thought. Her silent prayer had been answered. She waved happily as Liv and Olly headed for the door, then logged off her computer.

'You're rushing off quickly,' David observed as Hannah grabbed her bag and jacket from the back room. 'Going anywhere nice? Is Dan taking you out?'

'No,' she said sharply, then regretted it. David had no idea what had happened with Dan; it wasn't his fault for asking. 'Just going to do a bit of shopping.'

'Lovely,' said David, his eyes darting to the trainers Hannah had pulled from her locker.

Since she'd started running, Hannah found her trainers were much comfier than the tight, pinching work shoes. Even though they were battered and destined for the bin, they felt good on her feet. Especially now that her muscles were aching from her recent run. Hannah didn't care; in fact, she'd felt a glimmer of happiness as she'd hobbled in that morning. Didn't it mean that her body was getting accustomed to all the exercise? In that case, the pain was welcome.

Hannah threw her scuffed heels into the locker and headed out. Her mission?

To get herself some new running kit.

Since meeting Cassie and Malika, the issue of Hannah's sporty – or non-sporty, to be exact – wardrobe was an inevitable setback. Now that she'd officially started training, Hannah's ancient holey leggings and Dan's T-shirts weren't good enough. They were too thick, too uncomfortable. Hannah's trainers were also in dire need of replacement; they may have been comfy, but her feet were in danger of breaking through the soles. If she was going to run a marathon, she needed the proper attire.

Hannah stepped into Broadmead, into the throng of afternoon shoppers. She'd attempted to buy some running clothes days before, trailing through the high street in search of something cheap and cheerful. But her short-lived trip had only left her confused and self-conscious as twenty-somethings plucked tiny crop tops from the rails of sports-wear, items that looked more at home in lingerie ads than at the gym. 'Oh, that's just fashion,' Cassie had informed her nonchalantly before reeling off some alternatives.

Cassie had suggested a store on Park Street. 'You don't have to spend a lot,' she'd said, but Hannah wanted to treat herself, just a little. She made her way past the fountains and up the hill, feeling the strain on her legs as she marched on, determined to work through it. *It's all about recovery*, said Cassie's voice in her ear. *Don't overdo it.*

The shop's blue logo beamed out at her like a holy grail, its window boasting an array of outfits on mannequins, including a display of brand-new, brightly-coloured trainers. *This is more like it*, she observed.

Hannah felt the familiar tug of nerves. Clearly, this store was for serious runners, not newcomers, clueless to this new world and everything in it. But, catching the eye of the sales assistant, who gave her a welcoming smile, her mood lifted. Racks and rails of delights surrounded her. There were T-shirts and leggings in a variety of styles and colours that looked pleasantly soft and cool at the same time. She looked at the clothes hanging there, the plain shirts in black and blue, contemplating which kind to go for. All she needed was something decent to run in. It didn't have to be stylish.

That was until her eyes landed on a vest top. Hannah reached out to touch it, to feel the material against her hands. It was in a shade of bright pink, a colour she wouldn't normally go for, instead choosing to hide her body with darker colours. *They're more slimming*, she'd always told herself. But pink . . . could she pull this off?

Beneath it were matching leggings in a pink-and-black pattern. *Daring*, she thought. *But what the hell* . . . She picked up the garments and headed towards the changing room, stopping only to grab a sports bra from a nearby rail. Face flushed, aware of the sales assistant watching, she hurriedly rummaged for her size.

'Found it,' she whispered before the assistant could come to her rescue.

Hannah shuffled into a cubicle, shrugging off her jacket and Travel Town uniform. As her smart red skirt dropped to the floor, Hannah was faced with that long-time bogeyman – the Shop Changing Room Mirror. Hannah's pale, doughy skin shone out at her like a terrifying beacon. She prodded at her thighs, grasped at them, sighing a silent greeting to her old friend, cellulite. She turned away from her reflection and unhooked her faded grey bra, trying to ignore what she saw, even though she knew that the mirror told no lies.

That was her. That was Hannah, in full near-naked glory. And she hated every part of it.

Hannah reached for the sports bra, the Super Impact Shock Absorber. *Whoa!* she thought, carefully freeing it from its hanger and holding it out in front of her to inspect it. Its cups felt sturdy and as Hannah attempted to pull it on over her head, she suddenly realised she was stuck.

'Oh no,' she said, fumbling frantically in an attempt to unleash one of her arms, which had been caught in the straps.

This was no normal bra. Hannah felt the heat of panic course through her as she stood in the tiny cubicle with one arm captive in a bra that was nowhere near her breasts. Her eyes flitted to her reflection again and she was horrified.

I'm going to have to go and ask for help, aren't I?

Hannah wanted to cry. Just as she was about to make a sheepish SOS cry to the sales assistant, she finally managed to dislodge her arm from the offending bra, pulling the rest of it over her head, trying to calm herself. Pulling the elastic into place, she adjusted the cups and glanced down.

Wow.

Hannah had never felt so . . . pert. The Super Impact Shock Absorber had pulled her breasts into submission, the cups secure and comfortable. Impressed, she grabbed them in the mirror, grinning as she did an impression of Madonna from her 'Vogue' days.

She did a little jump, marvelling at the way her boobs stayed in place, a vast difference from her collection of old T-shirt bras that were in danger of breaking at any moment, like a humiliating game of Buckaroo.

Happy, Hannah pulled on the pink T-shirt and almost gasped at how much she loved it. Yes, it was bright, it was different, but it suited her. She reached for the leggings, feeling the strong fabric against her fingers. She pulled them on, expecting them to get stuck by the time they reached her knees, but to her surprise, they glided up her legs. They felt weightless, as if Hannah was naked. Giving the fabric a slight tug to ensure that it was real and that she wasn't in some kind of *Emperor's New Clothes* scenario, she closed her eyes and braced herself for her reflection.

When she opened them again, the shock almost made her topple backwards.

The image before her was completely unexpected. It almost didn't look like her, the Hannah of five minutes ago. The leggings clung comfortably to her skin, shaping the bum that she normally hated, that she always kept concealed beneath flowing tops and dresses. The thought of putting her figure on show would normally reduce her to an anxious mess . . . but not now. Her eyes were drawn to her stomach, another feature she feared showing off to the masses, which was now looking great beneath the pink top. It brought out the natural colour in her cheeks.

Hannah could see all the things she disliked about herself. They were still there, only hidden beneath not just a layer of clothes, but also a layer of brightness she didn't know existed until now. She felt different in these clothes. As though she could conquer the world.

Instead of seeing overweight, newly-dumped Hannah in her holey leggings, she saw someone new. *Hannah, the marathon runner.* She pictured herself running alongside Cassie and Malika, looking great as they zoomed past the finish line. Was that . . . *confidence?*

Then she noticed the fifty-pound price tag.

It hung from the shirt tauntingly, making her heart plummet. Together with the trainers she'd had her eye on, the whole bundle of clothes in her arms cost more than what she'd usually spend on clothes in a whole year. It cost more than the utility bill, sitting unpaid on the coffee table. She'd already sent Dan a text about it. The bills had been coming in and Hannah was paying them all dutifully, but she could only manage alone for so long.

The clothes would cost a small fortune, but they were a much-needed investment. She could hardly train in kit that was falling apart. They were a statement of a new beginning, a whole new self. Which is why she didn't mind putting them on the credit card she kept for emergencies.

Placing the clothes back on their hangers, Hannah dressed quickly and headed back to the shop floor. Just as she reached the checkout, a woman blocked her way.

'Excuse m—' Hannah began, then froze.

As the woman turned, Hannah's heart pounded so quickly she thought she'd keel over. In that fleeting moment, Hannah's world crumbled again. She remembered where she'd seen that sleek dark hair before, and that enviable figure and face that made her look like she'd just stepped off a TV set.

Sophia.

Sophia, young and gorgeous as ever, was standing right in front of her. Sophia, the woman who'd swiped the happiness from Hannah's life so breezily. Hannah had spent so many evenings looking into those brown eyes, analysing everything about her, wondering if Sophia knew just how much hurt she'd caused. Did she even care?

Hannah had pictured this moment a thousand times in her head. How she'd confront this woman, ask her why she'd happily break up a home. In her imagined scenarios, Hannah was brave and demanding. Feared. A woman like Sophia could have anyone, so why her Dan? But as she stood there, flummoxed, Sophia's eyes locked on hers, she couldn't speak. All the words had frozen in her throat, her body unwilling to do anything but stay glued to the spot.

Did Sophia know about her? It was one of the many questions Hannah asked herself. One of the things she wanted to know. Did Dan tell her about his wife, or did he avoid talking about her altogether? Had he lied to Sophia? Spun her a clichéd tale like 'My wife doesn't understand me?'. Surely, Hannah thought, that excuse was so overused that it didn't fool anyone any more? Had Sophia stayed up late at night poring over *her* photos? There was so much she wanted to ask, wanted to say.

The questions were there, on the tip of her tongue, but they wouldn't come out. Hannah wasn't ready. Standing there, her hands grasping the clothes, she saw Sophia's glossed lips turn into a smile.

'Sorry,' Sophia said, stepping aside. 'Didn't realise I was in the way.'

Hannah turned and scurried back to the changing room, pulling the curtain closed before the tears gave her away. Of *course* Sophia didn't know who she was. Of course Sophia didn't have a clue. Why would she?

Hannah was nobody.

She felt her new-found confidence ebb away, fragments of the person she'd only just seen in the mirror falling from her until she was face-to-face with the old version, complete with tears. She stayed there, crouched on the floor, hands still clutching the pink top. Refusing to move until she knew Sophia had gone.

A bus pulled up as Hannah left the store and she made it just in time, grateful to be heading home. As the doors closed with a hiss and the bus pulled away, Hannah spotted another familiar figure walking down Park Street, her curly hair tied back in a ponytail, her head down as she weaved through the busy afternoon crowd of pedestrians.

'Malika!' said Hannah, tapping loudly on the window.

Malika didn't notice.

Hannah would recognise that face anywhere. Though normally, it didn't look so sad.

You and me both, thought Hannah.

12

Hannah

'Yoga,' said Hannah with a shudder, standing before the studio door. She stared up at the logo, a green silhouette of a woman in what, she imagined, was meant to depict blissfulness and calm. To Hannah, it looked about as welcoming as a haunted, rat-infested cellar. 'I'm actually about to do yoga. I never imagined this day would come.'

Cassie sensed her displeasure. 'It's not as bad as it seems. You should be excited. First experiences and all that.'

'But all those . . . *bendy bodies*,' Hannah said quietly as a tall, slim woman with a pastel yoga mat and blonde topknot passed them and headed into the studio. Hannah edged further from the door as if the words 'yoga studio' were repelling her, like a vampire in a church. 'My body's only just starting to recover from this running lark. Now this.'

Cassie shrugged. 'Well, you've got to get yourself prepared. Twenty-six miles is a long run. Yoga will help to strengthen your muscles and improve flexibility. That's why I put it in the training plan.'

Hannah tried not to think about the four-page training plan that was stuck to her fridge next to the shopping list and council tax bill, detailing all the horrors that had yet to come. Cassie had even colour-coordinated it, including slots for conditioning exercises, so Hannah had no excuse not to follow it. It was daunting, but there was light at the end of the tunnel. Hannah was determined and even if following the plan meant getting up at the crack of dawn for a 6 a.m. run, then so be it. She'd be there.

Her encounter at the running store had followed her into the next day, her anxiety trailing her like a looming rain cloud threatening a downpour at any moment. She'd recounted it to Bronwen who, ever the dutiful friend, told her what she wanted to hear.

'He'll get bored, love. Just you wait. She's got nothing on you. You're smart and funny and gorgeous to boot.'

It was always nice to be complimented, but such sentiments didn't do anything to mend the heartache, to pick up the shards of self-confidence from her kitchen floor and glue them back together again. She knew that if she wanted to change things for the better, she had to go out and change them herself. She needed to run.

Plus, she'd already promised to help Malika raise money for Brake.

'I guess the alternative is being carried off in a stretcher before I've even done a mile,' Hannah commented.

'Trust me, you'll love it,' said Cassie.

Hannah wasn't so sure.

'So what do you do, then?' Hannah asked curiously as they stood waiting for Malika. 'As your day job. Do you work in fitness?'

Cassie laughed. 'Not at all. Nope, I'm a team leader in finance. Hardly glam or exciting, but I enjoy it.'

'And what about Jack?'

Cassie smiled. 'He works for a cancer charity. He's a communications manager.'

Hannah could sense Cassie's eyes were glinting with pride even beneath her sporty sunglasses.

'Love the outfit, by the way,' said Cassie.

Hannah tugged nervously at the pink top. She almost launched into her miserable tale of running into Sophia but decided against it. She didn't *know* Cassie. Not really. Plus, Cassie would probably only think she was being stupid.

'Here she is,' said Cassie as Malika jogged towards them, clutching a rolled-up yoga mat of her own.

'Oh no. Please don't say you're both experienced at this. Am I the only yoga newbie?' asked Hannah, worried.

'Nope!' Malika laughed. 'Definitely not. I've never been, but my housemate Kath does it sometimes. She's at work, so I borrowed this from her room.' She tapped the mat. 'She won't mind.'

'Great!' said Cassie. 'Seeing as we're all present and accounted for, let's get inside.'

The studio was tucked away in a side street, housed in a brown brick building near the centre of town, where the rows of new shops and towering office blocks gave way to the Bristol of old. Hannah and Malika followed Cassie into the large room, with its airy interior, high ceilings and – to Hannah's horror – an entire wall covered from floor to ceiling in mirrors.

'OK, I'm done,' said Hannah, turning to leave, but Cassie pulled her back. 'I can't stay in here,' said Hannah, her trainers squeaking against the glossy floor.

The three of them were a little early, but they weren't the first to arrive. Four other women had already positioned their mats on the floor in a practised fashion and were silently starting some warm-up stretches.

'Hannah, don't worry about it,' said Cassie quietly.

Hannah wandered tentatively to the very back of the room. 'OK. But I'm claiming this spot. I think it's best if I hide at the back.'

'If that's where you feel most comfortable, then that's fine. I'll just go and get you a mat. Malika, don't let her escape.'

Cassie hurried off, returning seconds later with a yoga mat. Hannah unravelled it, preparing her space on the floor between Cassie and Malika. She knew she'd feel safer at the back, where nobody could watch or judge, unlike the awful experience she called ZumbaGate that was still lodged in her memory. Hannah hadn't attended that many group fitness classes and in the rare instances she did, it was usually down to Bronwen's insistence that it would be a good idea, a gateway drug to a new-found love of exercise. Once, Bronwen had persuaded her to try Zumba, only for Bronwen, who was naturally good at it, to insist they stay at the front – no doubt to be closer to the rather handsome instructor. Hannah hadn't realised just how uncoordinated she was and spent the entire hour wishing the ground would swallow her whole.

Just thinking about it made her feel sick. Glancing around the yoga studio, Hannah immediately felt out of her depth, as though wading straight into the deep end with nothing but inflatable armbands. The women who surrounded her were poised and pretty, and they filed into the room as though doing this was the most natural thing in the world.

'If you really don't like it, you don't have to stay. Honestly,' said Cassie with a smile, sitting down on her own mat and stretching out her arms, her legs, a picture of elegance.

Hannah saw Cassie wave at some of their classmates as they came in and yet again felt like a fish out of water. She took off her new trainers and placed them carefully behind her as people took their places. The room was quickly filling up.

Hannah turned her face away from her reflection. She looked at Malika, who was stretching, too, looking fiercely determined.

'How are you feeling?' Hannah asked.

'Not too bad, actually. Kath's been trying to get me to do yoga with her for ages. I've just never fancied it. But if it helps with the race . . .'

I didn't mean about the yoga, thought Hannah. She wanted to explain that she'd seen her in town, looking terribly upset. But at that moment the door opened and the instructor breezed in, a petite, sixty-something woman with dark hair in a braid.

'Hello!' she boomed. 'I can see we have some newcomers joining us today, so welcome. Also, Anna has joined us again after the birth of her baby, so welcome back, Anna.'

A happy chorus of congratulations rose from the room. At the opposite end, an auburn-haired woman gave a shy wave. 'Thank you!' she said.

'So,' said the instructor, 'I'm Bel and for the benefit of newcomers – and Anna – we're going to start by doing the basic stretches and poses.'

Oh, God, thought Hannah. She glanced accidentally into the mirror, to see Cassie looking her way.

'Just relax,' she whispered as Bel launched into the down-ward-facing dog.

Hannah's jaw almost hit the floor. Cassie laughed but quickly stopped when she realised heads had turned, no doubt to see who was giggling at the back. Serious Cassie had returned.

As Bel raised her buttocks skywards, Hannah threw Cassie a smile. *Well*, she thought. *Here goes.*

Yellow light beamed in through the tall windows as the class began to pack up. Around the room, people were rolling up mats and pulling on shoes, heading back out into the midday sun.

'So. Thoughts?' asked Cassie, pushing her sports bottle into the side pocket of her rucksack. 'Did you hate it and still think I brought you here for deliberate torture?'

'You know what? I actually really enjoyed it,' Hannah replied.

She had to admit it – Cassie had been right. Just minutes into the class, Hannah had started to get into the poses. It had been difficult – incredibly difficult to imitate some of Bel's more intricate moves – but she did her best. Especially when she realised that everyone was too busy working on their own experience even to notice her. Nobody was judging her. Nobody really paid much attention to her besides Bel, who'd come over to assist the newcomers.

'I feel the ache,' said Malika. 'But I guess that means it's working.'

'Cass! Hey!'

All three of them turned to see Anna hurrying towards them.

'Anna!' said Cassie. 'Welcome back.'

'Thank you. It's so great to be back. It's nice to have an hour out of the house just to myself, you know? Not that I don't love the little bundle of joy, but sometimes I just miss my peace and quiet. It all changes. How are you?'

'I'm great, thanks. Oh, ladies, this is Anna; we've been coming here for the past two years. Anna, this is Hannah, and this is Malika. We're going to be running the Great South-West Marathon together.'

Anna's eyes widened. 'Impressive,' she said. 'I wish I could do something like that. But you know, with the baby . . .'

'Well, you—' Cassie started, but Hannah jumped right in.

'Congratulations!' said Hannah excitedly. 'Boy or girl?'

Hannah heard a low sigh from Cassie and instantly felt guilty.

Anna's face lit up immediately. 'A girl. Her name's Rosie. She's gorgeous. I love her to the moon and back, obviously, but life can be so exhausting right now. It's a wonder I even managed to brush my hair this morning, let alone get here.

But I had to. She's coming up to five months now and I need to get out again. You know how it is.'

I don't, thought Hannah, but she nodded anyway. Best to be polite.

As Cassie zipped up her bag, Anna's gaze suddenly fixed on her, enraptured by the twinkle of her engagement ring.

'Oh, Cass! Is that what I think it is? Did Jack propose?'

'He did.' It was Cassie's turn to glow with pride. Her pale cheeks flushed with a rosy hue. It suited her. 'It was such a surprise, too. We'd just finished working on the garden and I came home from work to find he'd put fairy lights all around the decking, and a bottle of champagne on the table. Then he got down on one knee. It was amazing.'

'Jack is so sweet,' said Anna. She took Cassie's hand, leaning closer to inspect the ring. 'I guess it won't be long until you two will be starting a family, then.'

Suddenly, Cassie's happy smile diminished for all of one second. But Hannah had noticed. She saw how Cassie's face fell momentarily before putting on a big grin for the benefit of Anna.

'Well, no. The thing is, we—'

'Honestly, Cass!' Anna interrupted, giving Cassie a playful nudge. 'A gorgeous man like that, a lovely house . . . you need a little one in your life. Trust me, you don't know real love until you've had a baby.' She glanced down at her phone. 'Well, I need to go. Food shopping awaits. Mum can only have Rosie until four. I'll see you next week.'

With that, Anna was gone, in a flash of pastel Lycra.

'She's very . . . full-on,' said Malika.

Hannah couldn't decipher the look in Cassie's eyes, much as she wanted to. 'Yeah. What was that about?'

'Oh, that's just Anna,' Cassie said, pulling the strap of her rucksack over her shoulder. '"You don't know real love until you've had a baby." How many times have I heard that rubbish? Anyway, I've got to head back now. See you at the park on Wednesday?'

Waving her friends goodbye, Hannah set off through town, wondering about Cassie. Anna's comment hung in the warm air, an unwelcome reminder. *You don't know real love until you've had a baby.*

Lucky you, Hannah thought. *Some of us never got the chance.*

13

Malika

'So what are your plans, then?' The voice of Malika's mother drifted down the phone. 'Will you be going out to celebrate?'

'Yep. Don't worry,' Malika added. 'It's Dean's birthday in two weeks. We'll do a joint celebration.'

'I was only wondering,' her mum replied. A somewhat defensive tone had crept in among the usual sweetness in her voice. 'I don't *always* worry.'

At that, Malika laughed.

'I know, Mum. Just ninety-eight per cent of the time.'

Standing on the quiet street, Malika gripped her phone with one hand and the flowers with the other, trying to disguise the sound of crinkling paper and cellophane. Plastering on her best smile, trying to emulate the perky happiness of her former self, she stared ahead at the lamp post that was tied with a fading blue ribbon.

'Mum, I've got to go. Love you!'

Hanging up, she exhaled into the light afternoon air. This wasn't the way she'd imagined spending her twenty-fourth birthday. Lying to her parents was bad enough for starters, but it had to be done. They couldn't know the truth; how low she was feeling, how most of the time she'd lost her feelings altogether. They'd drift away, seemingly forgotten until a spark broke through, normally one of anger or guilt.

Given that her parents had a tendency to worry – her mother especially – she chose to keep her feelings to herself, knowing that it would only make them more concerned. Her mother might even turn up on her doorstep, willing her to come back home.

Malika wasn't the naive student she'd been at eighteen, the one who her parents thought had needed protection. It had been the same since the day their only daughter had left for university in Bristol and they'd been the same with Khari, too.

'Don't worry,' he'd told her during freshers' week, when messages from Mum would appear on her phone several times a day. 'They bombarded me, too. They just care, that's all. We need to consider ourselves lucky.'

Malika knew he was right. But she also knew that if they had an inkling of what she was going through, her mum would be constantly on her case. So she figured it was best just to pretend.

Her parents knew about the marathon, as did Khari. He and his friends had already sponsored her.

'That's amazing,' he'd said. 'You're going to be brilliant.'

She hoped that was true.

Her birthday had arrived quietly, though she knew her housemate Kath had been busy making a cake while Malika was at work. Despite her denial, there was no hiding the lovely lingering smell of baking. Khari had sent her flowers. A sweet gesture, along with a voucher for clothes and a crude card to make her giggle, the kind they always sent to each other. Khari didn't know too much about Abbie, seeing as Malika had kept the subject quiet, choosing only to mention it to their parents subtly. They knew she'd been a colleague, but not one of her friends, someone she considered close. So he wasn't aware that flowers were something

Malika tended to avoid, as they reminded her too much of the days that had followed.

In the house, Malika had carefully lifted two of the blooms from the bouquet, one of each colour. Lilac was one of her favourites. She'd tugged gently at the stems to pull them free of their wrapping and lifted them cautiously from the bunch, being careful not to damage a single soft petal. Then she'd placed them in her flower press, listening to the slight crunch of the flattening petals. Beneath her bed she kept a scrapbook of memories: childhood, school, uni. Photos, ticket stubs and trinkets she'd gathered but wanted to keep. And once the flowers were ready, she'd add those, too. Preserve them. A memory set within pieces of pretty paper.

The rest of the bunch was held in Malika's arms as she walked up the long stretch of Gloucester Road and turned off towards Cotham, making her way through the terraced streets, grateful to leave behind the low roar of traffic from the busy streets beyond. It was quieter as she ascended, into the residential area that had been part of Abbie's daily route home. She'd lived only minutes from where it had happened. She'd been so close.

The sight of the lamp post made Malika's heart thud wearily, just as it had since she'd started coming here. Taped tightly to it were the remains of a bouquet crumpled in the sway of the breeze. Dried and darkened in the warmth of the sun, the lifeless blooms drooped within their faded paper. On the ground below, other bouquets had been left, equally dry and banded together with fading ribbons, making the scene look even more sombre.

Something terrible happened here. That was the image it portrayed. It was why the flowers had been left, not just by Malika but others too, until they'd stopped coming altogether. Now, everyone was forgetting. The little section of the road, where a car had zoomed round the corner just as Abbie was heading uphill, was peaceful. Normal. No different to how it was before it happened.

Malika reached into her rucksack, pulling out a crumpled carrier bag and a roll of tape. She pulled the dying flowers from the lamp post before scooping them into the bag and replacing them with the new bunch, wrapping the tape as tightly as she could. She admired how fresh they looked, how the lilac and white roses stood out brightly against the backdrop of pale biscuit-coloured brick.

From a bay window in a nearby house, a man peered at her curiously. The moment was quick, a vague flicker of interest before getting on with his day. Turning away, Malika headed down the street, alone in her thoughts, pondering how much different this birthday was to her last. Last year, she'd celebrated with her housemates and Abbie. They'd gone out, had a good time, drinking in pubs in town. This year, her only plan was to head back to the house, or maybe go out for a run. Usually, she'd be preparing for a fun evening, choosing her outfit, perhaps spending her birthday voucher on something new to wear. But now, it only seemed like more stuff to leave behind. When life was so fragile . . . well, what was the point?

Turning back, she took a final look at the flowers which, she decided, should really be the last bunch – did she really want to keep returning?

The answer was no.

Malika heard the forceful brake of a car, watching as it swerved quickly, dangerously round the corner before zooming away into the distance.

The flowers. She'd only just put the flowers there, yet the driver didn't even notice. Didn't care.

Anger began to boil away inside her. Standing on the pavement, Malika screamed.

'Are you fucking *stupid*?' she yelled at the top of her voice, pointing at the bouquet.

It was no use. The car had already gone.

This was why she was running. This was why she needed to help make a change, however small. Suddenly, she had an idea.

Malika hurried down to the main road, leapt into the first cafe she saw and sat down to write an email to the *Bristol Post*.

Life *was* fragile and Malika was prepared to fight for it.

14

Hannah

Hannah tossed and turned beneath her thin summer duvet. The room wasn't so warm now that the cloying heat that had cloaked the city, sweeping everyone and everything into its humid clutches, had eased off, but it was still far too stuffy. Hannah watched as the curtains swayed slightly in the breeze, jumped at the noise of a car horn somewhere in the street. As much as she hated to admit it, she wasn't fond of being alone.

It was near impossible for anyone to scale the back wall of her terraced home to get through the bedroom window, even though her brain told her otherwise. It happened every night – visions of masked burglars. Burly blokes hammering through the double-locked door to steal her telly and jewellery flooded her mind whenever it was time to sleep. It was a ludicrous notion, but Hannah couldn't help but feel vulnerable, all alone in the house.

During the day, all was fine. She still missed Dan, but loneliness tended to take a back seat during those daylight hours, when the noise of the neighbours' televisions, or people chatting as they walked past her house, would tell her there was life around her. That she wasn't *completely* on her own. She could focus her attention on other things. Work, running, household chores.

Hannah had returned to the house on Wednesday in a post-run high, cleaning everything around her, ridding her furniture of the sprinkling of dust that had settled, putting away some of Dan's things that were cluttering the living room. Out of sight, out of mind.

But at night, Hannah would be kept awake by all the noises of the darkness. The creaking of the pipes in her old house, a branch of the cherry tree in her back garden rapping lightly, annoyingly, against her bedroom window. Sounds that had never bothered her before, which went unnoticed in the blissful presence of her husband, all came out to play. She'd lie in bed, hearing them all at once, an unstoppable medley that would prevent her from drifting off, instead forcing her to watch the shadows dance on the dark ceiling.

Hannah curled up on the side of the bed in a futile attempt to get comfy. She had the entire bed to herself now, but she always kept to her usual side, her feet poking out of the duvet as they always did. There was something strange about taking up Dan's half, as if by shuffling over into the middle, she'd feel even lonelier. Loneliness was something she'd never encountered before. She'd been happy, happy enough that there was nothing spooky or untoward about a branch against the window or a pipe that, if she believed it enough, sounded like footsteps creeping through the house. But nowadays she always seemed to be fully awake. Night had taken on a life of its own.

She reached out to touch the space on Dan's side, remembering the warmth of his body as he slept next to her, his arms wrapping around her, pulling her closer as he turned over in his sleep. Small, intimate moments she sometimes took for granted, which she was now aching to repeat. The mornings where he'd wake with an eager smile, his hand softly caressing her body, working its way gently across her thighs, her stomach, her breasts. His lips against her skin, Hannah giggling like a teenager at the sensation of day-old stubble against her neck as he worked his way down.

She even missed his snoring. *I must be mad*, she thought.

Similarly, Hannah hadn't imagined just how empty the house could be without Dan. When they'd first bought it, Hannah and Dan had thought it modest. It was a three-bedroomed Victorian terrace, just the right size for a family home. When they'd first gone to view it, Hannah had wandered from room to room, imagining how she'd transform the well-worn carpets and lacklustre walls into something beautiful.

Hannah already had her heart set on a nursery. The smallest room, next to their own, would be perfect. She'd pictured freshly-painted lemon and white walls, perhaps a woodland mural on one, with ducks that would dance along its border. She saw it being filled with a brand-new cot and a chest full of toys. And then, when the baby grew older, he or she would move into the second largest room. Maybe, she hoped, there would one day even be bunk beds . . .

Now, in the space where Hannah had planned to put the cot, old boxes and suitcases stood in piles, ready to be hauled to the loft. A home treadmill that Dan had purchased years ago stood near the door. The room was used for nothing more than storage.

Finally, Hannah kicked off the duvet in frustration. She was awake now, restless. It was half past ten and the sunset had given way to a dusky sheet of darkness. As she lay there, her thoughts meandered down the risky path towards Dan again, wondering what he was up to. Her mind went over the possibilities, picturing him with Sophia. Were they cuddled up on the sofa, watching a film, just as he and Hannah used to? Or were they in bed, under Sophia's sheets – luxurious, she imagined – Dan's hands making their way over Sophia's svelte body . . .

No. She didn't want to go there. Just thinking about it was torture.

Yet, somehow, she couldn't will the thoughts away.

Hannah grabbed her phone from the bedside table. The light from her screen, from Instagram, illuminated the darkened room. Instantly, she was hit by that ever-familiar flurry of anguish that accosted her every time she dared peek. But she just needed to *know*.

She sat up, remembering that she had some wine left in the fridge. *Perfect*, she thought. She'd have a small drink, sit downstairs and scroll through.

Getting out of bed, she then padded into the hallway, switched on the landing light and made her way downstairs quietly, as though half-expecting to disturb some burglars. Sighing with relief that the kitchen was, as usual, empty, Hannah headed straight for the fridge. She caught sight of Cassie's training plan, attached to the fridge door with two large magnets in the shape of castanets, fun souvenirs from a Spanish holiday.

Three months until race day!

She'd written it at the top of the plan on the day the club had formed, complete with a little smiley face. But now there were only ten weeks left – ten weeks until Hannah was meant to run twenty-six (and a bit!) miles.

In the fridge, the bottle of rosé beamed out at her invitingly, beneath its own spotlight. Hannah reached out for it, but then her attention turned back to the plan. Cassie had spent precious time making it, filling it with colour-coded boxes and handy hints. *Ten weeks.*

Hannah felt more awake than ever now, but suddenly, drinking and sabotaging her own evening via Instagram no longer appealed. Instead, Hannah closed down the app, shut the fridge door and hurried back upstairs.

She needed something to tire her out.

So why not go for a run?

Ten minutes later, Hannah stood perplexed before her bedroom mirror, wondering just what on earth she was thinking. If being alone in the house made her jumpy, then why was she heading outside, where anyone could be lurking? *Murderers and all sorts*, she mused, telling herself not to watch any more crime dramas before bed.

Even though the evening was still warm, Hannah decided to take a jacket. She'd raided Dan's wardrobe yet again, fishing out a black hoodie he hadn't worn in years, stuffing her keys and phone into its pockets. She zipped it up and pulled the hood over her head to conceal herself from the potential gaze of nosy neighbours.

She locked the door and set off straight down the street, feeling safe and comforted by the glow of televisions and living room lights flickering cosily from nearby houses. She ran as far as she could along the main road before ducking quickly into a side street, where the pavement was encased in shadow, no longer illuminated by the street lights. Hannah's pace grew faster; she struggled but kept going, a personal race to get back out of the darkness, her eyes on the houses up ahead.

She felt determined. Exhilarated.

Just around the block, she told herself. *Then I'll go home.*

Hannah traced the route again, feeling the energy working its way through her body. She thought she'd be nervous, but it felt so *good*. She was proud of herself, remembering that first day, when she couldn't reach the end of the street before almost collapsing, and now she could keep going. And it was all thanks to the club.

As she approached the perfectly-trimmed hedge belonging to Mrs Gibson, Hannah noticed that her neighbours' curtains were open and the TV was on. She rushed by as speedily as possible.

Hannah knew she should head back home, but she wasn't ready to stop. The night air had gifted her with a fresh sense of ambition, a new-found solace in the silence and freedom of a night-time run. She carried on, turning down another side street, letting her feet lead her until she found herself on Bath Road. Hot and sweaty in the hoodie, Hannah ran, her breathing steady, feeling the strength in her legs, determined to run until she could run no more, playing out the *Rocky* training song in her head.

Just then, the wail of a siren broke Hannah's mental montage. Behind her, a police car was approaching.

What's going on? she wondered.

Hannah turned round, her feet slapping against the pavement, her breath hot and heavy. The piercing whirr drew closer and suddenly her path was bathed in the bright blue light of the police car that had just pulled up by the kerb.

'Shit,' Hannah said, tumbling forwards, managing to break from her running momentum.

She succeeded in stopping herself just in time, glaring like a rabbit in the headlights as two police officers stepped out of the car.

'Stop there, please,' barked the first one, a man, as he shut the car door.

Hannah stopped, rigid with fear. She'd been overzealous with the run, she knew that now, hence her frantic wheezing, now regretting not bringing any water.

'I . . . I didn't . . . *hello,*' she croaked.

The other officer, a female, stepped out to join her colleague. Both of them greeted Hannah with a curious gaze. Suspicious, almost. Without thinking, Hannah raised her hands in surrender. The female officer laughed.

'Don't worry,' she said. 'This isn't a Netflix show.'

'Thank Christ for that,' mumbled Hannah, shame-faced, dropping her hands to her sides.

Hannah peered up from beneath her hoodie, looking from the man's inquisitive pale eyes to the woman's kinder dark brown pair. To her dismay, she noticed that the male officer issuing her with such a piercing glare was, in fact, particularly attractive.

'Can I ask what you're doing, running around the area at this time of night?' he asked.

He moved forwards, looking at Hannah as she stood guiltily on the pavement. The policeman regarded her with suspicion. What was happening? She didn't dare ask. Instinctively she stepped back, wishing yet again that the ground would open up and swallow her. After all, this man was beautiful. Tall and broad, with light hair. Hannah couldn't make out if it was blond or auburn. She peered harder in the glaring light.

'Are you going to cooperate?' he asked, noticeably frustrated.

'Oh, God. Er, OK. What's this about?' she asked, stuttering.

Hannah had never been stopped by the police in her entire life, so wasn't exactly versed in this kind of scenario. As she stood, rooted to the spot, the female officer stepped forwards. She smiled. Hannah instantly felt a little better.

'So you're the good cop and he's the bad cop, then?' she asked, unable to stop herself.

The female officer laughed.

'I'm PC Meddings,' she said, 'and this is my colleague, PC Carrigan. I wouldn't say he's all that bad, not really.'

At this, PC Carrigan rolled his eyes.

'I'll ask again,' PC Carrigan said, addressing Hannah this time. 'What are you doing?'

'I was just out for a run,' Hannah replied.

'Out for a run.'

'Er . . . yes.'

'Really?'

PC Carrigan's stern eyes were on her. Hannah didn't know whether to back away or allow herself to melt into the pavement. He really was attractive. Gorgeous, in fact.

'Are you running from anyone in particular?'

'Steve . . .' PC Meddings began, but PC Carrigan didn't listen.

Hannah shook her head. 'Just myself.'

'Very funny. Look, we've had reports of suspicious activity in this area. A couple of people have reported their sheds being broken into, locks tampered with, someone in a dark hoodie trying to open car doors. You wouldn't happen to know anything about that, would you?'

'Honestly,' said Hannah. 'I'm training for a marathon. I couldn't sleep. I thought I'd just pop out for a bit.'

Steve pointed at her hoodie. 'In that get-up?'

Hannah glanced down. Her choice of attire didn't exactly help her defence. There she was, zooming round the neighbourhood in black leggings and a hoodie that covered half of her face. No wonder PC Carrigan was apprehensive. She looked as shifty as hell.

As soon as Hannah realised, the laughter came. She let forth a roar of laughter that set PC Meddings off, too. Hannah unzipped the jacket and pulled down the hood to reveal herself, in all of her red-faced, sweaty glory.

'Oh my *God*,' she said, almost choking with tears of laughter. 'You think I'm a *criminal*?'

'I tried to tell him,' chuckled PC Meddings, pointing at Hannah's feet. 'Those aren't any regular trainers, they're running shoes. He's a runner as well, he should know.'

Hannah observed a pink flush gracing PC Carrigan's cheeks.

'I guess I should have,' he said, grinning.

That smile, Hannah thought.

'Well, we can never be too careful,' said PC Carrigan.

'I swear I haven't pinched anything,' said Hannah. 'If I *was* into a life of crime, I'd probably be the behind-the-scenes sort of criminal, you know? I couldn't be trusted to make any quick getaway. Not that I'd do *any* crimes, of course. Please don't think I'm considering it.'

PC Carrigan grinned widely and Hannah was caught unaware at how blue his eyes were, especially in the light streaming from the headlights.

The feeling hit Hannah with gusto. He wasn't Dan. She liked him and yet *he wasn't Dan*.

'Well, we'd best let you get on,' said PC Meddings. 'Sorry about that. Bit of a misunderstanding.'

PC Carrigan headed towards the car and strangely, Hannah was sad to see him go.

'Sorry,' he said. 'But we have to investigate every line of inquiry. So unless you've got some power tools stuffed up that jumper, we'll be off. Good luck with the marathon.'

'Thanks,' replied Hannah. 'Good luck with catching the actual criminal. I promise I'll stay out of trouble.'

As the car sped off into the night, Hannah wondered why her heart was still fluttering even when the shock had worn off.

Part Two

Two months until race day!

15

Hannah

Hey, ladies! I've booked us all a surprise that'll help with conditioning. It's not yoga, but I promise it'll be just as fun! Meet me by the Watershed on Thursday at eight. No hints! (Bring comfy kit, tho!)

Mal

Xx

'*Belly dancing*?' shrieked Hannah. 'Are you bloody kidding?'

'Whoa,' said Malika, noticing the panic on Hannah's flustered face. 'If I'd told you beforehand, you wouldn't have turned up. Hence the surprise.'

'She's right,' Cassie commented as Malika pulled a smug face. 'In fairness, you enjoyed yoga in the end and you didn't fancy that at first, either.'

Hannah hesitated as they found themselves outside a building in the town centre. Malika hadn't revealed what the surprise activity was until they were standing outside, despite numerous guesses.

'Pilates?' Cassie tried, reeling off every slight possibility. 'Netball? Some kind of martial art? Um . . . archery?' She hadn't even suspected belly dancing.

Now, Hannah tugged down her T-shirt, suddenly feeling self-conscious. Something, she realised, she hadn't felt in a couple of weeks. Or at least, she hadn't thought about it too much.

'It's all right for you two,' she said, 'with bodies like yours. The last thing I want to put on show is *this*.' She prodded at her stomach, at the softness underneath her shirt.

'*That*,' said Cassie, 'is gorgeous. And anyway, nobody will be judging you. Just like they didn't at yoga.'

It'll be Zumba all over again, Hannah thought.

'I mean, we could always try pole dancing instead,' Cassie continued, straight-faced. 'I hear that's *really* good for body conditioning.'

'Oh, it is,' said Malika. 'Roz has done some classes. It's a great workout.'

'Nooo!' said Hannah, her voice rising an octave or two in fear. Sometimes, Cassie was so blunt that Hannah often didn't recognise when she was joking. 'No dancing of any kind, no . . . gyrating, or anything like that.'

She flushed, picturing herself wrapped around a pole, trying to move sexily and coordinated in time to the music and failing tremendously. Hannah hadn't thought of herself as truly 'sexy' in quite some time.

Briefly, Hannah pictured herself doing a sexy dance for Dan and in her vivid imagination, his expression morphed from one of longing to one of sheer amusement. The lust had long disappeared.

She wanted that lust back in her life. She wanted to feel sexy again.

'Anyway, Mal,' said Cassie, 'what's with this addition to the schedule? I thought we agreed to stick to the plan. Belly dancing isn't on the plan.'

Malika shrugged. 'I know. But Kath's girlfriend, Andrea, comes here sometimes and she told me how good it is. I thought it could be something for all of us to try. And

– confession – I quite fancied it but didn't want to go on my lonesome. Andrea's on holiday at the moment.'

'Well, I'm up for it,' said Cassie. 'That is, if we can persuade Hannah.'

Malika slipped her arm around Hannah's. 'Please? We've been doing so well over the past few weeks and we deserve a bit of fun. Sorry for dragging you both here. I just needed to escape the noisy house for a bit and it seemed like the perfect opportunity.'

Hannah wanted to ask why, or whether, it had anything to do with how upset she'd looked when she'd seen her on Park Street, but she didn't want to bring it up now.

'After all,' said Malika, 'aren't you Hannah Saunders, potential badass? Cops hot on your trail and everything.'

'Hey!' laughed Hannah. 'I can assure you that was an accident. Although I quite liked being a potential badass for all of three minutes. Can I keep the nickname?'

'Only if you go dancing,' said Malika.

'C'mon,' said Cassie. 'Be brave.'

Hannah considered this for a moment. *Be brave.* What did she have to lose? Besides having to endure another potentially humiliating exercise class, there was nothing really in her way. It had been two weeks since she'd been stopped by the police, which normally would have deterred her from any more night-time running. But in fact, she wanted to do it even more. She found it relaxing. At night, she could race against the cool air, feel the breeze whip softly at her face, listening to the thud of her footsteps. The sound soothed her as she ran off all of her restless energy, passing the houses, the signs of life behind the windows. She felt a new sense of freedom, moving until she was breathless, until she returned home to fall into a peaceful night's sleep.

Though she had, however, purchased some reflective accessories. Getting mistaken for a criminal wasn't an experience she wanted to repeat; although if it meant she'd bump into the lovely PC Carrigan again, she was tempted.

Malika's phone beeped with a new notification.

'Guys!' she cried, almost screaming with happiness. 'We've just hit three hundred pounds on Abbie's fundraiser!'

That was all Hannah needed to hear. After all, her race wasn't simply about her any more. She *had* to be brave.

'Right,' she said. 'Come on, we're going belly dancing.'

'And now for some hip twists!'

Hannah swirled her hips in a swift figure of eight, letting the music guide her. As the group twirled in unison before the vast mirror, she wondered why she'd allowed herself to get so frightened in the first place.

She'd watched the more experienced dancers take to the floor to demonstrate a particular routine they'd been working on in previous weeks. They'd moved with an air of grace and sultry sexiness, and Hannah had stared in wonder at the seemingly effortless ways in which their bodies moved, twisting and shimmying to the fun, upbeat tempo as they appeared to glide along the polished floor. And not one of them, Hannah noticed, looked to be under a size 16.

Just five minutes later, Hannah had felt confident enough to join in, laughing and grinning as she copied the moves of the other dancers. Some of the women had turned up in their regular workout clothes, whereas others had opted for more authentic attire, complete with jewelled belts that jingled when they shimmied. Hannah didn't feel out of place at all; in fact, she loved that women were happily showing off their midriffs, uncaring, simply focused on the music and the dance. Hannah felt nothing but happy determination.

She watched the moves carefully, her gaze shifting from the instructor at the front, to the other women, making sure she was keeping up the pace. Aware that she was grasping the moves much more quickly than she expected, Hannah had even moved towards the middle of the group, no longer wanting to hide at the back.

Behind her, Cassie and Malika were struggling. Cassie especially. Amira, the dance instructor, had hurried over to her rescue as she'd tried – and failed – to do a hip twist. Hannah watched in the mirror, seeing Cassie's effort look more like some X-rated thrusting than twisting.

'I'm sorry,' Hannah heard Cassie say. 'But this is so new to me.'

'You need to give more of a push. Like this,' said Amira, demonstrating the move perfectly in her long, flowing skirt.

Cassie tried again. Hannah stepped out of her place and hurried to the corner to help.

'You'll get it,' said Amira encouragingly. 'The more you practise . . .'

'I *should* be getting it,' said Cassie.

Hannah noticed that her cheeks were flushed pink and there was a look of sadness in her eyes.

'Hannah!' said Malika, who was no better than Cassie but was still trying her best. 'What do you think of the class? You're absolutely acing this.'

Laughing, Hannah shimmied her breasts, enjoying the way they jiggled as she raised her arms in the perfect belly dance pose. They were surrounded by music and all Hannah wanted to do was move.

'Come on now. I may be overweight and menopausal, but shimmying? You should have been clubbing with me twenty-eight years ago.'

Cassie dropped her hands to her shoulders in surrender. 'I give up,' she said.

It looked as though she was about to cry.

'Cass,' said Hannah, we haven't been in here that long. Give it another go. You told *me* to be brave . . .'

Cassie stood back up, watched the dancing, her lips a thin line of determination. She tried again, moved her feet in the same direction. It was harder than it looked, Hannah knew that. She was using muscles she didn't expect to be using, feeling them tighten as she followed the routine. But whereas Hannah allowed herself to let the music take her, let herself glide along with the others, Cassie couldn't seem to master it. If anything, she looked . . . wooden.

'I guess you can't be good at everything,' said Malika, performing a rather lacklustre shimmy of her own.

'Aw, Cass, don't worry about it. It's only meant to be a bit of fun.'

'It's . . . fine,' Cassie replied.

She smiled, but Hannah knew it was merely for their benefit.

'It's meant to be a workout and I can't even manage one move,' Cassie muttered.

Hannah was shocked. She'd never once seen Cassie give up so easily. Cassie, who was all about 'establishing the habit', who could draw up an entire marathon training plan, had lost all of her enthusiasm. Worse still, she seemed upset by it. *Wow*, Hannah thought as it finally dawned on her. *Cassie is competitive.*

Perfect Cassie, who could do anything she pleased with what seemed like expert precision, had discovered something she couldn't excel at, that she couldn't record in miles or minutes. And evidently, it hurt.

Hannah hated the idea of her friend feeling that way. Malika must have noticed it, too.

'If it makes you feel any better,' she said, 'welcome to my world. My brother was always amazing at everything. When we were kids, he was the sports star of the school. He even got better grades than me.'

'Ha! Oh, don't even start,' laughed Hannah. 'My brother's three years younger than me, but he was always the more sensible one. Even now. He's a doctor with a lovely wife and three kids. We used to drive each other crazy as children. He was a right pain in the arse. Still is sometimes, but to be honest with you, I wouldn't swap him for the world.'

A hint of a smile crept across Cassie's pale face. 'I don't have any siblings,' she said. 'Well, besides Jack's sister, of course. I never had any growing up.'

'Lucky you!' Hannah joked.

She'd often wondered, in jest, what it might have been like growing up without Ben. But it was true, she loved her brother dearly.

'Cass, are you OK?' Hannah asked outright. 'We can go if you want.'

'No! Let's carry on.'

There was reluctance etched into Cassie's expression, but Hannah didn't want to push the issue. Instead, they danced until the music stopped and Hannah's heart raced with happiness. For once, she'd found something she was truly good at.

As the class dispersed, they headed for the door, Cassie full of relief, Malika sweaty yet happy, and Hannah bursting with energy and pride. As they were leaving, the small, rushed footsteps of Amira could be heard behind them.

'Hannah!' she said. 'It *is* Hannah, isn't it?'

Hannah nodded.

'I just wanted to say, you were brilliant in class. You picked it up really quickly. Are you sure you haven't done this before?'

'Not at all,' Hannah replied. 'I wouldn't have dared try if these two hadn't forced me into it.'

'Well, a few of the class members are part of a dance group here. We perform at festivals and events all around the south-west. It's a bit more advanced than today's class, but if you're interested, we'd love to have you join us.' She handed Hannah a business card.

Hannah stared at it, flummoxed.

'A dance group? Well, I'll definitely have a think about it.'

Outside, the sky was turning to dusk. Hannah tried to make sense of the evening. The way she'd shimmied, the way the music had made her feel free. Confident. *Sexy*. And her weight hadn't stopped her – in actual fact, it seemed to be an advantage. So much so that she'd been scouted for a dance group.

Cassie was noticeably quiet as they walked back through town.

'Well,' said Malika, linking arms with the others. 'Hannah Saunders: belly dancing badass. What's next?'

'I don't know,' she replied, glancing up at the clouds. 'I really don't know.'

Who could tell what the future had in store? Maybe being brave was the way to go, after all.

16

Hannah

It's Sunday, and what better way to spend it than
with a proper healthy #runners breakfast and a long
training sesh with the girls? Getting ready to give it
my all today! Two months to go! #fitandfast
#marathon #runningintotrouble

Hannah woke before her alarm, nerves forming a tight
knot in her stomach. Today was the day of the first long
run. Hannah had known it was coming – the bright pink
reminder had beamed out at her each time she'd walked
past the fridge. But now that the day was here, nerves had
claimed her.

Hannah pulled on her new best friend, the Super Impact
Shock Absorber, followed by the rest of her kit, before
stuffing some essentials into her bag. Today, she was going
to meet the others in a Totterdown cafe for some breakfast
before they embarked on a six-mile run.

As she reached for her bottle of water from the kitchen,
Hannah's eyes fell on the latest electricity bill that had fluttered onto the doormat yesterday morning. She'd put it aside
to deal with it later. *Mr D Saunders and Mrs H Saunders.*
Looking at it, the envelope with its little logo sitting there
so innocently, Hannah felt a small surge of anger and tore

it open, staring at the quarterly bill. She pulled her phone from her pocket and called Dan.

'Hello?' he answered groggily.

Hannah could tell she'd woken him. Not that she cared. She thought of Sophia stirring peacefully beside him all princess-like, Dan trying not to wake her from her blissful slumber, and, strangely, didn't feel the hurt this time. Just impatience. If anything, she wished she had an airhorn.

'Han? What's happened?'

'Nothing's happened, Dan,' she said, hearing him quickly shuffle out of a room, closing a door behind him. 'But I need to talk to you.'

'Han, we've alr—'

'No,' she said firmly, holding the bill in her hand. She'd been living alone for almost three months, but some of the outstanding debt was his responsibility, too. It wasn't the only bill she'd been putting off. 'We need to work this out, Dan. We need to decide what's happening. Moneywise. I can't afford to live on my own for much longer.'

Dan let out a tired sigh. 'Bloody hell, Han. Do you know what time it is? Look, I'll call you soon, OK? We can sort it out. I promise.'

Hannah hung up. She took the bill into the living room and placed it with the others.

Things were about to change.

Hannah headed out into the quiet morning air, walking briskly towards Totterdown. It was a 25-minute walk if she was quick, but Hannah wanted to do it. The streets were still as steep as they'd been the first time she'd taken them on, but now her legs had become a bit more accustomed to the incline. From the top she could see the city again, the green of the parks below as the cluster of tower blocks stood tall in the far distance.

Reaching the top was worth the moment of breathlessness. One thing Hannah had learnt from the club, in just a few short weeks, was how much she didn't know about the city. How it looked first thing in the morning, before the day had truly begun. How the sunset looked over the harbour, how its beauty was often missed when witnessed from the haze of a pub, or through an office window. Being in the moment made it all special. She saw Bristol come to life; noticed how the high-rises, their tall structures visible for miles, shone at night with their many lights, their signs of life and activity, making her feel as though she could never be alone.

'Hey!' said Malika, waving brightly as Hannah entered the cafe.

Hannah knew they were already there, as she'd seen Cassie's car parked neatly outside.

'Where are we going today, then?' Hannah asked.

'Cassie's going to drive us down to Stoke Park,' said Malika. 'We'll be running through the woodland. It's the perfect day for it. Oh, and guess what? We've raised even more money for Brake!'

Malika lifted her phone to show the charity page. Malika had updated the photo from her initial selfie to one of the three of them. Below the picture, in bold red, was their current total amount. Nearly five hundred pounds.

'That's amazing,' said Cassie. 'Reckon Abbie would approve?'

'Oh, definitely. She'd probably be laughing at me right now, asking, "Mal, what the hell have you got yourself into?"'

Hannah peered gingerly at the menu, not at all hungry, yet her stomach was telling her otherwise. The low rumble emerging from the table was proof that she needed to eat something if she was going to complete a six-mile run.

'I'll go and order,' said Cassie, rising from her seat. 'Do you want a regular breakfast, Han?'

Hannah nodded, trying not to feel queasy at the thought of mushrooms, bacon and sausage, the grease rolling around in her sensitive stomach. Normally, Hannah would be all over a cooked breakfast, her mouth watering at the mere thought. Now, however? Her appetite had seemed to have upped and left.

'Are you nervous?' she asked Malika, who was scrolling through her phone. 'About today?'

'Of course,' Malika looked up, placing the phone on the table and picking up a menu. She traced her finger along the edge absent-mindedly as she spoke. 'If I was on my own, I'd probably still be hiding in my bed. But I'm with you two, so the company makes it better. We've only got eight weeks left until the big day. There's no backing out now.'

'I'm with you there,' replied Hannah.

Cassie sat back down at the table. 'You all right, Han? You look a bit sick.'

'I'm fine,' Hannah lied. 'Nerves.'

'Is everything else OK?' Cassie inquired. 'You know. With *Dan*.'

'You say his name like it's a curse,' said Malika. 'And I love it.'

'Too right,' Cassie replied, brandishing a butter knife as if it were a wand. 'A pox on that man's penis!'

All three of them collapsed into laughter.

'I don't know,' said Hannah truthfully. 'I called Dan this morning. I need to speak to him. I'm fed up of being in limbo.'

'Oh?' said Malika.

'I love him. I always will. And I miss him so, so much. But I can't keep waiting for him. We need to sit down and talk. Whatever happens, happens. I . . . I actually think I might be ready.'

Malika pulled Hannah into a hug. 'See? More badassery. But really, Han. You deserve to be happy.'

'Good for you, Han,' said Cassie. 'He's a knobhead.'

Wiping a stray tear, Hannah tried not to dwell on the subject. She didn't need tears, she needed determination to get through today. Hannah's attention was brought back to the present by the strong smell of bacon and eggs wafting in from the kitchen, permeating the entire cafe.

Just then, the door to the cafe opened and a look of faint shock, followed by irritation, flickered across Cassie's face when she caught sight of the figure in the doorway. A woman entered, noisily pushing a large pushchair that was laden down with her handbag and an additional baby bag. Hannah rushed forwards to help, noticing that trailing behind the woman, hand linked with hers, was a small blonde toddler in a pretty pink coat.

'Thanks,' said the woman, smiling at Hannah, pushing a lock of curly red hair behind her ears.

When Hannah returned to her seat, she found that Cassie was artfully trying to conceal herself behind a propped-up menu.

Too late, however.

'Cassie! I saw you in the window as I passed. Thought I'd pop in and say hi.'

Cassie replaced the menu and broke into a smile that both Hannah and Malika knew was entirely fake.

'Emily! Hi!'

Emily moved tables and chairs out of the way to make space, the wood scraping noisily against the floor. Cassie winced at the sound. Inside the buggy, a big-eyed baby gurgled, its gaze landing on Hannah. Instantly, she was smitten. The toddler rushed towards them gleefully.

'*Auntie Cass!*' she roared, throwing herself at Cassie with such excitement it was hard for them all not to smile.

As the little girl climbed onto Cassie's lap, Cassie quickly introduced them.

'Ladies, this is Emily, Jack's sister,' she said.

'Soon-to-be sister-in-law!' Emily clarified, grinning. 'My husband Carl's at work, so I'm taking the kids to the park for a bit.'

'Emily, this is Hannah, and Malika.'

Emily's gaze trailed across their outfits. 'Oh, so is this the club you're coaching?'

'It is, yes.' Cassie looked away quickly, almost sheepish.

Hannah noticed her trying to keep her composure, where it was obvious that she wanted more than anything for Emily to leave. The toddler was clambering over Cassie, making a grab for the condiments and Cassie's cutlery.

'Hey, Cleo!' said Cassie. 'I need that ketchup. How do you fancy going to the zoo with me and Uncle Jack soon? Would you like that?'

Cleo's scream of delight could have deafened the whole street, let alone the cafe.

'You have gorgeous kids,' said Hannah, and she noticed Emily's cheeks flush with pride.

Hannah looked at this woman, this rushed, slightly harried-looking mum in her daisy-print dress, denim jacket and what appeared to be a food stain on the front of her clothes, and wished she was in her place. What she would give for just a day.

'Thank you,' said Emily. 'They're a handful, but I love them. You should see Jack with them. He loves the kids. Doesn't he, Cleo? Uncle Jack loves you guys! This is Cleo, by the way, and this little guy is Harry. He's being quiet for a change.'

'Want to join us?' asked Hannah, pulling up a chair.

Cassie flashed Hannah a warning look.

Both Hannah and Malika registered the awkwardness on Cassie's face as she lifted little Cleo down from the table as if defusing a bomb. As Cleo's face grew red, the threat of wail looming, Emily ushered her back towards the pram.

'I'll see you again really soon, Cleo,' said Cassie kindly. She turned to her sister-in-law. 'We're just having breakfast and then we're off. Got to get back to the training.'

'Training. Yeah, of course,' she said dismissively. 'Oh, before I go, shall I come over at some point soon to have a look at some dresses for the wedding?'

'Ooh, you're picking out your dress?' asked Hannah. 'Exciting!'

Emily looked momentarily confused. 'Oh! No, Cassie has her dress. I mean for Cleo. There are just so many possibilities. We need to organise some sort of rehearsal, too. I mean, she's never been a flower girl before, so we want to ensure she has a good idea of what she'll be doing.'

Cassie began to rearrange her cutlery. 'The thing is, Em . . .'

Emily cut in excitedly. 'I've already checked with Jack. He'd be delighted to take the little cherubs off my hands while we have a look.'

'Right,' said Cassie.

'Anyway,' said Emily. 'Well, we'll be off. I'll give you a ring, Cass. Come on, kids, say goodbye to Auntie Cass.'

Hannah waved to the smiling baby before leaping up to help Emily with the door, watching fleetingly as they headed back down the street.

'So, that was your sister-in-law,' said Malika. 'She seems nice.'

'Don't get me started,' said Cassie.

Cassie nibbled at her toast as if to avoid elaborating. Hannah noticed her long sigh of relief. Her willingness to get this happy, bubbly, have-it-all mother out of her sight. She knew that feeling – the pain, the unwavering question that circled her mind at every waking hour. *Why me?* At one point, she'd even felt it difficult to be around Bronwen's kids. Little Ethan and Josh, the children of her closest friend, who treated her like a real aunt. She'd see them and her heart would plummet in the knowledge that the life she wanted, what *they* had, would never be hers.

She knew it all too well.

As they ran through the rolling fields of Stoke Park Estate, the yellow Dower House wide and castle-like on its hill ahead, Hannah watched Cassie with new interest. She mentally prepared all the things she wanted to say, wondering if she should even say them at all. When Malika sprinted on into the near distance, Hannah decided to go for it. She herself knew from experience that there was no use skirting the issue. If anything, she wanted to be there for her friend. To help.

'Look, Cass, I didn't know whether or not I should bring this up, but I see you as a good friend, so I thought, why not? I know what you're going through. I've been there, too. So if you ever want to chat, or vent, I'm here. I know that you can be a bit, you know, private, so I wanted to make it clear that you *can* talk to me.'

Cassie slowed her pace. 'Private?'

'You keep yourself to yourself. And that's great, Cass, but it's not good to bottle things up.'

'Han, what are you talking about?'

Hannah caught her breath. 'Children,' she said matter-of-factly. 'I saw the way you were with Emily. And Anna at yoga. I recognise it. Trust me, Cass, I've been there. I couldn't have children either and it was painful. It ate me up inside for a good few years until I finally accepted it, and

I still have bad days, where I see children and wonder what my life might have been like. And I wish I'd had someone to talk to back then. My husband was feeling the strain as well. My best friend couldn't understand. Not fully. She had two boys of her own.'

Cassie stopped running. Her feet came to an abrupt halt on the track. Malika was still ahead, only slower now, glancing back to check where the others were. There was silence as Cassie's face contorted into a look of incredulity and for a moment, Hannah wished she'd kept her mouth shut. Clearly, it was way too personal. She'd crossed a line.

'Oh, Han, I think you've misunderstood,' said Cassie, sadness in her eyes.

'I have?'

'It's not that I *can't* have children. I just don't want them. Ever. I'm child-free.'

17

Hannah

'Child-free?'

The word came out as a whisper. As though Hannah didn't want to release it, would have preferred to have kept it locked inside. She'd heard it before, that phrase. She knew what it meant. She'd read about it once, in a magazine. One of those thick, glossy tomes, with its twenty-something cover model, its pages brimming with the latest fashion trends she could barely afford. She'd flicked through it in the dentist's waiting room in an attempt to take her mind off a looming root canal, stumbling across this new term with piqued curiosity. *Child-free.*

At first, she'd thought it meant the same as *childless*. Like her. But she quickly learnt it was vastly different. A world so unfamiliar to her own, where the yearning she'd come to know, learnt to deal with over time, simply didn't exist. Yet, somehow, she couldn't quite bring herself to believe Cassie.

'Yes,' said Cassie casually. 'Voluntarily childless. I don't want to have children. I've never been maternal. And the trouble with Emily is that she just can't seem to accept that. In fact, hardly anyone can.'

Suddenly, Hannah felt as if she'd been winded. Child-free. It was absurd – at least, to Hannah. Who would volunteer to be childless? Cassie had everything going for her, yet here she was, dismissing the one thing that Hannah had wanted most in the world: motherhood. Cassie had the power to have it too, and yet judging by the look on her face at the mere suggestion of children, was casting it aside like old rubbish.

Hannah opened her mouth to speak, the word barely audible. And as soon as she did, she wished she hadn't.

'Why?'

Cassie spun round, trainers kicking up gravel. 'Because I don't want to. Because there's more to life than having kids. Because the idea of pregnancy is . . . well, it doesn't fill me with joy, I'll tell you that much. I never wanted children.'

'Not ever?'

'Nope. When I was younger I didn't and I thought, maybe I'm too young, maybe I'll want kids later. Then in my twenties, when all of my friends started having babies, I still had no desire to be a mother. I waited for that maternal instinct to kick in. It didn't. Part of me wondered why. There were all my friends, some I'd grown up with, blissfully journeying into motherhood. We grew apart then, I guess, because I didn't 'fit in' any more. Our lives are so different. I just didn't want their lifestyle; I wanted to keep travelling and keep living my own life. I wasn't *ready*.

'Then in my thirties . . . nothing. There was no yearning or sudden worry about my biological clock, despite everyone asking. Everyone thinks it's their business, as though all women are just walking incubators and we're weird if we don't want to do our "natural duty". It really pisses me off.'

Hannah walked alongside Cassie. There was so much she wanted to know. Her body shook with a rare feeling. Jealousy? Perhaps. She'd been used to that over the years. But this was different.

This was longing. A longing for something she couldn't have, that once took over her so thoroughly that it exhausted her. It had been a while since that feeling had surfaced, but now it had returned.

'Do you ever wonder, though?' Hannah asked. 'Do you ever look at children, or mothers, and think, I wonder how different my life might have been?'

Cassie shrugs. 'No, not really. I know if I'd had kids, I would have been unhappy. It's not the life for me and surely it's better to own up to that rather than live a life you don't want simply because society tells you to? Once you bring children into the world, there's no going back.

'People ask why, as though it's some kind of strange lifestyle, but I guess you could ask the same about those who *have* children. I like my freedom. I like the ability to go out when I want to, travel when I want to travel and not have to worry about "the kids". My life doesn't revolve around children. I don't have to adapt my schedule to work around naptimes and school.'

'I'm sorry,' said Hannah. 'I completely got the wrong end of the stick.'

'You did,' said Cassie. 'But thanks. You know, for offering to talk. I feel so terrible for snapping at you. I've just been tired of hearing it all of my adult life.'

'Don't worry,' said Hannah. 'It's hard for me to grasp, I'll admit. There's so much joy in having kids and yet you don't want it.'

'What about adoption?' asked Cassie. 'When you found out you couldn't have children? Or what about IVF?'

Hannah shook her head. 'IVF . . . We tried. Failed. We couldn't try any more; we couldn't afford to. I held on, thinking that maybe, *maybe*, some miracle would happen. It happens to some women, doesn't it? What if I was one of those lucky ones? And then I went through menopause and, well, knew the dream was over. I would have loved to adopt, or even foster. We had the room and plenty of love. But Dan . . . well, he wanted kids of his own. You know. Biologically.'

Glancing at the sky, sunny and cloudless, Hannah's world became dark, as it often did when she thought about Dan back then. *I want my own*, he'd said, brushing off the very suggestion. Hannah sometimes wished she could go back in time and argue her case. To tell him she didn't care. That being a parent didn't matter if the children were biologically *yours* or not.

There was once a time when she'd wanted the experience for herself; the ability to feel a baby grow inside her. She longed to experience pregnancy, and all its ups and downs. She dreamt of being pregnant alongside Bronwen, so they could share even more precious moments together. Going to baby classes, shopping, taking the kids to the park while they sat to talk about this new, wondrous stage in their lives. She might have wanted a baby of her own but, ultimately, Hannah knew that giving birth had nothing to do with truly being a mother.

'I'm sorry, Han,' said Cass. 'Dan really is a knob. I can put another spell on him if you like. Seeing as that's what we child-free "lonely old spinsters" do, apparently. Centuries ago, they might have put me on a bonfire.'

Hannah couldn't help but laugh. 'Speaking of men . . .' she said cautiously, 'what does Jack think?'

'Jack feels the same way,' said Cassie. 'We discussed that at the very beginning. Jack's happy not being a dad. The only problem is Emily.'

'How so?'

'She's constantly trying to talk us into having kids. I know deep down that Emily isn't a bad person. Somehow, she's just been led to believe that being a mum is the only thing in the world that's important and I can't have one visit from her without her trying to persuade me to think about it. She keeps saying things like, "You'd be such a good mum!" and "Don't you worry about getting older and having nobody to take care of you?" But some of us don't want to live life not being able to go to the toilet alone, or being forced to sit through hours of bloody *Paw Patrol*. I like my life. It's nice, it's peaceful. I wish people would stop trying to convince me to change it.'

Flummoxed, Hannah started to walk along the gravel path. Up ahead, Malika had stopped to stretch, her figure bathed in the glow of the sun. Cassie's revelation was still a shock.

'Look, Han, I'm sorry that you went through what you did. I just wanted you to know the truth, that's all. You may think Emily's lovely and sweet and yes, she is – but she's also so suffocating, trying to pressure Jack and me into having a baby whenever she can. It's as though she doesn't believe us and she keeps thinking that forcing her own children on us will suddenly make us change our minds. She says, "You'll want them one day." Do you know how annoying it gets to hear that continuously?'

Hannah shook her head.

'Very. Especially now I'm engaged. I dread people at work asking me. As soon as they catch sight of this' – she lifted her hand to display her engagement ring – 'the interrogation begins. As soon as I tell them the truth, I catch the looks on their faces. They think I'm strange. Or that I'm in denial. Or that I'm hiding the fact I *can't* have children. Why is it such a supposedly *terrible* thing to choose to be child-free?

'My parents are even at it. "When will you give us grand-children, Cassandra?" Don't get me wrong, I absolutely adore Cleo and Harry. I don't hate kids, not at all. I love them. I just don't want any of my own. As for our wedding, I'd rather it be a tiny event, to be honest with you. Just a couple of friends. But Emily is insisting that the kids play a part, as though the wedding is all about Cleo. Jack can't bring himself to say no.'

They walked together along the path, the words forming in Hannah's throat. So many words, so many questions, so many little things that she tried to make sense of in that particular moment.

'I hated people asking me, too,' admitted Hannah. 'Afterwards. When I found out it just wouldn't happen. People just assumed I was waiting, or it wasn't the right time. In the beginning, I loved it. People would ask me if we were "trying" and I'd get all giggly and excited. I couldn't wait to bring a baby into the world. But later, it was awful. People used to look at me all solemnly, as if they pitied me. I just don't understand how . . . I mean, having a family is all I wanted. And you've got Jack, and you could have a family, and just . . .'

She trailed off at hearing Cassie's disdainful sigh.

'Why is it not enough?' Cassie asked. 'Just to be happy?'

'But what if you change your mind?'

Cassie flashed Hannah a warning glare. 'Change my mind? I'm thirty-six now, Han. Surely I'd have known by now.'

'Right,' said Hannah, pondering to herself.

What kind of person didn't want to experience the love of becoming a mother? It was still hard to comprehend, even now.

At that, Cassie sped up again towards Malika, her angered face still fresh in Hannah's mind.

The conversation was over.

18

Malika

Malika glanced up at the clock behind the counter, nervously clutching her coffee cup. Amid the clinking of mugs and chatter of nearby customers was the sound of time ticking by, so much so that the cup seemed to be getting cooler by the second. Malika was hoping it would last. He was eleven minutes late.

Malika hadn't even wanted the drink. Her nerves were clamouring, making their ever-familiar way all over her body, but she couldn't just sit there with nothing. *Maybe it was a stupid idea*, she thought as she sat tucked away in the corner, glimpsing the road outside the cafe window, searching the neat row of shops for anyone who might resemble a journalist. *Maybe he's been called on a story*, she mused, taking a lukewarm sip. Something more urgent, something for the front page.

Considering this for a moment, she decided just to get up and head home, but as she got to her feet, the door creaked conspicuously, announcing a new arrival. She saw the man step in: tall, light-haired, a white T-shirt visible beneath his smart jacket.

He looked around, scanning the cafe until his eyes met hers. Hastily, she sat back down.

'Malika?' he asked. 'Malika Sade? I'm Tim. We spoke on the phone yesterday?'

'Hey!' said Malika brightly. 'Lovely to meet you.'

'Sorry about the delay,' said Tim. 'I was caught in traffic on the way here. Would you like another drink before we begin?'

Malika declined, watching as Tim strode to the counter to order something for himself. Her hands trembled slightly. *Am I really going to do this?*

When she'd gone to put flowers at the site of Abbie's accident, Malika's sadness had morphed into anger when she'd witnessed that car swing round the corner, seemingly oblivious to her presence, or the bouquet she had just taped to the lamp-post. She'd been so outraged, so hurt that she wanted to throw herself at the driver. Shout and scream until her voice was hoarse. But even if he'd slowed down enough to hear her, it would have been no use.

Instead, Malika had stormed into a nearby cafe, head and heart full of bold determination, and told the *Bristol Post* about her plight. The marathon, Abbie, Brake . . . it all flowed forth into the email that she fired off before she could stop herself.

So when Tim, a reporter, had phoned her two days ago requesting an interview, how could she refuse? After all, she wanted to raise as much money as possible for charity, so surely some publicity was a good thing? She'd even worn her running kit to jog the few minutes back home later, to make her feel that little more in control.

Tim returned, carefully setting down his coffee. Malika had suggested meeting in a cafe rather than her home, where her surroundings swallowed her, the familiar comfort letting her disappear inside herself.

'Thanks for meeting me,' he said. 'The marathon is such an exciting event and when I got your email . . . wow. You've got a lot of passion, I can tell. We're going to be running some features over the coming weeks about the marathon, so I'd love to know more about what made you sign up. Would it be OK if I get a photo of you, too?'

Malika nodded. 'Sure.'

'So are you a first-time runner?' Tim began, taking out his notebook and flipping it open.

'I am. I never thought I could do it. Never *wanted* to do it. My friend Abbie made me promise to run with her one day. I always joked, saying I would. I always thought, *like that'll ever happen!* But when she died, I realised that it would never happen at all now. I missed my chance to do it with her and I regret it. So now, I'm running *for* her.'

'So, were you ever into sports?'

'Never! My brother, Khari – he's the sports star of my family.'

'And what does your family think of your goal to run twenty-six miles?'

Malika smiled. 'Proud, I think. My brother definitely is. I guess none of them expected it. Me, of all people, running such a distance.'

She thought of Khari and his trophies. How, maybe one day, Malika would have a medal collection of her own. Strangely, she felt good being the underdog for once. And she knew Khari was rooting for her.

Tim took a sip of coffee. Malika sat back, hoping her nervousness wasn't obvious.

'In your email you mentioned joining a running club. Can you tell me a little more about that?'

Malika relaxed as she told Tim the story of their accidental running club. How she'd enjoyed training with these women she now thought of as friends. *Friends.* She wondered if they saw her in the same way and hoped more than anything that they did. They were an unlikely trio who somehow gelled so well together. Bubbly, funny Hannah and the serious, kind Cassie who'd taken the newbies under her wing.

Sometimes, she wondered if the events of the past few weeks were down to Fate. Finding Abbie's medal in the drawer, meeting Cassie and Hannah by chance in the park . . . it seemed too good to be true. And, some nights, there in the darkness, she asked herself if maybe, just maybe, it was down to Abbie. Was her friend arranging it all from the other side? It was stupid, she knew, but she couldn't help but wonder.

'. . . so we decided to keep training. Cassie is kind of our unofficial leader. She's amazing. Running is like her *life* and we've come so far in just a matter of weeks with her help.'

Tim scribbled furiously as Malika told him all about the Running into Trouble Club.

'We meet every Wednesday at Victoria Park.'

'At what time?' Tim asked.

'Seven pm. It's great fun. We train during the week, too. Sometimes together, but Wednesday is club day.'

Tim leant forwards, fixed Malika with a serious expression. 'Do you find that running has helped you to cope? In your email you mentioned the grief, the depression . . . how has running made you feel?'

Malika hesitated. Suddenly, she remembered just how much she'd said in that email, how much she'd unwittingly shared. She'd been on a roll, not caring that she was writing, merely focused on getting Abbie's story down before she could forget anything, because she was determined not to let her friend be forgotten.

She took a deep breath. 'Well, I didn't mean to have included all that . . . you're not going to put that in the article, are you?'

Tim gazed across at her, a caring smile on his face. 'You don't have to tell me anything you don't want to.'

Malika considered this. 'Thanks. I just haven't been coping well since Abbie's death. It's not something I've really shared. But running has actually made me feel loads better. It was hard at the beginning. I didn't even want to leave the house, but when you've signed up to a race like this, you can't exactly avoid it.'

She remembered the feeling, the marathon hanging over her head, a strong sense of dread following her everywhere until she made herself get up and run.

'After Abbie died, I didn't want to go anywhere, or do anything. I still don't. I went to work on autopilot and for a time I wondered if that would ever change, if things would ever go back to normal. Everyone tells you it'll get better, to take each day as it comes, but it's easy to tell someone they can move through it without offering the slightest hint of how. I was wading through life as if it were quicksand – I could barely move – and I thought that running through it would only make it worse. But it's helped me to cope.' Her cheeks flushed. 'That's off the record.'

Tim dropped his pen and held up his arms in mock surrender. 'Fine by me. So, how is the fundraising going? Have you raised much so far?'

Malika grinned. 'Yes! Nearly six hundred pounds. It's going well. We'll be running for Brake, the road safety charity.'

Tim gave a little cough. He regarded Malika with a serious expression before turning to a new page in his notebook.

'I wanted to ask you about that, actually,' he began. 'I understand that Abbie was a cyclist, killed in a traffic collision. You raised some concerns in your email about road safety in the city. There are talks of additional 20 mph zones being introduced to more areas in the city. What do you think of this? When they were first introduced a few years ago there was a lot of backlash. A lot of drivers aren't fond of the idea.'

Malika took another sip of cool coffee, just to give her a second to breathe. Her heart began to race.

'Probably because they think it's an inconvenience. It wouldn't be an inconvenience if they'd lost a loved one because of dangerous roads. Abbie was killed almost instantly. The driver didn't see her, but he turned the corner so quickly there was no chance for either of them to stop. One moment she was there and the next she was gone.

'I know accidents happen, but if there had been something in place to stop this, she might still be here. Abbie might still be alive if that car had been going at twenty.'

'Do you drive?' Tim asked.

'No,' she said sharply, slightly irked at his question. 'Would it matter if I did? I'd still back the restrictions. The thing is, road deaths happen so often that we don't really think much of it. People just say "how horrible" and move on. Why would it become national news when it happens all the time?' Malika stopped herself. 'I'm sorry, but it's not fair. And if there's a chance to help improve things, I'll take it. I don't want Abbie's death just to be a statistic.'

Tim nodded. 'Thank you. That's perfect.'

Surprisingly, the interview wasn't as nerve-racking as she'd thought. She'd expected something a lot more formal, but as she left the cafe with Tim, stopping for a quick photo – and feeling grateful that she'd chosen to wear her running kit – she was happy. Letting off steam, helping to get Abbie's story out there . . . just having someone to talk to about it all, well, it felt like a weight had been lifted from her shoulders. She ran all the way home, pounding the pavement. And this time, she was smiling.

19

Hannah

'What fresh hell awaits us today, then?' asked Hannah from the back seat of Cassie's car.

'Hey! Nothing too sinister,' Cassie replied. 'I'm not uttering a *word* about it until we get there, but I thought we could do something a bit different for our long run this weekend. So I signed us up to something.'

Malika threw Hannah a scared glance. 'Uh-oh.'

'You *what?*' said Hannah, incredulous.

'Like I said. Not. A. Word.'

Surrendering, Hannah leant back onto Cassie's plush seats, looking out through the window as the city rolled by. Cassie turned off the busy road and drove towards Keynsham as Malika turned to show Hannah her phone.

'Ladies! We have raised . . . drum roll . . . eight hundred pounds! We've had some donations coming in over the past two days. Cassie, are these from your colleagues?'

'Guilty,' said Cassie, grinning.

'This is fantastic.' Malika reached over to snap a selfie of the three of them.

Hannah smiled widely, even though her true mood was anything but elated.

'Eight hundred quid,' said Malika. 'That's much more than I could have imagined.'

'My turn,' said Hannah, holding out her phone for a photo of her own.

Recently, her Instagram account had attracted some new followers in the running community. Checking out their feeds only made her feel more inspired. As she went to upload it, she noticed a new notification.

'That's weird,' Hannah said. 'Dan's "liked" a few of my Instagram posts.'

'Really?' Cassie asked.

'Yeah,' said Hannah. 'Why is he doing that?'

Scrolling through Dan's account, she noticed he didn't have many photos and only three followers, one being Sophia. The pictures were generic, mainly snaps from days out, or the odd pint of beer. Dan usually wasn't into social media; he didn't see the point. She suspected it was something else that Sophia had got him into.

'Weird,' said Malika.

Very weird, indeed, Hannah thought. Although, admittedly, she was elated.

As they pulled up into a car park, Cassie surveyed the ground. The sky had given way to rain during the night, sheet-like and sudden, leaving the gritty surface of the car park glistening and full of puddles.

'Hmm,' she said, brow furrowed as she opened the boot of her car. 'The thing is,' she began, 'when I booked this, I didn't think it would rain the night before. So please don't hate me.'

'Why would we hate you?' asked Malika. 'Cass . . . what have you done?'

'I'm not going to like this, am I?' asked Hannah as Cassie passed each of them a brightly-coloured sheet emblazoned with a number.

Hannah stared at it.

'You just need to fill out the little form on the back in case of emergencies,' said Cassie, 'and pin them to your shirts. I've got plenty of safety pins. I booked us on a trail run!'

Grinning, Cassie waited for the excitement to kick in, but none came. Her jazz hands were regarded with a look of worry from the others.

'Trail run?' asked Hannah. '*Emergencies*?'

'You mean . . . hills?' asked Malika. 'Wet, muddy hills?'

Cassie pointed into the distance. The others followed her gaze across a well-kept playing field to the tall trees that rose up from the sprawling woodland behind it.

'Well, *some* hills,' Cassie reasoned. 'It shouldn't be all that bad. It's a 6k route. Trust me, I've done worse than this. We're so used to running around the park and the harbour, usually on a flat route, so I thought we could mix it up a bit. What do you think?'

Hannah tugged at the sleeves of her hoodie; because of the slight chill left over from the night's rain, she'd decided to bring along something a bit warmer. 'I don't know. Do you think we can do it?'

'Ideally, you need special trainers for trail running,' said Cassie, lifting up a leg to show her shoes, which were equipped with a thick grip.

Typical Cassie, thought Hannah, *always expertly prepared*.

'But you should be OK as this is only a short course. There'll be a lot of hills, so this run will be more about endurance and technique than speed. It just . . . well, it might be quite muddy, so bear that in mind.'

Hannah looked down at her trainers, her beautiful statement running shoes that she'd somehow managed to keep clean, imagining them caked in thick brown mud.

'It'll be fun,' remarked Cassie as though reading her mind.

'Fine. Let's do it, then!' said Hannah.

They attached their running numbers to their clothes before trudging across the car park towards the field. Runners had turned up in droves, some already doing stretches. Most of them were just as equipped as Cassie, with their special shoes and gloves and an aura of determination. As they gathered in their little groups, Malika started to jump on the spot.

'Just got the jitters,' she said as the woodland loomed ever closer. 'It feels like an actual race, with my race number. And the start banner. And all of these people.'

'Are you OK?' asked Cassie, noticing the fear on Malika's face.

'No.' Malika took deep, steady breaths. 'I mean, it seems OK, but I'm scared. What if I don't finish? And this is only a small run – compared to a marathon, anyway. Sometimes I want to give up.'

'Mal, try to stay calm. We're with you. I know it's nerve-racking,' said Cassie. 'It all seems so serious, when you're at the start line with everyone else and you automatically think everyone's better or faster than you. But it's not true and to be honest, it doesn't actually matter.

'When marathon day comes, you'll see so many different people: professional athletes, competitive runners . . . But there will also be people running who are physically disabled. I've seen people with one leg get around a course, because they're determined to do it. And there are people who are just doing it for a bit of fun, and there are people in costume . . . it's for everyone.

'As for this one, you can take it slow if you want. It's not an actual race, just a practice run. And to tell you the truth, one of the reasons I booked this for us was so that you could get a feel for what race day is like, so you know what to expect. Plus, you made me belly dance, so it's also payback.'

Malika let out a laugh. 'I'm sorry,' she said, finally letting go of Hannah. 'I was just having a silly moment.'

They followed the other runners, who were ambling further down the field, moving ever closer towards the start line. Hannah watched their confident strides along the grass. She trod carefully, seeing the hills up ahead, tall and foreboding. Everyone was raring to go. They took their places. And then, at the sound of a whistle, they were off.

'Er, guys? *Help*?!'

Hannah stood at the bottom of the small hill, trying her hardest to climb upwards, her feet slipping in the mud. It may have been small, but it was treacherous compared to the others she'd accomplished in the twenty minutes they'd been running. Well, not just running – climbing, walking, jogging nervously along the riverbank, and wading through thick sludge-like mud at the start of the course that had left their legs completely coated. Wet mud covered them almost up to their knees and Hannah had long since stopped caring about her once perfect trainers. Squelching along the next obstacle – a tree-lined path, its rocky surface keeping them at a slower, careful pace – they'd come face to face with the slope.

'OK, I definitely underestimated the rain,' said Cassie. Grabbing on to a thick branch of a nearby tree with one gloved hand, she reached for Hannah's with the other, hoisting her upwards to the safety of the flat path. 'I didn't think it would be this bad.'

'Don't worry; people pay a lot for mudbaths,' said Hannah. 'Good for the skin, apparently.'

They continued up the footpath, veering off from the safe gritty surface and into another section of woodland, where the ground dipped and the roots of the trees stood wide and threatening. The path itself was well trodden, a faint track of mud that was slippery with wear.

The route ahead seemed like an adventure, manned by marshals in hi-vis vests who led them on to the next hurdle – another mud-soaked trek through winding forest. The humid scent of rain and mud hung in the air as they dodged nettles and bark, trying to keep up with the others.

'Is it weird that I'm kind of enjoying this?' gasped Malika as they came out of the clearing, where a marshal shouted encouragingly at them to keep going.

'Glad *you're* having fun,' laughed Hannah. 'I'm covered in sludge.'

Hannah looked round in dismay, at her green surroundings, her fellow challengers who were almost as mud-soaked as she was. Some were passing with fierce determination on their faces. Others, like them, were wavering, trying to smile as they navigated their way through brambles and overhanging branches.

'We're almost halfway through,' Cassie informed them.

'What?' asked Malika. 'We're not even halfway done yet?'

They continued towards the next clearing, over a stile and towards the riverbank. A marshal was leading them to the safety of yet another path full of churned-up mud.

'*That* doesn't look promising,' said Hannah.

'Grab my arm!' said Malika. 'We'll do this together.'

They approached cautiously, arms linked as they trudged on through, trying to maintain some speed at least. Beside them, the bank sprawled outwards, leading down to the river, which glistened in the morning sunlight. They slid, laughing under Cassie's watchful gaze, as she held out a hand to steady them. But the mud was too thick, too slippery.

Edging forwards, Hannah felt her legs slide. She couldn't control them and before she knew it, she'd lost her balance, hurtling backwards into the dense mud.

'Oh no,' she said before the horrible feeling of falling overcame her. It felt like she was moving in slow motion. Legs first, then body, as she slid towards the riverbank. 'No no no . . .'

Unwittingly, she kept Malika's hand in a firm grip, pulling her down, too.

'Nooo!' said Malika. 'Hannah!'

But it was too late. Hannah was already on her backside, sliding straight towards the river. And Malika was behind her, still holding on, until she, too, was hurtling towards the water. Closing her eyes, Hannah felt the wet sensation of mud all over her body before she hit the water with a terrifying splash.

She was up to her waist in water, splashing frantically with surprise to the sounds of shouts and loud gasps from the crowd behind.

'Fuck!' she screamed, wiping muddy hair out of her face. '*It's so cold.*'

'Hannah! Malika!'

It was Cassie's voice, sounding distant among the chatter. Hannah turned to see her at the top of the bank with two marshals, who were hurrying over, their fluorescent vests like beacons.

Hannah and Malika trod water, their mud-soaked feet only making their escape even more difficult. Luckily, the current wasn't strong.

'I wanted to be in water,' said Hannah. 'But I was thinking of a lilo in a swimming pool, not being swept downstream in the bloody Avon.'

'Look up there,' said Malika, pointing up at the bank, where runners were still zooming on, with not even a glance to spare at the commotion. 'I guess they're really determined to get those personal bests.'

'Probably best they don't see us,' said Hannah. 'I'm so embarrassed.'

The tall figure of Cassie waved from the top. Her feet were perilously close to the edge.

'Stay put!' she yelled sternly. 'Stay calm! We'll come and get you out. I'll . . . oh . . . oh no . . .'

'Cassie!' yelled Malika in warning, but she didn't hear.

At the top of the riverbank, Cassie's top-of-the-range trail running shoes slipped on slick ground, sending her toppling down the hill on her bum. Everyone watched in horror as she slid, falling into a strange sort of roll before coming to an uneremonious stop, half in the water.

'Oh my God!' she shrieked, panic on her face as she struggled to get out.

Nearby, the first marshal, a tall, thin man with an overly serious expression, rolled his eyes in frustration.

'Stay calm,' Hannah mimicked, laughing.

'What? *Why are you laughing?* I'm soaked. We're *all* soaked.'

'Let's face it,' said Malika, 'it *is* funny.'

Hannah couldn't help but laugh, although she was praying nobody had their phone out, snapping away at the hilarity, ready to post it on social media. Still, in a strange kind of way, Hannah was glad to see Cassie stuck in the mud, too. It meant she wasn't so perfect, after all.

'My phone! My tracker! Shit shit *shit*,' Cassie shrieked. 'They're probably ruined. Why did I think this was a good idea?'

'And that's where using your bra as a phone holder can be an advantage,' said Hannah.

Malika took Cassie's arm. Slowly, with small, light foot-steps, they got out of the water, shivering, every inch of their bodies coated in mud.

'You didn't have to try to help, Cass. We would have got out OK. We'd have coped.'

'But it's my fault,' said Cassie. 'I shouldn't have brought you here. I knew it had rained. I just didn't think the course would be that dangerous. Don't worry. I'll put in a complaint about it. They should have closed the race. What if something worse had happened?'

'But it didn't,' said Hannah. 'Cass, it's fine. Calm down. It was *funny*. Humiliating? Yes. But totally fine. Nobody *really* saw us. We're all safe. We just need to get out and get dry, stat.'

'I just feel sorry for the state of your car on the way home,' said Malika, watching as Cassie's face paled in realisation.

On the bank, two marshals braved the mud, clambering down with shaky footsteps.

'Look at them,' said Malika, her feet swallowed by the unruly sludge. 'The way this is going, we'll *all* be in the water in a minute.'

'Ladies! Stay put, we're coming to get you,' said the first marshal, the taller of the two, shouting as though they were about to be rescued from a burning building or hostage situation rather than shallow waters.

Still, they couldn't get out entirely by themselves; the ground was simply too wet.

Behind him, his colleague made his way down too, striding shakily down the slope in an attempt to keep upright. As his face came into view, Hannah was overcome by a shock of recognition.

Those eyes. That hair. She knew that face all too well. It'd been particularly bright beneath the glare of police lights.

PC Carrigan.

'Oh no, hide me, quick!' said Hannah, ducking behind Malika.

'What?'

'I know that man! He's . . . the policeman.'

'The one who almost arrested you?' asked Cassie excitedly.

'Shh!'

Hannah watched as PC Carrigan approached, half tempted to throw herself back in the water to hide. She'd happily prefer another involuntary mudbath if it meant she'd escape the humiliation of the gorgeous PC Carrigan seeing her in such a state.

It was too late, however. As he moved closer, offering his outstretched hand, he squinted at Hannah, at what he could see of her that wasn't graced with a layer of thick mud.

'I know you!' he said, his blue eyes searching hers. 'I'm sure I've seen you before.'

'Er . . . I don't know,' said Hannah. 'In town, perhaps?'

Suddenly, his face broke out into a wide smile. *Gorgeous as ever*, she thought.

'Aha! You're that runner from the other week. I'd know that face anywhere.'

All eyes were on Hannah now. She nodded slowly, wishing the mud would swallow her up for good. It wasn't just the fact that she'd thought about PC Carrigan a few times lately, but because he was here, right in front of her, out of his uniform. Even in hi-vis he looked somewhat dashing. And Hannah was . . . well, a 'right state' would be an understatement.

'Er, yes,' said Hannah flatly.

'Are you coming, then?' he asked, reaching for her hand to pull her up. 'Or are you going to stay down here all day?'

Hannah felt the heat rise in her cheeks as she reached out for him. With a tug, he pulled her safely from the mud and led her to the side, where an old wooden fence ran back up to the route. Taking hold, she worked her way back up towards the main path as the other marshals assisted Cassie and Malika.

'Well, it can't get any worse from here,' said Hannah, taking in their covered legs. 'There's mud everywhere. It's even in my knickers.'

'Let's just go,' said Cassie. 'We can head back to the car.'

'We're not going to finish the race?' asked Malika, somewhat disappointed.

Behind them, the unflattering sound of shoes thudding slowly along the wet path caught their attention. They turned to see PC Carrigan making his way over.

'Hey,' he said with mild amusement. 'That was unfortunate. Are you all OK?'

'Yep. Just a bit embarrassed, that's all,' said Hannah. 'What are you doing here, anyway?'

'I'm off duty, as you probably guessed. I'm also a volunteer marshal.'

'When you're not catching criminals? Or, you know, perfectly innocent people?' Hannah joked.

Behind her, out of the policeman's view, Cassie and Malika grinned and gave her a thumbs up.

'We'll wait over there,' Cassie mouthed, winking as she and Malika slowly edged away.

PC Carrigan chuckled. 'I'm still really sorry about that. But no, I work at these events whenever I can. Keeping everyone safe. Or at least trying to. I'm Steve, by the way.'

'I'm Hannah. Thanks for pulling us free. Today didn't go as planned.'

'I can see that,' Steve laughed, looking Hannah up and down. 'It happens, though. You seem to have a knack for landing yourself in trouble.'

'Please don't remind me.'

'No! Honestly, it's a good thing. Maybe. At least I got to run into you again, say a proper hello this time. Do you need any help getting back?'

'It's OK,' said Hannah, nodding towards Cassie and Malika, who were making their way slowly down the rest of the track. 'I'll catch them up.'

'All right, then.'

Hannah stood, not wanting to move any further, even though she had to. She remembered how she felt last time PC Carrigan – Steve – had stepped into his car and out of her life, leaving her feeling strangely saddened. Now, the fluttery feeling had returned. She'd wanted to see him again and now here he was. Right in front of her. A second chance.

At what, though? Hannah wondered. He was just a man, an attractive one at that, but something made her excited to be around him. Even now, when she looked as though she'd just emerged from a swamp.

'Well . . . see you then, Hannah,' he said and started to walk back to his colleague. Then he turned round. 'OK,' he said, 'I wasn't going to ask, but I know I'll regret it if I don't. So, do you fancy going out anytime soon? Get coffee, go to a pub . . .'

Hannah faltered. Standing motionless on the muddy grass, she wondered if this was actually happening. *Is he asking me out? Is this handsome police officer asking me on a date?* For a second she stood, her face taken over by surprise, unable to think fully.

She looked at Steve, with his lovely big smile and eyes that crinkled in the corners from too much laughter over the years. Instinct told her to say yes, to do what she clearly wanted to do and accept his offer immediately. But her heart told her differently. *You still love Dan.*

Her mind was suddenly interrupted by Malika's words. 'You don't know what's around the corner.' Perhaps that was the advice she should be taking . . .

'You know what? I'd love to,' said Hannah. She gave Steve her number. 'Right, I'd better go. We're probably going to head home after that ordeal.'

'Home?' said Steve. 'Now? You've got a race to finish. Go and get that medal!'

20

Hannah

The medal hung proudly on Hannah's wall, on a photo hook above the mantelpiece. Behind it, the square of pale cream was visible. Noticeable. The ghost of an old photograph that was once a centrepiece.

The wedding photo was in a box now, piled up in a stack at the other side of the room. She'd taken it down, removed it from its pride of place, where it demanded the attention of everyone who walked in. There was something about it now that made Hannah want to hide it away from anyone's view, especially her own; it wasn't just the joyous formality of all that wedding photographs brought. Unspoken words that said, 'We are together. We are one. This is our happy home. This is *us.*' But something about Hannah's smile that was captured so wonderfully, in the way she looked at Dan all those years ago with such hope and excitement, made her turn away now.

She'd been ecstatic. The overwhelming happiness at things to come, immortalised on a large canvas. Even the style of her dress, which often made her chuckle now, endowed her with a pang of hurt. They were happy, once, and everything about that day was perfect. The local church, filled with all of their family and friends; the pride she felt when she walked down the aisle, giddy with excitement, followed by her bridesmaids in their lilac gowns. But now it was nothing more than an image and the thought irked Hannah. It taunted her, that picture of them both. Caught, preserved, in a happier time.

The wall had looked bare, so Hannah had taken her running medal – they'd each been awarded one for finishing the trail run – and placed it over the hook. It looked silly and out of place; this tiny square of metal on a little green ribbon hanging plainly on the wall. But it meant a lot. To Hannah, it symbolised happiness, the happiness of *now*.

'Are you sure you don't want these?' asked Malika, sifting through a pile of books.

Some of them were her own; well-read paperbacks she'd devoured on holiday and never got round to donating to the charity shop. A vast number were Dan's; books he'd bought and read once, never to revisit.

'*Golf 101*,' Malika read. '*Fly Fishing. The Ultimate Camping Survival Guide*. Basketball? Dan has a lot of hobbies.'

Hannah chuckled to herself. 'Dan *thinks* he has a lot of hobbies. He gets an idea and is overcome with the urge to be an expert at it. He lasted just one weekend at golf after buying all the kit. And camping? We rocked up to the campsite, started pitching the tent, then Dan got annoyed because it was windy. Then we gave up and went to a B & B instead. Bear Grylls he is *not*.'

'Twat,' said Cassie, who'd just arrived in the living room with fresh cups of tea.

Hannah pretended not to hear.

'Charity shop, then?' asked Malika, arms hovering over a big cardboard box, on which she'd scrawled 'DONATE'.

Hannah thought for a moment, wanting to agree – after all, he'd never look at those books again in a million years. But something made her shake her head.

'Hmm, just put them in the "Dan" pile. He can sort through it all himself.'

Hannah had considered getting rid of it all, but at the same time, she knew Dan would be annoyed if she got rid of his stuff behind his back. She decided to box it up, place it all neatly in the spare room. Because enough was enough.

It was time to start moving on.

Hannah didn't know if, or when, Dan would return, but living in the house alone, surrounded by his things, *their* things, a reminder of their life together, was only making her more depressed. She'd come in from work, or fresh from a run, only to be greeted by Dan's coats hanging in the hallway, his clothes in the bedroom. Everywhere she turned, there were framed photos of them together, fond reminders of past holidays or events, and it hurt Hannah just to look at them.

Since becoming a runner, Hannah had, to her amusement, become so much more energetic. She'd launched a new plan: to declutter the house from top to bottom. Not only that, but also de-Dan it. If her husband wanted to stay with Sophia, then so be it. He couldn't have it both ways. Until they'd decided what was to happen next, Hannah had accepted that she'd be living alone. And she was no longer prepared to sit around wallowing, waiting in a pile of memories. Not any more.

She'd enlisted the assistance of Cassie and Malika, who'd been all too happy to oblige, helping her to haul boxes down from the attic and sort through her life, deciding what to keep and what to bin once and for all. Initially, she hadn't wanted to ask the girls, but Bronwen was away on a training course and it was a task she didn't particularly want to face alone. The Running into Trouble Club had come to the rescue and she was grateful.

Cassie put down the tea and headed back out to the kitchen. She returned seconds later with a box of cleaning products from the cupboard under the sink.

'For the dust,' she said, running a finger along the coffee table.

She got to her knees and grabbed the stack of unsorted mail and old magazines that were gracing the bottom shelf. They landed with a *smack* on the top and, to her horror, Hannah saw a red "FINAL BILL" flutter out of the stack and onto the floor.

She reached down to snatch it away, but Cassie had already noticed.

She frowned. 'Is that what I think it is?'

'I think you can get rid of those Pizza Hut vouchers . . .' said Hannah, trying desperately to change the subject. 'They keep sending me those.'

'Hannah.'

Cassie reached over, grabbed the letter and tore it open. Hannah felt the colour drain from her face as her friend read it, sitting down on the seat next to her, wishing she could simply melt into the sofa and never be seen again. *It's odd to see Cassie out of her running get-up,* she thought, watching as Cassie perused the letter, brow furrowed, looking casual and unassumingly glamorous in her skinny blue jeans and oversized black top that hung off her delicate shoulders.

'It says here that you're overdue on your utility bill. Can you afford this? Be honest.'

'Yes! Of course I can,' said Hannah stiffly. 'Kind of. I just need Dan's help. I called him the other day. Just waiting for him to get back to me.'

'And when exactly was that? Why are you waiting on him? Han, this is serious.'

'You're talking as though I don't already know,' said Hannah curtly. She took a deep breath and reached for her cup of tea.

Malika, who was still placing things in the box marked 'DAN'S STUFF', called from across the room. 'Windsurfing? Does he actually *go* windsurfing? No? Into the box it goes . . .'

'If you don't want to talk to Dan about this, I can,' said Cassie. 'I can give him a call right now, if you like. This is what I do for a living, Han. I help people in these situations. And if the utter dick-brain has time to stalk you on Instagram, he has the time to pick up the phone. You can't just let him walk all over you. He's already left you for someone else, now he's dropped you in it with all the bills, too.'

'Thanks. Really, thank you,' snarled Hannah. 'As if I didn't feel like shit already.'

'I'm only being honest with you, Han. Why are you putting up with this? Do you still want him back?'

Hannah ran a hand through her hair. *Do you still want him back?* Truthfully, Hannah didn't know, but she knew deep down that her answer was, most probably, yes.

'It's not that easy,' said Hannah, staring at the carpet, at the table, at anywhere but Cassie's stern glare. 'We've been through so much together. I know how stupid this must sound, but I still love him.' The tears were in full flow now. 'You're younger than me, Cass. You don't know how it feels for me . . .'

Cassie rolled her eyes. '*I love him*,' she mimicked. 'Such a cliché. If he loved you, he wouldn't be doing this. He wouldn't have cheated on you. If things weren't going so well, he'd have talked to you, not run off with someone else. What are you, a doormat? Shall we go to the tattooist later and get "welcome" inked across your face? I'm only telling you this because I know you're worth so much more. You need to move on, Han. If he *does* come back, how long before he does it again?'

Hannah put down her tea. Her hands were shaking and she was in danger of dropping it, letting the mug fall, the dark brown liquid seeping into the beige carpet.

'Well, thanks for your lovely bout of concern, Cassie. I appreciate it.'

'Han, sometimes you have to be cruel to be kind. I'm not going to sit here and rub your back and tell you how everything's going to be sunshine and rainbows. I'm giving you the honest truth, take it or leave it. You're too good to be treated like rubbish by some dickhead who can't make up his mind as to what he wants from one minute to the next.'

'Cassie's got a point,' said Malika. 'Plus, what about Steve, the sexy marshal?'

'This isn't about Steve,' Hannah sniffed. 'Plus, "move on"? That's so easy to say. It's so simple for you, Cass, with your perfect life. If we sell this house, I have to start from scratch. All those years, all the work put in . . . and where am I supposed to live? In some crummy bedsit? Move back in with my parents? I'm nearly forty-nine. I can't do that.'

Malika spoke up. 'Kath's considering moving in with Andrea, so there's a chance her room might be available soon. You're always welcome to move in with us if you need to.'

Hannah thanked her, grateful for the generous offer. However, living with a group of twenty-somethings was out of the question. There was no way she wouldn't cramp their style. No, she'd probably prefer the bedsit. At least it'd be hers and hers alone.

'Han,' said Cassie. 'I'm surprised you're even standing for this. Let him go.'

'Plus, Steve's more attractive,' added Malika. 'Not my type, but I'm just saying.'

Cassie's words stung. Deep down, Hannah knew there was truth in her brutal honesty, but it hurt. Hannah felt a flash of anger at this woman, Miss – or soon to be Mrs – Perfect, who seemed to have life handed to her on a plate. And even *that* wasn't good enough.

'Thanks, Cass,' she snapped, 'but it's different for me. "Oh, just leave him," says Perfect Cassie, with her lovely fiancé and house, in a world where everything goes her way. It's obvious you've lived your life excelling at everything, never having to worry.'

'Han—'

'No. It's easy for you to look down on me because guess what? I'm not bloody perfect. I'm not like you or your mates, with your dazzling careers and fantastic fitness habits, off to get your personal bests so you can compare them in the office and tell each other how brilliant you are and give yourselves a giant pat on the back.'

'Hannah! I'm trying to help.'

'Is it helping, Cass? Not only do I have to endure you looking down on me, but I also have to hear you moan about not wanting kids. I've looked it up, you know. Child-free-by-choice, or whatever it is you call yourselves. I've seen those women on social media, whining about kids in restaurants or on trains, stating how so amazingly happy you are that you're not a "breeder" or a "mombie" and won't be blessing the world with your "crotch-goblins". You know what, Cass? That hurts.'

'We're not all like that. Han, my choice has nothing to do with this—'

'Wait, I'm not done. I'm nothing like you, Cass. So please, *please* don't try to tell me what I should be feeling. I'm not saying I want Dan back. I'm well aware that he's treated me badly. You don't have to keep reminding me. All I'm saying is that it's not as simple as it seems. I'm going to have feelings for him, for some time. Just accept that, OK?'

When silence fell, besides the sounds of Malika rummaging through boxes, Cassie spoke quietly.

'I know you're angry. But I'd be an awful friend if I only told you what you wanted to hear.'

Tearfully, Hannah put her head in her hands. Cassie stayed silent before hopping over to the sofa. She pulled Hannah in for a hug. It felt strange to Hannah, feeling Cassie's hands on her shoulders. She didn't think Cassie was the hugging type.

'You'll be fine,' she said. 'You can get through this. Try to focus on the race. If you can get through that, you can get through anything.'

Hannah nodded. 'I'm sorry. I didn't mean to—'

'Whoa!' came a shout from the back of the room, startling them both.

They looked up to see Malika, who was on her knees, rummaging through an old box. It was falling apart; one that had been long ignored in the dusty depths of the attic. She held up a handful of books in triumphant glee. Books with glittery covers that Hannah recognised immediately. Her stomach dropped as Malika flipped one of them open.

Her old diaries.

Oh no.

'Please don't . . .' said Hannah, almost launching herself across the sofa to shield Malika from her cringeworthy ramblings of the eighties.

But the damage was already done.

'Wow,' said Malika. 'Look at this! Can I read it, Han?'

Hannah's face was puce. Malika was already flicking through in apparent awe.

'Ugh, if you must.'

Malika read aloud:

So there's a disco on at the youth club next week and I really want to go. I bought a new dress. Mum went with me to get it, says it looks great. But you know when sometimes you think something looks great and you get home and it's anything but? Well, that's what happened to me. It's too tight and bright pink, and it pinches me in the ribs and makes me look like a giant ball of fluff. If I go to that disco, Bronwen will look gorgeous and I'll just tag along and people will laugh. They already laugh, so this will be a million times worse. And Mum is going to wonder why I'm not going and will be mad that I asked her for a new dress. She'll shout that we can't afford it, so I'll have to fake period pains, and Bronwen . . .

Hurriedly, Hannah reached over and grabbed the diary from Malika's grasp.

'Aaand that's enough of that. I'll take that, thank you,' she said. 'And those.' She swiped the whole lot.

Armed with the diaries, she wandered into the kitchen.

'Aw, come on, Han. I was enjoying that. Did you go to the disco in the end?'

Hannah shook her head. 'I faked the period pains. I just couldn't bring myself to go. Bronwen was annoyed, but then she ended up snogging the boy I fancied. Well, the whole school fancied him, really, so she wasn't too annoyed after that. To be fair, she was pretty smug.'

She took the first diary from the top, its cover decorated with a holographic horse, and flicked through. Pages and pages of her handwriting, large and neat. The pages bulged with the thoughts and dreams of teenage Hannah. Naive and oblivious as to what life held in store.

On 1 January 1988, she'd been seventeen and angry at the world. Life hadn't been going to plan, even then. She remembered wanting to give up those daily jottings, yet somehow, she hadn't been able to stop writing. Hannah ran a finger over the handwritten date and flicked through, her embarrassment tinged with a hint of sad nostalgia. Sometimes her writing was frantic, the frustration of her youth evident in the way her 't's almost tore through the paper, how the curled 'l's were straighter in times of annoyance with friends, with boys, with her weight. In all the books that stood next to her, stacked on the worktop, not once was she happy with the way she looked.

'This Bronwen,' said Malika.

Hannah turned to see that Malika had taken another from the pile and was already engrossed.

'She's in here a lot. Has she always been your best friend?'

'Yep.'

'Hmm,' said Malika, her expression unreadable.

Hannah didn't have time to dwell on it, as Cassie came to join them in the kitchen.

'I might still have all of my old diaries at my parents' house,' said Cassie, flicking through as she sipped her tea.

Hannah wanted to stop her looking, to save her embarrassment, knowing the childhood worries and anxieties those glittery books contained.

'What was in yours?' laughed Hannah. 'Let me guess. "Today, I aced my maths test *again*?" I bet all the boys fancied you.'

'Actually, they didn't,' said Cassie. 'Believe it or not, I had bad acne and braces for years. Super desirable.'

'I'm sorry for prying,' said Malika. 'I was just being nosy. It's hard to believe you wrote these before I was even born.'

'Don't remind me,' quipped Hannah.

'I love it,' said Malika. 'I kind of wish we could go back to this sometimes, you know? It's intriguing to read about what someone's school life was like before mobile phones and social media took over. It's a whole different world now. I've never even *been* to a disco.'

Hannah considered scooping up all the diaries and shoving them straight into the bin. But something stopped her.

'You've never been to a disco?'

Malika shook her head.

'I've only been to awful school ones,' added Cassie. 'And they weren't *real* discos. Just lots of Ricky Martin and fizzy pop. Actually . . .' Cassie turned to Hannah, a smirk of mischief forming. 'Han, you know it's your turn to choose an activity, right?' she asked. 'I chose yoga, Malika took us belly dancing. You need to pick one.'

The holographic horse stared back at her from the book. The expectant smiles of Cassie and Malika told her all she needed to know.

'You're right,' she said. 'And I now know what we're going to do. Ladies, we're going to a disco!'

21

Malika

'Let's get these down us, then!' Dean yelled, over the noise of the busy bar.

He appeared at the table to a collective cheer and began to distribute the array of shot glasses from a small tray. Malika took hers, hesitantly inspecting the green concoction. At the count of three, they all knocked back their shots. Malika grimaced as the liquid hit her throat.

'Whoop!' yelled Roz, raising her little glass to the air. 'Happy belated birthday, guys!'

The others swiftly joined in, clapping and cheering as Malika and Dean stood to take a bow. Since their birthdays were a few weeks apart, they'd gone out on a boozy joint night out ever since Malika had started living with the group.

'Thanks, guys. You really didn't have to do this.'

'Shh,' Dean pretended to whisper. 'Yes, they did. We deserve to be spoilt.'

You really didn't, she thought, trying not to think of her cosy bed, the lure of her little sanctuary that was waiting for her in their empty house. Instead, it was half past ten, and she and her housemates were spending their Friday night working their way through the many pubs and bars of Gloucester Road in celebration of Malika and Dean's birthdays. Malika hadn't particularly wanted to go out; she thought she did, thought it would do her good to spend time with her friends again, but as they'd walked into their third bar, Roz already tipsy, the unending noise, the heat of so many bodies crammed into one space was starting to make Malika feel uneasy.

She still hadn't thought it right to celebrate, to have the big night out that they usually did, where Roz, Dean, Kath, Andrea, Abbie and a couple more of their close friends who could make it would go out on the town to celebrate.

Yet for the past month, the urge had vanished, slipped away into a breezy night along with her yearning to do anything social that wasn't race prep. When she wasn't running, she was usually in her room. Running made her feel free, took her away from the harshness of life, fended off her anxiety even just for an hour or more. When she was out, her feet hitting the pavement, she was someone else; someone with a goal, a purpose. Someone who could put the regularity of her life behind her, if only momentarily.

She hadn't expected to meet Cassie and Hannah in the park that day. But since she had, her life had become that little bit better. It made her feel strange to admit it, but when she was part of the club, she felt . . . different. Like she didn't have to pretend. As though they understood.

Running had helped her. Just by being outside, she felt better. Her body felt better. And sometimes, it was as though she felt Abbie beside her, telling her to keep going. *Keep going, it'll all be OK if you keep going. We can do this together!*

Malika found solace in the rhythmic sound of her shoes, or the feel of the sun against her face. And the club, with Hannah and Cassie, only made it more fun. When the world around her began to feel distant, and the sky became grey despite the summer sun, she knew that a run and a chat could help her through.

Unfortunately, she knew that she hadn't seen enough of her housemates in recent weeks, so when Roz arranged the birthday night out, she could hardly refuse, instead deciding to do what she did most days: grin and bear it until she could get back home.

'What are you having?' Dean asked loudly over what seemed like a thousand voices.

They were all there now, around the wooden table, which was sticky with beer spillage. The place was packed. The varnished oak tables, surrounded by the old-fashioned decor that gave the small pub the air of an antiquated tavern, were hidden within a sea of people who battled to reach the bar. Loud chatter sounded from every corner and as Malika sat near the window, squashed in between Roz and Andrea, she wished she could be outside. She felt warm, trapped. She longed to be out in the cool air.

'I'm buying,' said Andrea.

Malika had an inkling of what was to come. Everyone would buy her a drink and she'd end up with far too much to force down before they headed to their next venue. She decided to put a stop to it, quickly.

'Guys, I totally appreciate this, but I'm fine, honestly. I'll just have one vodka and Coke.'

'That'll be a double, then?' asked Dean, grinning.

'No! Just a single. I can't drink much tonight. And I can't really stay out too long. I've got a run tomorrow.'

It wasn't a lie. Malika had planned to run around the marina again in the morning. The last thing she needed was a hangover.

'You *what*?' asked Kath incredulously, looking at her through her oversized glasses.

The whole table gawped at Malika. Expressions of amusement and slight shock greeted her as she shuffled uncomfortably in her limited space.

'Come on, Mal,' said Kath, 'you need to be out with us. Having fun, like we used to.'

'Honestly, I can't,' Malika replied, smiling apologetically at them all. 'Otherwise I'll be knackered tomorrow.'

'You're always running,' said Roz. 'We barely see you. Can't you just give it up for one day? It's not every day you turn twenty-four, you know.'

'Yep, you need to celebrate this glorious age,' joked Andrea.

Malika considered this, remembering what Cassie had said about keeping the habit. She knew that she could probably sit out one run, but for once, she didn't want to. It shocked her – the fact that just weeks ago she'd never in a million years have thought she'd prefer a run over a hungover, lazy Sunday with her best mates, complete with Roz's famous bacon sandwiches and strong tea.

Then again, she didn't think she'd lose Abbie, either.

'Look, I'd love to,' she said finally. 'But I have to keep this up. I can't just stop training.'

'Oh, don't worry about that,' said Roz. 'You're with us and we're going to have an ah-may-zing night, OK? Now, what are you going to have?'

Malika frowned. She had a sudden urge to cry but managed to stop herself just in time. She dabbed at her eyes with the long sleeve of her new black dress, pretending to fix her make-up. She was grateful for her friends, but in the weeks that had passed, she'd felt herself growing further and further apart from these people she'd once shared so much with. Was it because of what had happened to Abbie?

She knew she'd become quieter. Somewhat of a recluse, hiding up in her room like the safe, tall fairy-tale tower that it seemed to be in her eyes as she tried to process what had happened, thinking about the fragility of human life. She'd tried not to come across as too upset, in case it annoyed them, in case they thought her weak. Boring. And they'd tried; they really had. Yet, something was missing and Malika suddenly saw, flickering in the forefront of her mind, the possibility that she was drifting away from her best friends.

Abbie's not here. Malika knew she would be, if things had turned out differently. She'd be having a laugh alongside them. Somehow, Malika felt guilty for being out, when Abbie wasn't here to enjoy it, too. Yet, she knew that if she could, Abbie would be shouting at Malika to enjoy herself. It was a constant circle of guilt that threatened to consume her.

'How's the training coming along anyway, Mal?' asked Andrea. 'I saw that you've raised hundreds now. Well done.'

'Just be careful,' said Dean. 'People have died doing marathons, you know.'

His laughter came to an abrupt halt as everyone turned to look at him, horrified.

'Dean!' hissed Kath, throwing him a glare.

His face drained of colour at the realisation of what he'd said. Malika noticed a look that passed between her housemates and felt a jolt of unexpected anger.

'What's the matter?' she demanded, breaking the sudden silence. 'What's so wrong?'

'Well, you know,' said Roz, shifting awkwardly in her seat. 'We just . . . well, it's bad, isn't it? We shouldn't really be talking about death of all things, around . . .' She trailed off.

'Around me?' Malika finished.

Since when did death become taboo, an unspoken word? Come to think of it, Dean *had* been quiet lately. He was normally the biggest joker of them all and in possession of a dark, blunt sense of humour that she normally loved. So where had it gone?

Looking around the table, she recalled her interactions with her housemates of late. Kind. Supportive. Yet completely avoiding the subject. Talking to her with that forced, upbeat tone as though scared Malika would crumble, fall to pieces if they uttered something remotely upsetting.

'I need to go outside for a minute,' said Malika.

Squeezing past Roz and heading for the door, getting out of the bar seemed to take a lifetime. The smell of beer suddenly invaded her nostrils and made her slightly queasy, as did the warmth of the pub, the closed-in heat of all the people who blocked her path.

'Out of my way! I'm going to be sick!' she yelled, pretending, watching as the crowd parted like the Red Sea.

That trick always worked.

The cool evening air hit her immediately. She stood for a few seconds, just inhaling the fresh air, feeling the breeze on her face until Roz came out to find her.

'You all right?' she asked. 'You looked really upset in there.'

'I'm not all right. Not really,' Malika replied truthfully.

She moved away from the people who were milling around outside, the grey plumes of smoke from their cigarettes trailing into the night air.

'What's wrong?'

Malika hesitated. Cars went by on the busy road, loud music pumping from their windows.

'Honestly, Roz? I don't really know. I just know that I don't want to be in there and I'm sorry. I don't even really want to be out tonight.'

'Then why did you come? You could have just told us, Mal. We didn't force you.'

'I know. But sometimes it feels like you are. Like if I say no, you'll still try to persuade me. I feel so guilty. Really, I do. I just didn't want to upset you or seem antisocial. I know I haven't been the greatest of mates recently.'

Roz ran a hand through her newly cut pink hair. She'd added a flash of green to it. It was noticeable beneath the nearby street light.

'Mal, we're just trying to do the best for you. Make sure we're there for you. We're all looking out for you, but you don't really do yourself any favours. You rarely see us, or want to spend time with us. You don't want to watch movies with us, or come out, even though I invite you all the time. I don't know what else to do. It's like you're obsessed with running all of a sudden. You spend your time with that club but not us. What do you expect us to think?'

Malika sniffed, guilt creeping in now that she'd heard her friend's true opinion. She tried to fight back the tears.

'I know, and I appreciate it. But sometimes it's a little overwhelming. Sometimes I need you around me just to talk to, just to be there. I don't always want to go out drinking. Cass and Han are my friends, too,' she said. 'They talk openly about Abbie. They don't wrap me in cotton wool like you do. I saw it back there, you know. I watched you all freak out when Dean dared to say "died". Do you really think I'd get upset over that?'

She saw the look on Roz's face. *Yes* was the only viable answer.

'It hurts,' said Malika. 'I'm really sorry, Roz, but I can't do this. I can't sit there and pretend to be having a fabulous time when I'm not. I don't think I'm ready for all this yet. I think I'd rather be at home tonight.'

'Mal . . .'

Malika turned and began to walk down the street, her new heels click-clacking against the uneven pavement. She could hear Roz follow her to a point, but when she turned round, she saw the shock of pink hair disappear back into the pub.

She let the tears flow freely, mascara snaking down her cheeks as she walked to the bus stop.

22

Hannah

'What do you reckon, Dave? Does this cut it for an eighties night?'

Hannah stepped out of the Travel Town staff toilet and did a little twirl, fluffing up her hair as her boss surveyed her outfit. She'd gone for something subtle: skinny jeans, an oversized top and a pair of brightly coloured high heels that she'd seen on sale the other day, teamed with some bright accessories just like the ones she'd owned as a teenager. High street fashion had suddenly been graced with a hype of nostalgia and Hannah had revelled in it.

Not only that, but she also found herself having to buy new jeans. Her previous pair of skinny jeans – which resided in the back of her closet and were worn rarely – now hung from her waist and were baggy at the thighs. To her delight, Hannah had dropped almost two dress sizes. Running and her new-found determination to eat healthily were clearly working well for her. She had Cassie and her plan to thank for that.

Cassie. Hannah winced whenever she thought of Cassie and the argument they'd had at her house. Hannah had apologised profusely and Cassie had ensured her it was fine. Yet, Hannah couldn't help feeling that there'd been some truth in her words – it was hard to see how other people felt when you had everything you wanted in life.

'Looking great,' replied Dave. 'Very eighties. Could do with more glitter, though.'

'Not that you'd know, Dave,' piped up Hannah's colleague, Katarzyna. 'How old are you again? Twenty-seven?'

'I'm twenty-*six*!' he said, his cheeks reddening.

'I'm going to head off now,' said Hannah. 'See you tomorrow.'

She grabbed her tote bag, into which she'd stuffed her uniform and awful, pinching shoes, and headed out to meet the others.

She'd been working the late shift at Travel Town, so had decided to meet the girls straight from work. Malika was doing the same, so they'd agreed to have a quick drink before Cassie turned up. As Hannah walked through Broadmead in her yellow shoes, seeing the shutters of the shops close down around her, she caught sight of her reflection in the window of the bank. She looked tall, for once. Fun. *Sexy.* She tried a little strut, wobbling a little on the new stilettos before she became used to them, feeling as though she were in a movie, walking through the city in slow motion. *I can dream*, she thought.

Her phone pinged with a text. She rummaged in her handbag, assuming it would be Cassie or Malika – perhaps they were running late. Instead, an unknown number caught her attention.

Hello, Hannah! It's Steve, the policeman/marshal. Hope you remember me. Just wondering if you still fancy that drink?

Hannah's hands shook with elation as she typed back a reply:

Of course! Let me know when and where. X.

When she saw the little tick, the little notice that he'd seen it, Hannah felt elated. Excited. This gorgeous man wanted

182

to take her out on a date. She stole another glance in the nearby shop window. She was hot. She was ready.

But for now? It was time to go to that disco.

Cassie did a double take as she approached the nightclub, seeing the others waiting outside. Not that anyone could miss them.

'Malika? Oh my God, is that *you*?'

Malika sighed, nervously fussing with her hair, which she'd left natural and loose.

'I thought that by "eighties night" we were meant to, you know, actually *dress up*.'

'So she went full *Flashdance*,' said Hannah, howling with laughter. 'Honest to God, I nearly died laughing when she rocked up to Wetherspoons wearing that.'

'Oh, hilarious,' said Malika.

She grabbed her light jacket and hurriedly shuffled it on in an attempt to cover the leotard. There wasn't much she could do about the white tights and neon pink legwarmers, however.

'I was only joking. You look fantastic. You won't be the only one dressed for the occasion, I can assure you. Look, there's a guy over there in a luminous shirt.'

Cassie looked to where Hannah was subtly pointing.

'But is he dressed up for the party, or is it just vintage?' she asked.

'Your guess is as good as mine,' said Hannah. 'Anyway, by the time we're all up and dancing, nobody will care.'

'Now I feel underdressed,' said Cassie.

She, too, had gone for a more subtle look. She'd chosen a black shirt that was tucked into a pair of high-waist jeans with a pair of large hoop earrings. In her heels she was even taller than usual.

'I hope this venue is OK,' said Hannah. 'Seeing as nobody really does "discos" any more besides children, well . . . unless we want to gatecrash an actual kids' party, then a themed club night will have to do.'

They headed inside, where the light dusk gave way to a darkened foyer, illuminated by neon lighting. They were early, but there were already people milling about by the bar and surrounding nearby tables. Hannah could now see the dance floor, its shiny surface luring her in.

'Oh God, whyyy,' said Malika self-consciously as people passed, eyeing her outfit with curiosity. 'Why did I have to wear this?'

'Because we're celebrating?' asked Hannah. 'Well, not exactly, but we are here to attend the disco that I never did. Oh, and guess what? Steve asked me out!'

'The policeman-slash-marshal guy?' asked Cassie.

'I hope you said yes,' said Malika.

The grin on Hannah's face gave her away.

'So you're over Dan then, I take it?' asked Cassie.

Hannah's face flushed beneath the red and yellow lights that flickered over the bar area. 'You said I need to move on. So . . . I'm giving it a go.'

'I'll get the first round,' said Cassie dryly. 'Looks like we're going to need it.'

What's up with her? Hannah wondered as she moved towards the dance area, finding a small table in the corner of the room. Madonna's 'Holiday' pumped through the speakers and Hannah swayed in time to the music. By the time the others returned to the table, Hannah was in full swing, belting out the lyrics as she shimmied in her seat. Cassie poured out three glasses of wine as the music thumped and lights flashed, bathing them in an occasional red spotlight.

'Seeing as I never got to dance in 1988, I'm sure as hell going to now!' yelled Hannah, snatching up her drink and making her way to the dance floor, followed by Malika. 'Coming, Cass?'

'Oh no, not yet,' she said, shaking her head. 'I think I need a bit more liquid courage before I dance. As you've all witnessed, I'm so awkward. I'll make an idiot of myself.'

'I'm already in fancy dress,' said Malika, 'so dancing can't do much more damage. Sure you don't want to join us?'

'In a bit,' said Cassie finally.

There was something about her smile, Hannah noticed. It was curt. Forced.

Leaving Cassie at the table, the others hurried off to the dance floor. It was steadily filling up. It had been the first time in *years*, Hannah realised, that she'd been out, on her own terms, not concealed beneath the guise of a work night out. Or a drink with Dan and their mutual 'couple' friends at the local pub, where they'd chat into the night until it was time to wander home on wobbly legs. She'd been happy with that, happy for the company, but along the way she'd grown accustomed to habits. The need to please others. Dan wouldn't dance to Belinda Carlisle in a darkened club. He'd have laughed at the mere suggestion.

Hannah looked around at the people dancing, the faces and bodies she was moving among, noticing that they weren't all young. There were people in their late teens, thirties . . . even fifties. Couples, too. Why hadn't she been here before? After Bronwen had had the boys, their nights out had begun to dwindle. Bronwen's life had descended into happy chaos, consisting of trips to the park, baby swimming lessons and playgroup, and Hannah could do nothing but watch from the sidelines, looking in on the happy family like a strange, wistful voyeur. After that, their lives simply changed, and as friends and acquaintances became engrossed in marriages and motherhood, their friendship a patchwork of snatched moments, Hannah had no such reason to get away.

I could have been dancing, she told herself.

The dance floor was full now. The beat was almost euphoric to Hannah's ears, a reminder of days past. She used to wonder – in fact, it was in one of her diaries – what she'd think of herself looking back. When she was an adult, had worked hard, fallen in love and had it all, she'd planned to open those books, revisit her old life and think, *It was worth it in the end*. That's why she'd kept them all in that box in the attic. She remembered now.

Malika appeared to be having a good time, giving her all to Belinda. By the looks of it, she'd given up caring about her elaborate choice of outfit. She was even gaining some attention from an obvious hen party group, who'd pulled her into their tipsy dance routine. As the song faded into the intro of Salt-N-Pepa's 'Push It', to a thunderous cheer, Hannah looked over the crowd at Cassie.

Hannah saw that the wine had gone; Cassie had finished off the rest of the bottle and another had arrived. *She's had a lot*, thought Hannah, wondering if she'd have to lay off the drinks for the rest of the night in case she had to be the responsible one of the trio for once and take her home to Jack in a taxi with an apology. If Cassie was planning on running in the morning, and there was no doubt whatsoever about that, she was going to be mightily unhappy to have a hangover.

Cassie's brow was furrowed in concentration . . . or was it anger? Hannah tried to decipher the look amid the moving lights. Cassie's eyes were on her phone, then she almost threw it down on the table and poured herself another glass. Hannah felt a pang of annoyance. Cassie was meant to be having fun yet, clearly, she couldn't leave work alone for just one minute. Hannah weaved through the dancing bodies, congratulating the bride-to-be, who was decked out in a tutu and a pair of glittery penis-shaped deely boppers, and appeared at the table.

'You OK?'

Hannah surveyed the glass, the additional bottle.

'No,' Cassie hiccuped.

'Come and dance, Cass,' she said. 'Work will still be there in another hour or two. Can't you just leave it? You're always telling us about avoiding stress.'

'It's not *work*,' she replied tersely.

Even in the darkness, her blue-grey eyes looked teary.

'Then what's the matter?'

Cassie stayed silent. 'It's . . .'

She sighed before rummaging in her small bag for a tissue to dab her eyes, afraid of smudging her make-up. Hannah had never seen Cassie in make-up before, but she was clearly good at it. At that moment the song faded and the familiar sound of Kylie Minogue and Jason Donovan filled the club.

'Yes!' said Hannah, ecstatic. '"Especially for You"! I remember this so well.'

It was as though she'd been transported back to 1988, where she'd doodle hearts on her exercise book, harbouring a deep wish for David Macleod in the year above to ask her out. Which never happened. But it was a nice memory nonetheless.

'It's funny, isn't it, how you think your teenage years are the absolute worst, yet they have absolutely bloody *nothing* on adulthood. Devastating heartbreak on a whole new level.'

Malika bounded over to the table. 'I put in a request for you,' she said. 'I saw this top ten list in the back of your diary and this was number one. It's not bad. Cheesy, but not *too* terrible.'

'You're the absolute best. Thank you.' Hannah scooped Malika into a hug just as Cassie rose from her seat and tottered unsteadily towards the toilets.

23

Hannah

Hannah hurried through the crowd until she reached the cubicles, ignoring the curious glances of the two women applying make-up in the nearby mirrors as she burst through the door.

'Cass? Are you in here?'

A telltale sniffing noise gave her away. Hannah could see the strap of Cassie's red leather handbag peeking out from beneath a cubicle door. Hesitantly, she pushed it open to find Cassie, sitting on the toilet seat, sobbing.

'Whoa. Come on, Cass. No need to cry. It was only Jason Donovan.'

A faint smile appeared in the corner of Cassie's mouth. 'It's not that.'

'What is it, then? You can tell me, you know.'

Cassie emitted a long sigh, letting out the words between sobs. 'Me and Jack . . . had a . . . row.'

'Aw, Cass, don't worry,' said Hannah, rubbing her friend's arm. 'I'm sure it'll be OK tomorrow. You can work through it.'

Cassie shook her head. 'Not a chance. We haven't fought like this since . . . well, ever. I don't know what to . . . to do . . .'

Cassie grabbed her bag from the floor, in search of more tissue. Hannah pulled a wad of toilet paper from the dispenser instead and handed it over, watching as Cassie noisily blew her nose.

'What was this row about, then?' asked Hannah.

Cassie glanced down at the floor. She looked so different when she cried, Hannah thought. Hannah hadn't seen it before. She'd never been privy to the sight of a teary Cassie, she who normally had everything in check. She hadn't witnessed her with panda-like eyes, remnants of subtly applied purple coursing down her cheeks.

'He . . . he asked me if I wanted to have a baby.'

Hannah's stomach lurched.

A baby. The very thing that Cassie didn't want.

Hannah stood still, wondering how to process this information. A mixture of feelings jostled for the top spot and envy claimed the throne. Here was Cassie, with everything she ever wanted – including a generous, loving husband-to-be who was yearning to start a family. Why were some people gifted with all the luck?

'It came out of nowhere,' Cassie continued. 'Totally unexpected. We were washing-up and Jack asked if I'd ever reconsider it. Having a baby. It really knocked me for six.'

'Why?' asked Hannah. 'Why is he asking now?'

'Because we're getting married, I expect,' she said. 'Jack said, "Are you sure we shouldn't be thinking about it, after all?" I just burst into tears, started crying into the tea towel. Then we shouted. He backed down, but . . . oh, God, Han, I don't know what to do about this. I thought I could forget about it for tonight, but it's eating away at me. I can't focus on anything else.

'I was just going through all the photos of us on my phone and hearing the romantic songs just set me off, that's all. Nothing to do with Kylie and Jason. Sorry for spoiling things.'

Hannah managed a comforting smile.

'What did you say to Jack?' she asked. 'About having a baby?'

'What do you *think* I said?' Cassie almost snapped. 'I told him exactly what I told you before. *I don't want children.* I'm willing to bet his sister has been at it again, putting ideas into his head. When it doesn't work on me, she tries Jack. He said he was "just asking". And I . . . well, I—'

'Let me guess, you went off on one?'

'That's probably the most accurate way of putting it, yes.'

'Why would he "just ask"?' inquired Hannah.

'I don't know. But what am I meant to do? I have a choice now, Han. Have a baby, or leave Jack. I don't want to leave Jack. I . . .'

'You love him,' chorused Hannah. 'See? Not so easy now, is it?'

'Piss off,' said Cassie, but Hannah knew it was in jest.

Hannah leant over awkwardly in the cramped space and gave Cassie a hug, feeling her friend's arms snake around hers as she sobbed into Hannah's top.

'So, what did you do?' Hannah asked.

'I told him exactly how I felt and went running. Then I came here.'

Of course *she went running*, Hannah thought. It seemed to be the solution to all of Cassie's problems.

'Do you think Jack changed his mind, then? I thought you'd told him when you first dated?'

Cassie nodded. 'I did. On date number three, to be exact. I really liked him – we really connected with each other. And I thought, *I need to tell him.* Otherwise, what was the point? I'd met so many guys who wanted to settle down and have children, but I knew it wasn't for me. So I told him. Right there, as we were walking along the beach, feeling like a right weirdo for bringing up the subject of babies on our third date.

'I thought he'd run a mile. He didn't. But, secretly, I always worried this would happen.'

'And you're absolutely certain you can't work through this?'

Cassie burst into fresh tears. 'I love Jack more than anything. I can't bear to think of losing him. But this . . . well, if this is what he wants, I'm going to have to face the fact that we're not meant to be. It's unfair on him. I can't deprive him of that. He'll only regret it later. I don't know what to do. Do I leave, or do I have a baby?'

Agony circled Hannah, making her feel queasy, until all she found herself able to do was nod quietly. The words – she had so many. So many things she wanted to say to the woman in front of her, who didn't know how good she had it. A loving fiancé who wanted a family. A stable partnership and life. The ability to have children, to have the power to bring new life into the world and nurture, love and protect it. To be the one thing Hannah always dreamt of being: a mother. Yet here she was, casting it aside, unwanted. The gift that Hannah had longed for, prayed for, cried for, was potentially here in another woman's hands and she wanted none of it.

Why her?

Hannah wrestled with the anger, the urge to lash out, tell Cassie exactly what she thought. *You're ungrateful.* Instead, she tore out another handful of tissue and handed it over, prising the wet, snot-coated ball out of her friend's grasp.

'It might not be such a bad thing, after all,' Hannah suggested quietly.

Cassie looked up from her hot-mess state and glared. 'What?'

'Having a baby. What if you like it? What if it changes your life? So many people would kill to be in your situation, Cass, and you're just . . .'

'Just *what*?'

'You're throwing it away.'

Rage flickered across Cassie's face. Her cheeks reddened, her eyes burning with anger.

'Are you *serious*?!'

Hannah stood her ground. 'Yes. I'm being honest here, Cass. Do you realise how this all sounds from my perspective? It's selfish. *Selfish*, Cass. Every day I wonder what having a family might have been like and you get offered it on a plate but no, that's wrong. What if . . . you enjoy it?'

Hannah expected Cassie to rise from the toilet seat, give her a Medusa-like glare that would turn her to stone – or at least, a gibbering mass of tears. At the very least, Hannah expected Cassie to retaliate, to rush out of the disco and never return. But nothing like that happened. Instead, Cassie stayed put, a look of defeat on her small face.

'You think I'm selfish. *Everybody* thinks I'm selfish.' With that, the sobbing resumed.

Suddenly, Hannah felt awful. 'I'm sorry,' she said. 'Sometimes, it gets to me, that's all. Some of the heartache doesn't go away. Cass, I can't tell you what to do, but I *will* tell you that whatever you decide, you can get through it. You've always seemed stronger than me, yet I'm carrying on. If I can still get out and dance, so can you. We'll help you, OK?'

Cassie nodded. 'Thank you. Right now I need to make a choice. Jack means everything to me. I can't even picture being with someone else. Which means if I want to stay with him, I'm going to have to do this. I'm going to have to have a baby.'

Just as Hannah opened her mouth to speak, Malika's face appeared at the cubicle door. She peeked in curiously, her head adorned with the deely boppers. Two swaying plastic willies pointed skywards.

'There you both are,' she said. 'I was looking for you. Is everything all right? Why are you hiding in the loo?'

'I'm fine,' said Cassie, straightening up. 'Er, Mal, why are you wearing a pair of cocks on your head?' Cassie's amusement crept through the tears.

'Oh, there's a group of women on a hen do who for some reason think I'm also on my hen night. It's way too late to correct them now. So I'm just going with it. They're hilarious. I really didn't think I'd have this much fun. Want to come and join us? We're just about to order cocktails.' She held her hand out to Cassie, pulling her to her feet.

'Don't worry,' said Hannah, putting her arm around Cassie. 'Try to enjoy tonight. It'll all seem better in the morning.'

Hannah followed her friends back towards the bright lights of the disco, trying to undo the knot of pain that had formed, tightly, inside her.

24

Malika

Hi, lovely! I know I said I'd stop doing this. I know
you can't see this message (everyone must think I'm
a right sap!!), but I can't help thinking – hoping –
that somehow you can. It's still hard to accept
you're gone. Remember all those times you tried to
get me running? When you made me promise to run
a race with you? And I always laughed. (Argh, why did
I laugh?!) Well, I decided to take on a marathon. A.
Freaking. *Marathon.* My friends and I are raising funds
in your memory. We've raised nearly a grand so far!
It's race day in a few weeks and even though you
can't be here with us, I hope you'll be with us in
spirit.
Xx

Malika pressed Send and took a deep breath. A gentle breeze
whipped across her face as she stood outside the Rocket office.
She'd composed the message while walking up Park Street,
immersed in her world as the city yawned awake. Dropping
her phone into her blazer pocket, she stopped at the sight of
a blue bicycle, just like Abbie's, parked across the road.

A momentary flash of elation erupted in Malika's chest.
She's here. Malika looked over at the bike, its electric-blue

frame parked in Abbie's usual spot. Malika was filled with a rush of excitement until reality hit her and she remembered: Abbie was gone. The bike must belong to someone else. Abbie's bike had been crushed beneath the wheels of a car.

Malika felt unsteady on her feet. She leant against the wall to gather her thoughts, to wonder why her brain had let her forget for a second. As though for one nanosecond, she'd slipped into an alternate universe in which Abbie was still alive. It was a strange experience but, she realised, a revelation.

The sight of the bike had unearthed something new. A familiar spark of recognition, something old and almost forgotten, and Malika suddenly remembered the mornings when Abbie would be locking up her bike just as Malika would arrive, and they'd often get some coffee before the day began. A memory so vivid she was almost living it again.

Before, she'd blocked out all the memories. Unwittingly forced them away. Just thinking about Abbie was painful. Now, she'd somehow let them in. And this time, it was a comfort.

Malika pushed open the door to Rocket Recruitment, startled at the sight of Marc already there. He was at his desk, typing away, the whiff of berries from his bowl of porridge taking over the office.

'Oh! hi, Marc,' she said, putting down her rucksack. 'Didn't expect to see you in at this time.'

'Left the gym a bit early. Just fancied getting a head start. Just like you, I suppose.' He shot Malika a smile.

OK, she thought. Marc was usually the last member of the team to arrive. He often jokingly aimed comments of 'Swot!' in Malika's direction when she dared to start work early. But with Abbie gone, they were still sometimes struggling. Perhaps he was acknowledging this. Not that Malika was complaining; the team needed all the help they could get.

Marc glanced over, taking in Malika's outfit. 'Nice blazer,' he said. 'Looking smart.'

'Thanks. It's new. I've got that meeting with CallerArc soon and wanted to make a good impression.'

'Wow! Look at you,' said Eva, entering the office. 'And I think a congratulations is in order.'

Malika sat, turning on her PC. 'Congratulations? What for?'

'You don't know?' asked Eva. 'You're in the newspaper today. I just saw your article on *Bristol Live*'s site.'

Malika's eyes widened in astonishment. *The article.* She hadn't been told when it was going live and was certain Tim, the reporter, was going to let her know. Overcome with new-found excitement, Malika quickly logged on to the site.

'Accidental Running Club Takes On Marathon' roared the headline. Beneath it was Malika's photo. 'Malika Sade is running for cyclist friend killed in accident.' Scrolling down, she started to read, just as Eva sidled over to her desk.

'I've got to admit, though, I'm a bit upset that you didn't tell me,' said Eva.

'Tell you what?'

'About the depression. You could have told me.'

Malika felt as though the floor had given way beneath her feet. Dread enveloped her. *Depression.* How did she know about that? She'd told Tim that it was off the record. That she didn't want anyone else to know about her personal life. Her true feelings.

Feeling sick, Malika scrolled down slowly.

When Abbie died, I lost a true friend and it hit me hard
. . . at first, I found it hard to concentrate on anything
else, always asking myself a million questions . . .

'Oh no,' said Malika, clicking off the page. She wanted it
gone, out of sight. 'This wasn't meant to . . . oh shit.'

She fell slack against the back of her chair, breathing
deeply. *This can't be happening.*

'Mal! Mal, are you all right?' asked Eva.

'That . . . that stuff. About my depression. It wasn't meant
to be published.'

She grabbed her phone, ready to call Tim. Perhaps even
call his office, tell them how angry she felt. When she looked
at the screen, she saw the flurry of activity that made her
head swim.

Eight new messages.

Five missed calls.

Shakily, Malika scrolled down the call list.

Cassie. Hannah.

Mum.

Malika was suddenly unable to breathe. Her fingers
ventured towards Cassie's message.

**Mal! Saw the story. Congrats, but WTF? 'For Cassie,
running is her life??' Why did you say that? I didn't ask
to be part of this.** 🙁

She closed the message, only to be faced with a second
from Cassie:

**Why has the paper printed the details of our club like it's
official? We're NOT official . . .**

Aware of her boss watching her intently, Malika opened the page again. Her heart sank. There it was, at the bottom of the page:

Want to take on a new challenge? Run for fun? Make some new friends? The Running into Trouble Club meets every Wednesday at 7 p.m. in Victoria Park, Bristol . . .

No wonder Cassie sounded annoyed. Tim had printed a full invitation for all to join in. He'd clearly misunderstood when she'd told him about their club.

The phone began to vibrate with a call from Mum. Malika dropped it, watching it fall to the carpet with a sickening *thud*.

'I've messed up,' she said, dabbing at her eyes to stop the tears.

She felt sweaty beneath the blazer. Hot, as though shame were oozing from every pore. She was supposed to be raising awareness, telling the city about her cause. Not annoying her friends and, clearly, worrying her mother, who'd no doubt be calling her every five minutes.

Marc headed over to Malika's desk.

'Not being funny, but you look terrible,' he said. 'Why don't you go home?'

'Marc's got a point,' said Eva. 'Go home, clear your head. You rarely take a sick day. I think it's time.'

Malika shook her head. 'No. No, I can't, I—'

'Mal. Go home. We can cover you,' said Eva sternly, and Malika knew that was the end of it.

Gathering her things, Malika took a final look at her own grinning face as her picture beamed out from the screen.

What have I done?

25

Hannah

'I'm sorry, but you told a *journalist* of all people to keep things off the record?' asked Cassie, incredulously.

It was Wednesday and the club had met at their favourite spot in the park. Malika knelt on the grass by their usual bench. After the story broke, she couldn't apologise enough.

'It was stupid of me,' she said. 'I just . . . blurted it out. I didn't even realise.'

Hannah perched on the bench next to Malika. 'Mal, your article was fantastic. Why are you so upset? I mean, OK, you blabbed your innermost secrets and now they've been published for the world to see—'

'That's meant to be helping, is it?' quipped Cassie.

'Oi! I hadn't finished,' said Hannah. 'Yes, you shared your feelings. But is that such a bad thing?'

Malika nodded. 'Yeah. It is. I wanted to keep it to myself. It's bad enough that my housemates seem to mollycoddle me. I know they mean well, but they've treated me differently since Abbie died. And my parents are worried . . .'

'That's just parents for you,' said Hannah. 'That's natural.'

'Trust me,' said Cassie. 'My parents still fret now and I'm in my thirties.'

'I know,' said Malika. 'But sometimes it's overwhelming. Worse still, my boss has seen it. She already thinks it's affecting my job. So now I've pretty much confirmed it in print. All I wanted to do was drum up some more publicity for Brake, maybe get some more donations. Not put my life on show.'

Hannah nodded. 'I get that, I really do. But on the plus side, there might be others reading that article who are going through the same as you. You seem to put on this mask of happiness, but I had no idea that you felt that way. You should have told us.'

'She's right,' said Cassie. 'Don't beat yourself up about it. Try to see it in a positive light. Although, you *did* kind of make me look obsessed with running. I'm not over that.'

'And you're *not* obsessed?' said Hannah.

'OK, maybe I am. A little,' Cassie confessed as Hannah narrowed her eyes.

Suddenly, Hannah stared off into the distance. 'So you know what you were saying, Cass? About how this isn't actually a club?'

'Yes?'

'Well, if we're not, you might have to break the news to *this* lot . . .'

Cassie and Malika followed Hannah's gaze. Three women decked out in running kit were making their way through the gates. On the other side, beneath the backdrop of colour from Totterdown, a few more people were heading towards the path. A man among them spotted them at the top and waved in greeting before striding towards them.

As they drew closer, Hannah could see a mixture of ages. There was one lady who appeared to be in her late sixties, her short hair pushed aside by a pink headband, walking next to a younger woman. The man who'd spotted them first was in his fifties, and it became clear that even more people, men and women, had entered the park, making their way towards the small congregation at the top. Generations had gathered to see them, it seemed, and they all had one thing in common: each and every one of them was ready to run.

'Are you the Running into Trouble Club?' asked one young woman, her sleek blonde hair tied back in a ponytail.

'Must be,' said the woman with the headband. She nodded towards Malika. 'I recognise that girl from the paper. Malika, isn't it? Hope I'm pronouncing it right.'

'You are,' replied Malika, grinning in surprise. She'd expected one or two people to turn up, but not *this* many. 'Er, yeah. We're the club.'

'Welcome,' said Hannah, bowing theatrically.

The woman in the headband spoke first. 'I'm Angie, and this is my daughter, Marie. We saw your story in the paper and thought we'd give it a go as well. Brave woman,' she said to Malika. 'I'm sorry to hear about your friend. Life can really deal you some shit, can't it?'

'Yeah,' said Malika. 'Thank you.'

'I know how it is, love,' said Angie. 'And I'm sorry,' she boomed, gesturing to Hannah and Cassie. 'I meant women, *plural*. You're all brave. Rather you than me. But I might not say that in a year or so. Once I start, there's no stopping.'

Malika laughed. Hannah could tell that Angie was a character. Malika was grinning, Cassie was sharing a giggle. Maybe adding to the club wasn't such a bad thing, after all.

'Hannah here is new, too,' Malika said. 'Cassie is *way* more experienced, but it's her first marathon as well.'

'Have you run before?' asked Cassie.

Marie shook her head. 'Not really. We used to walk a lot, didn't we, Mum?' She turned back to Cassie. 'Then Mum was diagnosed with breast cancer six years ago and we didn't go for a while.'

'Oh, that's terrible. Sorry to hear that,' said Hannah sincerely.

'It's fine,' said Angie. Her tinkly laugh caught Hannah off guard. 'It was terrible at the time though.'

'I thought I was going to lose her,' added Marie.

'But you didn't, did you?' Angie linked her arm through her daughter's. 'I got the all-clear. Well, for *now*, anyway.'

'Mum!'

'Come off it, Marie. You never know what life's got in store for you, do you? Malika here understands, don't you, love?'

Malika nodded.

'In my opinion, when your time's up, it's up. Going through cancer was awful, but I was one of the lucky ones.' She gestured down to her running top. 'I lost both of my breasts, but I managed to keep my life. But when I was sick, I was full of regret. All that stuff I'd wanted to do but didn't because I "didn't get round to it".

'Then I thought that was it . . . I'm going to die. And let me tell you, that bucket list stuff? It's not the same as living in the moment. It feels a whole lot different when you've got a time limit.

'Then I got the all-clear. It was a kick up the arse for me to enjoy the life I've got left and so here we are. Other people don't have that luxury. So, Marie and I are going to sign up to a 10k.'

'That's amazing,' said Cassie.

Angie pondered for a moment. 'And after that, a skydive. I always said you'll never catch me jumping out of a bloody plane, but now I think it'll be thrilling.'

'Jesus Christ,' said Marie, sighing in exasperation.

Hannah chuckled.

That's fine, Mum, but please don't expect me to join you for that one.'

'Maybe *we* should have started small,' Malika said to Hannah. 'You know, with a 10k.'

'It's bit late now,' laughed Hannah.

A teenage girl stepped forwards. 'I'm Kirsty!' she said brightly. 'If this is a club, do we get T-shirts, then?'

'Er, not exactly,' said Hannah. 'Not yet.' She made a mental note to try to get some. *T-shirts*. The Running into Trouble Club was, quite possibly, popular enough to have T-shirts. Hannah couldn't believe it. 'But we like to go for a drink after most runs.'

Angie looked ecstatic. 'Bring 'em on!'

'So, are you all new runners?' Cassie asked.

There was a quick show of hands from at least two thirds of the group.

'OK. So we'll all do the warm-up together and then the more experienced runners can come with me, and the others can split into two groups, led by Hannah and Malika. We'll meet down at the gates in forty minutes.'

'What?!' whispered Hannah, sidling up to Cassie who, she noticed, seemed particularly smug. 'This is . . . no. I can't take on a group. I'm not that experienced yet.' She looked around fretfully at the expectant faces.

Angie had already launched into the warm-up and was on her second set of squats and lunges. Hannah had never taken charge of a group before, besides training new employees at work now and again. And a rundown of Travel Town's temperamental IT systems were a whole lot different to leading a group of runners. What if someone was injured? Hannah knew she should have taken that first aid course when David had offered it.

'What am I meant to do?'

'I'm not sure about this, either,' said Malika. 'I've never done this kind of thing before.'

'It'll be fine. Just do exactly what I've been doing all this time,' said Cassie. 'You both wanted a running club. Looks like you've got one, after all.'

*

Forty minutes later, Hannah's group made their final jog towards the bottom of the path to regroup with the others. Hannah could see them, sitting on the grass, stretching and relaxing in the evening sun. The downhill sprint was the easiest, she knew. It was more positive. The struggle was over and the endorphins flowed.

Altogether, there were eighteen people. Eighteen people who'd turned up especially to run with them. Hannah would never have imagined it and the thought filled her with pride.

'How are you feeling?' Hannah asked, turning to her group, in particular Angie and Marie.

They'd decided to take it slow; that way, they didn't have to worry about catching up or forcing themselves to do more than they felt they could. Hannah could hardly believe that these people were relying on her, pinning their determination on the group leader. She'd never been a leader and would never have pictured herself leading a running group in a million years. Just two months ago she'd have laughed at the mere idea of it, as she no doubt popped a few more biscuits into her mouth. But here she was. A leader – and a good one, it seemed.

They'd had a good time, too, having a nice chat as they made their way round the path, their footsteps weaving among the shadows of the surrounding trees. Angie had been dispensing her wisdom along the route, especially to John, a thirty-something who had some work-related woes.

'If you don't like it, pack it in,' she'd said. 'Obviously look for something else first, don't be a tit about it, but don't waste time doing something you hate.'

Angie's harsh truths were refreshing and Hannah wanted to talk to her more. She wondered how someone who'd gone through so much could be so full of positivity. It made her flush with slight shame at how she'd let Dan become the focus of her life, how her body issues had made her feel less worthy of happiness. Yet here was Angie, taking on new challenges after almost losing her life to cancer.

'I feel like I'm about to collapse. But in a good way,' Angie said bluntly. 'It's been a lovely time, actually. Do you meet every week, then?'

'Yep!' said Hannah. 'Sometimes we run together on the weekends as well. Feel free to join us if you fancy it. We can swap numbers.'

'That's a really nice idea,' said Jan, another member of Hannah's group, her grey ponytail swishing as she jogged briskly down the path, dipping in and out of the shade.

Hannah noticed that despite everyone looking a little worse for wear, they were all smiling. *Phew.*

'I've always wanted to give it a go, but it's hard on your own. Boring, almost. I've always wanted to be the kind of person who gets up and goes for a run, but when it actually comes down to it, I can never manage to get myself out of the house.'

'I was exactly the same,' replied Hannah. They were getting closer now, the gates shining beneath the sunlight. Malika's group had appeared too, gathering together as Hannah and her team took on their final few metres. 'Up until I met Cassie and Mal, I was terrible at going it alone. I was terrified. I was self-conscious and worried about what other people would think of me. I only forced myself to go out because I had to – I wanted to run the marathon. It's all about establishing the habit.'

Oh no, she mused. *I'm becoming Cassie.*

They sprinted to a halt on the grass by the others and Malika weaved her way through the small crowd, bounding over to where Hannah and Angie were stretching their legs.

'That was daunting,' she said, flustered. 'But it was great. I can't believe all these people turned up to run with us.'

'Warm down!' boomed Cassie.

Immediately, the entire group spread out on the grass to complete their final exercises.

'Let's stretch those muscles.'

Cassie was clearly brilliant at commanding attention.

'Does this mean we need official registration?' said Malika to Hannah as they kept their eyes on Cassie, copying her moves even though they knew the short routine by heart.

'Or newsletters?' asked Hannah. 'And a website? Wow. This is going to keep us all busy. This is all because of you, you know. Your article inspired people to come out today.'

'Maybe,' said Malika.

But Hannah saw an unmistakable flash of worry on her small face. She wanted to talk more, to say whatever she could to reassure her, but she didn't want to ruin the moment.

Once the warm down had finished, the group began to disperse as the runners headed off in all directions, vowing to return next week.

'Well, that was something,' said Cassie. 'In fact, it was, dare I admit it, fun. I take it back. I like this club.'

'Hey!' a voice called out from behind them.

All three turned to see Angie and Marie beckoning them to the gate. Not just Angie and Marie, but about six others were standing there, waiting for them to follow.

'Are you coming for a drink then, or what?' asked Angie.

26

Hannah

Hannah watched the lone tea light flicker at the centre of the table. All around her, people talked. They laughed too, clustered together and wrapped up in the warmth of the atmosphere of a small shared space. Hannah cast another glance out of the window, searching. She'd been lucky enough to pounce on a window table just as another couple were leaving and she sat up straight in the tall seat, reaching for her phone.

Hannah looked around the packed bar, watching the others, trying to emulate that cool, collected, 'I do this all the time' vibe. She shifted in her chair, attempted a nonchalant pose, all the while trying to fend off the worry that she'd been stood up.

Her phone screen lit up with a message and Hannah was engulfed by a sense of dread. *Here it is*, she thought, expecting the inevitable 'sorry, something came up' text that would send her running out of the bar and back home. As she swiped to read it, she saw it wasn't from Steve, after all. It was from the group chat with Cassie and Malika:

Cassie: Han! How's the date going?

Hannah tapped out a reply as a man walked bravely by with a tray full of drinks:

Hannah: He hasn't turned up yet. Honestly? I'm dreading this. First date in years! Will he even show up?!

Malika: Lol! Shush, he'll love you. You're A BABE XXX

Cassie: You'll be fine. Do you and Mal want to come to my house for dinner on Saturday? I'm doing pasta. I can give you recipes for some carb-loading foods! Exciting stuff.

Malika: Hannah might be getting some action tonight. That's exciting.

Hannah: Mal! I will not.

Cassie: Am waiting for inevitable flurry of hot cop jokes/ innuendos. Please don't disappoint me.

Cassie: But dinner . . .

Malika: Yes, I'd love to come to dinner. I can bring pudding.

Malika: Does it have to be healthy?

Malika: CASS!

Cass: Healthy? Hell no, it's dessert FFS.

Hannah: I'll bring gin!

Cassie: Yay! Now go have fun! X

Hannah laughed to herself as she read the messages, so immersed that she didn't see Steve approach until he was almost at the table. As he drew near, the nerves subsided, giving way to the fluttery feeling she'd grown to enjoy whenever she saw him. *Or thought of him.* It was a new kind of excitement, something she hadn't experienced for a long, long time.

'Hey!' he said, shrugging off his dark grey jacket.

Steve looked completely different in this setting, out of his police uniform or hi-vis marshal's jacket. Hannah watched as he took his seat, careful not to stare. Steve was wearing dark jeans and a T-shirt that fit his taut, broad body just perfectly. She caught a waft of aftershave: sweet, understated, unlike the strong sort that Dan would use, which would often catch in her throat as it wafted across the landing. A little goes a long way, she'd say, but Dan would never listen.

Don't think about Dan, she told herself. *Tonight is not about Dan.*

'Got to admit, I was a little worried. I thought you might stand me up. Luckily, I saw you in the window. I waved as I walked past, but you didn't see me.'

Hannah prayed Steve hadn't caught a glimpse of her phone as he'd walked by. On the table, more messages were coming through from the others. Hannah glimpsed a message about handcuffs and swiftly stuffed it into her handbag.

'Stand you up? Why would I do that?'

'You wouldn't have been the first,' Steve said, a sad look on his face.

Hannah couldn't believe it. If anything, she thought it would have been the other way round.

'Dating is . . . well, it can be difficult sometimes. I've found it that way, anyway. And yes, now I know I'm spoiling *this* date by talking about it. Tell you what, shall I walk out and back in again? Pretend this little intro never happened?'

Hannah laughed. 'No! Don't worry. I like it. That you're honest. I've been worried about this for days. I haven't actually . . . well, I haven't dated in a long time.'

'When you say "long time" . . .'

'Twenty years,' said Hannah. 'And more.'

'Wow.'

Hannah was suddenly hit by a crashing wave of self-doubt. *What am I doing?* Here she was, in this dimly lit bar, surrounded by all the people she was not. The twenty-something couples, the groups of friends who took up entire tables, voices loud over the soft rock music piping through the speakers. Hannah considered the black top she was wearing. It had made her feel so stylish before she left the house, but now she felt as if she was trying too hard.

'That's not a bad thing, you know,' said Steve.

He smiled widely and Hannah instantly felt comforted.

'You look worried. If you like honesty, then here goes. I started dating two years ago. It's fun, sometimes, but there's also the nerves. The doubt. That feeling of failure when you realise you just don't click with someone. That's happened.'

'Ouch.'

'I know. Wonderful, isn't it? Hey, let me get you a drink. What are you having?'

'Hmm, I'm not too sure,' said Hannah.

She looked towards the bar, trying to spot what drinks were on offer. The sight was mostly blocked by the crowd of waiting customers.

'I can recommend the cider,' he said. 'It's really good. Or there's gin.'

'Ooh! Go on, then, I'll have a cider,' said Hannah. She usually went for the wine, but hey, why not try something different? Just a half.'

She watched Steve as he headed for the bar, his tall body weaving through the crowd to the empty space at the far end. Hannah felt warm, almost blissful as she watched him, stealing a look as he awaited the barman, wondering how she'd been so lucky.

Dating. Hannah hadn't thought about it in many years. She didn't think she'd ever do it again. She'd almost forgotten how it felt the first time. The nervous excitement, the preparation, the butterflies . . . the fear. She remembered it, somehow. Those years in her early twenties before she met Dan. When Dan had come along, that was it. Dating was a thing of the past. Hannah had heard stories from her colleagues – Tinder dates that seemed more scary than fun, a whole array of unwarranted dick pics. It was like navigating an entirely new universe, one that Hannah wasn't cut out for.

Steve reappeared minutes later, placing a cold glass of cider on the table.

'Well,' he said, slipping into his seat, moving closer to the window. 'I hope you like the place. I haven't been here before, but a friend recommended it.'

'It's great,' she said. And it was. It was loud, and packed, but, Hannah soon realised, it had atmosphere. Company. The best kind of place to get to know someone. 'So,' she said, 'did you ever apprehend the criminal in the end? You know, the one you thought was me?'

'Ah! The shed burglar. Yes, we did. Meddings took the piss for a week after that. She says hello, by the way.'

'Ha! I feel guilty. Well, a little. So what's it like then, chasing down Bristol's wrongdoers?' *Do not stare*, Hannah told herself harshly, *no matter how gorgeous he is.*

Steve laughed. Hannah liked his smile. It was comforting. Genuine. Hannah felt that familiar, all-consuming flutter and willed it to go away.

'Not as exciting as you might think,' said Steve. 'But I've been in the force for years. It was always my big dream. I got into running before my training began; even ran the London Marathon once. *That* was an experience. I don't do it that much any more.'

'Why not?'

'Work, mainly. But I marshal at events, which is a lot of fun. I started doing it ages ago and I enjoy it. It's rewarding. I get to pull beautiful women out of rivers, for starters.'

'Very funny.'

'I'm serious! Plus, I have a special someone in my life who keeps me very busy, so I don't exactly have much time to train properly. I can't throw myself into running and the gym as much as I used to.'

Hannah's stomach dropped at his words. *A special someone.* For a moment, the disappointment rendered her silent and her head flooded with confusion. Why did his words feel like a gut punch?

Steve reached into his pocket to retrieve his phone. He turned it towards Hannah. 'This is Ivy.'

Hannah looked down at the screen. A little girl beamed back up at her. She was adorable, with auburn hair just like Steve's, a gap-toothed smile and the same bright blue eyes. She was wearing a baseball cap over her long plaited hair and was holding a football.

Ah! thought Hannah, relieved.

'She's my everything,' said Steve. 'Love her to bits.'

'She looks very much like you,' Hannah replied. 'A lot, in fact. Christ, you're like two peas in a pod.'

'Ha! I know. Poor girl,' said Steve.

He glanced down at the phone, his eyes gleaming with a smile. Love. It shone from his face. *She's my everything.* He didn't have to mention it; Hannah already knew. The way he smiled when he looked at his daughter made it impeccably clear. It was a beautiful sight, one that filled Hannah with an oddly delightful sadness.

'She'll be nine in October. She loves football, athletics, anything sporty. She stays with me a few days a week and some weekends. Her mum and I split when she was four.'

'Oh, I'm sorry,' said Hannah, cursing herself for feeling a pang of happiness at that revelation. 'Was it difficult?'

'Ivy was upset – what child isn't when their mum and dad have to split? It happened to me as well. I was eleven at the time. Luckily for us, it's worked out well. Me and Sarah are still friends. She remarried shortly afterwards.'

'What happened? Actually, you don't have to tell me. I'm being nosy. I'm sorry.'

Steve shrugged. 'Be as nosy as you like. Nothing happened exactly. We fell out of love. That's all it was. Sometimes two people just aren't compatible in the first place and it takes some time to realise that. It took us a few years, after we'd had Ivy.'

Hannah pondered this. She recalled how happy she and Dan had been. How they'd witness other incompatible couples and thank their lucky stars that it wasn't them. That they would be together forever.

I've been so, so stupid.

'Ivy's the best thing that ever happened to me, as cheesy as it is to say. If I could do it all again, I wouldn't change a thing. What about you? Do you . . .' He glanced downwards and his gaze landed on Hannah's hand. He straightened in his chair. 'Ah.'

Hannah realised just what he was looking at. The conspicuous telltale tan line from summer running that had formed on Hannah's ring finger. The gold band that snaked around it had gone; days before, Hannah had finally allowed herself to remove it. The ring that had symbolised her love for Dan now resided in her bedside drawer.

It was time.

'Um, it's a tricky one,' said Hannah.

She ran a finger around the faint line, the one that had once proudly showed off her set of rings. Even now, she felt a heart-stopping jolt of fear when she couldn't feel the gold band before she remembered she hadn't lost it. She'd removed it. It had been her choice and hers alone.

If Dan doesn't want me, then I'm not wearing it.

'I'm married. Well, we're separated.'

'Oh.'

The disappointment in Steve's voice was hard to ignore.

'He left me. For someone else.'

There was silence. Hannah took another sip of sweet cider, hiding her hand on her lap.

'It's what made me sign up for the marathon. Which is also a long story.'

'I understand,' said Steve. 'Do you have any children?'

Hannah shook her head. 'None.'

She looked at the table, at the small decoration in its centre that drew attention away from the old glossed wood. She didn't particularly want to elaborate.

'I guess that makes things a little easier, then,' he said finally. 'Not that it's ever easy, of course.'

Hannah nodded. They continued talking, enjoying the evening as it descended into night, and at eleven thirty they were still there. They'd discussed family, aspirations, their lives, their childhoods growing up in Bristol. Steve had always wanted to be a policeman, he'd confessed.

'When I was Ivy's age, I was putting on my fancy dress costume and pretending to arrest my parents for refusing me ice cream. I'm surprised I even had any friends.'

'Ha! I bet everyone loved that.'

'What about you? What did you want to be?'

Hannah stared out towards the window, where the street was quiet and the darkness had taken over. The word hung in the humid air. *Mother.* Hannah didn't admit this. She kept the word back, locked away for her and her alone.

'I don't know, actually,' she said, thinking of the times she'd feed and dress her baby doll. One she'd dropped so many times that its eyelid hung half open in a creepy way that would freak her mother out on the numerous occasions when she'd left it lying around the house. Not that that stopped her. 'I thought about lots of things,' she said. 'I wasn't really career-focused or academic, but I was happy. I always wanted to work in travel. I guess I thought it would be glam, you know? I loved going on holiday and at one point I wanted to be an air hostess, then I became a travel agent. And then I got married.'

'And life just got in the way? I think that happens to us all. Now you're a belly dancer, by all accounts.'

'I wish I hadn't told you that.'

'Why not? I'm impressed.'

They laughed as they finished their cider and last orders were called, sending the reluctant customers out into the cool air. Hannah and Steve headed out into the night, walking slowly towards the Victoria Street bridge, where traffic flowed and moonlight hit the water in a beautiful soothing pattern. Night-time in the city brought a sense of promise, an adventure. Hannah could feel the tipsy, warm euphoria of the night coming to a close and part of her didn't want it to end.

'I'll book a taxi,' said Hannah, fishing her phone out of her bag.

They slowed their walk by the water. The evening breeze swiped Hannah's face, making her skin feel cool, a stark contrast to how she felt inside – warm, ready, a frisson of excitement fluttering in her chest, yearning to make its escape. They stopped for a moment and looked out across the river as the waves seemed to sparkle beneath the soft light. Hannah could barely remember the last time she'd felt like this – exhilarated, happy enough to burst, confident that she could spend more hours laughing into the night air with Steve.

At first, she'd suspected it was the cider working its magic, lulling her into this pleasant sense of security, but deep down she realised that wasn't the case. It was *him*.

This handsome, funny, interesting man standing in front of her, who'd re-invoked a long-lost sense of delight that she thought had gone for good. He'd made her feel like a teenager again, giddy and starry eyed, only this time she was no longer being ignored.

'It's been a really nice evening,' said Steve. 'We should do it again. It's hard to believe that I've lived in this city all of my life and there are still places I've yet to explore. And it'd be nice to have someone to explore them with.'

'Me too,' said Hannah. 'I guess after a while you just get used to certain things and you forget about everything else.'

'Tell me about it. I mean, as you've probably guessed, I frequent most parts of this city on a nightly basis, but not in the same way.'

'Look at you, being all heroic,' Hannah laughed.

'Ha! I'm not complaining. That's how I met you, after all. Actually, I'm glad I very nearly arrested you now. But we should definitely do this again. I'll leave it to you to choose the date; I know how hectic your schedule is. Running, belly dancing . . . is there anything you don't do?'

'Going out again would be nice,' she said, almost adding, *it's been a long time since I had this much fun*, but quickly decided against it. She didn't want to look *sad*, not when Steve had assumed she had a busy, fun-filled life. Even so, she liked the idea of being a bit more mysterious. It was certainly more thrilling than the truth. 'I'd love to.'

They stood by the bridge, looking out at the view. She'd seen it a million times before, but it seemed different tonight. She took one last look, to keep the moment, and the renewed happy feeling, locked in her memory. She wanted to stay, but it was already late and the taxi was on its way.

Suddenly, she felt Steve's hand in hers and as she turned to face him, felt herself moving closer. His hand softly ventured around her waist and before she could stop herself, she was kissing him.

The feeling took her by surprise. Part of her wanted to stop, to slow down and enjoy every second as if it were her last. But she was too busy enjoying the moment, caught up in the excitement as they pulled one another closer.

Steve's kiss was gentle, his lips unexpectedly soft against her own. She let her hands wander into his jacket, feeling the taut body beneath it, covered by the thick fabric of his shirt. She hadn't expected this; to be spending the evening snogging a policeman on a public street as though she were a loved-up seventeen-year-old.

And she was enjoying it. Every. Single. Second.

Dan's face floated in her memory, a brief flicker, before it disappeared again. This was not about Dan. Dan didn't kiss her like this, didn't hold her in the way that Steve was currently holding her. The breeze was cold between them now and she clutched her jacket tighter around her, loving the way Steve's hands rested on her waist, how his light stubble brushed across her cheek. It made her feel wanted. Beautiful. *Sexy.*

'You're absolutely gorgeous,' said Steve as he finally pulled away.

Hannah didn't want him to stop, wanted to stay there in that spot by the river, unmoving, lost in each other.

'Sorry,' he said, leaning in to kiss her cheek. 'I just couldn't help it.'

'Me neither,' said Hannah.

She groaned as her phone trilled to tell her the taxi was approaching.

'I had a wonderful time,' said Steve.

Hannah pulled him closer and they kissed again until the impatient beep of a car horn finally made them let each other go.

They walked towards the waiting cab in silence, a thousand words forming in Hannah's head. A firework of joy and passion, being lit anew. As she bundled herself into the back of the car, she gave Steve a final wave, feeling the sticky, smudged lip gloss that had travelled halfway up her face and laughed. The cab pulled away and Hannah slumped back in her seat, her mind replaying what had just happened. As though she were a teenager, heading home to write in her diary.

It had been a long, long time since she'd felt this happy.

27
Malika

Malika twirled Abbie's medal around in her hands, watching the sunlight bounce off its silver surface. Her good luck charm. She felt the weight of it in her palm as she perused the meeting notes she'd worked on for hours the night before. As her housemates had spent the evening playing one of Dean's elaborate board games, Malika had locked herself away in her room, prepping.

The newspaper article had been a shock, but soon she realised Hannah had been right. Where was the harm in being truthful? If anything, the article had brought her more support. A flurry of donations had appeared on the club's charity page, not just from friends and loved ones, but also total strangers who'd heard about her plight.

In the days that followed, she was flooded with messages of support from her friends. Her housemates had seemed more understanding. And yes, while her parents may have sounded overwrought with concern during the numerous phone calls she'd received, she knew that it was because they cared about her so much.

'Are you sure you're OK? Do you want to come home for a little while? Are you eating properly?'

She pictured her mother, curled up on her favourite chair, worrying the day away.

'I'm fine, Mum. Please don't fret.'

Malika gave the usual stock answers, but this time, she felt better. As though an invisible weight had been lifted from her body. She felt lighter. More free.

What Malika was feeling was normal. Grief does that to you. She knew that now. And with the upset behind her, she was happy to be back at work.

Flicking on her computer, Malika sat back in the chair, reading the notes she'd rehearsed in her room, feeling somewhat silly as she spoke to the air. The small presentation she was planning to give CallerArc was almost perfect; she just needed to tweak it a little, make sure the words flowed. CallerArc were an established business about to open new offices in the city and were soon to be in need of some new staff. Malika was determined to get Rocket that contract. It was finally a time to show Eva what she was made of. If anything could demonstrate just how good she was at her job, it was leading this meeting.

She caught her warped reflection in the medal's surface. *Nailing it*, she thought. It was what Abbie used to say.

'Morning!' Marc said brightly as he entered the office.

Eva was already in, sitting at her desk, wearing a look of concentration, no doubt snowed under with emails. Malika watched as Marc took off his jacket carefully before slumping into his swivel chair.

'Good weekend?' he asked.

'Not bad, actually,' said Malika. 'It was fun and I also got in some swotting.' She held up the meeting notes and braced herself for the oncoming banter.

Marc frowned.

'Yeah?' he said, his expression maudlin. 'You seem like you're in a better mood. Which is nice. I hope you didn't let those trolls get to you.'

'Trolls?'

'Yeah,' said Marc. 'On your article? Wait. You haven't seen them? In that case, forget I said anything.'

Malika froze. *Trolls?* She hadn't looked at the article online since before the weekend. The comments she *had* seen were pleasant. Supportive.

'You can't say that then tell me to forget about it,' she said, already heading for the Bristol Live page. 'What do you mean?'

Marc shrugged, his face a picture of regret. 'Seriously, don't worry. It was a really nice article. Abbie would have loved it. Some people are just shitty. It's not even worth looking.'

Too late. The page loaded, displaying Malika's smiling photo. Her eyes flitted to the bottom of the page.

Fifty-seven comments.

Fifty-seven? The last time she'd looked, there were twelve. Her heart beat faster in her chest as the messages swam in front of her eyes. Marc was right. Among the supportive platitudes were some less than pleasant comments:

Isn't this the girl who's backing the stupid slow zones? Not sure why she's bothering to raise money. Too many cyclists with a death wish. Should be running for a more worthy cause!

Ha! That's one less irritating cyclist on the roads, then.

Can we cut all the sentimental crap and think about the poor driver who'll be forever traumatised because some entitled idiot zoomed into traffic?

Run all you like, love. Cyclists will never learn. I can tell you where to stick your 20 mph zones. Right up your . . .

Malika stopped. Her breath caught in her throat. She didn't want to read on, but curiosity got the better of her and she scrolled through, trying to maintain her composure as the hateful remarks glared out menacingly from the screen. Other commenters had leapt to her defence, accusing the trolls of being insensitive, but that only encouraged them further.

Abbie's death had been an accident. Nobody was to blame. A freak accident, which Abbie had paid dearly for. The driver of the car who'd hit her had been injured but was still alive, while Abbie's life had ended.

Anger rose inside her. Her hands drifted over the keyboard, ready to type out a response. Give them a piece of her mind. Fingers flying over the keys, Malika pounded out a message, words of rage pouring onto the screen. She went to hit Send.

Then she stopped. It'd be no use, she knew that. She'd be playing right into their hands.

Malika jumped as the phone on her desk rang, its shrill sound jolting her from her angry reverie. She didn't want to talk to anyone. Not right now. For once in her life, she'd happily have let the call ring out, but she was aware of Eva and Marc glancing in her direction. Closing the website, she reached for the receiver.

'Rocket Recruitment, Malika speaking.'

'Malika! Hi, it's Jenny from First Circle Solutions?'

There was an unfamiliar hint of uncertainty in Jenny's voice.

'How are you?' Malika asked.

'A bit confused, if I'm honest,' Jenny replied. 'I've had a candidate from Rocket turn up for an interview today, but his slot isn't until tomorrow.'

'Oh! Whoops. Well, I guess that's an easy mistake to make.' She'd had quite a few interviewees turn up on the wrong day. 'Embarrassing, sure, but no harm done.'

Jenny paused. 'Well, the thing is, he was adamant it was for today. He showed me the confirmation email and, well, he was right.'

What?

'I'm really sorry about that, Jen. I'll look into it right away.'

'Thanks. I didn't want to alarm you, but that's not the only mix-up we've had recently. I spoke to Eva last night about it. Someone else turned up yesterday for the contact centre job but thought she was interviewing for the accounting position. It was a little embarrassing for us. And another person attended for Jade Richardson's slot and she didn't turn up at all. I have a feeling something's gone wrong with the scheduling somewhere. We just need to clarify that everything's OK.'

The receiver shook in Malika's hand. Her breathing quickened and she tried to focus on letting it flow. In. Out. *Calm.* Naturally, it was no use. Panic was already rising in her chest.

'Can I call you back?' asked Malika hurriedly.

'That'd be grand.'

The formality hung in Jenny's voice like a threat. Before Malika had even hung up, the phone on Marc's desk began to ring and moments later, she could hear him trying to console an unhappy caller.

'I'm sorry,' he said. 'I'll find out and get back to you today, OK? I promise.'

He threw down the receiver. 'That was for you, Mal. Someone's gone to an interview, which she apparently didn't have today. Sounds like a right fiasco.'

'Oh, God.'

'Is everything OK?'

Malika felt as if she was going to be sick. Her morning coffee was gurgling away in her stomach, threatening to make a reappearance. As she rose from the desk, contemplating a

223

dash to the bathroom, Eva stepped out from her desk and beckoned her over.

'Can I have a quick chat, Mal?' she asked.

Forcing herself to breathe, to let her stomach settle itself, Malika padded lightly towards the back office, taking a seat opposite her boss. Eva's bangles clinked together as she pushed the door closed. It clicked with a sense of finality that Malika wasn't used to. The cheerful, jingling sound that always alerted the team to Eva's approach no longer seemed so light-hearted.

They were together now, alone in the cramped white-walled room with its faded posters about health and safety and team building that had been Blu-Tacked to the wall when she'd first started working at the company. Her gaze flicked between each of them as she willed herself not to get teary; as long as she didn't look at Eva and see the disappointment in her eyes, she could manage to hold it together.

Just.

'Malika, I need to speak to you and I want you to understand that you're not in trouble, OK?'

'So I'm definitely in trouble, then,' she laughed.

Her attempt at humour fell flat. She dabbed at her eyes with the sleeve of her blouse.

Eva didn't return her smile. She took a deep breath. Yellow light streamed in from the tiny window. Despite the lack of it, it was harsh.

'I had a call,' Eva began. 'Yesterday, after you left. Jenny rang and told me she'd been experiencing some issues with the interview schedule. I also had a complaint from someone who'd apparently missed an interview. I brought up your spreadsheet to have a look and it turns out that some of the information is incorrect.'

'Eva, I'm really sorry. I have no idea what went wrong.'

Then again, it wasn't exactly the first error she'd made. There had been times when she'd had to remember to concentrate.

'Well, clearly something did. Look, we can deal with this. I'll get on the phone later and make this all right. But having complaints like this is concerning. Remember what it took to secure the First Circle contract?'

Malika nodded, keeping her eyes on the table, where the ghost of a coffee ring took pride of place. It was a welcome relief from Eva's disheartened expression.

'You haven't been hitting your targets this month, either,' Eva added, 'but I wouldn't expect you to, not with what happened and the workload I've heaped on you, which I'm really sorry about. I didn't realise I was putting you under so much pressure. You should have told me you were struggling.'

'You didn't put me under pressure. I volunteered to take over Abbie's work, remember? I *wanted* to do it. And I thought I was doing well. If there's anything I can do to resolve this, I—'

'Mal,' Eva cut in. 'I think taking on additional responsibility isn't the best idea at this moment in time. I think you need to step away from it. From work in general, to be honest. Just for a little while.'

'What?'

'You need a break. I'm sending you home for two weeks.'

No. No no . . .

It was difficult to shake the panic from her voice. 'Am I being suspended?'

Eva's smile didn't reach her large brown eyes. 'Of course not. You've been an absolute asset to this team since you joined us. And we're short on staff at the moment as it is, so I wouldn't be doing this if I didn't think it was what's best for you. I feel as though being here right now isn't good for you, so I want you to take some time out. Focus on *you*. Don't think about work. Then once you're back, we can reassess your workload and go from there.'

'But I don't . . .'

Eva held up a hand, preventing Malika from continuing.

'Mal. Honestly. Take some time away. Being here is evidently causing you more stress. You've never made a mistake until recently. Clearly, you've been taking on too much and, for the sake of your health, I want you to go home today and return in two weeks. I'll sort out your pay, so don't worry about that. It's nice that you enjoy work, but you can't let it consume you. There's more to life than Rocket. Abbie's death made me realise that – she was always worried about work.'

Malika opened her mouth to reply but thought better of it. There was nothing she could say, no appropriate reply besides begging to stay, but she knew Eva would have none of it. Malika loved her job; she wasn't prepared just to let it go. She'd been determined to make sure the team didn't suffer with the sudden loss of their account manager.

Yet, evidently, her feelings were having a detrimental effect on her working life. She hadn't been thinking straight, her mind on other things while she was updating the schedules. On Abbie, on running, on just getting through the day. Her grief was taking over and it was officially winning.

Forcing back more tears, Malika slid from her seat, the scrape of metal against the floor piercing the new awkward silence.

'What about the meeting?' Malika spluttered, suddenly remembering her appointment with CallerArc. 'I have that big meeting next week. There's no way I can miss that.'

'Marc can cover it. Don't worry, Mal. The world's not going to end because you took some time off. Go and get yourself a cup of tea, shut down your computer and, when you're ready, head home. Try to relax.'

Malika's face burned with shame. Eva didn't believe that she was capable and she was right. Determined not to cry, Malika rose from her chair and moved slowly towards the door, trying to process the news. She'd never been in trouble at work before and now *this*. Even though she knew she wasn't in trouble, according to Eva anyway, she still couldn't bear the thought that she'd messed up.

She didn't stay for tea. She didn't think it possible to keep anything down at that moment, not when her stomach was churning, and she wanted to leave before the tears returned.

She stepped out of the back office and headed for her desk, where she shut down her PC in silence, grabbed her rucksack and shuffled towards the door, aware that she was being watched by Marc.

'You all right?' he asked.

But Malika simply nodded before rushing out and walking home on autopilot, unable to concentrate on anything but the one thing she'd learnt today.

She couldn't do the job, after all. She'd let Abbie down. She'd failed.

28

Hannah

Hannah dropped the bag of shopping on the doorstep as she fumbled for her key, sighing as a rogue onion made its escape from the bag and rolled along the path. Hannah made a grab for the runaway veg just as Mrs Gibson chose that moment to step out of her car, Hannah in her sights, no doubt to further question the whereabouts of Saint Dan, but Hannah launched herself into the safety of her hallway as fast as humanly possible.

After taking the shopping through to the kitchen, Hannah began to unpack: soups, fresh fruit and vegetables, some healthier-than-usual microwave meals for her lunch. Carefully, she pulled from the bag a bottle of red wine. It was a treat, something she'd make last. Enjoy. Since the start of their little running club, Hannah's penchant for wine had begun to diminish; after all, when she had to get up for an early morning weekend 10k, a hangover wasn't the best of ideas.

Hannah poured herself a glass, watching as it filled. *Just halfway*, she thought, feeling a flush of pride as she screwed the lid back on. It was a rest day, a day free of yoga or running, and a day Hannah now looked forward to as a way to focus on her self-care. After the busy eight hours at Travel Town, a glass of wine and a hot bath were exactly what she needed.

She took the wine and padded upstairs to the bathroom, pouring in a generous amount of the posh bubble bath her brother had bought her for Christmas before going to the bedroom to undress. She smiled as her skirt, once tight around the waist and starting to strain at the zip, came off easily with one shimmy. Alone in the house, Hannah had taken to practising some of her belly dance moves in the kitchen or the bedroom, albeit to Beyoncé – she made a note to ask the tutor for a good playlist to dance to.

It wasn't just the weight loss that had made Hannah happy. As nice as it was to shed the pounds, to feel the difference in the way her clothes fit, it was more than that. It was discovery. Hannah's weight had no longer become a priority in her life. Plus, Steve seemed to like her regardless.

Since the date, Hannah hadn't been able to stop smiling. Her colleagues had been wondering why she'd practically danced into work. She knew not to be too hopeful, but she couldn't help feeling positive.

Hannah marvelled at the way her body felt now, at its newness – how her legs felt tighter, how her stomach was getting tauter. The difference was slight, but to her, it was visible.

Naked now, Hannah headed to the bathroom, taking one of her soft towels from the cupboard. Just as she dipped her feet into the bubbly water, the doorbell sounded, the high-pitched, unexpected shriek sending her jolting backwards. Turning off the taps and pulling on her dressing gown, she edged towards the top of the stairs, peering over the banister in order to work out who the blurry figure behind the frosted glass belonged to. Thinking it was probably Mrs Gibson, she readied herself to head back up to the warm, foamy comfort of her bath, but the person behind the door was too tall to be her neighbour.

The doorbell sounded again. *What if it's an emergency?* Perhaps her shed had been broken into this time, she thought, imagining the disappointed faces of the would-be burglars when they prised open the old creaking door to get a face full of cobwebs and ancient half-empty tins of paint. Maybe even some rusty tools.

Pulling her dressing gown tightly around her, Hannah hurried downstairs and opened the door.

And came face to face with Dan.

Dan, her husband, stood expectantly on the doorstep, clutching the handle of their old suitcase. Hannah stared back, flummoxed, her heart pounding so scarily fast that she felt it was in danger of leaping right out of her mouth and flopping onto the well-worn doormat.

No. Not now.

'Are you going to let me in, then?' Dan asked, a sheepish smile on his face.

Silently, Hannah moved aside, the bath water pooling in a tiny puddle around her feet. She closed the front door, unable to speak, or let out anything other than a small, choked sigh.

Hannah watched as Dan walked through to the kitchen, one hand in the pockets of his dark jeans. *Clearly new*, she thought. She could see him cast a glance around the place, taking in the living room, the neat hallway, Hannah's running clothes on the washing line outside, visible through the back door. He nodded towards the training plan that was stuck to the fridge.

'You're doing well,' he said.

Hannah felt the heat rise to her face. She wiped beneath her eyes, where the steam from the bathroom had made her face shiny, smudging most of the eyeliner she'd applied for work, more daring now that she had achieved extra confidence.

She stared at him, standing there in the kitchen, suitcase in tow. He looked at it, contemplative. She wondered if he was going to empty it, pull out the clothes and load them into the washing machine, as if he'd never left. As if he'd just gone on a work trip for the weekend and not left her completely and utterly alone.

Hannah remembered how, only weeks ago, she'd longed for this moment. Yearned for him to turn up, to step back through the doors of their home and talk. Now, she was feeling anything but relieved.

Now? She wanted him out.

Dan rested the case next to the fridge and wandered into the living room. Hannah followed.

'What do you think you're doing, turning up out of the blue like this?' she demanded.

'It's still my house, too,' he said. 'I have every right to.'

'Really?' Hannah reached for the stack of bills on the coffee table and thrust them under his nose. '*Really?* Because it doesn't seem like it. You left. You left me for months. So no, you don't just "have every right" to swan right back in here and invade my living space. What if I had someone here with me?'

Dan's head whipped round. Hannah spotted a slight hint of fear working through his features, no matter how hard he tried to hide it.

'Are you saying you've met someone else?'

'What if I have? Does it matter to you?'

Dan opened his mouth to argue, then something caught his eye. He looked around at the altered living room, the shelves bare of wedding photos and shared knick-knacks. The neat stack of boxes that Malika had pushed to the far wall, all bearing his name.

'What . . . Han, what the fuck's all this?'

'This,' said Hannah, 'is your stuff. The rest is in the spare room, all boxed and ready. I don't know how you're going to get it all in that case, but I'm guessing you've got your van outside. Give me two secs, I'll nip upstairs and get changed, and then I can help you load it up.'

Dan stared at Hannah, his gaze flitting from the boxes, to her. 'Han . . .' he said, trailing off as Hannah simply stood there, arms folded in her fluffy dressing gown.

She watched as he crossed the room, plonking himself onto the sofa.

'We need to sort this out, Dan,' said Hannah quietly. She'd expected to be angry; livid, even. Yet, as hard as she tried to feel rage for everything he'd put her through, there was nothing. All she wanted was to go back to her nice peaceful evening. 'We need to work out how we move forwards. I'm assuming we'll sell the house. I've packed up your things, cleared out a lot of mine . . . we need to talk, Dan. Properly. If we're going to divorce, we need to sort it out sooner rather than later. You can't ignore me any more.'

'Divorce? You want to *divorce*?' asked Dan, incredulous.

He leant forwards, his face in his hands, looking much less confident than he did when he first walked in. Hannah couldn't face the idea of sitting down. She was agitated now, full of sudden energy.

'You actually want that?' Dan muttered.

'Well, what else are we going to do?' snapped Hannah. 'And no. I didn't *want* that. I didn't want my husband to cheat on me and leave me for someone else. I didn't *want* to have to contemplate losing my home and having to start my life again when I'm almost fifty. No. But I haven't exactly had a bloody choice. So don't ask me such a stupid question.'

'Han. Come here.' He patted the cushion next to him, just as he always did.

Reluctantly, Hannah wandered over, watching her husband, this man she once loved – and still did love, though it was different – take a deep breath. His eyes were unusually red. *Teary*, she noticed. So unlike the strong no-nonsense Dan.

'Do you really want to end this?' he asked.

Hannah nodded. 'I think it's best if we just get it over with. We can't move forward if we're still in each other's lives. You have Sophia now. I've accepted that.'

Dan reached out for her hand. She almost pulled it away, thinking of Steve. How Steve's hands caressed hers at the bar. How they pulled her closer to kiss. Just thinking of the kiss sent pleasant shivers all over Hannah's body. There was a time when Dan had kissed her like that, when just a touch had caused such sparks, but those days had long passed.

'The thing is, Han . . . I think I've made a massive mistake. Sophia's great, but . . . well, she's not you. I miss *us*.'

Hannah laughed, noticing Dan's disdain as she snorted into her dressing gown sleeve.

'You *what*? Come on, Dan, don't be stupid. What, has Miss Perfect dumped you for the next gullible idiot who's signed up to her spin class?'

'No,' he said, pulling his hand away. 'She hasn't. If anything, she wants us to move forward.'

'Well, why not? I'm trying to help her out here. Let's just get it done and dusted.'

'I love you, Han. I don't want us to end. When this all started, I thought it was what I wanted.'

'To cheat on your wife?'

Dan exhaled loudly. 'No. I was, like you say, a gullible idiot. I thought we were over. We both got too content, didn't we? We obviously had issues and we never talked.'

'Don't blame me,' said Hannah. 'Please, Dan, don't blame me for your shitty behaviour. I didn't do what you did.'

'I'm sorry,' he said.

The words were unfamiliar. Genuine. As if Dan were possessed.

'I came to see if you want to try again.'

Hannah smiled wearily. *Who was this person?* Hannah asked herself. It looked like Dan. *Her* Dan, with his kind eyes and slightly crooked smile, the features she'd been drawn to on the day they'd first met. Sure, he looked a little different now. Sophia's well-tuned new model. But he was still the same man, who'd seen her at her absolute worst and still loved her through it. How he'd used to cuddle her, wrap her in blankets and spoil her whenever she had the flu, sprawled on the sofa with a tissue in each nostril. The times when she'd come home from one too many Christmas parties; her head and the toilet bowl had been old festive friends. And of course, there were *those* years; where hope had made way for despair and denial, followed by a thick black cloud of grief that they'd existed beneath for a long time. Just when they thought it inescapable, they'd pulled through, together, because they were Dan and Han; a loving, unstoppable force.

This was the question she'd been waiting weeks for. Her wish had been granted.

'I know it'll be difficult, Han,' he said. 'With Sophia – I need to make it up to you. I'll do everything I can to make it up to you.'

Her heart lifted. Of course it was going to be awkward. And there'd be a lot of work ahead for the both of them. She knew that. It would take her a long time to erase the memories, the images of him cuddled up with Sophia when they should have been together. It would take time. Trust was so fragile, but it was worth it, wasn't it? She was willing to try to put their relationship back together, piece by fragile piece, until they were happy again. She could make him happy again. She was determined. And she'd surprised herself with her determination lately, so what was stopping her?

Steve. His face filtered through her mind like a movie montage.

But Steve wasn't the one she'd spent more than twenty years with. Steve hadn't seen her through those difficult times. And besides, what if everything with Steve went wrong?

One date. It had been *one date*.

Hannah shuffled closer to Dan on the sofa. She rested her hand on his knee. Noticed he, too, had removed his wedding ring. *Perhaps this'll be a new start*, she pondered. She could curl up in his arms again, maybe spend the evenings together like they used to. See how things go. Forgiveness was going to be difficult, but it could happen. Just as she'd trained her unwieldy legs to run, she could train herself to forgive him. *One day. Surely.*

'What do you think?' asked Dan as he softly kissed the top of her head. 'Shall we give it another go?'

'Yes,' said Hannah. 'We should. This time, no secrets.'

They sat for almost an hour. Hannah heard the clock tick while she rested in his arms, inhaling his scent. Beneath the new expensive aftershave and the new jacket was Dan. Her Dan. The one she loved, wanted. Being with him had made her remember.

They were Han and Dan. Always.

'I'll go,' he said, pulling away as the afternoon drew to a close. 'I'll explain everything to Sophia.'

She waited until the faint roar of his van could be heard before grabbing the bottle of wine from the kitchen and heading back to the bathroom. As the bubbles rose, she picked up her phone to send a message to Steve. Her heart sank as she noticed he'd already sent one:

Hi, lovely Hannah! I'm free on Thursday evening, do you fancy spending it with me? X

Hannah tapped out a response, hands trembling:

I'm so sorry, but I don't think we should see each other again. I had a great time but things are difficult right now. I'm so sorry, Steve. Xx

Hannah leant back as her tears dropped into the water. *It has to be done.*

Dan was back. Dan was back and everything was going to be fine.

It was all for the best.

29
Hannah

Hannah spotted Bronwen before she reached the cafe, her head of caramel hair visible in the window. She was wearing a loose pink jacket, one Hannah quite fancied for herself if she wasn't so adamant it would make her resemble a marshmallow.

'Han!' Bronwen called, gesturing to the comfy chairs in the corner that she'd managed to bag as the lunchtime rush bustled around her. 'Don't worry, I've got your usual!' she said just as Hannah was about to squeeze through the throng towards the queue.

Sure enough, Hannah's mocha was waiting on the small table, gloriously topped with whipped cream and sprinkled with chocolate. The cream had already begun to melt around the edges, and Hannah took her spoon and scooped a sneaky mouthful from the top, her own little ritual.

'Hannah!' said Bronwen brightly. 'How are things?'

Hannah reached for the mug. It warmed her hands as she readied herself to tell Bronwen the news. She hadn't told her about Steve. Normally, she'd share everything with her best friend, call her when something so big had happened. Hannah recalled their teen years when Bronwen would be straight on the phone, giving Hannah the low-down on her latest date. But something stopped her from sharing this time. Bronwen was too close to Dan. Too close to her former life, the life before the running club.

Former life. Only now, it wasn't her former life any more. Hannah was living it again. Dan was coming back, returning everything to normality. Hannah hadn't shared the news with Cassie and Malika yet; she had a feeling she knew what Cassie would say.

But it wasn't Cassie's life. It was hers.

'Did I tell you about Jo at work?' Bronwen asked excitedly.

Hannah listened, wondering whether to break the news of the Han and Dan reunion at this week's catch-up. Hannah listened intently, grateful that the subject had moved towards the safe confines of work gossip. Bronwen's job at the council was vastly different to Hannah's day-to-day life as a travel agent, but they loved hearing about each other's work woes.

It was nice to have a place to vent, to chat for hours about anything and everything. Their weekly catch-up had been a tradition that had held them together over the years. When their lives had left the carefree realm of high school and the world of work began, followed by marriage and, for Bronwen at least, a family – they'd promised never to let anything get in the way of their friendship.

'Especially not men,' Bronwen had joked.

But men did, eventually. Nobody was to blame. That was just how life worked. Things became more sporadic; nights out were less frequent, visits to each other's houses were rescheduled numerous times, especially when children came into the picture.

Hannah recalled the days when the boys were young, when Bronwen would manoeuvre her huge buggy containing Josh into the cafe as Ethan toddled closely behind. They'd still meet up for their catch-up sessions, the boys seeing it as a fun outing, an adventure of sorts, with their colouring books and small army of soft toys to keep them entertained while Hannah and Bronwen delved into work and family life. Often, Hannah would sneak a look at the boys, at the look of concentration on Ethan's face as he coloured a giraffe in a meticulous fashion, chubby-cheeked Josh gurgling away, and wondered when life would bestow upon her some of the luck and happiness that her friend had in droves.

Despite Bronwen's harried look and insistence that motherhood wasn't the image of sunshine and roses that people made it out to be, Hannah would have jumped at the chance. She told herself it was only a matter of time and wondered when that day would come, the day when she, too, would receive the happy news. That perfect, grainy black-and-white scan image that would tell them it was real. Hannah wondered when she, too, would be just as lucky.

Bronwen's phone pinged. She glanced down at her latest message, eyes wide with excitement.

'Ooh, I haven't told you! Ethan's got a girlfriend. Took him ages to bring her round to meet us, but she came over at the weekend and she's lovely.'

'Awww!' said Hannah, grinning. 'Bloody hell, it feels like only a year ago he was running round the house in his nappy.'

Bronwen beamed with pride. 'Here, I'll show you a photo . . .'

Bronwen lifted her phone for Hannah to see, displaying a photo of Ethan, who'd inherited Bronwen's pale eyes and cheeky smile. His arms were around a pretty girl with flowing black hair, grinning like the Cheshire cat.

'Oh, and there they are at school prom night. I mean, *prom*. It's all changed now, hasn't it? Remember when we had our end-of-year discos?'

Bronwen had swiped to the next image, but her son wasn't in it. She stared at the screen. Instead of Ethan,

Hannah saw a familiar face. Dan. In what appeared to be Bronwen's garden.

Before she could say anything, Bronwen swiped the image away.

'Whoops!' she said, but Hannah could feel the edge to her voice. 'Went a bit too far. Here we go.'

There was Ethan, standing proudly in his tux.

'What was that?' said Hannah, her voice high.

'What was what?'

'That other photo. Go back to that last photo.'

Bronwen placed the phone quickly back on the table and waved away the question.

'Don't worry about it. It's nothing important. Anyway, so this prom, you'll never believe what—'

'*Bron.*' Hannah was no longer smiling. 'Show me that picture. Please.'

The look of worry on Bronwen's face said it all. She was hiding something, Hannah knew it. Even in school, Bronwen's excuses for not doing her homework would fall flat. Hannah had to get her out of all manner of scrapes during their teenage years. She was, quite simply, a terrible liar.

Reluctantly, she picked up the phone again and scrolled through to the offending picture, showing it to Hannah.

'There,' she said. 'And yes, I'm sorry.'

Hannah felt her face drain of colour. There, right in front of her, was Dan. He was standing next to the barbecue, beer in hand, as Bronwen's husband, Mike, grinned in the background. Hannah snatched the phone from her friend's grasp, seeing her face fall as Hannah flicked through even more photos, feeling increasingly sick with each one.

Pictures of her husband and friends – *her* friends – beamed out at her in full mocking colour.

There was Bronwen herself, in a floaty orange top and a pair of sunglasses. Behind her, reclining on one of Bronwen's deckchairs with a glass of wine, looking glamorous in huge paparazzi-dodging sunnies and a messy bun, was someone she really, *really* didn't want to see.

'Please tell me that's not Sophia.'

Bronwen went to grab the phone, but Hannah was too quick. She turned round, zooming in on the awful image. *Yep, it was definitely Sophia.* Enjoying a barbecue in her best mate's garden.

'Look, I'm in a bit of an awkward position,' Bronwen pleaded. 'Mike and Dan work together. What am I supposed to do?'

Anger rose in Hannah's chest. 'Have you been spending time with Dan and his girlfriend behind my back?'

She handed back the phone with shaky hands, no longer wanting to see. Tears pricked the corners of her eyes. She really didn't want to break down in a sobbing fit smack bang in the middle of a busy coffee shop. She'd had enough humiliation in the past few months to last an entire lifetime.

Bronwen had the grace to look embarrassed, at least.

'Yes. Well, not exactly. The thing is, it was just a little barbecue Mike arranged. Of course Dan was going to be there, so I decided not to tell you. I wanted to, I really did, but . . . well, what would you do, if you were me?'

I'd be honest, Hannah thought through her tears. Although *had* she been honest lately? The social media posts, the pretence that everything was happy, that Hannah was embarking on a new life. She'd been just as bad for playing pretend. But, Hannah reasoned, her little white lies didn't hurt anyone. Everyone exaggerated on social media now and again. She wasn't betraying anyone, especially not her best friend since childhood.

'Han, I really didn't think he'd bring her. Honestly. I felt terrible when she turned up.'

Hannah *had* expected things to become a little awkward, given that Dan and Bronwen's husband worked together. In fact, Dan had helped Mike to get a job with his surveying company. But this? This was different. To top it off, their mutual friend Caroline was in the photos, too. Caroline who'd called Hannah shortly after Dan had left, proclaiming how she'd heard through the friend circle and that she 'can't believe he's that gutless. What an absolute fucking shitbag.' Clearly, judging by the way they were smiling and laughing together, clinking glasses in the picture, Dan wasn't such a shitbag, after all.

'You didn't think to tell me at all?' asked Hannah. 'You know how I've been feeling about all this, yet you've been spending time with him and didn't think to mention anything? I understand it's awkward. I'd just rather have known.'

Bronwen looked at the table, for which Hannah felt glad; seeing the guilt in her best friend's eyes would only set her off in a flood of tears. It wasn't just the fact that Dan had thought it appropriate to parade his new girlfriend around at parties with his friends – *their* friends – that made her feel so horrendous. The fact that Bronwen had concealed it from her was much, much worse.

'It's difficult,' she said finally. 'I can't exactly cut him off. Mike wouldn't have it.'

'Bron, he cheated on me. You've sat with me, listened to me cry, told me how what he's done is unacceptable. You're supposed to be my friend.' She stopped to take a deep breath, trying to will the tears away. 'I'm not asking you to cut him off entirely, but I *do* expect you to back me up a little. Make it clear to him how you feel. But no, there you are, pratting about with him and Sophia. What's . . .'

What's she like, anyway? She stopped speaking before the question escaped her. Did she actually want to know? It felt strange, knowing that she'd soon be back in his life. Back at those friends-and-family barbecues as if nothing had happened. Pretending as though Sophia had been a mere illusion, one that everyone should forget about, sharpish. Hannah knew there was no escaping that humiliation, but if she wanted it to work, it had to be done.

'What's she like?' asked Bronwen.

Of course; they'd been friends for so long that they often knew what the other was thinking. They used to joke that they had some kind of psychic bond. Which made the situation only more devastating.

'She's . . . all right. She's nice enough. Obviously, I don't want to be her best mate, but I had to be polite, Han. What was I supposed to do? Cause a massive row?'

Hannah looked at the drink, the frothy cream melting into an unappealing mass. She felt too sick to finish it.

'Why did you even take photos, anyway?' Hannah asked before the realisation dawned. 'Wait. Did you put these on Facebook?'

The guilty look in Bronwen's eyes told Hannah all she needed to know.

'We did. We made sure to hide them from your view. I just didn't want you to get upset, Han.'

The tears finally came. Hannah was powerless to stop them. They streamed down her cheeks and into her mocha, and she pushed the drink away, no longer in the mood for such sweetness.

There were a thousand things Hannah wanted to say, but she couldn't. Just like she couldn't with Dan, those months ago. Couldn't bring herself to argue. The emotion was too raw. The words were there and then they were gone.

Hannah rummaged in her bag for a tissue. She didn't have one, so she grabbed a napkin instead, dabbing at her eyes and letting out a loud, snotty sob as customers glanced in her direction. How many more people in Hannah's life was she about to lose?

Hannah pulled a five-pound note from her purse, placed it on the table and got up, weaving through the chairs and people as her former friend called after her.

'Han! Han? I'm really, really sorry.'

But she was already gone.

30

Hannah

'Cass! I'm so sorry I'm late.' Hannah stopped to take a breather as she rushed towards the marina, flustered from the annoyance of the packed bus. 'One of the girls at work went home sick, so I was inundated with customers. Barely had time to pee, let alone get home in time. Where's Mal?'

Cassie peeled her eyes away from her phone. 'No idea. She hasn't turned up yet. Has she sent you a text or anything?'

She hadn't, but Hannah pulled out her phone from her brand-new running belt and checked, just to be sure.

'Nope. I'll give her a ring.'

'Already tried,' said Cassie. 'Twice. No answer.'

'Maybe she's out,' Hannah suggested, but knew as soon as she said it that it was unlikely. Malika never cancelled and if she did, she'd certainly have let them know. 'It's not like her not to turn up.' Hannah listened as the phone rang, but eventually it went to voicemail. 'Malika, love? It's Hannah. Give us a ring when you get this. Just wondering if you'll be joining us tonight.'

Friday wasn't their official training day, but they'd decided to meet for an evening run around the harbour. They were edging ever closer to race day. In all of Hannah's fright, she couldn't help but imagine holding that finisher's medal in her hands, feeling it around her neck, wearing it with pride. She'd probably refuse to take it off for weeks.

'I've sent her a couple of messages . . . what shall we do?' asked Cassie. 'She could be on her way. What if she's forgotten?'

'Or lost her phone?' asked Hannah. 'That's more likely. There's no way she'd have just forgotten.'

Cassie surveyed the harbour area, which was bustling with people; evening walkers, drinkers, people on their way to meet friends at the nearby bars. Cassie watched, almost waiting to see Malika burst through the crowds, ponytail bouncing, but there was definitely no sign of her.

'You're right,' she said. 'Let's give her a few minutes, in case she's just a bit late. Could be on her way, for all we know. Shall we just run halfway to the bridge and back, then see if she turns up?'

Hannah jogged behind Cassie as she set off along the pavement, against the backdrop of colourful boats and glistening waves. Hannah couldn't help but worry about Malika and tried to bat the concern away in her mind. Malika was normally so upbeat, but she couldn't forget her face that day on Park Street.

Her phone pinged. Hannah glanced down to see that the message wasn't from Malika but Bronwen:

I still feel so bad about the other day, can we talk??

Hannah shoved the phone back into her belt.

Hannah still couldn't believe what her supposedly 'best' friend had done. Despite Bronwen's reasoning, it had been a betrayal, pure and simple. In all the years they'd been friends, Hannah had never expected Bronwen to do something like that. Had Hannah not accidentally seen the photo of their pleasant little garden party, she'd have been none the wiser.

Bronwen had tried to make contact; a flurry of 'sorry' messages had winged their way to Hannah moments after she'd left the cafe, but Hannah didn't reply. In the past, she'd never seen the appeal of such childishness. Her current ignoring of her almost lifelong friend was painful, akin to the 'I'm not your friend any more' arguments best left to the school playground. Yet, she couldn't bring herself to respond. Not yet. Not when she was still trying her best to heal.

Just as she and Cassie raced back to their starting point, Hannah's phone vibrated in her pocket. She reached into the fabric to see a message from Malika. Cassie had received one, too:

Hi, guys. Won't be joining you. Really not in the mood for running at all tonight.

'Shit,' said Cassie, frowning as she peered down at the screen.

'That doesn't sound like Malika at all,' said Hannah.

'What if she's sick?' asked Cassie.

'I think she'd tell us if she was. Do you reckon we should pop round? Just check she's all right?'

'Are you sure? Would she mind us just rocking up on her doorstep? Wait. Do you even know where she lives?'

'Roughly. I know what street she lives on, anyway. Keep trying her phone. If she doesn't answer, I can try to find out. Where's your car?'

'Just round the corner.'

'Brilliant! Let's go. Malika's never one to turn down a run. I'm telling you, something's up.'

Cassie swung her car into the first available space she could see in Malika's long street.

'So. Any idea which house is Mal's?'

'Not a clue,' replied Hannah. 'This is definitely the street, though. She told me. One sec . . . Time to do a bit of detective work . . .'

Hannah opened Facebook on her phone to Malika's profile page and began searching through the photo album. She scrolled past the many photos of Malika with her friends and a man who bore a striking resemblance to her. *Must be her brother*, thought Hannah, and as she kept looking, she came across a collection of photos of Malika and a woman with blonde hair. They looked happy, tipsy perhaps, on what appeared to be a night out. *That must be Abbie.* Looking at her now, this young, vibrant-looking woman, oblivious as to what was to come, Hannah felt a shiver.

Stepping out of the car, Hannah tore her eyes away from the photos and went back to the matter at hand until she found what she was looking for. Sure enough, there was a photo of Malika, wearing a hat and an oversized jacket, making a funny face at the camera. She was standing outside a house, a Victorian-style terrace that looked very much like all the others in the street.

'Aha! So Malika's house has a white door.'

'Well *that* narrows it down,' remarked Cassie. 'I think we need to do a bit better than that.'

'All right,' said Hannah. 'Keep your knickers on. Give me time.' Leaning into the shade cast over the car by a neighbour's overbearing hedge, Hannah zoomed into the photo. 'There are orange curtains in the downstairs window. I know what we're looking for. See? I could give Poirot a run for his money.'

Cassie rolled her eyes and started off down the street.

'So, did you speak to Jack?' asked Hannah.

The question caught Cassie off guard.

'No. I haven't.'

'Why?'

'I just haven't got round to it yet. Work has been pretty hectic and Jack's been staying late, and—'

'You need to speak to him soon, Cass.'

'And I will.'

She walked on and Hannah knew that was the end of the discussion. *So much for caring*, she thought. Hannah trailed behind, checking out door after door.

'Aha!' she said finally. 'That one.'

Up ahead, Hannah saw a house with a white door and on closer inspection, peeking out from a window half concealed by a sprawling overgrown conifer was the hint of an orange curtain.

'I'm sure that's it,' she said, pointing.

They crossed the road and as they approached, Hannah could see that it was definitely the same house. The flicker of a TV could be seen through the window. Cassie tapped softly on the door, but when there was no answer, she tried again, this time louder. A figure approached, getting closer from behind the glass pane, and the door opened to reveal a young woman in a green pinafore dress. Her blonde hair was swept up into a messy bun and her face was mostly taken up by a pair of huge, black-framed specs.

'Er, hi?' she said, her eyes travelling suspiciously over Hannah and Cassie, no doubt seeking out the pamphlets or brochures, or whatever diet shakes, local gym or religion they were undoubtedly there to tout.

'Don't worry, we're not here to try to sell you anything,' said Hannah brightly. 'You're Kath, aren't you? We're here to see Malika, if she's in.'

31

Hannah

Kath's face softened as realisation dawned. 'Ah! You must be from the running club. Yeah, she's in. I don't think she's very well, though.'

'Can we come in and see her?' asked Cassie.

Kath blinked. 'Yeah, sure.' She stepped aside to let them through. 'Mal!' she yelled, making Cassie and Hannah both jump. 'People to see you.' She turned to the others. 'Go on up. Top floor.'

They shifted up the two flights of stairs to Malika's room. Cassie rapped lightly on the bedroom door.

'Mal? It's us.'

'Hey,' said Malika's voice from inside. 'Come in.'

Malika was in bed, lying on top of her blue duvet. The room was warm, despite the cool breeze sneaking in from the small window. Malika closed her laptop, looking quizzically from Hannah to Cassie.

Hannah surveyed the room. It was small and the slanted ceiling made it appear even cosier, with a desk and a wardrobe on the far wall. There was just enough room for her desk, chair and double bed, and the walls were decorated with an array of fairy lights and photographs of a smiling Malika with her many friends. It wasn't big and it wasn't much, but Hannah knew at once that Malika felt safe in here, that this was her sanctuary. She looked to the window, which provided an amazing view of the city skyline.

'Whoa,' said Hannah. 'You can see a lot from up here.'

'Nice, isn't it?' said Malika. 'I love this view.'

Hannah stole another glance out of the window, where the tower blocks stood high in the distance. 'I've lived in Bristol all of my life,' she said. 'I never left. Never really wanted to. The novelty does go away and you sometimes forget what's around you – like this view. I think it's just a case of finding it again. That's what I've come to realise, anyway.'

'Very deep,' joked Cassie.

Hannah shrugged. 'It's true, though. So,' she said, taking a seat on the edge of Malika's bed. 'What's all this about? You never miss a running sesh. Hope you don't mind us stopping by, but we were worried.'

'Your message was vague,' added Cassie.

'If Cassie sent a message saying she didn't want to run, that'd be code for "I've been kidnapped". We're just being careful,' said Hannah.

Cassie rolled her eyes and laughed. 'You're not wrong. Anyway, Mal, it's not like you to pass up running either. We wanted to check you're all right.'

Malika shook her head. 'No, I'm not. I've failed.'

'Failed?' asked Cassie.

'Failed at what? You're twenty-four, love,' said Hannah. 'You're doing just fine. I mean, you haven't made half the silly mistakes I made when I was in my twenties.'

'Like what?' asked Cassie. 'Seriously, I'm intrigued.'

'That's a discussion for another time,' said Hannah. 'What makes you think you've failed, Mal?'

Malika began to speak, but the words came out in a splutter of tears. 'I . . . I think I've lost my job.

Cassie stared. 'What?'

'Well, I haven't *lost* it. Not yet. But it's only a matter of time. I made so many mistakes and . . . my boss sent me home.' She blew her nose noisily, took a deep breath before explaining what had happened.

'That's not so bad,' said Cassie. 'Maybe Eva has a point. If you're having trouble, then maybe you *should* take some time out.'

'It helps,' said Hannah. 'Honestly, it really does.'

Malika reached for another tissue from the box on her small bedside table. 'I've messed everything up. I was doing so well and then . . . I don't know what happened. I'm always so careful.'

'Things just slip your mind,' said Cassie. 'It happens. Don't beat yourself up about it.'

'I worked so hard, trying to keep everything together. Then I saw the comments on the website and . . . what's the point? I was getting there. I was just starting to feel better and then . . . then . . .' Malika trailed off, her words consumed by a fresh wave of tears.

'But all the money you've raised!' Cassie said. 'You've done so much for Abbie. You can't just quit now. Think of all the training you've done. And I know it might seem impossible at the moment, but try to remember how happy you feel when you're running. It helps you.'

Malika shrugged. 'It doesn't matter. People don't care. And it's not like Abbie's even here to see it.'

'What makes you think people don't care?' asked Cassie. 'And what do you mean by "comments"?'

Wiping her eyes, Malika reached for her phone, pulled up the Bristol Live article and handed it to Cassie. 'Look.'

Cassie scanned the comments before letting out a frustrated sigh. 'Oh, for God's sake, what's wrong with people?

Mal, these are just trolls. Insensitive idiots who post rubbish on the internet that they'd never dare say in real life. I see what you mean, though, they're horrid. But I take it you haven't seen the latest one?'

Malika shook her head, obviously bracing herself for whatever vitriol was lying in wait.

Cassie read it aloud:

It makes me so happy to read this – what a lovely cause. My son was killed in a crash eight years ago. He was cycling too, and a car pulled out from a side road and ploughed straight into him. The grief was indescribable. Sometimes I expect him to come bursting into the house, noisy as ever, but then I remember he's not here and I'll never hear him again. Keep running for your cause, Malika, we're all behind you!

'That's so sad,' said Hannah. 'I can't imagine how that must feel.'

'There are plenty more messages of support on there, Mal,' said Cassie. 'Don't let a few opinionated morons spoil it for you.'

She passed the phone back to Malika. The comment was still on the screen. Sarah Barclay smiled out from her profile photo, young and beaming, her arm around a little boy. The photo seemed old, a memento of Sarah and her son – the son who'd never come home.

Malika took a deep breath. Hannah saw her realisation that she had to finish the marathon. For Abbie, and for Sarah.

'As for your job, things will work out,' Cassie continued. 'And even if it doesn't, you can find another. It's not the end of the world. My company would snap you up in an instant.'

Malika smiled shyly. 'Thanks. I really want to stay at Rocket, though. I'm good at what I do. I guess I'll just have to see what happens.'

'Good,' said Cassie. 'Try to take your mind off it. Oh, and you're coming to my house for dinner tomorrow, right?'

'Of course. I wouldn't miss that,' said Malika. 'You really didn't have to come here, but it's nice. I feel a bit better already.'

Cassie leapt from the chair to join the others, cross-legged on the bed.

'Does anyone want a cup of tea?' Malika asked. 'And I just *have* to hear all about those mistakes of yours, Han.'

Hannah grinned. 'OK,' she began, 'It was 1991. The place: Ibiza . . .'

32

Hannah

Cassie lived in an ivy-covered house on a quiet street. Hannah pressed the doorbell, a bottle of pink gin in one hand as she nervously flattened down her new bird-print dress. There was laughter from inside and the door swung open to reveal Cassie, looking effortlessly glam in a pair of skinny jeans and loose blouse.

'Han's here! Oh, you really shouldn't have dressed up. Come on in. I'll pour us a drink.'

'Hey, Han,' said Malika, who was already making herself at home in Cassie's monochrome kitchen. The smell of pasta and a rich sauce permeated the air. 'Ooh, guess what arrived today . . .' She opened her rucksack and pulled out a small red bundle, grinning excitedly. 'Check it out!'

Hannah unravelled the red fabric. It was a T-shirt, with 'BRAKE' emblazoned across the middle.

'Turn it over,' said Malika.

Hannah did and saw her name making its bold way across the material.

'Mal, this is perfect. I can't wait to wear it.'

'I've also got something for you,' trilled Cassie.

She dashed into the living room and returned with two thin folders, and passed one each to Hannah and Malika. Hannah looked down at the folder, which contained three pages of A4 entitled 'Nutrition Plan'.

'These tell you all you need to know for the week leading up to race day. And I've put in a couple of meal suggestions, like pancakes for breakfast, with some blueberries—'

'Whoa,' said Malika. 'You really took some time making this. Thank you. You really didn't have to.'

'It's fun. I like it. I thought of starting a running blog in the past and never got round to it, so maybe I will. I've actually enjoyed training you guys and passing on advice. Why don't you go on through to the living room and I'll just finish up the food.'

Grabbing their drinks, Hannah wandered down the hallway, pushing open the door to the living room. She'd had an idea of what Cassie's home might be like: pristine, organised, minimalist. She was shocked to find that Cassie's place wasn't unlike her own. Cosy and lived-in. A bit cluttered. The living room opened up to a small dining area. There was a bookcase full to bursting on the far wall, along with a cabinet full of Lego models. Every shelf was home to framed photos of Cassie and Jack in various faraway places.

'Cassie and Jack? Total couple goals,' said Malika, flopping down onto the sofa.

'How many places have you visited?' Hannah called as Cassie joined them.

'Oh, lots,' said Cassie. 'All over Europe, mostly. That was when I was younger. And then Nepal, Singapore, Australia, New York, Canada . . .' She drifted off, looking dreamily at the framed photos. 'We haven't been anywhere for a few years while we've been working on the house. But someday soon . . .'

'Will Jack be joining us tonight?' Malika asked.

'Sadly not; he's out this evening.'

By the time dinner was ready, they'd worked their way through three quarters of the gin and all three were extremely hungry, no doubt because of the amazing smell wafting in from the kitchen. Cassie served up the food and they tucked in straight away.

'I'll have to make this myself,' said Hannah. 'It really is bloody lovely.'

'So, how's the wedding planning going?' asked Malika.

'Well . . .' Cassie began, then stopped.

There was a noise in the hallway, the sound of jingling keys, and all of a sudden, the house was filled with noise.

Small footsteps pounded through the hallway. There was a clattering in the doorway as Cassie's sister-in-law, Emily, battled with her pram.

'Bloody thing,' she said before a male voice sounded.

'Here, Em. Let me do it.'

Cassie put down her fork in disdain. 'Oh, for God's sake, not now,' she muttered.

The door swung open and in rushed Cleo, her eyes wide at the sight of Cassie.

'Auntie Cass!' she screeched, rushing over and wrapping her arms around Cassie's legs.

'Cleo! What have you been up to today?'

Hannah couldn't help but smile as Cleo launched quickly into the tale of her busy day at nursery. Her big brown eyes gazed up excitedly from her adorable round face. As she was talking, oblivious to Cassie trying to eat her dinner, a man walked into the room and gave Cassie a kiss on the cheek. It lingered for a moment too long and even though Cassie looked reluctant, there was no hiding their love. Hannah's envy returned.

'This must be the lovely Jack, then,' said Hannah. 'Hello.'

'Hi, ladies. I'm guessing you're the running club I've heard so much about. How's it going?'

Everyone smiled. Hannah's disappointment soared at the sight of Jack. He was lovely. He was tall, dark-haired and slim, with lovely blue eyes and a casual demeanour that made him seem very friendly and approachable, especially in his blue jeans and Superman T-shirt. A lovely man who wanted a family of his own.

'I've kept some dinner for you, Jack,' said Cassie. 'But I wasn't expecting . . .'

'Wasn't expecting *me*?'

Emily stood in the doorway, clutching baby Harry in one arm. 'Don't worry, I only popped in for a cuppa,' she said, smiling as she looked around the table. 'Really sorry, I didn't realise you had visitors. Hi again.'

Hannah and Malika waved. Glancing across the table, Hannah could see that Cassie was tense. Her smile had vanished. Cleo was still babbling away and Cassie was trying to be attentive.

'Sorry,' she mouthed to the others.

'Cleo, why don't you draw a picture?' Jack asked. 'Leave Auntie Cass to talk to her friends.'

'But I wanna stay heeere,' she whined. 'Can I draw my picture here?'

'It's no problem,' said Hannah.

Jack shrugged. 'Well, as long as it's OK with you. I'll go and grab her stuff.'

A few moments later, Jack returned with a cup of tea for Emily, and box of crayons and paper. Cleo dived thoughtfully into her latest piece of art.

'Here, I'll take the baby,' said Jack to Emily. 'Have your tea, Em.'

'Thanks. Got anything stronger? Just kidding. Sometimes I need it with these two. Sorry for interrupting your dinner, Cass. I won't stay long.'

Cassie smiled, told her it was no problem.

Cleo proudly held up her picture. 'Auntie Cass! Look, it's you.'

'That's lovely.' She leant over to give Cleo a hug.

'Wow!' said Hannah, looking at the picture. Amusingly, she could see the likeness, in the dark squiggles of Cassie's hair and big line of red Crayola smile. 'It looks exactly like you, Cass.'

Jack came over to take a look, the baby giggling in his arm, grabbing at Jack's shirt as he bounced him lightly around the room.

'Nice, Cleo. Maybe one day, when you're older, you'll be in one of those big art galleries in London. You can be a famous artist like Van Gogh.'

'More like Tracey Emin,' called Emily from the sofa. 'Actually, I'm surprised you're in today, Cass. You're usually out running. I hardly see you these days.'

'Well, the marathon is soon. Got to keep at it.'

'Every night?' Emily looked quizzically at Cassie before breaking into a smile. 'It's a very time-consuming hobby, isn't it?'

'It's worth it,' said Cassie.

'I imagine it is,' said Emily. 'When you said you couldn't help with Wednesdays any more, I thought it was just one evening. I can't even imagine what it's like to have all that freedom . . .' She trailed off wistfully.

'Wait,' said Hannah as Cassie's expression changed into a tight-lipped smile. A fleeting look of unease. Something stirred in Hannah's now tipsy mind. 'Wednesdays?'

Emily nodded. 'Yeah. I go to a gym class and Carl works late. Cass used to babysit. Not that it matters, though. Luckily, my friend Liz is happy to do it.'

Wednesdays. Suddenly, realisation dawned. That day, after their first run, when Cassie offered to train them. *How are you fixed for Wednesday evenings?*

Cassie had specifically asked them to train on Wednesdays. Hannah stared expectantly at Cassie, awaiting an explanation.

'Anyway,' said Emily, oblivious to the awkward silence that had hung in the air and settled on the table. 'I just needed to borrow the hedge trimmer from Jack and the kids wanted to come along. They love their Auntie Cass and Uncle Jack. You're so great with kids, you two.' She turned to Hannah and Malika. 'Don't you think so, too?'

'They are,' said Malika out of obligation.

Hannah nodded. *They definitely are*, she thought.

'I keep telling them, they should think about it,' laughed Emily. 'They're perfect. Jack's always loved kids. I mean, you've got this house. Look at that big garden. And that big spare room . . .'

Hannah, Malika and Emily, even Cleo, jumped as Cassie's cutlery clattered to the glossed wooden floor.

'Aaand here it comes,' said Cassie. She didn't reach for her fallen fork. Instead, she reached for more gin. 'That spare room is our *office*, Em. Can you leave it for just one visit?'

'What?'

'This "you should have kids" nonsense. I've told you before, we don't want any. And now you're trying to get my friends involved.'

By now, Jack had retreated into the kitchen. They could hear him rummaging in cupboards and talking to the baby.

'Jeez, Cass,' said Em. 'I was only saying. You said before, "once the house is sorted . . ."'

'Because it was an excuse to get you to shut up about it. Em, not everyone is like you. Some of us are happy with the way things are. And every damn time you come here, you spout the same overused lines over and over. "You're so good with babies! It's such a shame! The house would be perfect! Don't you want to know what it's like to be a mum?" No, Emily. I really don't.'

Emily was taken aback. 'Why are you so angry?' she scoffed. 'You always think you know better. I'm only saying these things because I think you'd make great parents. It'd be a shame if you and Jack missed out on that. You haven't exactly got forever.'

The room fell silent. Everyone looked at Cassie, whose face had lost all hint of joviality and was now turning as pink as the gin. She looked as though she'd been slapped; confusion at first, before ascending into full-blown rage. Words lay unsaid, but they were waiting, lingering, ready to be unleashed at any moment. It was only a matter of time.

Cassie rose to her feet.

'"Always think I know better?"' Cassie screeched. 'No, Emily. *No.* You're being ignorant. Please get it into that thick skull of yours that not every woman wants to be a mother. I love your kids, Em, but that life isn't for us. So give us a break. Stop with the stupid, *stupid* lectures. Stop trying to force parenthood on us.

'And yes, when I agreed to babysit, I meant now and again, in an emergency. Not a regular thing, which you quickly turned it into. I opted out of having children, Em, and so I don't want to look after yours all the time. I'm sorry if that makes me sound like a bitch.'

'Cassie,' said Hannah carefully, shielding Cleo's ears. 'It's OK. Calm down.'

Cassie rounded on the table. 'No! I will not *calm down.* It's *not* OK, Han. You don't have to deal with this all the time. I've explained time and again. I'm sick of it, from everyone.'

'Did you agree to train us to get out of babysitting?' asked Malika.

'No. Yes. Fine, OK, I did, initially. But in my defence, it wasn't just Wednesday. Emily is constantly asking us to help with the children.'

Nobody had noticed Jack reappear in the room. He glanced around at the scene, at Emily in tears on the sofa, at Cassie, red-faced and shouting. Malika looked on silently. Hannah was busy distracting Cleo with more coloured crayons.

'Cass? What's going on?'

'Your sister is being a pain in the arse. As per usual.'

Shocked, Jack rushed over to console Emily. 'What's all this about?'

'I only asked,' said Emily. 'I just said you'd make great parents.'

'We're. Not. Having. Kids,' Cassie yelled, banging her empty gin glass down on the table. 'I'm not interested, nor is Jack.'

Emily raised her head, casting a look of slight defiance in Cassie's direction. 'Are you absolutely certain? Do you know that's what he wants?'

Cassie stared at her fiancé, searching his face for a response. 'Jack? Are you going to tell her?'

'Come on, Cass . . .'

'Well? Where's your answer?'

Jack said nothing. Simply sighed and looked away. Emily got to her feet, loading her bag into the pushchair with haste, strapping in the baby and taking Cleo.

'Byyye, Auntie Cass,' called Cleo from the hallway as the front door slammed shut.

Cassie looked at Jack for an answer, for some kind of reassurance. Nothing came. The anger drained from Cassie's face and in its place was pure realisation. Hurt. Jack stepped out of the room to help his sister and Cassie slumped down on the chair, legs folding beneath her as if they'd given up.

'Um, that was awkward,' said Malika. 'Cass, are you all right?'

'What do you think?' she snapped.

'Seriously, try not to let this get to you,' Hannah advised. 'Some people just enjoy motherhood so much and they don't understand why anyone else wouldn't.'

'What's hard to understand, exactly?' Cassie snapped. 'I've explained so many times. It hasn't worked on me, but now Jack's clearly broody. This is it. It's over.'

'Look, love, I'm only trying to help,' said Hannah curtly. She couldn't keep her anger in for much longer. 'And let me tell you something. You've got everything. Some of us would give anything to have what you have. So before you rant about how terrible it is when people keep asking about babies, spare a thought for those of us who were never even given the choice.'

'Don't you start!' yelled Cassie. 'Don't lecture me, Han. You're one to talk. You let a cheating arsehole walk all over you. You lie about your life on social media. Life's just not fair, OK?'

'Don't you dare . . .' Hannah began, tears pricking her eyes, but was interrupted by Malika.

'Why don't you both just *stop*?' she yelled. 'Does it matter? We don't all want the same thing. You're being just as bad as each other now. For God's sake, just be grateful you're both still here.'

With that, Malika left the table.

'Thank you for dinner, Cass. I'm off. Seriously, guys, fighting isn't going to solve this.'

There was silence, punctured only by the sound of Malika pulling on her coat and the front door closing with a thud.

'I'm going,' said Hannah. She headed for the hallway, leaving Cassie at the table, sobbing into her sleeves. 'Cass . . .' she said, but Cassie pointed to the door. *Dismissed.*

Some people just don't know how good they've got it, Hannah thought.

33

Hannah

The sound of the letter box startled Hannah. She put down the jar of honey that she was busy spreading onto her toast and padded into the hallway. Something had thudded onto the doormat: a large white envelope. She moved closer, curiously. Had Dan sent her something?

She felt at its contents. The address was typed and there was something small inside. Hannah tore it open to find that it was from the Great South-West Marathon:

> *IT'S ALMOST RACE DAY! Please find enclosed your*
> *race pack, containing a handy route map, start times,*
> *your timing chip and race number . . .*

Hannah reached inside the envelope and pulled out a brightly-coloured race number, adorned with her name. She ran a finger over the letters, over the number that would be pinned to her shirt on race day. Her hands shook with a strange mix of both excitement and dread.

Hannah pulled out the map. The course began in the centre of the city and tracked out towards Bath: *26-and-a-half miles*.

This was it. It was official. There was no going back now.

'Honeytrap 'em,' Angie's voice called over the group in between exhausted breaths. 'That's one way to find out your other half's true feelings. Get someone to investigate. Like a honeytrap.'

'I think there's a legality issue there, Mum,' said Marie, running alongside her. 'You can't be serious. What would that even achieve?'

'The truth! If Hannah's husband can really be trusted, we need to find out. If he could be tempted by that Sophie woman.'

'Sophia,' Hannah corrected. She almost hissed the name.

'Sophia, then. But if he's really learnt his lesson, he won't do it again. So I reckon we send someone in . . . Kirsty here will do it.'

'Don't look at me,' said Kirsty. She slowed to take a drink of water, keeping up her pace next to Hannah. 'I'm not getting involved in your soap opera schemes.'

It was a sunny evening in the park, even though the weather had gradually become cooler, the branches of the trees shaking in the breeze, giving them a welcome burst of cold air as they passed beneath. Hannah had finally admitted the sorry tale of her marriage to the club and was now enjoying Angie's attempts at helpful advice in the form of revenge tactics.

Admittedly, Hannah was now starting to regret keeping it under wraps. She hadn't been the only one with issues, as it turned out. Practically everyone in the group had a story to offer in terms of past relationships and were more than happy to divulge. She was pleased that the club had been officially formed. In some ways, it was like therapy.

It would have been more enjoyable if Cassie had turned up. Since the argument at dinner days before, Cassie hadn't been in contact. She hadn't responded to any of the messages Hannah had sent – or Malika, for that matter.

Maybe she just needs time, thought Hannah. Especially since she and Jack obviously had a lot to talk about.

'So, have you heard anything from that lovely policeman lately?' Angie asked.

'No,' she answered, shaking her head as they headed up the bank. 'I think that's well and truly done for. The thing is . . . I told him it's best if we don't see each other. I didn't mention Dan specifically but, well, everything is up in the air right now.'

'You dumped him?' asked Kirsty.

'But you love Dan,' said Marie. 'Don't you? So you're doing the right thing.'

Hannah nodded, making a final sprint towards the bench. *I hope so.*

When the session was over, Hannah's group trooped down towards the gates. After the warm down, which Hannah took over in the absence of Cassie, Malika hurried over.

'We need Cassie,' she said. 'We're not *our* club without Cassie. We're just not experienced enough to take over. What are we supposed to do?'

'I have a feeling that turning up at her house won't be the best of ideas,' said Hannah. 'We'll keep trying to contact her, but it might be best to leave her be. I think she's had enough of people prying recently.'

'I guess so,' said Malika. 'I just hope she's OK.'

On their way to the pub, Hannah pulled out her phone and sent another quick text to Cassie.

Missed you at club – come back soon! Please call if you need to talk. Xxx

Then, before she could decide against it, she opened up a new message to Dan:

> Hey, Mr S, just wondering when you're coming round? xx

Time. That was all anyone needed, it seemed.

34

Malika

Malika unfurled herself from beneath the duvet, slowly and with reluctance. She pushed a foot out from her warm cocoon, feeling the cool draught of her bedroom. Since the summer had come to an end, saying its long goodbye with an evening chill, Malika's attic room had lost its heat. Instead, the rain pelted softly against the slanted window and the breeze whistled through its tiny gap. Normally, Malika found it comforting; it made her feel calm and safe as she snuggled under the covers with a hot drink.

Today, however, it was different. The rain outside was looming, threatening. The alarm on her phone sounded and she reached to switch it off, knowing there was no way she could snooze. In just two hours she was due back at Rocket Recruitment, for the first time since Eva had sent her home.

Two weeks. It didn't sound long, but it had felt like a lifetime. Unable to concentrate on barely anything else, running seemed to be Malika's only solace. The only downside was that Cassie still hadn't joined them. She had sent a message – blunt, to the point, as was her usual fashion, to say that she was having a 'particularly busy week'. Yet, after days had passed, the Running into Trouble Club was still missing a member – a *leader* – and it just wasn't the same.

The grey clouds filled Malika with trepidation as she traipsed up Park Street. It felt like a lifetime ago that she'd walked up the hill, a distant memory. Nerves wrapped around her like the wind as she approached the door of Rocket Recruitment, a tight knot of dread forming in her stomach. Deep down she knew there was nothing to be scared of; she wasn't about to be sacked, punished, judged in any way. But as much as she wanted to stride in, brimming with confidence, her anxiety kept her from doing so.

Malika had got to the office before the day began, to have a chat with Eva and catch up on any Rocket goings-on before tackling her undoubtedly full-to-bursting inbox. She wanted to get back into her job with a fresh clean slate.

Pressing her face against the window, Malika saw Eva, typing away at her desk.

'Good morning,' she said brightly as Malika entered, pulling her into an unexpected hug. 'You're here early. I'll make us a cuppa and then we can have a quick chat.'

Malika didn't stop to take off her jacket, just headed on through to the kitchen in Eva's wake. She looked around the office, expecting it to have changed, somehow surprised that it hadn't, besides the vacancy posters in the window.

It's only been two weeks, she told herself.

She followed the sounds of Eva clattering around in the kitchen, the soft roar of the old kettle.

'Come on through,' Eva said, leading her into the little back office with its foreboding white walls, a bad reminder of the last time she'd been in here.

'So, as you can imagine, I'm delighted to have you back,' Eva began. 'It's been strange without you. How have you been?'

Malika paused. She wanted to come across as calm. Casual. Anything but the ball of nerves that she currently felt. She wanted to prove she was better than before. Focused. *Capable.*

'It's been good, actually. I took some time out to myself, as you suggested. I spoke to my doctor too, which helped. I feel much better. I'm glad to be back, though! All those times I moaned about Rocket being so busy and it turns out I've actually *missed* it.'

Eva smiled. The tension in Malika's shoulders eased slightly.

'Well, we've certainly missed you. It's been busy, but we've managed. Marc's done a great job of handling most of the queries while you've been away and the meeting with CallerArc went really well. I'm sure he'll tell you about it this afternoon. We'll have a quick get-together, just to get you up to speed. But everything has been dealt with, so don't worry – you're not walking straight back into Armageddon!'

Relief flooded Malika. 'That's good to know.'

'However, I thought I'd better let you know that I'll be advertising Abbie's job shortly, Mal. We've been coping, but it turns out it's all a bit much for the three of us to handle. We need an assistant manager, and ideally soon. I know it'll feel a bit strange at first, for all of us, but we do have to think of the business. I wanted to give you a heads-up, that's all.'

The room suddenly felt colder. The time had finally come – Abbie was being replaced. She pictured someone new; in her mind, a faceless individual stepping into the office, full of cheery hellos, claiming Abbie's desk, her space, her *presence*. And they'd all have to carry on, a happy team again, Abbie's memory slowly erased with time.

A new season was on its way. First autumn, then winter. A Christmas that Abbie would miss, a new year she'd never get the chance to celebrate. Malika had feared this moment and now, here it was. It was happening.

'That's understandable,' she managed, sitting up straighter in the uncomfortable chair, determined not to let the hurt show.

'Of course,' Eva added, 'even though we'll have to advertise the role externally, there's nothing stopping you from going for it. You *have* been doing the job, after all. It'd be a great step up. I just wanted to make you aware. And we're not forgetting Abbie. Please don't think that's the case.'

Once the discussion was over, Malika stood and Eva gave her another hug.

'Now, let's get back to it,' she said happily.

Stepping out into the main office, Malika stopped in her tracks. There was Marc, in his blue suit, standing by Malika's desk. He hadn't noticed her come in. She stood stock-still, not moving an inch, watching him as he rifled briefly in her paper-filled in-tray before slowly pulling open the top desk drawer.

'Marc?'

Marc whipped round, spotting Malika in the doorway. He looked momentarily startled before his features returned to his usual cheeky smile.

'Mal! Finally, you're back. How's things?'

'Good. Were you looking for something?' she asked, ignoring the pleasantries.

'Post-its,' replied Marc. He turned to the desk and reached for the neon cube from beside her monitor. 'Found some! Sorry. I didn't realise you were back so early. I didn't think you'd notice if I nabbed some.'

'Oh! No worries. Take them. I've got plenty,' said Malika, feeling a strange surge of relief.

She shrugged off her jacket and placed her rucksack under the desk.

It was only when she was on the way to the coat stand that she noticed something odd. Glancing across the room,

Malika saw a half-used stack of Post-its beaming out from the corner of Marc's desk in their bright pink glory. He didn't need any, after all.

Eva's voice rung out in her mind. 'There's nothing stopping you from going for it . . .'

She was struck by an awful thought.

He wouldn't . . . would he?

Part Three

One month until race day!

35

Hannah

By the time Hannah reached the park, she was already soaking from head to toe. The recent arrival of September had brought with it the obligatory spell of rain.

For Hannah, September was a time of new beginnings, an untold tradition that stemmed from her schooldays. The nostalgic feeling had stayed with her through the years. The descending chill signalled the start of a new term and even though the beginning of the school year came with its own fresh sense of dread, that promise of newness hung in the air, one that couldn't be replaced by the chiming in of January, the promises made, bleary-eyed, after one too many glasses of champers. Promises she'd never get round to keeping, passionate missives of 'our year' falling swiftly by the wayside.

Which is why Hannah had taken to spending her days off sorting through more of the house. She'd started on her clothes, bagging up anything that was way too big; things that she'd kept 'for best' but were hardly worn, which now hung awkwardly off her smaller body. She didn't want a reminder of her old self, the unfit, unassuming Hannah who'd mistaken being content for being truly happy. So in they went, folded nicely in the bag, ready to be donated to the local charity shop. Then she got to work on her other clothes – the bobbly, comfortable leggings and oversized tops she'd spent years hiding behind. They went into a different bag, ready to be binned altogether.

Dan was yet to move back in, but he was working on it. *Just finalising a few things*, he'd messaged her earlier that week. Things were changing. Hopefully, this time, for the better.

Habits. There were good ones and bad ones. Hannah looked at the wall of boxes in the little room, the one she once had great plans for. Her life, and Dan's, stacked up like Jenga blocks. She'd thought everything was OK, when it wasn't. Before she closed the door, she wondered if all that stuff, all that routine, that ordinariness, was what had driven Dan away. Maybe she hadn't cared enough to see where it was all going wrong. That was her bad habit. He'd wanted more and he went for it.

He'd needed change. Perhaps, she hoped, he'd see just how much she'd changed now, too. And they could unpack their lives again, together, rebuild it slowly.

Because of the weather, Hannah hadn't expected much of a turnout at the weekly training session, but when she arrived at the gate, a small huddle of people were standing in wait.

'Hey, Han!' yelled Malika.

'We thought you'd chickened out,' laughed Angie, peeking out from beneath the hood of her jacket.

'I didn't think you'd come, either,' said Hannah, looking around and counting.

There were around nine people this week, all ready and raring to go. Two of them were in Cassie's group.

Hannah let out a small groan. 'I'm afraid Cassie's still sick,' she said sadly. 'Do you want to run with us?'

Luckily, both runners were happy to.

'We'll have to keep to the paths this time,' said Malika as they looked for space on the path to begin the warm-up.

The heavy rain had turned the grassy banks into a potential slip-fest and unless they wanted to recreate that awful muddy trail run, there was no way they'd be attempting *that*.

'Oh, we haven't told you!' said Marie mid-stretch. 'Mum and I have officially signed up to our first official run.'

'That's great news,' said Malika.

'Yep,' said Angie. 'We'll be running the Bristol 10k next May. So you'll be seeing quite a lot of us.'

'I'm a bit scared,' Marie confessed. 'Running in front of all those people.'

'Get used to it,' said Angie, ''Cause we'll be doing it in fancy dress.'

'You'll be fine,' said Hannah. 'So, when are you doing the skydive?'

Hannah chuckled as Marie's face turned a fetching shade of green.

'Please,' she mumbled. 'Don't remind her.'

'Er, Han . . .'

Hannah turned round and followed Malika's gaze. There, rushing through the gate, was a figure in a light running jacket, complete with hood. But there was no mistaking who those confident strides belonged to.

'Right, guys,' boomed Cassie. 'Call that a warm-up? Let's *go-go-go!*'

'Cassie?' asked Hannah, but before she could reply, Cassie was already leading their obedient club into a series of forward leg swings.

Cassie looked over and smiled.

'She's back!' said Malika happily. 'Cassie is back.'

*

The Running into Trouble Club had taken over the back table of the pub. It was becoming a common occurrence; Angie and Marie would seek out a table before the drinks would flow, warming and well-deserved. Hannah wiped the rain from her face as she perched on the end of her chair. Cassie scooted in next to her, placing her own drink on the table.

'I owe you two an apology,' she said.

'You do,' said Hannah. 'We were all worried about you. That dinner was—'

'Disastrous?' asked Malika.

'That's one way to describe it,' said Cassie, gazing out of the window, where a woman walked by, holding tight to a pushchair as she battled against the rain. 'I lashed out at you and I didn't mean to. Emily's just been so frustrating. I've calmed down. I drove out to Weston and ran along the beach, did a lot of thinking. I'm sorry if I seem insensitive to you, Hannah, but *you* need to understand, as well. I can't live a certain life just because others aren't able to.'

'I know, Cass,' said Hannah. 'I realised later that I was out of order. But you could have called me, could have shouted and sworn down the phone. It's better than radio silence. I'm your friend, OK?'

'Life has been a bit hectic, I'll admit,' said Cassie. 'And the argument with Emily just made everything worse. I'm fed up with the pressure, that's all. As for the training, Em's been on some kind of one-woman mission to lure me into the world of Yummy Mummies ever since Harry was born and she's been planting seeds in Jack's head, too, and now, obviously, he's really into the idea. So when I met both of you and figured you might need training, the idea just popped into my head. Then the club was formed and here we are. I didn't expect all this to happen.'

'Have you talked to Jack yet?' asked Hannah. 'Have you decided what to do?'

Cassie shook her head. 'Nope.'

Noticing that Angie and Marie had overheard the whole thing, Cassie stopped to explain what had happened.

'Sometimes it feels like whatever you do, it's not enough in someone else's eyes,' Cassie said. 'I'm not truly successful until I've become a mum, apparently. Sorry,' she said, catching Angie's eye, her daughter sitting right next to her.

'No need,' said Angie. 'We can't win sometimes, you know? If you want to be a mum, it's not enough. If you want to focus on a career, that's not enough, either. It's like you've got to have it all these days.'

Cassie nodded. 'Exactly. And I was just starting to get over all that, when Jack launched that firework of a dilemma at me. So I'm sorry. I shouldn't have just ignored you all like that. It's just not been a good few days, that's all.

'Jack went to stay with his parents for a bit, but he's back now. He wants to sit down and talk it through properly, but I know what that means. He'll just try to talk me into it. His parents have dropped the hint on numerous family get-togethers. But I just don't want to. I don't know *what* to do right now. I don't want a baby. But I don't want to lose him, either.'

'Cassie, love,' said Angie, sipping her vodka. 'You have to do what makes you happy. You only get one life.'

At that moment, Hannah's phone pinged. The screen lit up, displaying a message from Dan:

Hey, sexy! How's your day??

The group fell silent. Hannah looked up to find the entire table were leaning in, staring at the phone.

'Hannah?' said Cassie curtly. 'Is that message from Dan? Are you back with Dan?!'

All eyes turned to Hannah for an answer.

You only get one life.

All at once, she knew she'd made a huge mistake.

36

Malika

Ladies, GUESS WHAT?! It's officially ONE WEEK until race day!

x

The sun had yet to rise over Park Street as Malika turned on her office PC. She was on a mission.

As she waited for the screen to load, she opened her rucksack, pulling out a handful of files – a small stack of A4 folders that she'd taken from the stationery cupboard when nobody was looking. Opening her desk drawer, the one in which she kept all of her candidate files, she carefully added the folders before snapping a quick photo, just as Eva walked in.

'Finished your application yet?' Eva asked.

Malika shook her head.

'Not yet. I was thinking of taking some time over the weekend. Right now, I'm too focused on the marathon.'

'OK. Well, let me know if you need any help with it. I know Marc's applying, too. Obviously, it won't be me recruiting. It'll be someone from the regional office, so I can help both of you with your forms if need be. Feel free to ask.'

'Thanks, Eva. That would be amazing.'

She watched as Eva retreated to the back office. One thing was certain: Malika would definitely be applying for Abbie's job. She knew she was good at it. She'd been doing it so well until her supposed mistakes. But after seeing Marc lurking suspiciously around her desk the other day, she'd been plagued by thoughts that she just couldn't shake.

Could Marc have set her up?

It was stupid. She knew that. At first, she'd tried to swat the speculation from her mind. He was just looking for Post-its. He wasn't up to anything suspicious. *But the Post-its were in front of him . . . so why was he looking in the drawer?*

There must have been a genuine reason. They'd been working together for quite some time. Marc was nice. A bit cocky, perhaps. A typical lad. The kind who referred to himself as 'Captain Banter' and liked to check himself out in reflective shop windows. But he'd always been kind and supportive, and . . . well, *Marc*.

Was it all an act?

She wouldn't have even thought about it had it not been for the news of Abbie's job. Sure, Malika had taken over in Abbie's absence, but it was only temporary. Just until things returned to some semblance of normality. Malika hadn't actually wanted the job, she just wanted Abbie back. She was only being helpful.

But now there was a promotion up for grabs.

Taking a sip of her coffee, Malika logged in to her computer and opened up her spreadsheet. The database of candidates and interview schedules that she kept thoroughly updated. She kept it in the shared drive so that the others could access it, just in case she ever had to call in sick. She typed in the details of her six new candidates, the ones who were now nestled neatly in the desk drawer, and hit Save.

*

After lunch, Malika took off her jacket and sat. Pulling open her drawer, Malika did a quick count of all of her files.

One was missing.

'Marc?' she asked, making her way across the room, smiling at the candidate Marc was in the middle of registering. 'Have you seen a file around here? For a Sarah Castleton?'

Malika looked around the room, humming a tune as she did so. She could sense Marc's eyes following her. She rummaged through the tray by Eva's desk, checked the cupboard at the back and then the photocopier. Where, sure enough, it was poking out untidily from a small pile of paper.

'Found it!' she said cheerfully, heading straight out to find Eva.

'Are you sure?' Eva asked, brow furrowed.

Malika had clicked the door to the back office closed, slapping the file down on the desk.

'Are you one hundred per cent certain?'

'I know it sounds wild,' said Malika, 'but I wouldn't be telling you if it was only a sneaking suspicion. I caught him. I didn't have a clue until I saw Marc hanging around my desk the other day. Then it dawned on me. He's been setting me up the whole time.'

Eva slunk into her seat, her wide smile gone. She rubbed at her forehead and let out a deep sigh as Marc remained in the office, oblivious. *The scheming bastard*, Malika thought, trying hard to keep her composure. It wasn't easy. Tears were threatening to unleash themselves and she didn't want them to show. Not now.

'This file,' Malika said, 'isn't real. There's nobody called Sarah Castleton on our records. I made it up. I had a feeling Marc was messing with my things, so I made up six fake files and put them in with the others to see what happened. Lo and behold, this one went "missing".

'And my spreadsheet. I *know* I'm careful, Eva. I *know* I didn't make all those mistakes with the schedule. I might have been grieving, and I know that sometimes my mind can wander. But I even put my fake candidates on the spreadsheet and emailed it to myself as backup to see if anything changed.

'I never thought to before, because I trusted everyone in this office. I seriously believe the interview schedules were messed with, to make me seem incompetent. And it worked, didn't it? I got sent home. As soon as I'm out of the picture, the more chance Marc has of bagging Abbie's job.'

Eva stared, watching as Malika paced around what space remained in the little room. She couldn't sit down; adrenaline was coursing through her, her hands shaking with anger. Never had she been so furious.

'All the mistakes I made, all the times I supposedly wasn't concentrating. I was just trying to get through the day, Eva. I was devastated when you sent me home. I really thought I'd messed up for good. What if I hadn't noticed him snooping around? It would probably just keep on happening. You'd have let me go. I'd have lost my job. Who wants to hire someone *that* unreliable, right?'

'I can't believe it,' said Eva quietly. 'All this time. I knew he was ambitious, but I didn't think he'd—'

'Stoop *that* low? I didn't, either. What an absolute f—'

'Mal . . .'

Finally, Malika took a seat.

'And the promotion? I don't care if I get the job or not. All I wanted was to make sure everything was OK after

284

Abbie died. I wasn't doing it to rise up the career ladder. I mean, I don't *want* someone new coming in to replace her either, but I know it'll happen. I don't want to compete. I just want to do the job that makes me happy.'

Eva stood. 'And you will. For as long as you want it. Leave this with me, Mal. I'll sort it. I promise.'

37
Hannah

'He *what?*'

Cassie put her fork down so abruptly that a blob of curry splattered onto her blue striped T-shirt.

'He was setting me up the whole time! I still can't believe it. I wasn't going crazy, after all. I hadn't done anything wrong. Marc had been moving my files, changing dates and times, just to make it look as though I couldn't be trusted to do my job properly. I've never been so angry in my life.'

'That's disgusting,' said Cassie.

'What an absolute prick,' said Hannah, louder than she expected in the busy restaurant.

A couple on the next table with their young child shot her a look.

'Oops.'

'Nasty, isn't it?' said Malika, prodding at her plate of chips. 'It hurts that he could have been so calculating in the first place, but the fact he used Abbie's death to try to win a promotion is just the worst.'

It was the day before race day. Hannah, Malika and Cassie had met for dinner in a local restaurant by the harbour in order to have a big pre-race meal. Carbs, of course. Cassie thought it might be a good way to keep the nerves in check. The sky was an unappealing shade of light grey, but the light still danced on the waves outside the window. Hannah recalled the last time she was at the harbour; standing by the water in the darkness, starlight bouncing on the waves, hand in hand with Steve.

Steve, who hadn't left Hannah's thoughts, however hard she'd tried to put him at the back of her mind. It was impossible. Steve made her feel something she hadn't felt in years; an excitement she'd yearned for since their date.

Since Dan's planned return, the initial excitement had waned. Hannah knew deep down that it was wrong to take him back. Yes, she loved him, but not in the same way.

Not any more.

Hannah looked away from the window, away from the taunting waves.

It's almost race day, she told herself. *You need to get through this!*

'So what happened?' asked Cassie. 'Please tell me Marc isn't still working there.'

'He's been let go,' said Malika, grinning. 'Eva confronted him about it. It turns out he *had* been altering the spreadsheet. Deleting documents from the system. He denied it at first, but then Eva called his bluff, said she'd been in touch with IT about it. He confessed. He tried to call favouritism, saying he only did it because he knew I'd get the job over him, because Abbie and I were close and I was temporarily doing the job.'

'Is that true?'

'Not at all,' said Malika. 'It's not favouritism. I only offered to take over for the time being because I knew the way Abbie worked. It was just for a little while until we got back on our feet. And as for the promotion . . . well, Marc's figures rank so much better than mine. Despite everything, he's a really talented recruiter. He's much more experienced than me. Eva isn't even the one hiring, so it's very likely he'd have got the promotion. That's the sad thing. He went to such lengths for absolutely nothing.'

'I want to punch him,' said Hannah, stabbing at piece of spicy chicken with her fork. 'Hard.'

Malika shrugged. 'I did too, at first. But now all I can do is feel sorry for him, really. Anyway, he's gone. And we have a new temp called Robyn. She joined us yesterday. We went to lunch together and she's really lovely and bubbly, and I . . . hope she stays.'

Malika's voice became squeaky and she reached for her napkin.

'Malika? What's the matter?' asked Hannah.

'It's still weird to me. I dreaded this whole thing. You know, a replacement.'

'Change?' asked Cassie.

Malika nodded. 'I think so. It's all happened sooner than expected and when I was at lunch with Robyn, I found myself having fun and I felt guilty. I felt like I was forgetting Abbie. That I've left her behind.'

'You haven't,' said Cassie. 'That's just the way life is. You've got to move on at some point. You won't forget her, but you have to make room for the new. You can't stay in the past forever. Abbie trained you, remember, and you became friends. You're just doing the same with Robyn. It's a good thing. Trust me.'

'And speaking of new,' said Hannah, 'in a matter of hours, we'll be running a bloody *marathon*.'

38

Hannah

Race day is here!! Today, I will be running 26.2
miles. Up early and race-ready with a runner's
breakfast. Porridge, honey and blueberries, with
some banana to get me in that running mood!
(Yummy!) Wish me luck, people! #fitness #runner
#marathon #runningwiththegirls #ohgodhelp
68 likes, 49 comments

Looking down at the porridge bowl, Hannah fought off a
wave of nausea. The breakfast had looked appealing enough
on her photo, artfully arranged beneath a bright filter, the
blueberries bobbing neatly on the surface among streaks
of golden honey, the banana laid out beside it. Hannah
Saunders, paragon of fitness. In truth, just looking at it all
made Hannah want to retch into the toilet bowl for the
third time that morning.

I'm running a marathon today.

She'd set her alarm for six o'clock, only to wake up at five,
the fear forcing her eyes open. No matter how many times
she'd tried to snuggle back beneath the duvet, to get that
last remaining hour of sleep, her body refused to comply.

There was nothing she could do besides accept it. She
got out of bed and padded downstairs to the living room,

where she'd laid out her running kit on the sofa for a photo the night before. Her leggings. The Super Impact Shock Absorber. Her vest top and Brake T-shirt, complete with her race number already safely pinned on. Trainers, on which she'd fastened her timing chip that she'd checked about fifty times before she'd headed to bed, and two pairs of running socks. And the belt that she'd bought, with space for various bottles of water and accessories, which made her feel a bit like a budget Batman.

And then there was her emergency kit. Stuffed into the belt were her plasters, painkillers, moisturiser, tissues, as many jelly babies as she could safely cram in and a miniature tub of Vaseline. Everything that she could possibly need on a 26-mile course, with just enough space for her phone.

Hannah headed for the shower, trying to sing along to Dolly Parton as she scrubbed to take her mind off the oncoming race. As she stepped out, a message had arrived from Malika:

HELP! Couldn't sleep. Nervous as hell. THIS IS IT!! Why do I feel like backing out? X

She typed back:

Me too! Don't worry. No backing out! You're not allowed. I need you to carry me when I pass out! X

Now, looking at the breakfast she'd prepared, she couldn't face it. The thought of just one spoonful was enough to make her feel sick again. *It's just first-race nerves*, she reasoned, staring down at the blueberries drowning in the sticky beige sludge. She *had* to do it. She knew that she'd feel worse if she didn't eat a thing. In just three hours, she'd be at the start line.

As she stood in the kitchen in her dressing gown, eyeing her banana with disdain, the doorbell sounded. Rushing into the hallway, Hannah saw the outline of someone she really didn't want to see at that precise moment.

Dan.

'Hello,' he said, smiling widely and stepping into the house. 'I came to wish you luck.'

'Why?'

Dan's smile faded. Hannah stood there, in the middle of the hallway, blocking his path.

'Why now? You said you were coming back. You wanted to "try again", but I haven't heard from you for days. Text messages don't cut it, Dan.'

'Not now, Han. I just came by to—'

'To what?' By now, Hannah's nerves had vanished, replaced by irritation. 'You don't want to try again, do you? You just want to keep me waiting, keep the door open just in case things fall apart with Sophia. My guess is that they already have. But don't worry, you've got nice devoted doormat Hannah to fall back on. I don't think so, Dan. This isn't happening.'

Hannah stomped back into the kitchen, taking the warm porridge bowl and forcing down spoonful after spoonful.

'Don't mind me,' she said, between mouthfuls of blueberry. 'I'm just going to eat while you formulate an excuse.'

Dan's mouth opened then closed. Anger crossed his face. 'That's not what it is, Han . . .'

'Well, whatever it is, it's over. I've had quite a lot of thinking time recently, when you've been silent. I love you, Dan, but not like I used to. I spent a lot of time thinking I missed you – but I guess I just missed the company. You treated me like dirt, Dan, and I'm not going to let it happen again. I can't believe it took me so long to figure it out.'

'Hannah, I really do love you, I—'

'Forget it. It's over. It's all done, Dan.'

'Is that all you've got to say? Bloody hell, Han. You don't want to talk about this properly?'

'Yes,' said Hannah nonchalantly. 'I could stand here arguing for hours, but it's not worth it. I've got nothing else to say, other than please leave. I have other important issues to attend to.'

Such as one that stretched on for twenty-six miles.

'Han!' Malika's excited voice carried from the other side of the street.

Hannah could see Malika and Cassie as she crossed the road among a small crowd of people in running kit. Malika almost leapt into Hannah's outstretched arms for a hug.

'It's race day!' Malika shrieked. 'It's here. Finally, it's here.'

'I think I put on too much Vaseline,' said Hannah. 'I'm sliding everywhere. In places you wouldn't imagine. Look, we can do this. Er, Cass? You all right, love?'

Beside her, Cassie's face had turned even paler than usual.

'I'm fine,' said Cassie. 'Sorry. It's just nerves. I've spent so much time psyched for this day and now it's here, I'm fretting like mad. I've worked so hard to get this personal best. What if I don't hit it? I've been prepping for this moment for months and now it's here, I have this horrid feeling it's all going to go wrong. Like I'm a singer about to go to that all-important life-changing audition and I get on the stage and my voice has gone.'

'And you croak out the opening line, everyone laughs and then they send you home?' Hannah asked.

'Thanks. Thanks for that,' said Cassie.

'We'll all be fine,' said Hannah, putting an arm around each of her friends. 'It'll be great.'

They headed towards the starting area in Millennium Square, over the bridge and through the side streets. It was a crisp Sunday morning and the sun was peeking out through a sky of light clouds. There was no rain forecast, but as Hannah had come to learn, a bit of rain was often a welcome treat. All around them, entrants walked in the same direction, filling up the normally quiet streets with chatter and brightly-coloured outfits.

Out of curiosity, Hannah looked around at her fellow runners, her heart pounding in her chest with the sheer panic of what she was about to do. How far she was about to push herself. There were people heading through the streets alone, some in groups; three women with identical charity shirts power-walked past them as they turned the corner, as well as numerous couples, and lone runners fully equipped with their running accessories, their gloves and trackers attached to their wrists. Some, Hannah noticed, took it way more seriously than others.

Cassie was decked out in her professional gear, too. She was clad in her purple leggings, her Brake shirt and a head-band, ready to get that personal best. Black running gloves covered her hands and she was wearing a small backpack, a water bottle on each side, making her look more like she was fully equipped to go trekking up a mountain rather than a flat-surface run. Malika had brought a belt too, Hannah noticed with relief. She didn't feel so underprepared.

Millennium Square was packed with people. As they turned the corner, all Hannah could see were runners. A sea of people rose ahead, people of all ages, shapes and sizes. Each one was wearing a race number. Hannah looked down at hers, tracing the number on her bib with a finger, trying to prove to herself that this was happening. That this was real.

'Your race number is a different colour to ours, Cass,' said Malika, peering down at her own.

Cassie's was orange, whereas Hannah and Malika's numbers sat on a background of pink.

'That's because I'm in a different pen to you,' said Cassie. 'It's based on times. More experienced runners who are likely to finish in a shorter time start first. You'll start in the last wave. But it doesn't matter – you can go down a pen, just not up. So I'll start the race with you guys.'

'Are you sure?'

'Of course,' said Cassie, her scared expression softening. 'We have to start together. We're a club.'

They made their way into the throng, squeezing through the crowds of people who'd gathered by the mirrored dome that stood in the centre of the square. Strangely, Hannah's panic had subsided, replaced by an odd sense of excitement. The crowd was what had scared her, but looking around at everyone now, many appeared to be just as nervous as she was, doing their stretches, stuffing down hasty last-minute breakfasts and attaching their race numbers.

'Let's go to the starting area,' said Cassie.

The others followed, Malika holding on to Hannah so as not to get separated in the crowds. There was music playing in the distance, pop tunes thumping out from large speakers. As they made their way past more people and into a bigger area signposted with banners, Malika stopped walking.

'I can't do it.'

'What?'

Cassie and Hannah turned round, narrowly avoiding bumping into someone in a giant cow costume.

'I can't. There are too many people. I just can't.'

'Mal, it's going to be fine. Everything's going to be fine.' Hannah handed over some water as Malika tried to steady her breathing. 'Don't worry. We'll stay together.'

'You can do this,' said Cassie. 'Just remember, if you really, really can't do it, you don't have to finish it. You *can* quit the race, you know. Whenever you like, OK?'

'You've got this far,' said Hannah. 'You might as well give it a go. And I'll be next to you the whole time.'

Nervously, Malika tugged down her T-shirt. 'OK,' she said. 'I'm in.'

Hannah reached into her belt for her phone. 'Right, then. Selfie time.'

They huddled together, smiling their nervous smiles.

'I need to pee,' said Hannah suddenly. 'Sorry, it's the nerves.'

'Loos are over there,' said Cassie, pointing to a long line of Portaloos in the distance. 'Do you see that huge crowd of people?'

'The one as big as the crowd at Glastonbury?'

'Yep. That's the queue.'

39
Hannah

'Ready?' asked Cassie.

Hannah reached down for the neon yellow belt clipped around her waist to check it was still there. Of course it was; she'd panicked over supplies for days. She did another mental inventory of its contents: water? *Check*. Emergency jelly babies? *Check*. Plasters, Vaseline, painkillers? *Check, check, check*. They all jostled for space in her close-to-bulging running bag.

Sanity, however? She wasn't so sure about that.

As the crowd moved around her, a throng of bodies, jumping, stretching, cheering excitedly, gathering closer in preparation for the moment, Hannah stood frozen to the spot.

'You OK?' asked Malika, who bounced nervously beside her as she gazed ahead at the sheer amount of people in one place. Thousands. 'Do you need the loo again? Only the queues are snaking right round the block.'

'It's just first-race nerves,' said Cassie. 'Try not to worry.'

The crowd began the countdown. Loud chanting rose from the mass of people, all decked out in their best kit. One minute to go. Hannah may have had everything ready, but she felt anything but prepared. Voices screamed in deafening excitement, their shouts carried through the crisp morning air of a new autumn.

'*Thirty seconds to go!*' yelled a voice over the loudspeaker.

'Whoop!' shouted Malika. 'Oh, God. Look at us. We're actually doing it!'

Hannah moved forwards, driven by the crowd. She felt the sudden soft grip of Malika's hand in hers. Cassie reached for her other hand, her expensive running glove in Hannah's sweaty, nervous grasp, and Hannah wanted to hold on for dear life.

'Get ready,' said Cassie, grinning.

Then the klaxon sounded and the sea of people moved forwards in unison, sweeping the three of them up and into it like an unruly wave.

I'm not ready, thought Hannah, her heart pounding. *I'm not ready at all.*

What the hell have I done?

They were off. The crowd flowed, slowly at first, and Hannah felt herself propelled forwards. There was nothing to do but move. Thousands of people, all in one place, all moving at once. Still gripping on to her friends, Hannah edged towards the start line, the thud of footsteps like a stampede over the hard ground, the constant *thump thump* of trainers on pavement loud enough to rival the beat of the music.

With a final surge of movement, the people in front sped up and Hannah let her feet take her, faster and faster, until they had finally passed beneath the huge starting banner.

It was official. They were doing it.

Hannah was actually *running a marathon*.

The crowd screeched and cheered with excitement. Safely behind the barriers at either side of the road, spectators whooped and applauded, waving banners in the air as the pink wave of runners set off on the first part of the course.

'And so it begins!' said Cassie. 'How are you feeling?'

Hannah couldn't answer. The words fought to get out but Hannah failed to let them. It was a rarity that she couldn't speak, that excitement had made her nothing more than breathless, and not because of the running. The atmosphere had blown her away. She couldn't remember the last time her words had been stolen, swept away in all the intensity of the scene around her.

Dan.

He fluttered into her mind, a somewhat faded image. OK, she was wrong; there *was* a time when she'd been left with nothing to say. When Dan had announced he was leaving. She recalled looking for that answer, trying to grab it in the stuffy air of her living room, warm and stifling within those four overbearing walls. It was nothing like this. Now, she felt free. As though the world was hers again.

They followed the runners in front. Hannah had no time to linger with thoughts of Dan, not when she was watching the pavement, the colourful trainers pounding in unison, the route ahead filled with people, filled with hope. As they turned the first corner into a side street, fringed by more spectators, Hannah felt like some kind of celebrity. They were *all* celebrities. Hannah, Malika, Cassie, the team of women all dressed in pink sprinting ahead of them, the young men in silly hats, their charity T-shirts eye-catching and bright. The fancy dress costumes. The joy.

For the first time in what felt like forever, Hannah didn't mind being on display. She didn't want to shy away, hide her body from the passing people, afraid of what they'd think. *Not now.* She didn't mind people looking, watching her as she rushed on ahead, feeling like some kind of superhero. She was doing such an amazing thing. Terrifyingly, mind-blowingly amazing. She *wanted* them to watch.

Then she was hit by a sudden uncertainty.

'Oh no,' she said, calling over the noise of the music, the beat of a local brass band that were playing up ahead especially for the event. 'This is just the nice bit at the beginning, isn't it? Then it's all downhill from there. If only it was literally downhill. I'll collapse. It'll be like my auntie's wedding, where I thought taking part on the karaoke would be a good idea until I almost toppled off the stage.'

'Oh, you'll reach that point, all right,' yelled Cassie, sneaking a glance at her tracker. 'Probably about halfway through. Your legs will want to give in. You'll want to pass out. But you have to carry on.'

'And you're telling us that *now?*' called Malika at Hannah's side.

Runners weaved in and out, through the gaps in the crowd. People in costumes, some more elaborate than others, hurried alongside them before disappearing into the crowd and out of sight, making Hannah wonder just how slow she must be if two people crammed into a panto horse could bound past them fast enough to rival Mo Farah.

'I wasn't going to tell you before, was I?' Cassie said, giving them a wink. 'You should see your faces right now. Just remember what I said, just keep moving, don't stop. Even if you're walking, just keep moving.'

Hannah didn't know if she was capable of stopping. Her legs were guiding her and she kept her pace just right. As much as she wanted to sprint on, she didn't want to make herself exhausted so early in the race. *Preserve your energy.*

The route had led them through the city centre and the runners had begun to spread out on the road, separating from the crowd and finding their own areas of comfort. Hannah watched as a girl who'd slowed down to a brisk walk at the side of the road, the back of her shirt displaying a photo of her grandmother, was joined by a man who stopped to offer encouragement. They quickly picked up the pace together and jolted on ahead.

Hannah couldn't stop – she was enjoying it too much, laughing as she thought of her very first run. The achingly terrible attempt at a jog down her street, during which she'd nearly collapsed. It felt so long ago. A lifetime ago.

A lifetime without Dan.

She tried to swat the thought away. *Why now?* Why was Dan invading her head when she was currently doing the most exciting thing she'd ever done in her life?

Before long, they'd reached mile two and Hannah ducked to high-five a little girl who was holding a banner as she passed.

'Isn't it weird,' said Malika, 'how people are coming for a day out to watch this? Watch *us*. It's almost as though *we're* the inspiring ones.'

'We are,' said Cassie.

Would Dan be here? Hannah wondered. Would her husband be here in the crowd, waiting for Sophia to rush by in a flash of ponytail and bronzer? Would he have made her a banner with something cheesy and romantic on it? The thought crossed her mind.

And she laughed.

Hannah couldn't help it. The laughter came loudly and happily, flowing out of her as though she'd heard the best joke of her life. Tears flowed down her flushed face as Malika and Cassie glanced at her in confusion.

They turned the corner now, to more people, more music that felt as though it went on forever, the atmosphere so carefree and joyful and exciting that she wanted to reach out. Grab it, bottle it, keep some of that positivity for later when she truly needed to feel alive and wonderful and strong.

'What's funny?' Malika asked.

'Nothing.' Hannah wiped her eyes.

Nothing but her life.

She wasn't the old Hannah any more.

'OK, Cass, I think you'd better leave us,' said Malika as they approached mile three. 'We're only keeping you behind. Go and get that personal best!'

'Are you sure?' Cassie asked. 'I feel guilty, but . . .'

'But you want to kick ass? We know,' laughed Hannah. 'So bugger off.' She shooed Cassie away playfully. 'We're quite capable of finishing. I think. Maybe. Anyway, it doesn't matter – you need to go and get that PB! It's what you've been working for.'

Cassie pulled them both into quick hug. 'Right, then. I'll see you at the finish line!' And she sped off, disappearing swiftly into the crowd.

Hannah could just about see the slip of red shirt and short, swishing ponytail before she vanished completely.

'And then there were two,' said Malika.

40

Malika

The route took them out of the city centre and towards Clifton, where the houses stood tall and striking, pale brick against the backdrop of the city. Surprisingly, they hadn't walked at all yet, keeping their pace nice and steady, although Malika could feel an ache in her thighs. For a while, she'd worried that she'd finish last, casting nervous glances at the crowd behind her, expecting to see only a handful of people trailing behind her. As it turned out, there were still many people – thousands, possibly – making their way towards the Clifton Suspension Bridge. She'd spent so long worrying about this day; what if she didn't make it to the end? What if she ambled in last, dragging her tired, unruly legs across the finish line hours after everyone else had gone home for dinner? She couldn't bear the humiliation.

Look at you go!

The voice shocked her. She could hear it, loud and clear in her head. That happy voice, strong and fun, that she'd missed. She'd missed it so much.

Told you you could do it!

The realisation stung. That voice, a fresh memory in her mind, as new and clear as the day she'd last heard her friend speak. The day she'd heard it for the final time, when she'd had no idea that she'd never hear it again. Malika had been

302

frightened that Abbie's voice would fade. She knew that happened sometimes, when memories lose their clarity with time, fading into the past, never to be retrieved.

It had happened with her grandad, when she was little. Years of bedtime stories that she'd cherished. That deep, soothing voice that would lull her to sleep. *The Twelve Dancing Princesses.* It had been her favourite book, memorised in those comforting tones, until one day, it was gone. Years later, she'd spent time trying to recall that voice, to bring back the memory, but Grandad had gone.

That was until she'd found herself in the local Tesco Metro behind a man who'd asked for a lottery scratch card in an almost identical voice to that of her beloved grandad. She'd been so shocked that she'd dropped her basket where she stood and left.

Ghosts. Malika had believed in ghosts once, but not any more. And she knew that the voice she could hear in her head, Abbie's voice, was nothing but a memory. Just Abbie being Abbie, her usual encouragement and smile that could brighten a room. Perhaps it was the shock of the race. The adrenaline. Something had made the memory resurface, one that had been locked away.

Keep going, Mal. We'll do it together!

Malika pictured Abbie running alongside her, in that blue jacket she always wore. There were photos of her in it on her Facebook page, from before it had become a memorial. Pictures of her running, posing with her medals. Now, it was as if Abbie was there next to her, their shoes hitting the ground in unison.

The sky had cleared, making way for the sun, and above them, the tall, iconic structure of the bridge came into view. The sight of it made Malika gasp; she'd seen the bridge so many times. Seen it in the distance, watched with Roz and

Kath and Dean as the air balloons from the yearly Balloon Fiesta floated beautifully above it into the sunset. She'd never imagined that she'd be running over it, running a *marathon*.

She cried, softly at first, trying not to let the tears blur the view. I can do this, she said, *I can do this for Abbie*. She still saw her, Abbie's form, blissful and blue, which seemed to vanish into the crowd, and suddenly Malika knew why she was doing this. All around her, people were running in their charity shirts. There were photos of loved ones pinned to the backs of many:

In Memory of Robert.

Let's kick cancer's ass!

Running for Rosie.

Miss you, Mum.

Mum. A man beside her was running for his mum. There was a photograph printed on the back of his T-shirt. A woman with a dazzling smile. And as the wearer of the shirt turned to speak to his running buddy, his young face told Malika that he was just a teenager.

A teenager who'd lost his mother.

All these runners. All of these people racing for a reason. An array of shirts that filled the bridge with colour. A smiling elderly man ran by, noticing Malika's teary face.

'Keep going, love,' he said. 'Cry when you get your medal!'

All at once, the worry subsided. Malika was doing this for Abbie. For people *like* Abbie, like Sarah Barclay and her son, who'd died in that tragic accident. A feeling of pride rose inside her and she sprinted for a while, pulling Hannah alongside her as they crossed the other side of the bridge. All around them, people cheered and chattered, this strange collective of grief in a joyous union of excitement and pride. Vivid colours and funny costumes and laughter. So much laughter. To celebrate what life had to offer rather than hide away from it.

She wasn't scared any more.

I'm still here. I can make a difference.

If Abbie had shown her one thing, it was how to be a good friend. Supportive, encouraging, fun to be around in every way. Abbie had gone, but that didn't mean she couldn't live on.

Maybe it's a sign, she thought. *Maybe she brought me here in the first place.*

And she knew that Abbie would have absolutely *loved* this.

'You don't have to say anything,' said Hannah, 'but trust me, she'd have been proud.'

Hannah was right. Not only was Malika actually running the race – after all the times she'd laughed at the mere idea of running a 10k, let alone a marathon – but she'd raised money for charity. Awareness. She was responsible for creating a running club. A network of like-minded people who were brought together by one goal. To run.

And Malika was going to run like she'd never run before.

41

Hannah

'No. No more, Han,' Malika said as she hobbled unsteadily at the side of the road. 'How are we only at mile sixteen? We've got ages to go.'

'It's over,' moaned Hannah. 'I swear my legs are completely done in. Seriously. My feet were practically sliding around in my trainers with the Vaseline and yet I can feel the blisters already.'

Malika opened another bottle of water, took a big swig, poured some down her shirt and threw the rest over Hannah, who was incredibly grateful. She'd finished all the water she'd been carrying in her utility-slash-running belt, had stopped at a grand total of three Portaloos, and there wasn't another water station for at least half a mile. She'd even munched through half of her stash of jelly babies and was down to rationing the last five miniature bags. Half a warm bottle of Evian poured down her cleavage wasn't exactly the cooling shower that Hannah was fantasising about, but it'd do.

They'd just trudged breathlessly past the sixteen-mile banner, and the excitement and morale of earlier had begun to ebb away.

'This is it,' said Hannah. 'We'll pass out. A marshal will find us in a dried-out, dehydrated heap on the side of the road. We'll be in the *Bristol Post*. Tragically stupid. Might scoop a Darwin award for agreeing to do this bloody run in the first place. Ouch.'

The Great South-West Marathon had taken them out of the city of Bristol and on towards Bath. The road stretched out ahead, flat and dry; they were thankful for the lack of hills, at least. They weren't the only ones who were feeling burned out. Along the route, runners adorned in their pink numbers had slowed to a walk, some stopping altogether. They'd seen two people so far being tended to by paramedics. All around them, runners carried on as best as they could, slightly bedraggled, their faces pink and sweat-drenched.

Malika and Hannah were well aware that they were looking worse for wear, but that didn't stop them from walking as fast as they could along the road. There wasn't much of an audience at that point, not when the road stretched for miles into this distance, the surrounding fields giving them a glimpse into nature beyond the tall structures and the city skyline they'd been so used to. So far, they'd conquered the city centre, the Suspension Bridge with its stunning views and part of the countryside, where the air surrounding them felt fresher, cleaner.

They'd jogged leisurely past houses, parks, hidden nooks and areas of the city they hadn't visited before, seeing the residents watch and wave from their windows. By now the sun was out in force, making the road glow with a pretty yellow light as the slight chill swiped their skin in a deliciously welcome breeze. They felt it more now that they were walking, which they had been for the past fifteen minutes. It was their strategy: run, walk, run, walk. It was the only way to ensure they could keep going.

'We'll do it. We'll finish it,' said Malika. 'We might just have to crawl home, but we'll finish it. I can just picture the scene. A hot bath, laden with bubbles, a big glass of wine . . .'

'Please don't.'

'And you just step in, your tired legs sinking into the nice-smelling water . . .'

The thought alone made her want to cry. She would cry, later, when she could hobble towards the bathtub and get in. She could see it like a mirage in the middle of a desert.

'Keep going, ladies,' yelled a particularly happy woman, who was racing through the crowd. 'Wooo!'

'I need my positivity back,' Malika complained. 'And I need that bath. What are you going to do this evening? After the race? After we've all celebrated, of course.'

Hannah pictured an evening relaxing, soaking her weary limbs before spreading out in front of a nice film. A pamper session, all to herself. Now that she'd passed the dreaded halfway point, she couldn't wait for the run to be over – at least, in that present moment. It was the moment that Cassie had warned her about. Where the ache kicks in. Where the euphoria dies down, to be replaced by a jolt of reality and tiredness. And it hurt. It really, really *hurt*. Hannah could feel the ache rising all over her body, but she was determined.

Then she remembered Dan. Her decision. The work she'd have to do, everything she'd soon need to sort out.

'My plans?' said Hannah. 'I'm going to celebrate, then go home and celebrate again. I saw Dan this morning.'

'Really?'

'Yep. It's over. For good.'

Malika slowed down. 'I'm really sorry, Han. But isn't this a good thing?'

Hannah turned round to Malika, her grin as bright as the sunlight that illuminated the route. 'It's the best thing. I'm starting over and you know what? I'm not frightened any more. I'm going to get on with my life and whatever it brings next. I've been so, so stupid, Mal. Embarrassingly stupid. Never again.' And she laughed before breaking into a sprint. 'Thirty-second sprint. Let's go.'

Hannah had cried two miles ago at the realisation. She was a new person. It had become so startlingly clear when she'd turned off the long street that they'd been running down, one that overlooked the city. She could see it in the distance, tall and inviting and illuminated, and just the sight of it made Hannah want to reach out and grasp it. The excitement rose inside her, a feeling of discovery that she hadn't experienced in years. Was it new, or had it always been there, lying dormant, waiting for a moment like this?

Just months ago she wouldn't have dreamt of running down the street, let alone a marathon. Never in her wildest dreams would she have believed she could do such a thing. Yet here she was, feet pounding against the tarmac, along-side runners. Proper runners. She was one of them now.

The music had gone now, its thumping beat left long behind her in the distant crowds, but she could still hear it pounding in her ears. The noise of the bystanders. The cheering, the shouting, the pure positivity. Her limbs may have grown tired, but that didn't stop pure contentment, pure pride, from coursing through every muscle. Every nerve. Every part of her moving, aching, imperfect, beauti-ful, strong body that was capable of carrying out this amazing feat.

A body she was proud of. A body she could love.

Hannah hadn't looked at the scales in her bathroom for weeks. She hadn't wanted to. Hadn't needed to. The weight wasn't important any more.

It hit her with a force so emotional that she nearly stum-bled into another runner who was approaching to the left of the road, his T-shirt covered in hearts. Mum. He'd lost his mum. Hannah wanted nothing more than to stop him, hug him, sweep him up in a wave of love and assure him it would be OK. Wrap her arms around this grieving man, no older than twenty, and make things right.

She couldn't, of course. Nothing could make that right. Nothing could help in the ideal way. All the love Hannah could offer couldn't bring back the boy's mother, because life just worked in that unfair way; it had the power to throw you off guard, sweep the happiness from beneath your feet, just like it had with Hannah, when life didn't provide the one thing she ultimately wanted. The one thing that would have made her happy.

That's not true. Her own voice broke through her thoughts. The voice of happy Hannah. The Hannah who ran. Hannah who belly danced. Hannah who led a team of newbies through the park, who spent time with people she loved, who raised money for charity. Who had time for her friends and had everything to offer.

Hannah *was* happy.

She'd never have believed it. And when she thought about Dan, all she could do was laugh. At all the times she wanted to fight for him. At all the times she thought herself unworthy. The only person unworthy was Dan.

Sophia's welcome to him, Hannah thought. But she didn't want to feel bitter. Because at that moment, it was clear that she had needed Dan, after all. If only to show her what she was missing.

Twenty-six (and a bit!) miles was only the beginning of Hannah's adventure.

She was finally, finally free.

42

Cassie

With each mile marker she passed, Cassie grew more and more determined. Even the slight weariness creeping through her limbs was nowhere near enough to deter her. This was Cassie's moment. This was her *day*.

I'm going to smash this.

The thought of the medal propelled her forwards. It drove her, filled her with a passionate energy she'd never before experienced. That beautiful piece of carved metal, weighty around her neck. Proof that she'd done something extraordinary. She craved it. She pictured herself standing at the finish line, pulling it over her neck, feeling the ribbon against her warm skin. She'd touch it, run a finger along its engraved surface before taking it into the office and hanging it up by her desk. Putting her achievement on display for all to see. Who wouldn't? It was something to be proud of. Her colleagues would see it as they walked past.

'Did you hear about Cassie?' they'd say. 'She ran a marathon.'

Keep pushing.

The thought of closing her hand around that medal only powered her speed. She could see the next milestone in the distance, a banner of bright orange fluttering in the breeze – 25 miles. *Almost there.*

Cassie had already flown past most of the runners with their pink race numbers, leaving them behind ages ago. As much as she'd have loved to run with Hannah and Malika, she was delighted that they'd made her carry on ahead. This was no time to be slow; she'd worked hard. So hard. Trained so much, put in hours of precious time to tone her body and make it ready to push it to the absolute limit. This marathon was hers for the taking.

Keep going. Must keep going.

A few yards away, a man in a bright yellow running vest darted along the course. Cassie had been close to him for a few miles now. They'd overtaken each other, determined in their unspoken competition. During a big run, Cassie always liked to focus on someone and pretend they were racing against each other. It helped her to keep up the momentum.

There was a flurry of excitement around her now – they were nearing the finish line. She was coming up to the twenty-fifth mile, the marker in her sights. Spectators lined the road, cheering, yelling and waving banners in the air to inspire the runners. Cassie wondered if Jack was among them, if he was stationed in the crowd somewhere, ready to call out for her when she passed by, whether his voice would be lost in the noise and excitement of the crowd.

Jack had always gone to her races, standing on the sidelines, waiting to catch a glimpse of her. He'd meet her in the finishing area and she'd run into his arms, and he'd tell her how proud he was. How beautiful she looked. How he'd always be there for her, no matter what. She didn't know if he'd want to be there today and the possibility made her heart hurt.

Jack had always been supportive. Cassie knew that. *So why can't I do the same?* she wondered.

Cassie looked but couldn't see Jack's face among the hundreds of others. There was too much noise for her to hear anything but cheering, whistling, the approaching *thump thump thump* of music as they raced towards that final stretch. She kept her eyes on the road ahead that was littered with empty water bottles as her mind erupted with thoughts of Jack.

I hope he's here, hope he's waiting for me. I want him to know what this means to me.

As she ran, she imagined Jack right at the end, beneath the billowing FINISH banner, arms outstretched . . . before the image in her mind changed. In this altered version, Jack was clutching a baby in one arm. Small and chubby and gurgling away . . .

Babies. Cassie didn't know why she was thinking of babies all of a sudden, at such a vital moment. She'd almost finished a marathon, yet her head was filled with babies, with Jack. She pictured herself running with a baby growing inside her, wondered how it would feel. This tiny being who relied on her to nurture it, to care, to bring it into the world with love. She pictured her belly huge and rounded, Jack's hands caressing it. Maybe her child would like to run, too. She could join the other mums in the park. She knew she wouldn't be lonely. *Would it be worth it?*

Could I have a baby?

Sports days, Christmases, football practice, first days of school . . . all appeared like a movie montage in Cassie's overworked mind. Footage of a movie that didn't even exist. *Wouldn't* exist, unless Cassie made that all-important choice.

Cassie tried to swat the thoughts away, letting the pulsating beat of the nearby band carry her away from this world her brain was creating. *Why babies? Why now?*

You're just stressed, she told herself. *You're overthinking things.*

Cassie didn't see the kerb. Didn't see where she was going as she followed the crowd. She didn't feel herself veer towards the left, where the pavement rose from the road. She felt it first. Her breath caught in her lungs as she realised what was happening, that split second of terror before she felt herself toppling forwards.

Pain. Searing pain in her ankle before she landed on the cold, hard ground.

She heard the gasps, felt the spectators stare from behind their barriers. Cassie felt that the whole world was watching. Eyes closed, she reached out to touch her foot. *Agony*. She took deep breaths, trying to ignore the pain in her hands from the fresh grazes she'd gained from smacking them against the pavement. Her purple leggings were torn.

No. No. Please, no . . .

Cassie tried to stand, tried to pull herself back up on her feet to carry on. The man in the bright vest was long gone now. But the pain was too much; quickly, she fell back down. There was no way she could run now.

Devastation washed over her. Cassie burst into tears as her fellow runners rushed on by.

Her race was over.

43

Hannah

'This is it! Final stretch, Han. *Final stretch!*'

Hannah inhaled deeply then surged ahead as fast as her legs could carry her. Not that it was much use. They were well and truly vanquished. As the 25-mile banner swayed in the distance like a beacon of hope, Hannah and Malika edged slowly towards it, forcing their aching limbs to walk the distance.

'I can't believe it,' said Hannah. 'We've almost done it. Even if we don't, we've made it through twenty-five miles at least.'

Keeping to the side of the road to let the faster runners pass, Malika continued to power walk. All along the route, the spectators were cheering, yelling lines like, 'You can do it!'; 'Keep running!'; 'You're amazing!' in a bid to be inspiring.

'The end is near!' shouted a woman in a jacket and scarf, who was balancing a toddler on her shoulders.

'It very well might be!' Hannah called back.

'Don't be silly! You can do it! Go-go-go!'

Hannah was overwhelmed by their audience all the way round the course, the voracity of their shouts, their unending support for a bunch of strangers. It felt nice. Warming. How people she didn't know would stand outside for hours to watch out for a loved one and while they were at it, shout encouragement to every runner they thought needed some.

They'd seen banners of all kinds, from the inspiring to the downright funny. 'THINK OF THE WINE', one had read, waved by a young man back at mile fifteen. Hannah had cheered at that one.

They'd also passed the charity tents along the route, with volunteers on hand to cheer and wave at their passing supporters. Brake was there, too. A loud cheer went up as Hannah and Malika had scurried by.

Despite the exhaustion, despite the pain, it had so far been an amazing day.

Suddenly, Malika slowed to a walk. She pointed up ahead, where a woman was sitting on the ground, her shoulders moving up and down as though she was crying. A paramedic was tending to her foot. Hannah felt sick.

'That's Cassie, isn't it? Oh no . . .' said Malika.

They hurried as fast as they could, as fast as their worn-out bodies would let them, to where Cassie was slumped on the pavement.

'Cass, what's happened?'

Cassie turned round. Her face was streaked with tears.

'I fell,' she managed, her voice just breaking through the sobs. 'I've twisted my ankle. I can't run.'

'Of course you can!' said Hannah, smiling. 'Come on, get up, you can do this.'

'She can't,' said the paramedic sternly. 'If she runs, she might make it worse. I wouldn't advise it at all. But she refuses to move, so I don't know what to do.'

'This is it,' said Cassie, gazing longingly at the runners who were jolting past, racing towards the finish. 'It's over for me. All that training and I'm out. I only had a mile and a bit to go. I feel so stupid. I wasn't looking.'

'You're not stupid. Accidents happen,' said Malika.

'It's my fault. I got distracted . . .'

'Don't beat yourself up about it, Cass,' Malika said. 'It happened. You can't change it now.'

'You're not the only one who's fallen today,' said the paramedic. 'Try not to be too upset. There's always next year. You made it to twenty-five miles! That's still amazing.'

This only made Cassie cry louder.

'We'll stay with you,' said Hannah.

'No! You need to finish the race. And why the hell are you standing still, Hannah? *I told you to keep moving!*'

Hannah and Malika launched into star jumps.

'I know. But we had to stop. Is this OK?'

'No!' Cassie thrust her arms frantically towards the finish line. The last mile. 'Now go! *Go!* You're wasting time.'

Hannah and Malika exchanged a glance. *Poor Cassie*, Hannah thought. Of all the people it could happen to, it had been her. She'd poured so much time into her training. She wanted that medal just as much as Hannah and Malika did . . . quite possibly more.

'Could she walk the rest of the way?' Malika asked the paramedic. 'With help?'

'What?' Cassie shrieked.

The paramedic considered for a moment.

'You'd have to be extremely careful. I wouldn't advise it, but . . .'

'Right,' said Hannah, reaching out for Cassie's arm. 'See if you can pull yourself up. You're coming with us. Mal, get her other side. Slowly, slowly . . .'

Cassie laughed, wiping at her teary face. 'Are you serious? What are you doing? It's another mile, Han. A *mile*. Just over a mile, actually. We won't make it.'

Hannah and Malika heaved Cassie to her feet. Cassie put an arm around each of them so that she was fully supported.

'If we don't make it,' said Hannah, 'then we don't make it.'

Cassie sniffed. She held on tightly to her friends as they set off slowly, gripping onto one another as runners hurried past them in the final sprint to the finish line. Cassie hobbled wearily, trying to keep the speed up even as she struggled with her injured leg.

'Hate to break it to you, Cass, but you probably won't be hitting your estimated finish time now,' said Hannah.

'I know,' said Cassie, laughing now. 'I'm way out. But I can still win a medal. And we can finish the race together.'

'Exactly,' said Hannah. 'We weren't going to leave you behind, Cass. We're a club.'

The crowd roared as they made their way along the road, passing the 25-mile banner and heading towards their final destination: the finish line. People clapped and cheered, whooping as they shuffled along, Cassie hopping in the middle and smiling through the pain, to the applause of bystanders.

'So, regretting it yet?' asked Cassie.

'Would it be weird to say this has probably been the most surreal, fun day of my life? Pain included.'

'Hannah's left Dan,' Malika added. 'Good and proper, this time.'

'Oh?' Cassie turned to Hannah.

'Yep,' said Hannah, sounding delighted between tired breaths. 'Torturous hours of running really gives you time to think, doesn't it? I was blaming myself for so long, for something that wasn't my fault. This whole race – pain and all – has just proved to me that I'm worth so much more. Dan has made his choice. He made me feel like I wasn't good enough. I am more than good enough.'

'Told you,' said Cassie smugly.

They continued, walking on among the finishing crowd, watching as their fellow runners sprinted towards the final, most important part of the course. The finishing banner was up ahead now, towering above the sea of people hurrying through, cheering, waving their arms in the air as they passed with proud relief. Cassie, Hannah and Malika stayed quiet, focusing their energy on getting there. On actually making it.

'Hannah!'

Hannah heard a voice call out from behind, barely audible among the cheering. She turned to look, but all she could see were crowds of people. She continued on.

'Han!'

There it was again. A man's voice. *Must be calling for another Hannah*, she thought, carrying on, their pace faster now, as speedy as they could manage while being mindful of Cassie's injury.

The end was in sight. The huge, sprawling banner: GREAT SOUTH-WEST MARATHON – FINISH! The sight was almost heavenly. Gripping each other tightly, they surged forwards, not stopping, their breathing quick as they walked as fast as they could towards that giant arch, towards the people, towards the yelling and the thumping music and the excitement.

Their feet stepped over that magical line in unison.

They'd done it. They'd completed a marathon.

44

Hannah

The noise of the crowd pounded in their ears. The music blared and sunlight beamed through the crowds onto Bath's Royal Victoria Park. Hannah had never seen a more beautiful sight, hadn't felt so proud, so elated, so wonderfully swept away in the intensity of the moment. She was still holding on to Cassie as they were ushered carefully past the finish line and towards the marshal, who presented them with their medals.

Hannah's hands shook as she accepted the prize. The large silver medal felt cool and heavy, its details so intricate and precious. She could barely peel her eyes away from it and only did when she had to, when they had to step away to collect their finishers' goody bags.

'I can't believe it,' said Malika.

Hannah turned to see that she was crying. Huge tears streamed down Malika's face as she placed the medal around her neck.

'I did it. I always told Abbie I couldn't and I bloody did it!'

Wincing, Cassie moved over onto the grass and spread out like a starfish. She kissed her medal and held it into the air.

'Me too! OK, no PB, but do I care? No! That was amazing. Ladies, we did it. Although I might need to go to the medical tent.'

'Selfie first!' said Hannah.

Dropping down onto the grass, Hannah pulled out her phone and snapped a photo of the three of them. She glanced down at it, smiled and opened Instagram.

My club is the best ever! JUST FINISHED THE GREAT SOUTH-WEST MARATHON! Here's to a life full of new adventures. #ibloodydidit #running #fit #friends #runningintotrouble

Hannah hit Upload. No filter. No fakery. No little white lies. No worrying about what others would see. Because in the photo, they were amazing. Sweaty, dishevelled, bruised, tearful, together. And smiling the biggest smiles possible.

For the first time in her life, Hannah looked exactly like the person she'd always dreamt of being.

45

Malika

As Hannah helped Cassie walk to the medical tent, Malika sat on the cool grass. Above her, the the sky was clear, cloudless, and she lay back, enjoying the sensation of the ground against her warm skin. Her entire body ached. Every part of her was drenched in a layer of sweat. She was completely and utterly worn out. Yet at the same time, she felt absolutely fantastic.

Told you you could do it!

Abbie's voice came to her yet again. She closed her eyes, clutching her medal in one hand. She pictured Abbie there, slumping down on the grass next to her. Just like they used to do on College Green some lunchtimes, when the sun was out and they'd go for an iced coffee and a chat, away from the stuffy office.

'I know,' she whispered. 'I'm sorry I didn't believe you.'

She pictured Abbie smiling into the sunlight before getting up and walking away. Disappearing into the crowd. She imagined her soft footsteps among the other runners, blissful and unaware, showing off their medals and taking photos. Creating memories. Malika could see her now, the vivid brightness that was once her friend, those blue trainers stepping through the crowd before fading away altogether.

'Mal!'

The voice broke through her thoughts. Malika clambered to her feet just in time to see Khari rushing through the crowd towards her.

'Khari? Oh my God. You're here!'

'As if I'd miss this,' he said, wrapping his arms around his sister and lifting her off her feet. 'Surprise! Mum and Dad are here, too.'

'What?' Malika scanned the crowd and saw her parents nearby.

They hurried over as soon as they caught sight of her, scooping her into more impromptu hugs.

'Malika! It's so lovely to see you,' said her mother. She reached over and touched the medal. 'This is amazing. We're so proud of you.'

'Really proud,' said her father. 'We wanted to come and support you. We watched you at the end, you know. You were brilliant.'

'I can't believe you came here just to see me.'

'Why wouldn't we?' asked Khari. 'You were running a marathon. That's big, Mal. And we weren't the only ones.'

'What do you mean?'

Khari pointed into the distance, where a familiar shock of pink hair stood out in the sunlight.

'Maliiikkaa!' a familiar voice yelled and before she had time to process what was going on, Roz, Dean, Kath and Andrea had pounced on her with hugs.

'Mal! You were absolutely amazing! Well done!' shrieked Kath.

'Thanks, guys,' said Malika.

'That medal, though!' said Dean.

Malika noticed he was holding a banner, reading 'GO MAL GO!' in huge bright letters.

Malika couldn't help it; the tears came at full force yet again.

323

Roz spoke. 'We had to come and see you for ourselves. We didn't want to tell you we were coming in case it put you off, but we watched you go past at the third mile. We called out for you but you didn't hear us.'

'I wish I'd seen you,' Malika said, wishing she wasn't so sweaty in front of all of these people.

'Aaand we have a surprise for you,' said Kath.

She pointed to a large paint can that Roz was holding. She held it up, grinning in the manner of a magician's assistant. It had been decorated to read 'MALIKA'S MARATHON' in a rainbow of colours. Roz leant in closer and prised it open.

'Ta-daah!'

Malika peered in and her heart did somersaults. The paint tin was full of cash. Notes peeked out from a pile of pound coins that nearly reached the top. She even spotted some twenty-pound notes.

'What's this?'

'We've been helping you to raise money for Brake,' said Roz. 'It started off with a donation tin on the bar at work, and then Dean and I decided to do a weekly charity pub quiz.'

'Andrea and I did a craft stall for a few weekends,' said Kath.

Malika stared at the money. 'This is . . . wow. This is really too much.'

'We've done a quick count,' said Dean. 'There's over a grand in there altogether.'

Malika's legs were already unsteady. The shock made her almost tumble and she grabbed Roz for support. No wonder Cassie had advised them not to stop moving; now that the race was over, reality was taking over her weary limbs.

'I can't believe it! Thank you so much.'

Over a grand. Malika rummaged for her phone to check her online donation page. Altogether, the Running into

Trouble Club had raised nearly three thousand pounds for charity.

'You did so well,' said Roz. 'Abbie would have been so proud of you.'

Roz pulled her into another embrace and they all joined in.

'I've missed you all,' said Malika.

She had. She really, really had.

46

Hannah

Hannah escorted Cassie to the medical tent, hearing her friend's shrieks of 'Ow, ow, ow!' with every step.

'I'm trying my best,' said Hannah, holding on to Cassie and guiding her hopping form across the grass. 'We're nearly there. Just a few more steps.'

They were spotted by a member of staff, who quickly helped Cassie to one of the beds. Carefully, she eased herself onto it, wincing as she rested her leg on its surface.

There was sudden movement behind them and they turned to see a figure sweep through the makeshift doorway.

'Cass?'

Jack stood there, taking in the scene, his face etched with worry at the sight of his pained-looking wife-to-be being tended to by medical staff. His gaze landed on Cassie's bandaged foot and his shoulders sagged with relief.

'I thought it was serious.'

'This *is* serious!' snapped Cassie. 'I—'

'I meant *serious* serious, Cass.'

Just then little Cleo bounded into the room, clutching a banner that was almost as big as her. 'GO AUNTIE CASS!' was emblazoned across it in felt pen and glitter. Evidently Cleo's work, but she'd had some assistance.

'Look what I made,' yelled Cleo proudly. 'Mummy helped with the letters, 'cause I can't do them all big yet.'

'That's so lovely,' said Cassie quietly. 'And that was so thoughtful of Mummy.'

Hannah stepped away to leave, but Cassie grabbed her arm.

'Stay, please?' she whispered.

Hannah sat on a nearby chair, glancing around in the hope of finding a leaflet, or anything to focus on that would make her feel less awkward. Eventually, she settled on inspecting her medal again.

'What happened?' asked Jack.

'Sprained my ankle, I think. I went down right at the end. I still can't believe it. All that training—'

'Thank God.'

'What?'

'Thank God that it's minor, nothing worse. I came looking for you and couldn't find you. Went searching only to find you here, lying on a bed in the medical tent, and my heart stopped. For a split second, I thought something else had happened to you.'

'Like what?'

Jack moved closer, taking Cassie's hand in his. His fingers moved over her engagement ring.

'I don't know, Cass. You've been so stressed lately. I didn't even tell you I was coming in case it tipped you over the edge. I've heard stories of people dropping dead at the finish line and when I saw you . . . well, my mind went places.' He looked away. 'What if something *had* happened to you and the last time we spoke was an argument? I don't want that, Cass. I don't ever want that to happen. I need to talk to you, to clear all this up. I've been trying to all week and it feels like you've been avoiding me.'

'Best do it now,' piped up Hannah. 'Do it while she can't run away from you. Sorry, Cass.'

Cassie shot Hannah a warning glare, but Hannah didn't care. Jack was right. Life was too short for fighting. If only she'd realised it sooner herself.

'Thanks, Hannah, I will,' laughed Jack. 'Look, Cass, I think you might have misunderstood when I asked you about children.'

'Misunderstood?' said Cassie tersely. 'How could I have misunderstood *that*?'

She lay back on the pillow as a paramedic came over to check on her foot, pulling off her shoe as carefully as he could. Taking deep breaths, she focused on Jack as she tried to work through the pain. Hannah cringed at the thought of it. How *she'd* managed to get through the race unscathed was anyone's guess.

Cleo rushed over to Hannah, still holding the banner with tiny hands. 'Is Auntie Cass poorly?' she asked. 'Will she have to go to hospital?'

Cassie continued, 'You knew at the very beginning that I didn't want kids. I've always been honest about that. I thought we were both set on that decision. And then you go and ask me that question . . . it's all I've been able to think about since.

'I haven't wanted to face you, because I was dreading it. I've spent every waking moment since then trying to work out what to say, what to do. What am I *meant* to do? Bring a baby into the world who I don't want, or lose you? It's been eating away at me.'

'Cass—'

Cassie held up her hand. 'Just listen,' she said, a pleading look in her eyes. 'I love you, Jack. I love you more than anything and I want to be with you for the rest of my life. But I've made my decision. I can't do it, Jack. I don't want to be a mother.

I made my choice years ago and I'm sticking by it. I'm happy with my life and ideally, that life includes you. I really, really wish I didn't have to tell you this, but if you want to have children, I think it'd be best for the both of us to end it now.'

Tears poured down Cassie's cheeks as she gripped Jack's hand.

'It's unfair on the both of us to live a life we don't want. If having children will make you happy, you need to go for it, Jack. You need to be with someone who can give you that. Who *wants* to give you that. I wish it could be me, but . . . well, it's not.'

Silence fell around the bed.

'I'll . . . be right back,' said the paramedic, hurrying away.

Jack looked thoughtful for a moment before his face broke into a smile. 'Cass,' he said. 'This is one of the many, many reasons why I love you. You're not afraid to be honest about what you want. Yes, you're prone to overreacting, but—'

'Overreacting?'

'Yep, there she goes,' said Hannah.

'Yeah,' said Jack. 'Come on, you can't say I'm not wrong.'

Cassie sighed theatrically.

'But anyway, I love that about you, too. The thing is, Cass, I didn't ask because I *want* children.'

'Then why did you?'

'You never gave me time to explain.' Jack let out a breath. 'To be honest, I've never really wanted children. I thought maybe one day I might have some, but it's never bothered me either way. I love our life together. I love how we have our own time to spend doing what we want, even if we're just being lazy, just *being* with each other, you know?

'I can see us growing old together, just you and me. And it's not like I don't have kids in my life. Cleo and Harry are amazing. I love spending time with them, watching them grow, influencing them. Doesn't change how I feel about us, though. Being an uncle means I get the best of both worlds. Nothing anyone can say will change that.

'But recently, someone at work mentioned children. He said his wife had never wanted a baby until she fell pregnant accidentally and now their world has changed. They love it. And then I thought, *shit*, what if *you* felt differently?

'We haven't talked about it for ages and I had no idea Emily was making you feel genuinely upset. I know you've said you won't change your mind. I get that, Cass, but I suddenly worried, in case it *was* something you'd been thinking about but didn't want to mention. Because let's face it, you're stubborn.'

Cassie laughed, poking Jack in the stomach. 'Is there a reason I'm here getting roasted? I'm injured! You're meant to be nice to me. You two are harsh,' she said as Hannah and Jack exchanged amused glances. 'Are you serious, Jack? You don't actually want to have a baby?'

'Nope. I'm happy with the way things are. I just wanted to check that we were still on the same page. Maybe my words didn't come out as I'd planned. Cass, I would never, *ever* pressure you into making a decision like that. It hurts that you thought I would. I want you to talk to me, that's all. You can't run away from all of your problems and you don't have to, because I'm here.'

A soft sniffing noise came from Cassie before she erupted in a full-blown sobbing fit.

'I . . . love you . . .' she cried, pulling Jack into a hug, seemingly forgetting about her foot.

Unless, Hannah wondered, *that was half the reason for the waterworks.*

'Right, I am *definitely* leaving you two to it,' said Hannah, pulling herself up from the chair and waving goodbye to Cleo.

Just getting to her feet was hard work; her muscles had already started their notorious post-race ache. Hannah stepped out of the tent, her muscles feeling tight as she limped back out into the busy finishers' area, rummaging in her goody bag for the water she'd stuffed inside.

'Hannah!'

There was that voice again. The one she'd sworn she'd heard on the route. One that, now closer, sounded remarkably familiar. As she glanced up, squinting in the afternoon sunlight, she could see that she'd been right all along.

Standing before her, in his blinding hi-vis vest, was Steve.

47

Hannah

Steve.

'Hey,' he said, his smile wide, the smile Hannah realised she'd yearned for lately.

It made the much-missed, fluttery feeling return, rendering her even weaker on her aching legs.

'You were amazing. I did call out to you, but you didn't hear me.'

'I did,' she said. 'I thought I heard someone shout. I just didn't think . . . well, I didn't think it would be you.'

He nodded towards the medal hanging proudly at her chest. 'Congratulations!'

Hannah reached out for it, to feel it once again. 'Thank you. It was hard work, but worth every second.'

'How's your friend now?'

'She's fine. Hurt her ankle, but hopefully she'll be able to run again soon enough. I can't imagine what Cassie will be like if she can't run for weeks!'

Steve laughed. It made Hannah remember their evening out. Hours spent talking, laughing, reminiscing about life and not wanting to come home. Feeling like a teenager . . . that kiss by the bridge . . .

The kiss. Hannah tried to swat the memory away. Every time her mind ventured back to that kiss, she was greeted by a pang of longing. There was no use in longing, not now.

'Glad to see you're doing well,' said Steve. 'I'm sorry.'

'Why?'

'I think we moved too quickly on that date. I might have come on a bit too strong and I'm sorry about that.'

There was a look in his eyes and Hannah tried to decipher it. Sadness. It looked a lot like sadness.

'No! Steve, that wasn't . . . that was nothing to do with the date. In fact, the date was amazing.'

'Honestly?'

'Honestly. Things just got complicated, that's all. It's hard to explain.'

'I understand. I'm glad I got to see you again, anyway. Even if it was just to say hello. To be entirely truthful, I volunteered to marshal this race for a reason.'

'Really? What reason is that, then?' Hannah asked playfully.

'Take a wild guess. It involves a particular runner. Who also has some belly dancing moves, if I recall correctly. You look lovely, by the way, Han.'

Hannah laughed so hard she practically snorted. Here she was, pink-faced, her body a throbbing, pained mess. She was covered in so much sweat that her hair, her clothes, *everything* was sticking to her. Her feet were covered in an awful mixture of Vaseline and sweat, and no amount of emergency body spray could save her now. She absolutely *needed* a bath. Yet here was Steve, insisting that she was *lovely*.

'I mean it,' he said. 'That's why I wanted to come and speak to you. Got to admit, I was pretty devastated when I got your message. I thought I'd screwed up and just wanted to explain myself.'

'You don't need to. I should have told you the truth about my situation.'

'The truth is, I really like you, Han. I had more fun on that night with you than I've had in years and we only went out for a drink. I just seemed to click with you. You're fun, you're hilarious, you're down-to-earth, you're smart and, to top it all off, you're gorgeous, as well. I've been in a similar position. I'm divorced. I know how difficult and confusing it can be. But I like you. I just want you to know that. And if you ever want to go out again in future, even as a friend, well, I'd like that.'

All around them, runners were hurrying towards their friends and family. Chatting excitedly, snapping pictures, giving congratulatory hugs. The atmosphere must have been rubbing off on Hannah. She reached out for Steve's hand.

'Well, how about tonight?'

'Tonight?'

'Yes. It's come to my attention today that I've been seeing things in the wrong light. I've been letting people treat me badly. Heck, I've been treating *myself* badly. Life's way too short for all that. From this point on, I'm going to do what's right for me. I'm not wasting another minute of my life. So if you want to go out again . . . well, I'm ready.'

'Does that mean I can kiss you again?'

True to her word, Hannah didn't waste a moment. She moved forwards, reaching for him, feeling Steve's soft hands around her waist, feeling his lips on hers, and for a brief moment all the pain was gone. The ache in her muscles subsided as she felt herself melt into Steve's embrace. Kissing him felt so new, so real. So exciting in more ways than one. This man, this lovely, kind, caring – not to mention handsome – man wanted her for *her*. The Hannah he'd come to know; the real Hannah. Hannah the runner, with her muddy shoes and new-found confidence and, as of that moment, a brand-new life.

A brief thought punctured her happy bubble. *What if it all goes wrong?* Hannah laughed it away. *So what if it does?* Being here, her arms wrapped round Steve, having just achieved something amazing, was happiness as she'd never known it before.

'Hannah?!'

The voice came from beside her. Turning quickly, Hannah took in the long coat, the sunglasses, high heels sinking into the soft grass. Bronwen was standing in front of her, mouth open wide in shock.

48

Hannah

Bronwen held a banner that read 'RUN NOW, DRINK LATER!' It was decorated with pictures of red wine.

'Get it?' she muttered, looking from Hannah to Steve. 'Because you got drunk and signed up to the race?'

'I get it,' snapped Hannah defensively.

'I don't,' said Steve, clearly amused. 'You'll have to explain that one later.'

Bronwen's face had turned a funny shade of pink.

'We came to cheer you on,' she said. 'The boys and me. Sadly, the lure of the hot-dog van was too strong so they're queuing. I knew you'd be around here somewhere, though.'

Hannah stood, flummoxed, unaware of what to say. She cast a glance at the banner that someone – most likely Bronwen – had made especially for her, which warmed her heart, even though she didn't want to admit it.

'I've told you I'm sorry,' said Bronwen. 'I don't know what else to say. I really am sorry, Han. If it helps, I've told Dan the truth. About what an absolute imbecile he's been. Didn't exactly get in Mike's good books, but what can I say? I want my friend back.'

Bronwen's eyes were still trailing over Steve. Luckily, he'd turned away to answer a phone call.

'I'm needed over by the bag drop,' Steve said, giving Hannah a kiss on the cheek. 'I'll catch up with you later. Bye!' He shot Bronwen a huge smile before heading off.

'Er . . . are you seeing that guy? "Hot" is an understatement. How did you meet *him*?'

'I might be,' said Hannah proudly. 'And it's a long story. One I'll tell you tomorrow, if you're still up for our usual catch-up and coffee?'

Relief flooded Bronwen's face. 'Are you serious? I thought you were going to tell me to piss off. And I wouldn't have blamed you, either.'

'I'm serious. But you need to promise me something, Bron. Can you just be honest with me in future?'

'I told you, I just didn't want you to be hurt—'

'Not just about Dan,' Hannah cut in. 'About everything. Just be honest with me. I know you only try to spare my feelings, but you'd be a better friend if you just told me the truth. Even in school, you only told me what you thought I wanted to hear. It didn't spare me any heartache. It took the torture of reading my ancient diaries to make me see that, but I'm glad.'

Bronwen nodded. 'Jesus. I've been a shit friend, haven't I? I'm sorry, Han. Come here.' She pulled Hannah in for a hug, sniffing loudly. 'You smell awful. Is that honest enough?'

'It's a good start,' said Hannah.

'Oh, just so you're aware, Dan's over there in the crowd,' said Bronwen. 'I saw him earlier, skulking about while Sophia and her girly mates were huddling together taking pictures.'

Hannah laughed. 'Good.'

'Good?'

'I don't care about Dan any more. It's over. I'm done. I'm not *me* any more, Bron. I just want to move on.'

Hannah reached for her medal again. She had to keep touching it, had to know it was there. To feel that it was real and not some figment of her imagination, a dream she'd wake from and find herself disappointed. She'd cherish that medal forever. She'd hang it up, in her new bedroom perhaps, so it'd be the first thing she saw when she woke up. A reminder of her amazing feat. Her amazing strength. Her amazing friends.

It would remind her of a time when she truly felt alive.

EPILOGUE

Two months later

The air was cold now. The ground wore a thin blanket of frost, the kind that crunched beneath your feet. Malika walked on, searching, past the tall, bare trees and the grassy path that separated the two rows of headstones. They, too, had been graced with a dusting of ice; picturesque, restful beauty among the sadness and silence.

She found it quickly. Abbie's grave wasn't far along the row and as the breeze whipped around her face, Malika placed one gloved hand into her pocket and pulled out something round and silver on a ribbon of blue. Taking a deep breath, she bent down and placed it next to the headstone.

She spoke quietly. Across the way, a middle-aged couple had come to visit a grave and she didn't want them to hear. Not that it would have mattered. That's why people came here, after all, wasn't it? To pay their respects. To talk, in the hope that they'd hear. To be with lost loved ones; to know they were close, even though they were gone.

'Hey, lovely. This is probably going to be the last time I speak to you. I keep doing it and I know you can't answer. So I think it's best if I stop.

'I've brought your medal. The one I found in your drawer, the one that inspired me to run. I thought you might want it back. I've got one of my own now, but you already know that. At least, I hope so. I still think it was deliberate. That you set the whole thing up. I know, I know. That's silly. But sometimes I like to think that that's what happened.'

The couple nearby had started their slow walk back, meandering through the neat rows of stones. The man peered up from his scarf, battling with the harsh breeze, and gave her a smile.

'I'll miss you, Ab. I still think of you all the time and I always will. Especially when I'm running. I hope you'll be there alongside me, telling me everything's all right. I'm determined to have enough adventures for both of us. I hope I've got years of them left, but as we both know, we can't always be sure. I guess you could say you taught me that, that life can be short, so we have to make the most of it.

'So . . . well, goodbye, Abbie. Maybe one day I'll see you again.'

Malika tried to stop herself from crying, but she couldn't help a rogue tear from escaping. The wind was so bitingly cold that she feared it might freeze on her cheek. She'd cried enough over the past few months. Now, it was time to be brave.

Especially now. In two days' time she was going to speak at a local community meeting with the council, to discuss the improvements that could be made to local roads. Not to mention training with the Running into Trouble Club, which was growing by the week. Malika, Cassie and Hannah had all signed up for the Bristol 10k with Angie and Marie, and hoped to raise money for Angie's chosen breast cancer charity.

Things were happening. And with Christmas in a matter of weeks, a new year was swiftly heading towards them. A new year, full of new challenges. Just months ago, Malika had hated the idea of a new year, a new season without

Abbie, another horrid, lurching reminder of the passage of time. Recently, however, she'd been seeing things in a more positive light.

Trudging down the path, Malika could see a figure waiting for her by the tall iron gates. She turned round once more, taking a final glance. Wanting to remember her last visit.

'You all right, love?' asked Hannah.

Malika stepped out through the gates and closed them behind her.

'Aw, come here.' Hannah threw her arms around Malika. 'She'd have been proud,' she said. 'Always remember that.'

'Thanks,' said Malika.

They stood for a moment, Malika crying soft tears into Hannah's padded coat.

'I'm sorry,' she sniffed. 'Where are we meeting the others?' she asked.

'Here!' Hannah gestured across the road, where Cassie's car was parked up.

They crossed over and squeezed into the back seat.

'Get in!' said Cassie brightly. 'We're going for a countryside pub lunch.'

'Whoop!' said Hannah.

Malika squeezed in next to Hannah and Steve in the back. Cassie and Jack were in the front, dancing along to eighties pop music.

'I've got Kylie and Jason lined up on the playlist,' said Cassie.

'Sorry in advance,' Malika warned Steve. 'We've started doing singalong sessions on our runs.'

'Oh, and before I forget, here you go,' said Cassie.

She reached into the glove compartment and pulled out two gold envelopes, one each for Hannah and Malika.

Hannah opened hers to find a beautiful, crisp wedding invitation inside.

'Guys,' said Malika. 'This is beautiful. I'd love to come.'

'And, Hannah, I wanted to ask. . . .' said Cassie, almost sheepishly, 'would the belly dance group want to perform at the reception?'

'Definitely,' Hannah replied.

She'd taken up the offer of joining the group. She'd enjoyed it too much to turn it down. And as Hannah was also looking forward to seeing in a new year full of fresh opportunity, she wanted to do as much as she could. She'd packed up most of the house after agreeing to sell. Dan had expected more of a fight, seemingly a little disappointed that she was ready and raring to go. *Especially* disappointed when he'd heard from Bronwen about the handsome policeman, Steve.

Hannah had already taken to Rightmove, scoping out some cosy studio flats, in search of somewhere to rent for a little while. It was no longer daunting. In fact, it was yet another adventure.

A new year. A new life. A whole new beginning.

'So,' said Cassie. 'I read something about the London Marathon last night and I was wondering . . . who's up for another one?'

Acknowledgements

It feels so strange, sitting here writing the acknowledgements page of a novel that will one day be in people's hands. It still doesn't feel real, but I know that it is, and that this book wouldn't be here without the help of some truly brilliant people.

The biggest thank-you of all goes to my wonderful editor Katie Brown, who saw promise in this book, and helped shape it with her guidance. Katie, you have helped to make a dream come true – I cannot thank you enough. A massive thank you also goes to the amazing team at Orion who have worked on bringing this book to life.

A big shout-out goes to Writers' HQ for their hugely supportive network and day-long retreats (during which I tend consume a lot of caffeine, write a lot of words, and go home feeling great). Big thanks to Amanda for running the Bristol retreats.

To my wonderful partner, friends, family and colleagues who have shown constant encouragement throughout the writing process - I'm so, so grateful for all your kind words and support.

To Nanette, Julie, Sharon and Linda – this book was inspired by running with friends. I will not forget the fantastic time I had training for a half marathon with you. The company, the laughs - and the aches! - made it even more fun. Even the muddy trail run.

Thank you.

Credits

Trapeze would like to thank everyone at Orion who worked on the publication of *Running into Trouble*.

Editor
Katie Brown

Copy-editor
Claire Dean

Proofreader
Karen Ball

Editorial Management
Sarah Fortune
Charlie Panayiotou
Jane Hughes
Alice Davis
Claire Boyle

Audio
Paul Stark
Amber Bates

Contracts
Anne Goddard
Paul Bulos
Jake Alderson

Design
Loulou Clark
Lucie Stericker
Joanna Ridley
Nick May
Clare Sivell
Helen Ewing

Finance
Jennifer Muchan
Jasdip Nandra
Rabale Mustafa
Elizabeth Beaumont
Sue Baker
Tom Costello

Marketing
Lucy Cameron

Production
Claire Keep
Fiona McIntosh

Publicity
Alainna Hadjigeorgiou

Sales
Laura Fletcher
Victoria Laws
Esther Waters
Lucy Brem
Frances Doyle
Ben Goddard
Georgina Cutler
Jack Hallam
Ellie Kyrke-Smith
Inês Figuiera
Barbara Ronan
Andrew Hally
Dominic Smith
Deborah Deyong
Lauren Buck
Maggy Park

Linda McGregor
Sinead White
Jemimah James
Rachel Jones
Jack Dennison
Nigel Andrews
Ian Williamson
Julia Benson
Declan Kyle
Robert Mackenzie
Sinead White
Imogen Clarke
Megan Smith
Charlotte Clay
Rebecca Cobbold

Operations
Jo Jacobs
Sharon Willis
Lisa Pryde

Rights
Susan Howe
Richard King
Krystyna Kujawinska
Jessica Purdue
Louise Henderson

346